Praise for *Out of Bounds*

Shortlisted for the Theakston's Crime Novel of the Year Award

Shortlisted for the 2017 McIlvanney Prize

"In this genre [McDermid] has few equals . . . The sleuthing is satisfyingly involved and compelling . . . A refreshing and convincing addition to the crime canon." —*Independent* (UK)

"Thirty books in, most crime writers start to flag, but not Val McDermid. . . . As slickly plotted and polished as her earliest works, and that's saying a lot because McDermid's work always slashes like a knife." —*Globe and Mail*

"Readers will easily connect with Karen, whose unwavering confidence is tempered by a strong dose of kindness and sense of justice . . . Satisfying investigative detail, swift pacing, and realistic mysteries steeped in the intricacies of Scottish law; a sure fit for fans of Tana French and of Denise Mina's Alex Morrow series." —*Booklist* (starred review)

"Engaging . . . McDermid's 30th novel offers fascinating insights into the ethical dilemmas thrown up by advances in forensic science." —*Sunday Times* (UK)

"Cold-case detective Karen Pirie has her hands full tracking a break in an unsolved murder, a suspicious suicide, and an alleged IRA bombing from years before, tangling her in issues such as inheritance, privacy, and migration." —*Boston Globe* ("Best Books of 2016")

"Edinburgh's Master of Crime Fiction . . . McDermid demonstrates an enormous amount of empathy with her characters." —*Literary Hub*

"McDermid's expertly juggled plotlines and masterful handling of pace and tension tick all the best boxes, but what makes this book a real cracker is Pirie herself—grieving, insubordinate and dogged in her pursuit of the various culprits."

—*Guardian* (UK)

"The entertainment in McDermid books comes from every direction. That's especially true of the Karen Pirie series . . . From [the] tantalizing opening, the story continues to get even more intriguing in inventive McDermid fashion."

—*Toronto Star*

"No one writes sturdier mysteries than Val McDermid. But what's notable about her fourth book featuring DCI Karen Pirie, head of Scotland's Cold Case Division, is the warmth it draws from her hero's interactions with the female experts she turns to in investigating a pair of unsolved crimes . . . McDermid juggles all these elements with great aplomb."

—*Chicago Tribune*

"It's a treat to watch DCI Pirie once again as she pursues a tantalizing forensic trail through a brilliantly realized Scottish setting . . . The three plotlines are interwoven with consummate elegance."

—*Scotland on Sunday*

"None is more deserving of the queen-of-crime mantle than Val McDermid . . . I would like to see a great deal more of DCI Pirie."

—*Irish Times*

"*Out of Bounds* snakes and slithers just like Ross Garvie's wildly out-of-control vehicle at the novel's opening. Karen Pirie is a terrific and complex character with a real sense of justice and fair play . . . . Val McDermid is always great to curl up to, and I am confident many readers will do just that as they enjoy her latest thriller while winter storms blow just outside their windows."

—*Bookreporter*

"The need to find out who perpetrated the crime is only half the reason why Val McDermid's *Out of Bounds* stays on the mind any time you put it down. It is more the need to know how Detective Karen Pirie is faring that prevents the novel from staying closed for long . . . McDermid gives us the female heroine that doesn't fit the mold, and in the best way." —*National Post* (Canada)

"What superlatives are there left to describe the phenomenon that is the multi award-winning McDermid? . . . Told with McDermid's legendary verve and eye for detail, it grabs the reader by the throat and never lets go." —*Daily Mail* (UK)

"Engaging . . . Pirie, a tough heroine cut from the same cloth as McDermid's other fictional stalwart, Carol Jordan, never backs down from a thorny question or a seemingly impossible case." —*Publishers Weekly*

"Packed with intrigue, warmly drawn characters and dollops of tension, McDermid's 30th novel leaves the reader looking forward to the 31st." —*Irish Independent*

"The queen of psychological thrillers returns." —*Grazia* (UK)

"McDermid delivers a fun and exciting police procedural for fans of Stephen Booth and Anne Perry in this fourth series installment." —*Library Journal*

"McDermid is one of Scotland's (and the UK's) best-loved crime writers . . . *Out Of Bounds* . . . [is] the kind of pacy, intelligent page-turner we've come to expect."
—Susan Mansfield, *The Scotsman*

"It is evident in her 30th novel that her mastery of the crime has matured well . . . McDermid skillfully exposes the human side of her flawed but likeable heroine who is as prone to self-doubt, fatigue and the odd erratic judgment as anyone . . . The main story unfolds beautifully in the final chapters where the twists take some very unexpected turns. What gives the fast-flowing drama oomph is her attention to detail, particularly on forensics and the convincing dialogue . . . *Out Of Bounds* is a classic page-turner that would translate easily and well to the small or big screen." —*Sunday Express* (UK) (4/5 Stars)

"Val McDermid is arguably the doyenne of Great Britain crime fiction . . . She has set the standard . . . [with] dense plots and people you can get a scent from. She's a pro."
—*Durango Telegraph*

OUT OF BOUNDS

Also by Val McDermid

A Place of Execution
Killing the Shadows
The Distant Echo
The Grave Tattoo
A Darker Domain
Trick of the Dark
The Vanishing Point
Northanger Abbey
The Skeleton Road
Insidious Intent

TONY HILL NOVELS
The Mermaids Singing
The Wire in the Blood
The Last Temptation
The Torment of Others
Beneath the Bleeding
Fever of the Bone
The Retribution
Cross and Burn
Splinter the Silence

KATE BRANNIGAN NOVELS
Dead Beat
Kick Back
Crack Down
Clean Break
Blue Genes
Star Struck

LINDSAY GORDON NOVELS
Report for Murder
Common Murder
Final Edition
Conferences Are Murder
Booked for Murder
Hostage to Murder

SHORT STORY COLLECTIONS
The Writing on the Wall and Other Stories
Stranded
Christmas is Murder

NONFICTION
A Suitable Job for a Woman
Forensics

OUT OF BOUNDS

VAL McDERMID

Grove Press
New York

First published in Great Britain 2016 by Little, Brown

Printed in the United States of America
Published simultaneously in Canada

First Grove Atlantic hardcover edition: December 2016
First Grove Atlantic paperback edition: December 2017

ISBN 978-0-8021-2726-6
eISBN 978-0-8021-9015-4

Grove Press
an imprint of Grove Atlantic
154 West 14th Street
New York, NY 10011

Distributed by Publishers Group West

groveatlantic.com

17 18 19 20   10 9 8 7 6 5 4 3 2 1

This is my 30th novel. And it's for the indestructible, indefatigable, implacable Jane Gregory who has been my agent and my friend from the very beginning. Respected, feared and beloved in the literary world, she has fought my corner, had my back and through it all, her laughter has rocked my world.

1

'**S**ome night, eh, boys?' Ross Garvie flung a sweaty arm round the neck of Wee Grantie, his best mate in all the world.

'Some night, right enough,' Wee Grantie slurred. The two youths swung their hips in rough unison to the deep dark bass beat that shuddered through the club.

The two friends they'd been drinking with since they'd preloaded at Wee Grantie's sister's flat earlier jumped up and down, punching the air. 'We are the boys,' they chorused. 'We are the Arab boys!' Their Dundee United football shirts provided the explanation for their apparently bizarre chant, their team having scored a rare victory that afternoon.

'Ah want to drive all night,' Ross shouted, his body bouncing with the mix of Red Bull, vodka and some chemical cocktail that didn't even have a name.

Wee Grantie slowed as the music segued into the Black Eyed Peas' 'I Gotta Feeling'. 'You dinnae have a car. None of us has a car.'

Ross stopped. 'Have you no ambition?'

Wee Grantie looked at his feet, knowing there was no right answer.

Tam and Tozer, their partners in mayhem, punched each other in the shoulder. 'That's it,' Tam shouted. 'Tonight's gonna be a good, good night. Like the song says. Gonnae do it, aye?'

Wee Grantie frowned. 'How?' He stuck his hands in his jogging bottoms and adjusted himself.

'Come on, let's get out of here. There's no talent anyway. None of us is going to pull, we might as well hit the street.' Ross was already halfway to the door, not needing to check whether his posse was on his tail.

Outside, urgency kicked in as the chill air wicked the heat from their bodies. The young men shivered. Tam and Tozer slapped their bodies with soft arms. Nobody else was around; it was still too early for punters to abandon a club they'd paid to enter.

'Come on, Rossi boy, if you're gonnae do it, do it before my balls climb so far inside my belly they'll be sticking in my throat,' Tozer whined.

Ross scanned the patch of rough ground that acted as a car park for the nightclub, looking for something easy to break into, simple to hotwire. The answer was in the middle row, high enough to be instantly visible above its compact companions. 'There we go,' he said, breaking into a run, jinking between parked cars till he got to the Land Rover Defender. One of the new generation, still clunky as fuck to drive, but a piece of piss to steal.

'Find a rock,' he called out to Wee Grantie, who obediently started frowning at the ground. He knew from experience what he was looking for – heavy enough to make an impact, pointed enough to break the toughened window glass. There were plenty of candidates compressed into the car park surface, but by the time he found one and heeled it out of the ground, the other three were dancing on their toes round the driver's side of the vehicle.

Ross snatched the rock from him and set it just right in his hand, balanced and steady. He pulled his arm back and with a swift straight jab, he smacked it into the driver's side window. The glass cracked and starred but didn't break. That took a second blow. Then they were all inside, bouncing on the seats like toddlers needing a toilet break, while Ross took out his Swiss army knife, adeptly freeing wires, cutting them and reconnecting the ones that made the engine cough into life.

'Ya beauty,' he yelled, switching the headlamps on and grinding the car into gear. Barely seventeen, no licence, no lessons, but Ross Garvie had all the confidence of a boy who'd been stealing motors since he could reach the pedals.

The Defender lurched backwards, crunching into the headlamps and radiator grille of a VW Golf. Then into first, leaping forward, glass tinkling in their wake. The tyres screamed as Ross whipped the unwieldy Defender out of the car park and into the street. He hammered through the city centre, running red lights and cutting up sedate late-night drivers who didn't want to draw attention to themselves.

The city lights slid past in a blur. The three passengers whooped and yelled as Ross delivered all the thrills of a car chase without the pursuit, not caring when his handbrake turn smacked them into the hard edges of the door furniture.

And then they were on the Perth road, pedal to the metal, flat out. The Defender protested when the speedo needle hit eighty, but it felt a lot faster because of the lumbering sway of the two-ton monster. 'Who needs a fucking Porsche?' Ross yelled as they thundered towards a roundabout. 'I'm going right over the top of that fucker. Off-roading here we fucking come.'

Hitting the roundabout kerb at top speed threw the four lads into the air and back down in disorganised heaps. Ross's feet left the pedals and for a few seconds he felt he was in zero gravity, only his grip on the steering wheel keeping him in contact with the earth. 'Way-hey,' he screamed as he hit the seat and hammered the gas again. Somehow the Defender stayed on all four wheels, ploughing deep furrows through grass and flower beds before emerging on the other side.

'Fuck the Young Farmers,' Tozer gasped. 'We are the country boys.'

A wobble over the far kerb and they were back on the dual carriageway. But now they had distant company. Far back, Ross could see the faint shimmer of a flashing blue light. Some bastard had phoned them in and the five-oh were coming to get them. 'No way,' he shouted, crouching over the wheel, urging the Defender onward as if that would make a difference to its paltry turn of speed.

The next roundabout loomed, higher in the middle. He wasn't daunted. He wasn't wasting time going round when he could go over. But this time, he misjudged the obstacle. Beyond the kerb was a low wall that struck the Defender at precisely the wrong point. For a long moment, it seemed to teeter between the tipping point and stability, before gravity finally won. Once it started turning, momentum took over. The Land Rover rolled end to end twice, tumbling the four youths head over heels like dice in a cup.

Then it clipped the far side of the roundabout, which hurtled it sideways, catapulting it into another complete roll in a different direction. As it smashed into the crash barrier across the carriageway, the engine cut out amid a shower of sparks. The only sound was the creak and grind of metal on metal as the Defender settled.

The two-tone siren of a police traffic car split the quiet, braking to a halt, its blue strobing light bathing the battered vehicle in an unreal glow. It illuminated dark stripes, stains and spatters on the inside of the windows. 'See that?' the driver said to his rookie colleague.

'Tell me that's not blood?' The rookie felt slightly dizzy.

'It's blood all right. Stupid wee bastards. Looks like we'll not need to bother with an ambulance.'

But as he spoke, the crumpled driver's door of the Defender creaked open, spilling the ruined torso of Ross Garvie on to the tarmac.

'Strike that,' the cop sighed. 'That's what you call survival of the unfittest.'

2

K inross was a small town, but it was big enough to have more than one kind of pub. There were hotel bars that supplied food as well as a predictable offering of beers, wines and spirits. There was one where younger drinkers congregated to drink fruit ciders and vodka shots to the accompaniment of loud music. There was another where patrons played pool and darts and watched football on a giant TV screen, washed down with cheap generic beer. And there was Hazeldean's, tucked away off the Kirkgate, its wood-panelled décor apparently unchanged since the 1950s, its regular customers held fast by a range of craft beers and an eye-watering selection of malt whiskies. The walls were lined with padded booths, the tables topped with beaten copper. Bar stools were lined up along one side of the L-shaped bar; the other side provided a brass rail for customers to rest one foot on as they drank at the counter. It was the kind of pub where everyone knew their place.

Gabriel Abbott's place was on the bar stool nearest the corner. Hazeldean's was one of the fixed points in his universe, a reliable anchor when he felt he was navigating turbulent waters. To an outsider, it might seem that there was little in Gabriel's existence to justify that sense of instability. After all, he didn't have a job to worry about. He had a comfortable home, the rent taken care of without any effort on his part. He'd had some gnawing concerns about recent government policies that might affect his benefits, but he really didn't think anyone could argue that he was well enough to be in work.

The reasons that made him unemployable were the same ones that filled him with a sense of turmoil. However hard he tried to appear calm and normal, he knew people thought him eccentric and strange. He couldn't help his enthusiasms getting the better of him and making him garrulous and excitable. It was when he didn't keep his mind busy with his interests that the trouble started for Gabriel. That was when the paranoia started to creep in, eating away at his peace of mind, robbing him of sleep, pushing him back to that terrible pitch of anxiety where he thought his head would explode with its overload of conspiracies and fear. He felt like a piece of paper torn up and scattered to the four winds.

It always ended the same way. He'd surrender himself to the medical profession again. A hospital bed. Drugs. Talking therapies of one sort or another. And they'd help him gather himself together again. He'd re-emerge into the world, fragile but recognisably himself. Till the next time.

He knew he didn't look threatening. His untidy mop of black hair and his wardrobe of charity shop tweed jackets, shirts and trousers – never jeans – gave him the slightly dishevelled air that people imagined absent-minded academics to affect. Often, when he was sitting looking out over Loch Leven or walking from his cottage into town along the waterside path, strangers would strike up a conversation. And within minutes, his tongue would run away with itself and he'd be off on one of the obsessions that had filled his head for years, obsessions that had helped him to build an extraordinary network of contacts in a dozen countries. He could see the appalled expressions on the faces of those unsuspecting strangers as they tried to figure out how to escape a lecture on the resistance movements of Myanmar or the internal politics of North Korea.

But in Hazeldean's, they were used to him. He went there most evenings, walking the couple of miles along the lochside path in all weathers. He'd arrive around nine and have two pints of whatever was the guest beer of the week. He'd exchange a few words about the weather with Jock the barman or Lyn the barmaid. If Gregor Mutch was in, they'd talk politics. If Dougie Malone was there, he'd join in. They both indulged his fascination with the history and geopolitics of South East Asia but they knew him sufficiently well to say when enough was enough and, although it was hard for Gabriel to switch off, he mostly managed it.

That Sunday night, though, Gabriel was troubled. Gregor was in, his bulk perched on the neighbouring bar stool like a turnip on a toothpick, and Gabriel started even before his first pint was put in front of him.

'I'm worried,' he said. 'Very worried.' Jock set his drink in front of him and he took a long swallow.

'How's that?' Gregor asked warily.

'You remember me telling you about Saw Chit? My friend in Myanmar? The one who's been trying to document corruption in the political movements there?'

Gregor grunted noncommittally. Gabriel wasn't put off. If Gregor wanted him to shut up, he'd tell him. 'Well, I had an email from him last week, saying he'd uncovered some very important material relating to some very powerful figures who have made a big deal about being incorruptible. Apparently, Saw Chit has proof that they've been dealing in black market rubies—'

'Black market rubies?' Now he had Gregor's attention. 'What do you mean, black market rubies?'

'Most of the big-name jewellery companies like Tiffany and Cartier and Bulgari won't use rubies from Myanmar because of the absolutely deplorable conditions in the mines. It's virtual slavery, and they've never heard of health and safety. But nevertheless there's a huge market for high-quality gems. So there are always black marketeers who provide rubies with a false provenance. The whole supply chain is breaking the law, and the people at the very top turning a blind eye are the very ones who shout loudest about defeating the smugglers.'

'And your pal is going to name and shame them?'

'So he said in this email. But he's afraid, obviously. And with good reason. He doesn't know who to trust, who might betray him for their own advantage. You know how it is. So he's made a copy of his evidence and posted it to me because he can trust me, he says. I thought he was overreacting, I'll be honest. And then tonight, just before I came out, I had an email from his brother.'

'Don't tell me, let me guess,' Gregor said. 'Your pal's been killed?'

Gabriel frowned. 'No, not that. Actually, probably worse than that. No, he's disappeared. His house has been trashed and he's missing. Nobody saw anything or heard anything, which is frankly incredible. But if I lived there, I'd make a point of selective deafness and blindness.' Gabriel had never been further east than a holiday in Crete, but his imagination was more than adequate to the task of picturing life in the countries he'd made his life's study.

'So why's his brother got in touch with you?'

'He was hoping Saw Chit had managed to escape. To get away before whoever smashed up his house got to him. He thought if Saw Chit had made it, he would have contacted me. Because naturally he'd want someone outside the country to know what had happened. I probably need to speak to a journalist. There's someone at the *Guardian* I've talked to before. Or maybe our MP? Or should I wait for the mail? What do you think?'

Gregor drained his pint. 'I think you've maybe been reading too many of those John le Carré novels, Gabe. Do you not think somebody might be jerking your chain?'

Genuinely puzzled by what seemed to him to be a bizarre conjecture, Gabriel shook his head. 'Why would anyone do that? Besides, I've been friends with Saw Chit for years.'

'But you've never met him.'

Gabriel grabbed a handful of his hair. 'You don't have to meet someone to know them.' He took a breath and gathered himself, laying his hands flat on the bar. 'Why would he make up something like this?'

'I don't know. But if what you say is true, why is he sending the stuff to a guy on the dole in a wee Scottish town instead of 10 Downing Street?'

Gabriel smiled. 'Because he doesn't know the Prime Minister. He knows *me*.'

Gregor clapped him on the back. 'Right enough, Gabe. Better wait till you get the post, though. So tell me, did you see Donald Trump's latest?'

And that, Gabriel knew, was the kind way of shifting him off his personal soapbox. He bit back all the things he wanted to tell Gregor about illegal ruby smuggling and tried to concentrate on the three-ring circus that was American politics. He'd made the right noises in the right places, he thought, finishing his second pint and rising to leave.

Outside, the air was cool and the sky was clear. It was a fine night for a walk. Not that the weather made much difference to him. He needed the fixed mark of Hazeldean's and the only way for him to get there and back was on foot. He'd never driven and he couldn't afford taxis. Gabriel stood in the

Kirkgate, gazing up at the stars, trying to quiet the cacophony in his head. Saw Chit and Myanmar was bad enough, never mind the other thing. That business that had come at him out of nowhere and set everything in his world spinning like the plates in a circus show. All he thought he knew had been called into question. If the answers he found were the wrong ones, it could go very badly for him, and that was a terrifying thought.

He remembered once seeing a machine that tumbled dull rocks till they became polished gemstones. The inside of his head felt like that tonight. Lots of jumbled thoughts banging into each other, confused and indistinguishable one from the other. He knew from past experience that the walk wouldn't turn those thoughts into sense. But perhaps sleep might help. Sometimes it did.

As long as his thoughts didn't spiral out of control between here and home.

3

She walked. Whenever sleep slipped from her grasp, she walked. It occurred to her that her life had come to resemble the first draft of an advertising script for Guinness or Stella Artois. 'She walks. That's what she does.' Except that there was no brightly lit pub full of cheery faces waiting to greet her at the end of her wanderings.

Often at the end of the day, she knew there was no point in stripping to the skin and sliding between cool sheets. She would only lie stiff as a corpse, thoughts of murder running in her head, frantic hamsters on a wheel.

Sometimes, if she was tired enough, sleep would creep up on her and pin her to the bed like a wrestler faster and stronger than she was. But it never lasted long. As soon as exhaustion relaxed its hold on her, she'd surface again, eyes gritty and swollen, mouth dry and tasting of death.

And so she would walk. Along the breakwater, tall apartment blocks to her left, the choppy waters of the Firth of Forth on her right, the night breeze filling her nostrils with salt and seaweed. Then she'd turn inland, past the twenty-four-hour Asda and across the main drag into the old village of Newhaven. She'd pick random routes through the huddled streets of fishermen's cottages, then work her way inland and upwards, always trying to choose streets and alleys and quiet back lanes that she'd never entered before.

That was part of the point. She had chosen to move to Edinburgh precisely because it was unfamiliar. She'd grown up a mere forty-minute train journey away, but the capital had always been exotic. The big city. The place for a special day out. She'd only been familiar with the main streets of the centre until work had started to bring her here from time to time, opening up small windows on disconnected corners. But still, Edinburgh was not a place laden with memories to ambush her in the way that her home town was. Deciding to live here had felt like a project. Learning the city one street at a time might take her mind off the grief and the pain.

So far, she couldn't claim it had worked. She was slowly beginning to understand that there were some feelings nothing could assuage. Nothing except, possibly, the passage of time. Whether that would work, she couldn't tell. It was too soon.

And so she walked. She wasn't the only person out and about in the small hours of an Edinburgh night but most of them were cocooned in cars or night buses. She'd developed a surprising fondness for the night buses. Often she was a long way from home when tiredness finally claimed her. But she'd discovered the impressive bus app for the city. However obscure her location, it plotted a route home for her and, in spite of her initial apprehension, she'd found a rich seam of humanity huddled on the buses. Yes, there were the obnoxious jakies reeking of cheap booze, the zoned-out junkies with blank eyes, but they were outnumbered by others seeking a little late-night camaraderie on their journey. The homeless looking for a bit of light and warmth. The cleaners finishing late or starting early. The shift workers, sleepy-eyed on minimum wage or less. Different accents and tongues that made her feel as if she'd travelled a lot further from the Western Harbour Breakwater than she actually had.

That night, she was plotting a zigzag course along the edge of Leith when she came across the start of the Restalrig Railway Path. She'd encountered the far end of it once before, when she'd found herself down by the shore in Portobello. The disused railway line had been tarmacked over and turned into an off-road route for cyclists and walkers to cut across the city. Street lamps stretched into the distance, giving a sense of safety to what would otherwise have been a dark and uninviting cutting sliced through some of the poorer areas of the city. She decided to give it a try. Worst-case scenario was that she'd end up in the middle of the night in Porty, reliant on the night buses once again.

She set off, thinking about the hidden ways that snaked through the city. Edinburgh had more than its fair share, from those streets in the Old Town that had simply been buried beneath new rows of houses, to the closes and stairways and ginnels that made a honeycomb of the Old Town. Here, there was no clue to what the path had once been except steep banks of untended undergrowth and the occasional straggly tree trying to make something of itself in unpromising circumstances. Every now and then, a heavy iron bridge crossed the path, carrying a road metres above her head. The stone walls supporting the bridges were covered in graffiti tags, their bright colours muted in the low-level lighting. Not exactly art, Karen thought, but better than nothing.

She rounded a curve and was surprised by the glow of some kind of fire underneath the next bridge. She slowed, taking in what lay ahead of her. A knot of men huddled round low tongues of flame. Overcoats and beanie hats, heavy jackets and caps with earflaps, shoulders hunched against the night. As she drew nearer, she realised the centre of their attention was what looked like a garden incinerator fuelled by scrap wood. And what she'd taken for beanies were actually kufi prayer hats.

It didn't occur to her to be nervous of half a dozen men of Middle Eastern appearance gathered round a makeshift fire in the middle of the night. Not in the way she would have been if it had been a bunch of drunks or teens off their heads on glue or drugs. She wasn't heedless of risk, but she had a good estimation of the air of confidence and competence she exuded. Besides, she reckoned she was pretty good at telling the difference between 'unusual' and 'threatening'. She still held fast to that conviction, in spite of the unlikely event that had robbed her life of its meaning.

As she approached, one of the men spotted her and nudged his neighbour. The word went round the group and the low mutter of conversation ceased. By the time she'd broached the loose circle around the flames, they'd fallen silent, a ring of expressionless faces and blank brown eyes fixed on her. She held her hands out to warm them – who could begrudge her that in the chill of night? – and gave them a nod of acknowledgement.

They stood around in an awkward grouping, nonplussed men and a woman who could afford to be relaxed because she believed she had nothing left to lose. Nobody spoke, and after a few minutes, she nodded again and went on her way without a backward glance. Only another oddity to chalk up to her nocturnal ramblings.

She was beginning to feel that sleep might be a possibility, so she cut down Henderson Street, past the Banana Flats where occasional lights gleamed, down towards the wide mouth of the Water of Leith. Not far to go now. Then she would fall into bed, maybe not even bothering to undress.

At last, she'd lose consciousness for a few hours. Enough to keep her functioning.

And tomorrow morning, Detective Chief Inspector Karen Pirie, head of Police Scotland's Historic Cases Unit, would be ready to deal with whatever crossed her desk. Hell mend anyone who suggested otherwise.

4

oland Brown always left his house in Scotlandwell in plenty of time to cycle the six miles to his office in Kinross. Truth to tell, he set off ridiculously early because that way he could escape the hell that was breakfast with his three children. Other people's kids seemed to be able to rub along pretty well, but his daughter and two sons existed in a state of constant warfare that had only intensified now the teenage hormones were starting to kick in. It started as soon as their eyes opened in the morning and carried on relentlessly till bedtime. Which was another source of perpetual battles. He'd recently come to the conclusion that although he loved his children – at least, he supposed he did – he really didn't like them. It was a realisation he could share with nobody except the birds and the wildlife on his way to and from work.

Unlike humans, they wouldn't judge him.

So he'd hammer along the Loch Leven trail, muttering his current annoyance as he pedalled, ridding himself of his rage with every downward thrust of his legs. By the time he reached the office, he was calm, unflustered and ready to settle down to his clients' VAT returns and tax problems.

At that time of the morning, it was a peaceful ride. Unless it was raining or snowing, there would be a scattering of dog walkers who would raise a hand or nod their heads in greeting as he hurtled past. In the summer, he'd occasionally encounter cyclists on touring trips. But generally, it was just him and the things he knew he should never say to his ungrateful, ill-mannered, self-absorbed children. People spoke about blaming the parents, but Roland refused to accept that he and his wife had been particularly catastrophic in their child-rearing. Some people were born twisted.

He rounded a long curve, the loch on his left, the early morning sun hitting his shoulder as he emerged from a clump of trees. Ahead he could see a clearing with a bench that took advantage of the view up the loch towards the Lomond hills. A figure was hunched on the wooden seat. Roland had never seen anybody sitting there before, and it was a surprise to see someone sitting down on what was a cold spring morning with a real nip in the air. There would be dew on that bench, no doubt about it.

As he drew nearer, he could see the man wasn't so much hunched as slumped. Had he taken ill? Was that why he'd gone to sit down? Did he need help?

For a split second, Roland considered ignoring the man and pretending to himself there was nothing out of the ordinary going on. But he was a decent man at heart, so he slowed to a halt and wheeled his expensive mountain bike across the grass. 'Are you all right, pal?' he called as he approached.

No reply. Now he could see that the man's head was at an odd angle and he seemed to have something brown and sticky matting his hair. Roland drew nearer, his brain refusing to process what he was seeing. And then it was impossible to ignore and all at once Roland's bike was on the grass. Vomit sprayed the ground at his feet as he realised the man on the bench was never going to be all right again.

5

Nine o'clock and Karen was in the poky office at the back of the Gayfield Square station that housed the Historic Cases Unit. They were squeezed into the furthest corner, as if the high command wanted them out of sight and out of mind. Except when they cracked a major case, of course. Then Karen was dragged out of her remote cubbyhole and paraded in front of the media. It made her feel like a prize pig at an agricultural show. However, they were generally ignored for the rest of the time, which suited Karen. Nobody was looking over her shoulder, checking out what she was up to when she hunched in front of her computer screen, blowing on a flat white to cool it enough to drink.

First task of the day was to check her email, to see whether any of her pending cases had inched forward thanks to the forensic scientists who routinely re-examined evidence from old unsolved cases. Their results were often what set a fresh investigation in motion. Without a solid piece of new evidence, there was nowhere for Karen to go.

She was still skimming her mailbox when the door slowly opened to reveal the other half of the cold case team, precariously balancing a paper plate supporting two bacon rolls on top of a large cardboard cup. Detective Constable Jason 'the Mint' Murray was as dexterous as he was quick on the uptake, which made Karen fear for the fate of his breakfast.

'Morning,' he grunted, miraculously negotiating his arrival without spillage. 'I brought you a bacon roll.'

The gesture touched Karen more than it warranted. Jason seldom thought beyond his own needs, which was fine with Karen. She didn't need a daily reminder of what she'd lost. 'Thanks,' she said, conscious of sounding less than grateful.

'Any news?' Jason took one of the rolls and handed Karen the plate. He yawned as he dropped into his chair. 'Late one last night.'

'Where were you?' Karen really didn't care. But she knew the value of small gestures when it came to cementing team loyalty. Even if they were only a team of two.

'I went through to Kirkcaldy for my cousin's birthday. We ended up on tequila shots in somebody's kitchen. That's the last thing I remember.'

'I hope you got the train in this morning,' Karen said sententiously.

'Och, I feel fine. I'm a polis, nobody's going to do me on a morning after.'

'Not the point, Jason.' Before she could deliver a lecture, her mobile rang. 'DCI Pirie, Historic Cases Unit.'

The voice at the other end had the unmistakable vowels of Dundee. 'Aye, this is Sergeant Torrance from Tayside. Traffic Division.' He stopped abruptly, as if he'd given her enough information to be going on with.

'Hello, Sergeant. How can I help you?'

'Well, I think it might be me that can help you.'

More silence. Clearly she was going to have to work at extracting information from Sergeant Torrance. 'An offer of help always gets my day off to a good start. What is it you think you've got?'

'You maybe saw on the news we had a bad crash at the weekend?'

'Sorry, that one passed me by. What happened?'

'Ach, a stupid boy showing off to his pals, more than likely. They lifted a Land Rover Defender and somersaulted it over a roundabout on the Perth road in the wee small hours. All three passengers smashed to bits, dead on arrival at Ninewells.'

Karen sucked her breath over her teeth in an expression of sympathy. She'd seen enough road accidents in her time to know the level of carnage they could produce. 'That'd piss on your chips and no mistake.'

'Aye. One of the officers attending, it was his first fatal RTA. I doubt he'll get much sleep for a wee while. Anyway. The thing is, the driver's still alive. He's in a coma, like, but he's hanging in there.'

Karen made an encouraging noise. 'And you took a sample to check his blood alcohol.'

'Correct. Which was, by the way, five times over the limit.'

'Ouch. And I'm presuming you got the lab to run DNA?'

'Well, it's routine now.' Sergeant Torrance didn't sound like a man who thought that was a good use of Police Scotland's budget.

'I'm guessing that's why you're calling me?'

'Aye. We got a hit on the DNA database. I don't pretend to understand these things, but it wasn't a direct hit. Well, it couldn't have been, because it ties in with a twenty-year-old murder and this laddie's only seventeen.' The rustle of paper. 'Apparently it's what they call a familial hit. Whoever left his semen all over a rape murder victim in Glasgow twenty years ago was a close male relative of a wee Dundee gobshite called Ross Garvie.'

*

The adrenaline rush of reopening a cold case never faded for Karen. The rest of her life might have gone to hell in a handcart, but excavating the past for its secrets still exerted its familiar pull on her. Yesterday she'd never heard of Tina McDonald. Today, the dead hairdresser was front and centre in Karen's consciousness.

After she'd finished extracting all the information she could from Sergeant Torrance, Karen called the Mint over to her desk. 'We've got a familial DNA hit on an open unsolved rape murder,' she said, her fingers battering the keyboard as she googled the victim. She skimmed the thin results of her search, leaving it for later. There were more important things to set in motion.

Jason slumped into the chair opposite. In spite of his posture, his expression was alert. 'I'll not bother taking my jacket off, then.'

Both halves of the suit might have looked better if he'd taken it off before he went to sleep in it, Karen thought. 'Tina McDonald. A hairdresser from Partick. Raped and strangled in Glasgow city centre on May seventeenth, 1996. A Friday night. Twenty-four when she died. You know the drill.'

Jason crammed the last chunk of his bacon roll into his mouth and nodded, chewing vigorously then swallowing hard. 'I've to go to the warehouse and pull the files and the physical evidence. Take the evidence to Gartcosh to have the DNA checked again, then bring the files back here.' It was the first phase of every cold case resurrection. He recited it like the mantra it had become for him.

'Away you go, then. If you're lucky with the traffic, you'll be back by lunchtime and we can get stuck in this afternoon.' Karen returned to the screen, flinching as Jason's chair legs screeched on the tiled floor. These days, all her nerve endings seemed to be closer to the surface.

There wasn't much online. Back in 1996, the news media

hadn't really embraced the idea of digital platforms. There was plenty coverage of the Dunblane primary school massacre that year, but most of that was retrospective. What had happened to Tina McDonald had probably been well covered at the time, particularly by the tabloids. But it had more or less sunk without trace since.

Karen finally hit pay dirt with a website devoted to Glasgow murders. It spanned almost two hundred years and showed a devotion to detail that made her faintly queasy. She wondered whether her colleagues in the city knew about the site and the identity of its creator. He might be a bona fide obsessive. But he might be more than that. For now, however, she was grateful for his diligence.

When Tina McDonald left her cosy single-end flat in Havelock Street on Friday the 17th of May 1996, she couldn't have known she'd never return. Twenty-four-year-old Tina was off on a girls' night out with three workmates from the Hair Apparent salon on Byres Road to celebrate the birthday of Liz Dunleavy, the salon owner. Tina was wearing a new outfit from What Every Woman Wants, a figure-hugging red dress with a sequinned swirl from shoulder to waist. Her shoes were new too, a smart pair of low-heeled red patent leather pumps.

Petite blonde Tina took the underground into town from the Kelvinhall station to Buchanan Street then walked the short distance to the Starburst Bar on Sauchiehall Street where the girls were already ensconced with their drinks. Tina was drinking vodka and coke. According to Liz Dunleavy, quoted in the *Daily Record*, they had several rounds before leaving the Starburst for Bluebeard's nightclub in a side street off George Square.

The club was packed and the dance floor was full of bodies. At first, the girls stayed together but during the course of the next couple of hours they split up and danced with various men. Liz Dunleavy said they lost track of each other for a while. Little did they know the horror that was happening to Tina as they were dancing the night away without a care in the world. When they came back together around 2 a.m., of Tina there was no sign.

But none of them were worried. It wasn't unknown for one or other of them to pair up with a man and either go on to another club or go home with him. So even though Tina didn't generally behave like that, the other three didn't think anything was amiss. They queued up for a taxi from the rank at Queen Street station and went home, thinking Tina was having a good time with someone she'd just met.

Next morning, there was a big shock in store for Sandy Simpson, the early barman at Bluebeard's. Sandy's first job of the day was to deal with the empties from the night before. He wheeled out the first tub from behind the bar into the lane where the club's glass skips were situated. And there, stuffed behind one of the wheeled skips like a discarded piece of rubbish, was the battered and strangled body of poor Tina McDonald.

Strathclyde Police struggled with the case. They revealed Tina had been brutally raped, beaten about the head and manually strangled. They later admitted they had DNA evidence, but no suspects to match it against. Literally hundreds of people who had been out in the city that night came forward to be interviewed and tested, but it seemed that nobody had seen Tina with a man and all the DNA tests came back negative. The last definite sighting of her was touching up her make-up in the ladies toilet of Bluebeard's at about one in the morning. And then it was as if she had disappeared in a puff of smoke only to reappear the next morning as a murder victim.

All these years later, still no one knows who took Tina McDonald's life that spring evening. Nobody has paid the price for this cruel and heartless act that caused so much grief and loss to the people who loved Tina. It remains one of the shameful Glasgow murders that has no solution.

Behind the sensationalism and the bad prose were the bare bones of a case that had remained a mystery for the best part of twenty years. No witnesses, no suspects – at least, none the police were prepared to go public with – and no closure for the people who had loved Tina.

Now at last, here was a lead that might take them to the door of a man who had escaped justice for years. For Karen, the punishment wasn't the most important aspect of her job. In her experience, the overwhelming majority of killers didn't simply shrug off what they'd done and carry on as if nothing had happened. Their lives were distorted in one way or another by guilt and shame. More often than not, that final confrontation with their crimes seemed almost to come as a relief. In her book, the law's retribution was only the final stage of punishment.

What mattered most to her was answering the questions of those left struggling with the aftermath of sudden violent death. The survivors deserved to know how – and sometimes why – and by whose hand the people they loved had been snatched from them. It was easy to sneer at the idea of closure, but she'd seen at first hand how the cold case team's results had allowed people to come to terms with their grief and loss. It didn't always turn out that way, but it happened often enough to make her feel proud of their work.

Karen printed out the blog entry and while she was waiting for the printer to warm up and spit out the pages, she searched for images of Tina. And there was the poster Strathclyde Police had issued in a bid to jog the memory of potential witnesses. It had obviously been blown up from a snap taken by a pal on a night out. In the age of selfies and camera phones, it was easy to forget that back then there were far fewer images to choose from when you were trying to encourage people to remember what they'd seen. When you were using film, you couldn't tell what your pictures were like till you had them developed. And then the moment was past, with only a fistful of rubbish photos to remind you of a memorable occasion.

The head-and-shoulders shot of Tina that accompanied the request for information was fuzzy and indistinct. She was grinning at the camera, a cocktail glass in her hand. A tumbled halo of blonde hair surrounded a face that might charitably be described as heart-shaped, with a pointed chin and sharp features. Narrow shoulders and a dress that made the most of her breasts. Plenty of men would have found her attractive enough to chat up, Karen reckoned. The problem was that there was nothing particularly distinctive about her. She wouldn't have stood out in a crowd. And that was why they'd had so much difficulty in finding any decent leads, she supposed.

Karen printed out the photo sheet and collected it from the printer tray. She rearranged the contents of one of their whiteboards to make room for the new investigation and attached what little they had. With luck, Jason would bring something more substantial. And then they could get down to work.

6

U sually when a new case hit the Historic Cases Unit, Karen had to be pried away from her desk at the end of the day. She always felt driven to absorb as much as she possibly could right from the start. First impressions were important; she would drill down into the detail afterwards, but she liked to have a sense of how the previous investigation had taken shape.

But not on Mondays. Monday evenings were her time. Monday evenings were when she and Detective Chief Inspector Jimmy Hutton sat in her living room drinking gin and staring out across the glitter and swell of the Firth of Forth towards the clustered lights of the string of Fife towns from North Queensferry to Kirkcaldy. Karen had tried to tell Jimmy it wasn't necessary any more. That she wasn't going to fall apart. But Jimmy refused to take a telling. She suspected he needed their Monday evenings as much as she did.

Long months before, Detective Sergeant Phil Parhatka had been killed in the line of duty. That was something that almost never happened in Scotland; there was no routine protocol for getting past it. Phil had been Karen's partner. The love of her life. She'd fallen for him the first week they worked together and for years she'd been convinced it would never be reciprocated. And then it was.

After they got together, Phil had moved from the HCU. He became Jimmy Hutton's bagman, his trusted lieutenant in the quaintly named Murder Prevention Team. He'd been fascinated by his job and never imagined it would be the death of him. And then it was.

After the funeral, Karen ignored the advice of everyone who told her not to make any major decisions for a year. She sold the house in Kirkcaldy that Phil had left to her. She sold her own house to the couple who had been renting it from her. With the proceeds, she'd put down a substantial deposit on the flat on the Western Harbour Breakwater with the sensational view and absolutely no memories.

Two weeks after the funeral, Jimmy Hutton had turned up on her doorstep on a Monday. 'I thought you could maybe do with some company,' he'd said, proffering a bottle of gin – The Botanist from Islay.

'I'm fine,' she'd said. But she was leaning against the door for support. Kindness, she'd recently discovered, was her undoing.

Jimmy had sighed. 'No, you're not. And neither am I. I've not come to be maudlin. We've both taken a body blow, and we're neither of us in a position to let that show in the day-to-day. I could talk to Phil and so could you. I thought maybe we could talk to each other instead?'

And so she'd opened the door wider, saying, 'I've got Fevertree tonic in the fridge.' It had since become a Monday evening ritual. Gin sampling and conversation. They didn't talk much about Phil. They didn't need to; they'd both absorbed the terrible blow of his death and understood the cost of his loss. But when they did touch on him it was with affection and wry smiles. What they talked about instead was their work. Each had become a sounding board for the other. And in the process they'd worked their way through a series of interesting and sometimes challenging gins. Karen had a decided preference for Miller's Westbourne Strength with its notes of cucumber, while Jimmy's current favourite was Caorunn from the Highlands with its distinctive tang of rowan berries.

Tonight they were going to broach Jimmy's latest discovery – Professor Cornelius Ampleforth's Bathtub Gin. And much as she loved her job, on a Monday night there was no competition. Besides, she'd already made a first pass at the Tina McDonald case. They hadn't gone through the hundreds of statements yet, but just by looking at the way the paperwork was organised, she could sense that the initial inquiry hadn't been a fuck-up. It looked at first glance as though the i's had been dotted and the t's crossed. What they'd lacked was an even break.

Which was where Ross Garvie's familial DNA came in.

Karen was looking forward to telling Jimmy all about it. But as it turned out, he jumped in first with one of his own. Partly because he wanted it to be a cautionary tale for Karen. He knew about the walking and it made him uneasy. He knew what late-night streets in a big city could be like and he didn't want Karen to come to harm. After Phil, that would be unbearable.

'I can take care of myself,' Karen had protested the first time he'd raised the subject.

'Aye, and so could Phil. It's not you that's the issue, it's the bampots and bawbags out there.'

It was a topic he'd come back to more than once, sometimes directly, sometimes circling round it. Tonight was one of the more oblique ones. 'Did you hear they had a murder last night up by Kinross?' Jimmy swirled the ice cubes in his drink, clinking them against the sides of the tumbler. He sniffed at the glass, his nose wrinkling as he savoured the gin's complex blend of botanicals.

'What? One of yours?'

He shook his head. 'No, thank goodness. I only know as much about it as I do because we're working with the victim's social worker on another case altogether. She was telling me about it when I stopped by this afternoon.'

Back at the breakfast bar, Karen filled a bowl with crisps and headed back to the far end of the living room where two sofas were angled together in a V-shape to maximise access to the view. 'A domestic?' She sat down and plonked the bowl on the triangular glass coffee table.

'No.' Jimmy helped himself to a handful of crisps. 'Quite the opposite, really.'

Intrigued, Karen raised her eyebrows in a question. 'What's that, then? The opposite of a domestic?'

'Well, for a start, the victim wasn't in any kind of relationship. As far as Giorsal knows, he'd never—'

'Did you say, "Giorsal"?' Karen interrupted.

Jimmy's eyebrows twitched upwards. 'Aye. Giorsal Kennedy. She's the senior social worker in the case.'

'We were at school together.'

'Aye, she mentioned she used to know you.'

'We used to be pals but she went off to study social work in Manchester. Amazing. Giorsal Kennedy, as I live and breathe. Last I heard, she got hitched to some guy from Liverpool. When did she come back to Fife?'

Jimmy shrugged. 'I'm not sure. We've been working with her a wee bit more than a year now. You should give her a ring, I bet she'd be pleased to hear from you.'

Karen snorted. 'Now who's the social worker? I've not seen the woman for more than fifteen years, we'd likely have nothing in common. Still, Giorsal Kennedy ...' She pulled herself back to attention. 'So, tell me about this non-domestic murder.'

'The victim was a guy called Gabriel Abbott. A bit of a loner, by all accounts. He lived in a wee cottage near the Orwell standing stones.'

'What? The ones that look like a pair of massive dildos in the middle of a field?'

Jimmy laughed. 'One-track mind.'

'Hey, come on, what else do they make you think of? There's nothing symbolic about them, Jimmy. They're two giant willies. End of.'

He shook his head. 'Have it your own way. Anyway, apparently it was his habit to walk home from the pub in Kinross along the Loch Leven trail. So yesterday morning, some guy was cycling from Scotlandwell to his work in Kinross when he notices a man slumped on a bench at a viewpoint a few feet off the path. He thinks he's maybe taken a turn of some kind. So he stops and checks it out, and lo and behold, it's Gabriel Abbott.'

'Dead already?'

'Oh aye, dead a few hours at that point. At first they thought it might be suicide. Gunshot to the head, gun in his hand.'

'But?' Karen leaned forward, scenting something more.

Jimmy pulled a wry face, setting his glass down on the table. 'The entry wound was here.' He pressed his fingertips to his right temple. Then he waggled the fingers of his left hand. 'But the gun was in his left hand. So unless he was a contortionist ...'

'... he was helped on his way by someone who wasn't quite as smart as he intended to be.' She shook her head, puffing her cheeks as she exhaled. 'Easy done, if you're panicking. If you're an amateur. So what's the story?'

'There is no story at this point. It's as mysterious as that banker who got shot on his own doorstep in Nairn a few years back. You remember?'

Karen nodded. No enemies, no debts, no motive. No witnesses, no trace-back on the gun, no viable DNA. 'So what did this Gabriel Abbott do for a living?'

Jimmy picked up his drink and savoured a sip. 'Nothing. I kind of like this one, Karen. I'm getting a hint of coriander and cinnamon. Might be the perfect curry aperitif.'

'You could be right.' She took another swallow. 'Spicy warmth. Nothing clinical about this one. But going back to the dead guy: how old was he?'

'Around thirty, I think. Giorsal says he was bright, but he had some mental health problems going way back. He'd never been able to hold down a job.'

'It's hard to see how he would piss somebody off enough to murder him.'

'It doesn't always take much.'

'True.'

'Maybe he was just in the wrong place at the wrong time.' Jimmy looked at her over the rim of his glass. 'That's why—'

'Stop right there,' Karen said. 'I'm not in the mood for one of your heavy-handed morality tales. Bad things happen in the dark. I get it. But bad things happen in the bright light of day too. Phil didn't die because he was walking the streets at night, Jimmy. I know how to take care of myself. I know how to be safe.'

Jimmy sighed and ran a hand over the undulating bumps of his shaven head. 'Sure you do.' His voice was heavy with the weight of disbelief.

'So the local lads are struggling with this one?'

'Aye. No witnesses. Nothing.'

'Interesting.' Karen stared out over the water. Sometimes

she hankered after a live case. She loved what she did, but she couldn't kid herself that it carried the same adrenaline buzz as the quest to build a chain of evidence in real time.

'I'll tell you what's really interesting, Karen. Twenty-two years ago, Gabriel Abbott's mother was murdered. And nobody spent so much as a day in jail for it.'

7

Karen let the Mint drive to Dundee next morning. Not because she was worried about how much gin she'd drunk the night before but because she wanted to mull over the case Jimmy Hutton had brought up. There were a lot of things that ran in families, but murder wasn't one of them. Not even in families who made the criminal records computer ka-ching like a slot machine that had hit the jackpot. But there was nothing dodgy about Gabriel Abbott's family.

Equally, there was nothing similar about the two murders. After Jimmy had left, Karen had gone online to see what she could find out about the death of Abbott's mother. It hadn't been anything like she'd expected.

Caroline Abbott, a successful West End theatre impresario, had made the fatal error of travelling in a small plane with a former Secretary of State for Northern Ireland at a time when the IRA and its assorted splinter groups had been flexing their terrorist muscles. When the plane blew up over the Scottish Borders, the four people on board had died instantly. It looked open and shut, even though nobody had claimed responsibility. 'Probably forgot the bloody code word,' she'd muttered, thinking how often she ended up on the phone to her bank because she'd forgotten her memorable word.

Later, as she'd walked along the coast in the small hours, she'd thought about Gabriel Abbott, a man whose life must have been defined by that early loss. A year ago, she wouldn't have made much of that. But now, she had also become someone defined by loss and she couldn't help feeling an odd kinship with the dead man. Instead of paying attention to her surroundings, she worried at the handful of details she'd learned online about the catastrophic event that had turned his life upside down, as Phil's murder had done for her.

On the face of it, there was nothing to link the murder of Caroline Abbott with that of her son. A terrorist bombing and an up-close-and-personal shooting. Just a tragic coincidence.

Except that Karen didn't believe in coincidence.

The Mint slowed as two main roads merged on the approach to the Forth Road Bridge. The journey north from the capital had been less congested in the months since HGVs had been banned from the bridge because of fears that the whole thing might collapse and dump its users into the freezing waters of the estuary below. The haulage companies were grumbling at the detours that had been forced on them, but Karen had little sympathy. It was their heavily laden behemoths that had done the damage in the first place.

'I love that bridge,' the Mint declared, taking one hand off the wheel to gesture at the railway bridge, its cantilevers a dark red diagram sketched with careful accuracy against a blue sky.

'Me too,' Karen admitted. To someone from Fife, someone like her, it was a border crossing as definite and iconic as Checkpoint Charlie. It marked the southern frontier between the Kingdom of Fife and the rest of the world. Fife was different. Everybody knew that.

The road bridge was what mostly carried her across the

Firth of Forth these days, and that meant she was hardly ever conscious of its span. But the railway bridge was irresistible, a monument to Victorian engineering that had given a fresh idiom to the English language. 'Like painting the Forth Bridge,' described a never-ending Sisyphean task. Except that, these days, the idiom was a dead letter. Now the industrial chemists had come up with a paint whose topcoat would last for twenty years. It had made Karen wonder which of the other apparent certainties she carried in her head were equally invalid.

The Mint flashed her a quick glance. She'd schooled him well; he knew not to interrupt her if she was lost in thought. Karen reckoned he'd tossed out the comment on the bridge to see whether there might be an opportunity to talk. 'Something bothering you, Jason?' she said. 'And by the way, are you actually trying to grow a beard or did you just sleep in every morning for the last week?'

'It's going to be a goatee when it's finished.' His attempt at dignity was touching but unsuccessful.

'You do know it's coming in ginger?'

'Auburn, boss. Auburn.' He frowned, concentrating on the road ahead.

'Your hair's auburn, if you stretch a point. Your beard is the colour of Irn Bru. Trust me, Jason, it's not going to be a babe magnet. I say that in the spirit of kindness. Other people may not.'

He stuck out his lower lip, like a mutinous toddler. 'All the other guys in the flat have got beards.'

'Maybe so, Jason, but they're all students. They've got a licence to walk about looking like numpties. But you are a polis and you need people to take you seriously. Now, was there something other than facial hair you wanted to ask about?'

He moved into the fast lane as they reached the end of the

roadworks. 'How are we going about this, boss? Have we got a plan of action?'

'First stop, the ICU at Ninewells.'

'Why are we going there? I thought Ross Garvie was in a coma?'

'Because it's not Ross Garvie we're interested in, is it? Even if he's up for a conversation, which seems, frankly, a long way from likely, what's he going to be able to tell us? He wasn't even a twinkle in his daddy's eye when Tina McDonald was attacked. But the traditional place to find the parents in a situation like this is the bedside vigil.'

Light broke across the Mint's face. 'Right,' he said, extending the word to three syllables. Karen stifled a sigh. Sometimes she wished for a bagman with a few more functioning synapses. But Jason was willing, he was loyal, and because he didn't have his eye on a bigger prize, he gave every investigation all he had. And for that, she could forgive his lack of brilliance. 'So we'll have a wee word with them and then we'll see if we can persuade Stewart Garvie to part with a DNA sample.'

'And if we can't?'

Karen shrugged. 'We'll just have to arrest him.' It was a last resort, but Tina McDonald's killer had been walking the streets for twenty-odd years, and she was determined not to let him carry on for a day more than necessary. She looked out of the window at the rolling green unfolding on either side of the ribbon of motorway. This had once been mining country, the heart of the West Fife coalfield. In her youth, the landscape had been peppered with winding gear that looked as if it had come from the same drawing board as the railway bridge – a metal skeleton painted the identical dark red. Now it was country parks and fields and people doing jobs that men like her father didn't comprehend.

Before she could take the idea any further, Loch Leven

sparkled into view on the right, a reminder of Gabriel Abbott's violent death. All Karen knew about Loch Leven came from her childhood – an uncle who had fished for trout there at weekends to escape his termagant wife; a castle on an island where Mary Queen of Scots had been imprisoned, miscarried twins and abdicated the Scottish throne. Sometimes they'd gone on family outings on Sundays to nearby Kinross, where a vast covered market sold everything from underpants to sausages. The journey provided views of the loch, but she'd usually been too busy reading a comic or a library book to pay much attention.

But now she was interested. She craned forward in her seat to see past the Mint. The brutal bulk of the Bishop was reflected in the still waters, casting a shadow over half of the western end of the loch. One shore in shade, one in sunlight made for a dramatic scene. But not one where you'd expect a murder. Karen pulled out her phone and called Jimmy Hutton.

'Hi, Karen,' he said, his voice brisk. 'What can I do for you?'

'Have you got a number for Giorsal Kennedy?'

'Aye. Like I said, we liaise with her. So you fancy catching up on the old days after all?' He sounded upbeat.

'Why not?'

'I think the pair of you will get along gangbusters. I'll text you the number.'

Karen leaned back in her seat and smiled. Gabriel Abbott wasn't her concern. She knew that. But that didn't mean she couldn't take an interest. 'Jason?'

'Yes, boss?'

'How would you feel about getting the train back from Dundee?'

He gave her a puzzled look. It was the expression of his that she knew best. 'What for?'

'I think there's something I want to do on the way back. Somebody I want to go and see.'

'I could wait,' he said.

'It might take a while.'

He shrugged. 'I don't mind waiting.'

'That's good of you, Jason. But I think it would be better if you took the train home.'

This time he understood it wasn't really a suggestion. 'OK, boss,' he sighed. 'But what if we have to arrest Ross Garvie's dad?'

'We'll burn that bridge when we come to it.'

8

E ven with the pallor of unconsciousness and the partial shaving of his thick black hair, Ross Garvie's good looks were evident. Straight dark brows, long lashes, a neat nose with a hawksbill curve and a generous mouth with a natural quirk at the corners that made it look like he was on the edge of a smile. Easy to see how he'd been a leader of the pack, Karen thought. Chances were that would be beyond him in the future, if the nurse's verdict was on the money.

'Subdural haematoma,' she'd said.

'What's that?' Jason clearly wasn't watching enough episodes of *Casualty*.

Karen was happy to find that the nurse responsible for Ross Garvie was the talkative sort. She smiled at Jason and said, 'When you get a blow to the head that damages a blood vessel in the brain, blood leaks out and forms a clot that puts pressure on the brain. It causes brain damage. The severity varies according to how bad the original damage was and how long it is before we manage to relieve the pressure on the brain. Ross took a bad knock on the side of his head and another one on the back of his skull. The chances are he's going to have quite a bit of impairment to deal with once he wakes up from his coma.'

'Will he definitely wake up?' Jason again. Leaning over the bed and peering at Ross as if he was an exotic specimen in a zoo.

The nurse looked a bit more wary. 'It's too early to say. Coma's a very unpredictable state.'

'What about his other injuries?' Karen gestured towards the cage supporting the bedclothes.

'Fractures to the left tib and fib, and the right ankle. Pelvis pretty much shattered. Five busted ribs. Right arm and wrist will need surgery and pinning. He's looking at a long hard journey back to anything like mobility,' she said, matter-of-fact now. 'Not much of a future for a good-looking young lad like him.'

'Even less of a future for the three lads who were with him in the Land Rover,' Karen pointed out. 'So, are his parents not here?'

The nurse shook her head. 'They were here all day Sunday. She came back yesterday, but we asked her not to spend all her days and evenings here. It's better all round if we can get the families not to do that. It means we can get on with the work of the ward, which can be quite traumatic sometimes. And it means they don't get worn out in the same way. Left to themselves, they put their own health at risk, sitting at bedsides day and night. It's only natural to want to do whatever you can to support somebody you love, but it helps nobody if your own body breaks down in the process.'

'What did you make of them?' Karen said, stepping away from the bed and moving closer to the nurse, inviting a more intimate response. She was good at making people relax into revelation. She thought it was something to do with her apparent lack of sophistication. A few extra pounds (less than there used to be, but still . . .); a wardrobe that always looked slightly rumpled; a haircut that had defeated hairdressers all her life. Women never felt threatened by her and men treated her like a wee sister or a favourite auntie.

Now the nurse was seduced into confidences. 'They were stricken, but it was like they weren't surprised. Like they were resigned to something bad happening to the boy. His mum was definitely more upset. His dad ... it felt like he was more angry than sad. Mind you, it's often the same with men. They don't know how to express their feelings, so they hide behind being gruff.'

Karen remembered. Phil had been like that in public. But it had been a different story when they'd been alone together. Then, he'd found the words to anatomise his responses to the people and the situations he encountered at work. His hidden sensitivity was the key to his success in the Murder Prevention Squad, a success that had ended up costing his life. Karen gave herself a mental shake and focused on what the nurse was saying.

'But I had the definite feeling he couldn't wait to get out of here on Sunday night. It made him uncomfortable. I asked her if he was coming in yesterday, but she said he'd gone to his work. He needed something to keep himself occupied.'

'What does he do? Did Mrs Garvie say?'

'He's something to do with the redevelopment down by the station. Where the V&A's going to be.'

'What about her? Does she work?'

'She works from home, she said. She's a freelance transcriber.'

'What's that?' Jason had drifted across to join them.

Impatient with the interruption, Karen explained. 'When people dictate stuff, or when people need a hard copy of an interview or a meeting, they ping the digital recording over to somebody like Linda Garvie and she turns the audio into a document.'

'Sheesh. Who knew that was a job?'

'How did you think our interviews end up as court documents?'

The blank look he gave her said it all. 'I never thought about it,' he said.

Karen turned the full beam of her attention back to the nurse. 'So you reckon she'll be at home now?'

'Well, she said she'd be in this afternoon, so you'll probably catch her. But I don't think she'll be able to tell you anything about the accident.'

Karen smiled. 'We're only looking for a bit of background. You've been very helpful.' She took Jason's elbow and steered him towards the door. 'Time to let these good people get on with saving some lives, Jason.' *While we set about throwing a hand grenade into others.*

There was nothing remarkable about the Garvies' house, nothing that made it stand out from its neighbours in the quiet residential street off the main Perth road. A traditional Scottish stone semi-detached villa with a dormer window thrusting out from the roof. There would be an attic bedroom behind it, the roof and walls intersecting at odd angles apparently designed with the sole intent of cracking the heads of the unwary. Karen wondered if that was the room where Ross Garvie had grown up. Lads from streets like these were supposed to confine their teenage rebellion to tiny acts of nonconformity – stealing a nip of vodka from the bottle in the cupboard, swearing in front of their granny, toking on a skinny joint in a friend's bedroom. Not getting lashed to the gills and stealing cars. That was supposed to be confined to the underclass. The neighbours would be agog.

Unless of course any of the dead boys were neighbours. Then the atmosphere would be different. Vengeful and poisonous, rich with recrimination and blame. For Linda

Garvie's sake, Karen hoped Ross's victims lived on the other side of town. Whatever her stupid son had done, it wasn't her fault. As for Stewart Garvie – if the DNA lab had got it right, he might have worse things to occupy his mind and his neighbours before too long. 'Let's do it, then,' she said.

They walked up a path of neatly laid stone slabs that bisected weed-free gravel, a perfect oval flower bed on each side, miniature daffodils and grape hyacinths adding a splash of colour to the grey. Karen rang the bell and took a step back so she'd appear less intimidating. A long silence. She was about to ring again when the door inched open. In the gap she could see a wedge of dark hair and one blue eye with a dark smudge beneath it. 'I've got nothing to say,' Linda Garvie said, her voice loud and harsh. 'I told you people. I've got nothing to say.'

'I'm from Police Scotland,' Karen said quickly. 'Not the press.' She held up the ID she had at the ready.

The eyebrow lowered over the eye as Linda peered at it. 'Oh, I'm sorry, I thought you were another journalist.' The door opened wider to reveal the rest of her face, pinched with misery and lined with anxiety. She was a short, stout woman dressed in black trousers and a pink mohair sweater. Her hair looked dry and mussed, as if she'd slept on it and not bothered with a brush. She sighed. 'You'd better come in.'

Karen stepped inside, intrigued that the woman hadn't assumed their presence meant more bad news. In her shoes, Karen's first thought would have been that the police were there to reveal that her son had died. Linda gestured vaguely to the doorway on the left of the hall. 'In you go. Take a seat. Do you want a cup of tea or anything?'

'We're fine, thanks.' Karen turned into a living room as neat as the front garden. A sofa, two armchairs, occasional tables set with coasters, a plasma TV hanging above the fireplace where previous generations would have had a mirror or a picture. A display cabinet on the back wall contained glasses and bottles and a shelf of family photographs. Karen recognised the boy in the hospital bed.

Karen and the Mint perched side by side on the unforgiving sofa. It wasn't a piece of furniture that encouraged slumping, she thought. Linda Garvie hovered for a moment, then lowered herself gingerly into an armchair, as if she expected it to bite her. She crossed her feet at the ankles and raised her chin in an attempt at defiant propriety. 'We already spoke to the police,' she said. 'We had no idea what Ross was up to. He told us he was having a sleepover at his friend Grant's house. We've met Grant's parents, they seemed perfectly responsible, perfectly respectable. We had no idea the boys were drinking and going out to clubs.' She shook her head. 'He's got a job. An apprenticeship.' She screwed up her face, battling tears. 'He's had a wee bit of trouble in the past, but we thought he'd put all that behind him.'

A wee bit of trouble. That was one way of putting it. Fourteen-year-old Ross Garvie had a nice line in breaking into garden sheds in Strathmartine, helping himself to whatever he could carry off. He hooked up with an older lad who had a clapped-out van and together they sold off Ross's loot at Sunday-morning car boot sales when his parents thought their son was off playing tennis. When the police had finally rumbled the racket, Ross had been lucky to get off with a caution. There were no details of how he'd pulled that off, but Karen would have placed money on his parents and his school weighing in at his back. He'd stayed out of formal trouble since then, but she'd managed to track down the local intelligence officer, who had described Garvie as 'one step away from everything going tits-up'. The boy had been on the fringes of the kind of small-time stuff that had eventually sucked him in and spat him out. And this buttoned-up wee woman in her buttoned-up house looked like she'd been forcing herself to be completely clueless about that inevitability. It was an oblivion that she might well have chosen to apply to her husband as well as her son, Karen thought.

'You must be worried sick about Ross,' Karen said. 'I'm sorry to be bothering you at a time like this.'

Linda stretched her lips in a parody of a smile. 'I can't sleep. I can't concentrate on anything. I keep praying he'll be all right, and then I think he'll never be all right again. Not with his three friends on his conscience. And he'll be going to the jail, won't he? And that'll be the end of everything.'

She was right about that, at least. Karen tried to look sympathetic. 'I'm not actually here in relation to Ross's accident,' she said. 'Detective Constable Murray and I are attached to Police Scotland's Historic Cases Unit.' That always sounded better than the more truthful, *We ARE Police Scotland's HCU.*

Linda folded her hands tightly in her lap and frowned. 'I don't understand.'

'At the hospital, after the accident, a routine blood sample was taken from Ross. It has to be analysed so we know his blood alcohol level at the time of the crash. In these circumstances, it's Police Scotland's practice to do a DNA test as well. The results of that test are compared to the national DNA database—'

Linda's fingers fiddled restlessly. 'I still don't understand,' she interrupted. 'Are you trying to pin some crime on Ross? Because he's not a criminal. He's just young and daft.' Her voice cracked. She was trying hard to convince herself, but deep down that was a battle she knew she'd already lost. 'We did our best for him.' Her fists clenched and her eyes glistened.

'I'm sure you did. But it's not Ross we're interested in. The blood sample that was taken from Ross is an indirect match for an outstanding crime.'

'What do you mean, "an indirect match"?' Linda butted

in again. One of those who could never manage to wait for the explanation to finish, Karen thought. She bet Stewart Garvie never got to finish a thought uninterrupted. 'What outstanding crime?'

'I know it's hard to get your head round, but the DNA tells us that a close male relative of Ross was involved in a case a long time ago, a case that we didn't manage to solve at the time,' Karen said.

'But we still have the evidence,' the Mint added, trying to be helpful.

Linda shook her head. 'You've come to the wrong place. Just because Ross did a bad thing, it doesn't mean we've got anything to do with something that happened years ago.'

Karen tried again. 'There's no arguing with the science, Mrs Garvie. There's no doubt about what the DNA is telling us. But before we speak to your husband, I need to ask you a few questions.'

'This is ridiculous,' Linda protested, getting to her feet and reaching out to steady herself on the chair. The colour had left her face, emphasising the dark bruises under her eyes. 'You're barking up the wrong tree. My Stewart has nothing to do with any crime you're trying to pin on him.'

'Were you actually married to Mr Garvie twenty years ago?' the Mint barged in again. 'Only, if you weren't, you won't have any notion of what he might have been doing then.' He caught Karen's withering look. 'I'm only saying.'

'You're not listening to me,' Linda said, her voice rising. 'I don't care what your DNA says, this has got nothing to do with Stewart. Some detectives you are. Whoever did your crime, it wasn't my husband. And you know how I can be so sure of that? Because Stewart isn't Ross's father.'

9

Karen's first thought was that Linda Garvie had apparently not always been quite so strait-laced. Had she had an affair? Or had she been a single mum when she married Stewart Garvie? She didn't have long to wonder.

'Ross was adopted. He came to us when he was five days old. We're not his biological parents. Whoever your DNA connects to, it's not Stewart.' That explained why the boy in the photograph didn't look like either of his parents. Linda had sounded almost triumphant. After a few days of everything going against her, she'd finally scored a point.

Karen was taken aback. Suddenly what had seemed like a straightforward march to resolving a cold case had turned into a multilayered problem that she had no idea how to attack.

For once, Jason got to the point ahead of her. 'Where from?' he asked.

'What?' Linda seemed distracted now.

'Where did you get him from?'

'Was it a private adoption or through a formal agency?' Karen clarified.

Linda's face cleared. 'It was a charity. I can give you the details. But I'm not sure if they still exist.' She moved towards the door. 'I'll look them out, I know where they are.'

'Before you do that, Mrs Garvie—' Now Karen stood up too. 'Do you know the name of Ross's real father?'

Linda's eyes narrowed in a hostile glare. 'Stewart's his real father.'

Karen was momentarily furious with herself for the kind of tactless misstep she'd have hammered Jason for. 'I'm sorry. Of course. I meant his biological father.'

There was no relenting in Linda's harsh expression. 'We were never given those details. We didn't want to know. As far as we were concerned, Ross was ours from the moment he was put in my arms. I don't even know what his birth mother had named him.'

'Has he never wanted to know?' Jason said, scrambling to his feet as if he'd just realised he was the only one still seated.

Linda dropped the hard stare and turned away. 'No. Because we never told him. As far as Ross knows, he's our son. We never wanted him to feel like he didn't belong.'

That had turned out well, Karen thought. All teenagers wanted to believe they were changelings, cuckoos dropped in some completely rubbish nest. If you really were an outsider, she suspected you must be conscious of that at some subliminal level. The logical result of that would be to wage war against the world you knew wasn't yours. She wasn't thinking to excuse Ross Garvie, but maybe the extent of his rebellion had its roots in this ill-fitting respectability. 'And you never felt curious?' she asked.

Linda met her eyes again. 'I didn't want to know. Everybody talks about nature versus nurture. Well, I knew we could nurture him better than his birth mother could.' She gave a sharp, harsh bark of laughter. 'I didn't want to know if we had anything to fear from his nature. We were arrogant enough to think that the home we gave him, the love we gave him was enough to overcome any bad blood that was in him.' She shook her head, a bitter twist to her mouth. 'Shows how stupid we were.' Then with an abrupt, jerky movement, she hurried from the room.

'Is that us buggered, then?' The Mint spoke softly, leaning so close to Karen that she caught a whiff of bacon from his jacket.

'Could well be. I know nothing about the legal position.' Then she smiled. 'But I'm pretty sure I know somebody who does.'

Giorsal Kennedy had always known she'd never move back to Fife until she'd made something of herself. Now she'd reached the lofty heights of Area Team Leader in the Social Work Department, she reckoned nobody could fold their arms across their chest, purse their lips and accuse her of returning with her tail between her legs. Even if her marriage had collapsed in a cacophony of recriminations, leaving her with two kids and a divorce settlement barely worthy of the name.

But moving back to Fife from Beckenham had meant her share of the equity in their tiny suburban box went a lot further. Their modern house in Glenrothes felt palatial after their cramped existence down south. They even had a garden backing on to a clump of conifers you could almost call woodland. Thirteen-year-old Jess and eleven-year-old Becca seemed to think having separate bedrooms as well as a TV and games room of their own was a reasonable trade-off for the absence of their father. Not least because he'd hardly ever been there. Apparently, being a shift leader in the Fire Service meant you had to play a lot of golf when you weren't actually hanging around waiting to put out fires.

There was no doubt about one thing. She was getting a lot

more support with the kids now she'd ditched Victor than she had when they were married. Living a five-minute walk from their grandparents made childcare easier and there was no question that the girls liked hanging with Giorsal's parents far better than any after-school club.

She'd been back a shade over a year now, and Giorsal was beginning to feel confident that she'd got the measure of her team. She'd accompanied them on home visits, sat in on client interviews and reviewed their strategic provisions. Based on what she'd seen and heard, she'd drawn up new guidelines and programmes for her staff to incorporate in their work. She'd been accused of micro-managing in the past but she considered herself merely to be thorough. It wasn't her fault if other people were too lazy to know exactly what was happening on their patch. When some child was tortured and murdered by its mother's boyfriend, or a paranoid schizophrenic jettisoned his medications and stabbed somebody on a bus, or an elderly person lay dead and undiscovered for weeks in their own home, time and time again it was the team leader who took the rap, not the frontline worker. Somehow, they could win sympathy by claiming overwhelming caseloads; managers were supposed to take that in their stride. So Giorsal made sure she knew exactly what the story was on her watch.

Now she'd come to terms with the workload and the personalities, it was time to build a social life. She'd been invited out by her colleagues for drinks, birthday meals, leaving dos. Even a Ladies Day trip to a Raith Rovers match, for God's sake. As if there wasn't enough suffering in the job. But Giorsal liked to have a private life that was separate from her professional world.

So she'd asked her mother who was still around from her schooldays. It was a good bet that there would be a fair few. A lot of Fifers were disinclined to move away from their roots. She remembered a song her dad used to sing: 'Fife's got everything, just the place for tourists'. It had been darkly satirical, she recalled, but at its heart lay an unacknowledged truth that plenty of Fifers believed the chorus line to be nothing less than the reality. It had been no surprise when her mother rattled off half a dozen names without pause for thought.

Giorsal recognised them. Girls she'd been pals with lower down the school, but none she'd been close to. 'And then there's Karen Pirie.' Etta Kennedy's voice dropped, giving full weight to the syllables. 'Did you see her in the papers?'

Even down south, it had been impossible to miss. The murder of a police officer was rare enough to be splashed on the front of every daily paper and most internet websites. Giorsal vaguely remembered Phil Parhatka – she'd been in the Guides with his sister – but she hadn't realised till she'd seen the stories that he was Karen Pirie's bidie-in. 'That must have been terrible for her,' she said. Karen as a teenager was vivid in her memory – quick with a quip, clever enough to get away with backchatting the teachers, a bit on the chubby side. Always looked like she'd been dragged through a hedge backwards, even in her best Saturday-night outfit. She liked Karen. They'd been pals, but never best pals. It had been a genuine surprise when someone with so little respect for authority had joined the police. Giorsal hadn't known quite what to make of it. So when she'd gone off to university, they slipped out of touch.

But now, Karen Pirie might possibly be the sort of woman who could be a friend. They were both recently single, for very different reasons. Between that and their history, there might be enough common ground to forge a friendship. So when work had thrown Detective Inspector Jimmy Hutton into her path, she'd asked about Karen Pirie.

'Good lassie, good polis,' he'd said. Succinct as he always

was. She liked that about Jimmy. Even though the work his unit did crossed paths with some of the hardest parts of her own job, he didn't beat about the bush with euphemisms and jargon. When a man battered his partner, Jimmy didn't talk about anger issues. He talked about making bad bastards' lives hellish. Then he and his squad set about making good on those promises.

Research had shown that men who engaged in domestic violence often led lives of low-level criminality. The sort of pettiness that made them feel big but didn't generally attract much attention from the police. Jimmy and his Murder Prevention Team took a different line. They prosecuted every tiny infringement as hard and as often as they could. She'd once overheard his response to a bully accusing the police of harassment. 'You fuck off out of her life, and we'll fuck off out of yours,' he'd snarled. Sure enough, the man had packed his bags within the week.

'Are you not simply kicking the can down the street?' she'd asked him.

'If every division plays the same game, they're going to run out of street,' Jimmy had said grimly. 'Zero tolerance and no hiding place. That's what we're aiming for.'

So Giorsal had been more than willing to take Karen at Jimmy's estimation. She'd put contacting Karen somewhere near the middle of her To Do list. One day soon, she'd promised herself. She hadn't imagined that it would be Karen who'd make the first move. Giorsal had been sitting in the bright little cupboard of an office that was technically an interview room but which she had annexed in flagrant defiance of the department's hot-desking policy, reading the pathologist's report on Gabriel Abbott's autopsy, when her landline had rung.

'Giorsal Kennedy speaking, how can I help you?' Just because you were a boss didn't mean you should stop making an effort with people. Too many senior managers answered the phone sounding like you were deliberately messing with their day simply by daring to call them.

'Gus?'

The teenage nickname knocked Giorsal off her stride. Nobody had called her that since she went away to university in Birmingham and reinvented herself. 'Who is this?' Her warm tone had shifted towards caution.

'I don't know if you remember me from school? Karen Pirie?'

Giorsal couldn't quite believe it. 'I was only talking about you the other day,' she said.

'Snap,' Karen said. 'Jimmy Hutton said he's been working with you.'

'That's right.' She took a deep breath. 'It's amazing to hear from you. My mum was saying we should get in touch now I'm back.'

'Well, here I am, in touch,' Karen said. She sounded a bit embarrassed, Giorsal thought.

'That's great. Jimmy said you were in Edinburgh these days, but maybe we could meet for a drink? Or a pizza? Or something? If you're ever over this way?' Shut up, girl, you're sounding like a needy teenager.

'I'd like that.' Pause. 'But I was wondering if you could spare me half an hour later today? Business rather than pleasure, I'm afraid. But we could make plans to link up in our own time.'

Disappointment burst Giorsal's bubble. Why had she expected anything else? Karen must have her own life, her own friends. Why would Giorsal expect someone so well established on their old patch to be interested in a school-mate tainted with the aura of failure that came with divorce? 'Sure,' she said, trying for breezy. 'What can I help you with?'

'I don't know if Jimmy said, but I head up the Historic

Cases Unit. I could use some advice about adoption law. It's relevant to a case that's just come in, and I thought of you.'

'Well, it's not my specific area of expertise ... '

'You must know more than me.' Karen chuckled. 'Our dog knows more about it than me, Gus.'

Giorsal laughed. The 'our dog knows more' line had been the staple sarcastic put-down of their French teacher. With that single phrase, Karen had broken through Giorsal's self-pity. 'I've got a decent grasp of the subject. Are you in Edinburgh?'

'No, I'm in Dundee right now. Can you squeeze me in later?'

'I've got a meeting at three, but I'm only playing catch-up with my in-tray till then. Come on over. I can offer you a decent cup of tea or a truly terrible coffee. You know where I am?'

They sorted out the practicalities then said goodbye. Giorsal did a little dance in her chair. Fuck Victor, she could make a life on her own. Why had she ever doubted it?

10

Karen wouldn't have minded an office in the Social Work Department in Glenrothes. Modern. Designed for what it was being used for. Big windows and car parking. Everything her office was not. 'You sure you don't want me along, boss?' The Mint's raw-boned face looked troubled. 'I mean, this could be evidence, right?'

The requirement of the Scottish legal system for corroboration was the reason officers conducted interviews in pairs. Sometimes Karen felt as if she was attached to Jason by a judicial umbilical cord, perpetual parent to a slow learner. 'It's all right,' she said. 'It's only background. I need to find out how the land lies. There's plenty of experts we can wheel out if we need to spell it out in court.' Karen opened the car door.

The Mint's expression cleared, replaced by his usual bovine placidity. 'OK. So, have I to go back to the office, then?'

She paused, one foot on the ground. Did he seriously think she would tell him to call it a day when it wasn't even lunchtime? 'Go through the files, make a list of the officers who worked the original inquiry and track down contact details for them.'

'What? All of them?'

'Just the CID, Jason. Start with the SIO and work your way down the pyramid. We need to talk to them, find out what's not in the paperwork. You know how it goes.'

He nodded and smiled. 'Sure thing, boss. The names they never write down, the gossip they never nail down, the theories they never set down.' Another of Karen's mantras that she'd managed to instil in him.

'Exactly. Somewhere in there, the name of Ross Garvie's dad or his uncle is lurking. He's been walking around for twenty years thinking he's got clean away with what he did to Tina McDonald. And we are his worst nightmare, Jason. We are always his worst nightmare.' Karen pushed herself out of the car and closed the door behind her. She was done with talking to the Mint. Time for grown-up conversation.

She fully expected that from Giorsal Kennedy. Gus, as she'd chosen to be known to her friends, had never been a silly wee lassie. She'd always been thoughtful. She didn't rush into things, always considering the possible outcomes before she made her choices. Even so, in a teenage world that valued conformity masquerading as rebellion, Gus had never been short of friends. She'd definitely been more popular than Karen, who hadn't yet learned the techniques that these days spared Jason the rough side of her tongue. Back then, Karen had refused to suffer fools, gladly or otherwise. It hadn't made her many friends, but she and Gus had always been pals. As she walked into the social work office, Karen surprised herself with a sense of happy anticipation. It had been a while since she'd felt something so uncomplicated.

Karen had expected a secretary or an assistant, but Giorsal herself came down to meet her at the reception desk. She hadn't changed much. Her long hair was still obviously thick even though it was tied back in a ponytail, no apparent strands of silver in the brown yet. She was still slim to the point of skinny, though she'd filled out more in the bust. That was what child-bearing did for you, Karen thought without a shred of envy. The severe rectangular glasses were new, though. They raised Giorsal's status, making her look like someone who took decisions and made things happen.

As the two women stepped into an awkward hug, Karen wondered what Giorsal saw. How much had she changed from that awkward overweight teenager who never seemed to know what to wear or how to style her hair? Now she was a slightly less overweight thirty-something who still stared into her wardrobe with an air of bewilderment and still never managed to make her hair look the same as it did when she walked out of the salon. She had more frown lines than Giorsal, which surprised her because she reckoned social workers were one of the few groups who were exposed to even more horrors than cops were.

'Karen,' Giorsal exclaimed, holding on to Karen's shoulders and stepping back from the hug to look her up and down. 'My God, I'd have known you anywhere.'

'Check you out with your scary specs,' Karen said. 'You're looking good.'

'Liar. You could pack for a week's holiday in the bags under my eyes.' She let Karen go and waved an arm towards the stairs. 'Come away up and we'll have a proper blether.'

'It's good to see you,' Karen said to Giorsal's back as they climbed up to the first floor. 'Whenever I've heard news of you over the years, I always felt sorry we'd lost touch.'

Giorsal gave a quick look over her shoulder. 'I was so impressed when my mum told me you'd made DI. Serious business, that. And now DCI. Check you out, girl.' She led the way into a small office. It was tidier than Karen could have managed. She expected to see photos of Giorsal's kids on the desk and said so.

Giorsal dropped into her chair, gesturing towards the two visitors' chairs facing her. She made a wry face. 'I don't like to shove my good fortune in people's faces.' Then she straightened up and leaned forward, forearms on the desk, face sombre. 'I heard about your man,' she said. 'That's a helluva thing to get past.'

'I'm not there yet. Nothing like there, actually.' Karen cleared her throat. She wasn't ready to get into this with Giorsal. She half-hoped there would be a time when she would be, but it would be a way down the road. 'Nice office, by the way.'

Giorsal snorted. 'Make the most of it. We're being shunted out of here in a few weeks. The council sold the building to CISWO for buttons and we're joining the happy band at Fife House.'

'CISWO?'

'The Coal Industry Social Welfare Organisation.'

Karen nodded her understanding. Thirty years since Thatcher had killed off the Fife coalfield, and still the damage reverberated through the local economy and the communities who had depended on it. 'Fair enough, I suppose,' she said.

'They need somewhere since the council decided to bulldoze their building to redevelop the town centre. But you didn't come here to talk about town planning.' She gave the engaging grin that Karen remembered, eyebrows steepling at an acute angle.

'No. Look, Gus, I'd genuinely like to get together and have a proper catch-up, but I've picked up a case that I need to make some progress on, only it's complicated and I don't know my way through the complications and I think you probably do.'

Giorsal smiled. 'If I can help, I will. On condition that we have a night out very soon.'

'Deal.'

'You said on the phone it was about adoption law?'

Karen gave Giorsal a swift but comprehensive outline of the situation Ross Garvie's recklessness had provoked. 'I thought I had nothing more to do than take a buccal swab from Stewart Garvie and I'd have an overnight result.' She shook her head. 'I should have known better. I've been doing cold cases long enough to know it's seldom that easy.'

Giorsal made a rueful noise. 'Well, when it comes to adoption law, you're better off here than if you were down south, that's one good thing.'

'How's that?'

'OK, first the history lesson. Scots law enshrines the principle of forced heirship. In other words, you can't disinherit your kids. They're legally entitled to between a third and a half of what's called your movable estate – cash, stocks and shares, that sort of thing. Until the law changed in the 1960s, that applied to all your biological children, even if they'd been adopted. It doesn't apply to adopted children any longer, but the laws that were put in place to make it possible for them to uncover their history stayed the same even though their inheritance rights disappeared.'

'OK, that sort of makes sense. So what's the score?'

'When an adoption takes place, a new birth certificate is issued in the names of the adopted parents and the first name of their choice. And an extract of that is held on the Adoption Register. That's held separately from the births, marriages and deaths registers that the public can access.

'Once the adopted person turns sixteen, they have the right to access their original birth certificate. The records will either be at the Court of Session in Edinburgh or the Sheriff Court that authorised the adoption or at General Register House in Edinburgh. You write a letter to the National Records of Scotland and they'll tell you where to go looking.

Then you rock up with photo ID and they'll open up your original birth certificate extract.'

'That's all? Just the short form of the birth certificate?'

'Yes. But that's not the end of the story. You can go to the courts and ask for more information. You should be able to get your hands on the original petition to adopt, the report of the Court Reporter or Curator, the social work report, the circumstances of the birth mother, the reasons for the adoption, her address and where the birth took place. There might even be reports from the local authority or the adoption agency, if one was involved.'

Karen felt the warm glow that came with forward movement on a case. 'I had no idea that adopted kids could access so much of their background.'

'It's a good thing, I think. Generally, the adoption records are well kept and pretty comprehensive.'

'So, is it just the adopted person who can access the records?'

Giorsal pulled a face. 'The general rule is that it's only the adopted person or someone specifically authorised by them.'

'That suggests there might be exceptions to the general rule?' Karen wasn't too hopeful, knowing only too well the hurdles of bureaucracy.

But before Giorsal could reply, a brisk tattoo of knocking broke into the conversation. Without waiting for a response, the door swung open and a tall thin man in black trousers, a black polo neck and a black leather jacket walked in. Salt-and-pepper hair en brosse, narrow sunbed-tanned face bisected by a perfectly trimmed Clark Gable moustache, Detective Inspector Alan Noble always made Karen think of the Milk Tray man, only more sinister. He looked surprised to see her, but didn't let that break his stride.

'Hello, ladies,' he said, brisk as the wind off the North Sea. 'Well, well, well, look what the breeze blew in. I didn't expect to see you here, Karen. I thought you'd abandoned us for the fleshpots of the capital.'

Three sentences in and already she was weary of his overblown archness. 'Hi, Alan. I needed a wee steer on adoption law, and who better to ask than a social worker?'

His face creased in a smile. 'Aye. Like the old joke, eh? What's the difference between a Rottweiler and a social worker?' Both women sighed. 'You can get your kids back off a Rottweiler.' He giggled, a ridiculously high-pitched sound coming from a man with his image.

'See, the thing about jokes, Alan? They're supposed to be funny,' Karen said wearily. 'Do you need me to step outside so you can talk to Giorsal?'

'No, no. No need for that. Nothing confidential here.' Without waiting for an invitation, he sat in the other visitor chair, carefully pinching the knees of his trousers to preserve their crease. 'I'm only here for a bit of background. Like you, except my case isn't cold yet.'

'Is this about Gabriel Abbott?' Giorsal cut in.

'The same. First thought was a suicide then we decided it was a murder. Well, now the pathologist has had a look at the body and the gun and he thinks we might have been right in the first place.'

'What? He thinks it's a suicide after all?'

DI Noble gave a condescending nod. 'Got it in one, Giorsal.' He mispronounced it, enunciating each vowel with deliberate clarity, as if he despised her for being saddled with something so outlandish as a Gaelic name. 'The suicide we thought was a murder turns out to be a suicide after all.'

11

Karen leaned back in her chair, crossing one leg over the other. Things that turned out not to be what they appeared were what she enjoyed most. The prospect of unravelling a tight, intractable knot was what had drawn her to cold cases. 'What changed his mind?' she asked.

Noble looked smug. 'I did. I took another look at the gun. It's just a wee one, a Smith and Wesson 457. They stopped making them nearly thirty years ago, but they were quite the thing for a few years. With it having a short barrel, it would be possible for Abbott to have shot himself in the right temple with the gun in his left hand. The bullet trajectory would have been angled a bit towards the back of his skull rather than straight across, so I asked the pathologist to check. And lo and behold' – he spread both hands in a gesture of generous munificence – 'it turns out I was absolutely spot on. And since we've no evidence of anybody else at the scene or in his company, I'd say suicide is definitely the more likely option. Especially since we already know we're dealing with one of the mentally afflicted.'

'I don't like that terminology,' Giorsal said.

Noble smirked. 'I've never been awfully good at that political correctness thing, ladies.'

'It's not political correctness,' Karen said. 'It's about dignity. Respect.'

'Christ, Karen,' Noble drawled. 'The guy was in and out of mental institutions and residential care half his adult life.'

'And now he's dead. In my book, that entitles him to a wee bit of respect.'

Noble shrugged. 'What. Ever. Bottom line is, I need to know what kind of frame of mind he was in lately. When I spoke to you before, you said you'd actually sat in on a meeting he had with his case worker recently?'

Giorsal nodded. 'I've been trying to assess as many of my team in the field as I can. I met Gabriel with Ian Lesley, his key worker, about six weeks ago. By chance, I ran into Gabriel a couple of weeks ago in Kinross. He stopped me in the street and we had a bit of a chat. But I wouldn't say I was an expert on his state of mind.'

'How would you characterise his personality? His state of mind generally?'

'Is this a formal interview?' Giorsal said, frowning.

'No, no. Just a wee off-the-record chat to help me see how the land lies.' Noble raised his palms as if to ward off an attack. 'Obviously, it might come to a more formal interview before the Fatal Accident Inquiry, but we'd do that down at the station. So, how would you describe him?'

Giorsal fiddled with a pen. Karen could see that she wasn't entirely happy with the situation, but she would go along with it rather than get into a ruck with a senior police officer. Karen knew of old that Giorsal liked to keep her powder dry for the fights that really mattered. Talking about a man who was already dead by his own hand probably wasn't one of those.

'Gabriel had a major breakdown in his final year at

university. He never really recovered. As you said, he'd often been in residential care when he couldn't cope with taking care of himself and functioning in the outside world. He wasn't schizophrenic but he did have episodes of paranoia where he was convinced he had been the victim of a conspiracy to destroy his life.'

Noble snorted. 'What? He thought he was the rightful heir to the throne?'

Giorsal glared at him. 'No. He was never very specific. If he was questioned, he'd veer away from the subject. He'd say it was too dangerous to talk openly about what had been done to him. You're probably aware that his mother died when a plane she was travelling in was blown up by the IRA. I think that situation fed into his paranoid fantasies. Caroline Abbott was collateral damage in the bombing, but Gabriel seized on her death as evidence that he was in danger.'

'But was he suicidal?' Noble tapped the fingers of his right hand on his knee.

'I didn't see evidence of that,' Giorsal said carefully.

'But he had episodes of paranoia, you said. What if he killed himself and tried to make it look like murder as a way of saying, "See? I told you somebody was after me."'

'"I told you I was ill,"' Karen muttered.

'What?' Noble swung round to face her, baffled.

'Spike Milligan's epitaph. Sorry, not an occasion for frivolity.'

'You're the last person I'd expect to be making jokes about death,' Noble said acidly, pointedly turning away from her. 'So, what do you think, Giorsal? Is that what was going on here?'

She sighed. 'It's a possible interpretation, I suppose.'

'It's a bit of a stretch,' Karen said.

'It fits the crime scene and the dead man's mental history,' Noble said stiffly.

And it lets you off the hook of a difficult murder inquiry, Karen thought but didn't say. Impenetrable murder mysteries were fine for Scandinavian TV series on Saturday nights, but the reality was something few cops relished.

'You should talk to Ian Lesley if you want a more nuanced picture of Gabriel's mental state,' Giorsal said. 'If that's all, DI Noble, I won't keep you.'

Noble took his time getting to his feet, smoothing down his trousers and shrugging his shoulders to get the set of his jacket right. 'We'll be in touch,' he said. 'Thanks for your help in clearing this up.'

'What about forensics? Gunshot residue?' Karen asked when he was halfway to the door.

Noble turned back, his eyes narrow. 'There was some GSR on his left hand.'

'Aye, but the gun had just been fired. You'd expect to find some GSR transfer from it, regardless of whether he pulled the trigger. What about his clothing?'

Noble breathed heavily through his nose. 'His jacket's with the lab. I'm not expecting any surprises. Now, I'm sure you've got cases of your own to keep you occupied without sticking your nose in mine.'

Noble closed the door firmly behind him. Giorsal looked troubled. 'I'm surprised,' she said. 'I didn't think Gabriel was suicidal. But he had a history of emotional volatility, so it's quite possible.'

'Did he have any family? Could they cast any light on his state of mind?'

'Not close. He had a brother, Will. He lives in London and runs a computer gaming company. Must be doing all right because he paid his brother's rent and that wasn't cheap. Gabriel lived in a cottage about quarter of a mile from the path round the loch. Just a wee place, but a very desirable location. He'd never have been able to afford it on benefits.

He once said his brother was happy to pay the rent as long as it was far away from him and his family.'

'How did he sound about that? Bitter? Angry?'

Giorsal shook her head. 'Sad. He was a sad man, Gabriel. I did warm to him, though. He was obsessed with South East Asian history and politics. I don't know why. Ian Lesley said once he got going on the subject he became a different person. Coherent, cogent. But you don't want to hear about that. We hadn't finished talking about adoption law. You were asking about exceptions?'

'That's right.' Karen didn't mind moving on. She was intrigued by Gabriel Abbott's suicide/murder/suicide but not enough to divert her from her main concern. 'Are there any?'

'It's very rare. The only incidences I've ever heard of have been on medical grounds when the person concerned wasn't able to give consent.'

'Ross Garvie can't give consent.'

'Yes, but accessing his adoption records won't affect his medical state.'

'So I'm screwed?'

Giorsal smoothed her hair back from her forehead. 'Not necessarily. You can still go to court and ask for the extract of the original birth certificate to be opened for you.'

'That would work?'

'Maybe. The obvious argument against it is the European Convention on Human Rights, which is incorporated in the Scotland Act. You'd be in breach of Article 8 in respect of Ross Garvie, who is entitled to a private and family life. And as far as a future accused is concerned, it could be argued that you're in breach of Article 6 – that's the right to a fair trial. I think your suspect might complain that he's being accused of a twenty-year-old offence on the basis of a process over which he'd had no consent.'

'But that's all legal hair-splitting, surely? Who's going to stand up in court and oppose us?'

'His adoptive parents, for a start. You said they've never told him he's adopted. So they could argue you're not just breaching Garvie's Article 8 rights but theirs as well.'

Karen digested this for a long moment. 'Would any court hearing be in private?'

'Totally. It would be heard in camera.'

'So I'm not breaching their human rights if I don't tell Ross Garvie when he wakes up, am I?'

'Now who's hair-splitting? Surely it would all come out in open court if you finally nail someone and he goes to trial?'

Karen shrugged. 'Maybe not. I don't think we'd have to name Ross Garvie. We could ask the court to preserve the anonymity of the familial DNA source. Make the human rights legislation work for us, not against us.'

'I don't know anything about criminal court proceedings. I suspect that the family court would ultimately decide for giving up the info, but it might take a bit of strenuous argument. You'd need a good advocate. The court might also say, There's no rush. Let's wait and see whether Garvie recovers consciousness. Your case has waited twenty years already, a wee bit longer won't hurt. And of course, if Garvie doesn't recover and dies, the court will give you whatever you want because dead men have no human rights.'

Karen groaned. 'See, that's the kind of thing courts say because they're run by lawyers who don't know what it's like to live with all the uncertainties that go along with not knowing who killed your daughter, your lover, your friend. The way I look at it is every day that killer walks the streets is a day that the justice system has failed Tina McDonald. And there's a very potent argument for not waiting.'

'What's that?'

'Police Scotland is a very leaky sieve. It's only a matter of time before somebody hears we've reopened the case and sells us out to their favourite hack. And if our killer's still around? He might decide that, rather than chance it, he'll flee the jurisdiction.' She gave a wry smile. 'Do we have an Ecuadorian embassy in Scotland?'

12

Assistant Chief Constable Simon Lees had fared pretty well in the reorganisation that had followed the creation of a single Police Scotland force. He'd maintained his rank with a small but well-deserved uptick in his salary. He'd been able to escape the Neanderthals of Fife and base himself in the infinitely more civilised Edinburgh. And his natural talent for administration and management made him well-placed to shine. Really, he had no complaints.

Strike that. He had one complaint. Detective Chief Inspector Karen Pirie was still under his direct command. He'd thought he would be escaping her when he moved to Edinburgh. But her notable successes running cold cases in the former Fife force had brought her to the attention of the big bosses and they'd picked her to run the national Historic Case Unit. Even so, she should have been someone else's problem. Then that someone else had a heart attack and Lees' reward for his perpetual overweening careerism was to be given oversight of the HCU.

Karen infuriated him. She had a complete disregard for his rank, treating him with a bland condescension that bordered on insolence but never quite crossed over into insubordination. Or rather, by the time he'd discovered her sidestepping of his authority, she'd achieved another success that made her untouchable. And that was the worst of it. She was defiantly good at what she did. Sometimes unorthodox, sometimes out on a very shaky limb, but more often than not successful. And dramatically successful with the kind of cases the media loved. Karen bloody Pirie, whose every triumph reflected more glory on her boss, who had to smile and smile through gritted teeth.

Almost as irritating was his discovery that she'd been responsible for coining his nickname. He'd always craved the kind of handle he'd heard in the squad rooms when he was climbing the greasy pole – Hammer, Batman, Sherlock and the like. But she'd condemned him to the Macaroon, after Lees Macaroon Bars, a typically Scottish item of confectionery made traditionally with icing sugar and mashed potatoes. It wasn't a nickname calculated to cast fear into the hearts of criminals or subordinates.

The international fallout from Pirie's last major case was still troubling his inbox. And now here she was again, slumped in his visitor's chair, hair tumbled as if she'd just got out of bed, suit rumpled and slightly too big for her. Either she'd lost some weight or she'd conceded the battle and started buying bigger clothes. There was nothing shambolic about her gaze, however. Her blue eyes were calm and untroubled, but he always felt pinned down by them, as if she could see beyond his well-groomed, scrubbed façade to the insecurities that lurked inside. She stretched out her legs and crossed them at the ankle. 'You're not going to like what I've got to say,' she said.

Nothing new there, Lees thought. 'That's very direct of you, Inspector.'

'No point in beating about the bush,' she said. 'We've got

a very good opportunity to clear a case from 1994 – a violent rape murder in Glasgow. We got a familial hit on the DNA register over the weekend. But it's problematic.'

What else would it be with her involved? 'How so?'

Karen outlined the key elements of the case to date. 'If we're going to make any progress, we need to get our hands on those adoption records.'

'So what are you suggesting?'

'We need to go to court for an order to access Ross Garvie's original birth certificate.'

Lees sighed. 'Can't you deal with that yourself?' A forlorn hope, at a guess.

'Not if we want to win. It's not straightforward. There are human rights arguments against it. And the court will want to hear from his adoptive parents.'

Lees huffed. 'Can we not push it through quickly without involving them?'

Karen gave him a long, measured look. 'Even if we could, the blowback would be catastrophic when they found out. We'll need an advocate who knows about adoption law and human rights legislation.'

Lees pictured numbers clicking over like a cartoon cash register. 'That sounds like a budget-buster.'

Karen shrugged herself into an upright position, leaning slightly forward. 'If there was an alternative, I'd be proposing it.'

'Why can't we wait and see whether this joyrider recovers consciousness? Or dies? Surely that would put an end to any talk of human rights?'

Karen's expression hardened. 'Right enough. We could wait and see whether Ross Garvie wakes up or goes away the crow road. And in an ideal budgetary world, that would solve the problem. But I think there's more urgency here because there's a leak somewhere in our system. The media gets to hear about the cases we're working way earlier in the process than I'd like. Sometimes that works in our favour, and we get witnesses coming forward who said nothing at the time, for whatever reason. But I worry about perpetrators who've got used to walking around feeling like they've got away with something. They hear we've got new evidence, they're going to be away on their toes. Frankly, if it was me, I'd already have the false ID set up and the overnight bag packed. But thankfully most villains aren't that smart.'

'So because we've got a leak that you clearly know about but have done nothing to plug, this department's going to be stuck with a massive legal bill?' The burn of self-righteous anger was a feeling Lees had always enjoyed.

Karen rolled her eyes. 'It's pretty obvious there's a leak. I know it's not coming from me and I'd stake my pension that DC Murray isn't sneaking round talking to journalists behind my back. So it must be coming from admin or the forensics division out at Gartcosh. Neither of which is my responsibility.'

'Be that as it may, you should have reported your suspicions to me.' Lees glared at her. It wasn't often he got Karen Pirie on the back foot and he was happy to make the most of it.

Karen gave a tight smile. 'Sorry, sir. I didn't think I had to waste your time stating the obvious. I'll leave it in your capable hands now. But the fact remains that we don't know how long we can keep secret the fact that we've reopened the Tina McDonald case. Especially since I'm about to start interviewing the investigating officers and the witnesses. Not to mention talking to the family. So we need to get this moving. I need to get an advocate on the case and we need to get it in front of a judge as soon as possible.'

Lees groaned. 'How certain are you of getting a result if I do authorise this ridiculous level of expenditure?'

'There's no guarantees. Chances are the birth certificate won't give us the father's name. But it will tell us where to start looking. Without it, we've got nothing. With it, we could get the answer we all want.'

'Or we could get nothing.'

'That's always the way with historic cases. If you did a cost–benefit analysis at the start of any of my investigations, the accountants would have a fit. But you know that when we do resolve cold cases, it doesn't just give closure to the friends and families of the victim, it makes us look good. It raises people's confidence, and I don't think you can put a price on that.' Karen glowered at him.

'We don't usually have this level of expenditure up front, though. Look, you said this case is unusual. Can you not get an advocate to do it pro bono? For the prestige?'

Karen sighed. 'There is no prestige. It'll be heard in camera. Look, the world is going to hear we've reopened this case. I'm going to have Tina McDonald's family on my back as well as the media. Do you really want me to have to tell them that we're not proceeding with the investigation because you won't authorise the legal fees?'

Lees sighed. As usual, she'd backed him into a corner. 'Fine,' he growled. 'But don't go for a QC.'

Karen stood up, beaming. 'I'll get cracking, then.'

Before he could say more, she was out the door, showing a remarkable turn of speed. Lees squeezed his eyes shut. One day, he promised himself. One day he'd get rid of Karen Pirie for good.

13

Sometimes Karen's need to walk herself to sleep was thwarted by the weather. This was one of those nights. A sharp east wind drove in from the Baltic, cutting through clothes like a skinner's knife, carrying bitter gouts of rain that stung the skin like flying nettles. She could have quartered the city on the night buses, but she'd learned from experience that that didn't satisfy her need for movement. Instead, she made a cup of tea and settled down at her laptop. It was a picture of warmth and cosiness. But if she got too comfortable, a turn of her head would bring the sea into sight, white horses topping the heavy swell that hit the sea wall with jagged towers of spray. You could build walls against the wild, but you could never ignore its presence.

Because DI Noble's interruption to her day was still fresh in her mind, Karen decided to see what she could find out about the murder in 1994 that had apparently set Gabriel Abbott adrift from his moorings. Karen had still been at school then, so it hadn't made the sort of impression it would have done if she'd already been a cop. But she did remember the plane crash in the Borders and the shock as it had quickly emerged that this was no ordinary aviation accident but the result of a terrorist bomb.

Six years before there had been the horror of the explosion that had ripped through Pan Am flight 103 in the skies above Lockerbie and it had still been fresh in people's minds. Coupling the words 'plane' and 'terrorism' in 1994 was enough to provoke ripples of panic in the public consciousness. And when an RAF Chinook helicopter carrying twenty-five senior intelligence operatives was blown out of the skies en route from Northern Ireland a few weeks after the small plane came down, the national press flung themselves into a series of hysterical diatribes against the IRA and all their works. Nobody who took to the skies was safe, some commentators implied. But starved of detailed information, the story soon slipped from the headlines and joined the long tail of the Troubles that mostly happened somewhere else.

Karen typed in 'Caroline Abbott plane' to the search engine. The first hit was a Wikipedia page. It was as good a place to start as any. She was accustomed to bringing a healthy dose of scepticism to whatever information crossed her path. Much healthier for a police officer to assume every source was suspect rather than being seduced by appearances.

1994 Cessna Skylane explosion

From Wikipedia, the free encyclopedia

Cessna 182 Skylane, similar to the bombed plane

Accident summary	
Date	5 May 1994
Summary	Incendiary bomb
Site	Glendearg, Scottish Borders Latitude : 55.6625 Longitude : -2.8583
Passengers	3
Crew	1
Injuries (non-fatal)	0
Fatalities	4

Survivors	0
Aircraft type	Cessna 182 Skylane
Operator	Private
Registration	G-JPST
Flight origin	Elstree Aerodrome United Kingdom
Destination	Fife Airport, United Kingdom

On 5 May 1994 a Cessna 182 Skylane exploded in mid-air above a hillside at Glendearg near Galashiels in the Scottish Borders. The aircraft was en route between Elstree Aerodrome and Fife Airport by Glenrothes.[1] There were no survivors among the four people on board, who included former Secretary of State for Northern Ireland Richard Spencer MP, TV presenter Ellie MacKinnon and West End theatre promoter Caroline Abbott.

Aircraft[edit]

The aircraft involved was a UK-registered Cessna 182 Skylane, tail number G-JPST, construction built in 1975. At the time of the accident, the aircraft had completed 4,845 hours total time and 4,352 cycles.[2]

Accident flight[edit]

The Skylane took off at 10.17 local time from Elstree Aerodrome, with a destination of Fife Airport in Scotland. The flight had been uneventful until, without warning at 12.43, according to eyewitnesses the plane disintegrated in a ball of flame above a hillside at Glendearg near Galashiels Golf Course in the Scottish Borders. Burning wreckage was spread over a wide area.[3] There were no survivors from the explosion.

Casualties[edit]

All four occupants of the aircraft (pilot Richard Spencer and three passengers) perished in the accident. There were no physical injuries on the ground.

Crew

Pilot: Richard Spencer MP

Passengers

Mary Spencer, wife of the pilot

Caroline Abbott, theatre impresario

Ellie MacKinnon, television presenter and writer

Investigation[edit]

An investigation was conducted by the Air Accident Investigation Branch (AAIB), Lothian and Borders Police, assisted by the National Transportation Safety Board, the aircraft manufacturer, Cessna and the engine manufacturer, Pratt & Whitney Canada.

The AAIB published its formal report into the accident on 4 January 1995. It concluded that the mid-air disintegration of the plane had occurred as a result of an Incendiary device which had detonated and caused the engine of the plane to explode. The device was of a type typical of terrorist activity.[4]

A Fatal Accident Inquiry into the death of the four victims opened on 31 January 1995 in Edinburgh. The inquest concluded on 10 February with verdicts of murder being returned in all four cases.

Karen cross-checked the facts with a couple of other news stories on the crash itself. On the face of it, there was nothing to argue with. Her next step was to follow the thread of reportage from the breaking news via the finger-pointing to the definitive version of events that had become set in stone. She worked her way through a series of archived newspaper reports as well as random posts by conspiracy theorists, aviation geeks and Ellie MacKinnon fans who were apparently still mourning her passing.

The picture that emerged wasn't complicated. Richard Spencer, forty-nine, had been a commercial pilot before he became an MP and he'd kept his pilot's licence current even after he took up his seat. His private plane, a four-seater single-engine Cessna, was kept at Elstree Aerodrome in North London, a couple of miles from the home he shared with his wife Mary, forty-four, and their two children – fourteen-year-old Chloe and ten-year-old Guy. Richard loved to fly and, whenever there was an opportunity, he would take to the skies. He regularly used the Cessna to commute between London and his constituency in Birmingham.

On this occasion, he and Mary were flying to Scotland to attend the wedding in Perth of an old university friend of Mary. Ellie MacKinnon and Mary had also been friends since university and when Mary discovered Ellie and Caroline Abbott were also attending the wedding, she'd invited them to fly up with her and Richard, the way old friends do. Caroline also planned to visit her young son Gabriel who was at boarding school near Perth.

They'd set off in fair weather and passed all the waymarks on the route north without incident. Then, without warning, the plane had disintegrated in flames above a Scottish hillside. Shocked eyewitnesses spoke of a giant fireball falling from the sky.

Because Richard had been a Northern Ireland minister, outspoken against terrorists of every stripe, it didn't take long for speculation about terrorism to run like wildfire through the media. Some kind of incendiary bomb, it appeared. Set on a timer, presumably.

There was outrage in the predictable corners of the press. How was it possible that a plane belonging to an obvious terrorist target had been left vulnerable to sabotage? Was this what our politicians deserved in return for their service? Must innocent bystanders pay the price for the failings of the security service and the police? And so on. Karen had wondered about that too, until she'd found a few paragraphs buried deep in the *Telegraph*'s coverage. The small hangar where the Cessna was customarily stored was locked and alarmed and checked twice daily by the local police. The aerodrome didn't have the level of security of a commercial airport, but it was patrolled by security guards and there had been no signs of a break-in.

That didn't mean there hadn't been a breach, Karen thought. Just that it hadn't been an obvious one. Money might have changed hands; the security guards might not have been vetted thoroughly enough. There were plenty of possibilities. Nowhere was impregnable if someone wanted to break in badly enough.

She squeezed the bridge of her nose to stop the tears that had sprung up from nowhere. This was the point in her research where she would customarily have turned to Phil and run through what she'd read and what she was thinking. It wasn't that she couldn't work things out for herself, but the process of talking always helped her clarify her thoughts. And because their minds worked in different ways, he had a knack for picking up on the odd thing that had slipped past her.

Karen swung round in her chair and stared out at the turbulent sea. At moments like this, Phil's absence was a physical pain in her chest. A clench of misery and rage that wiped out everything else. She'd heard people talk of being heartsore and had always thought it was a metaphor. Now she knew otherwise. She hung her head, ran a rough hand across her mouth and turned back to the screen where Richard Spencer's face smiled out at her with the measured care of a man who knows he's trying to win your vote. Loaded with gravitas but leavened with approachability. He reminded her of the actor who played Inspector Lestrade in *Sherlock*. If he'd lived, she wondered if that would have played to his advantage.

Spencer's political career had the most extensive coverage, combed through to establish why he, in particular, might have been a target for the IRA or one of the other Republican splinter groups. The prevailing view seemed to be that he'd been chosen not for his specific achievements in office but because his hobby of flying presented an easy target, compared with the activities of his colleagues.

He had of course been elevated by his martyrdom to a saintly figure. A first-class constituency MP, a stalwart of the progressive wing of the party, a loving husband and a devoted father. Karen wondered how much of that was wishful thinking. She wouldn't mind betting she'd have formed a very different picture if she'd interviewed people the week before Spencer's death.

Ellie MacKinnon's career as a popular TV presenter had earned her a fair share of column inches too. She'd started out as one of a bubbly young quartet fronting a Saturday-morning kids' cookery programme, but her star quality had shone out and she'd soon been poached to join the nation's favourite kid's show, the teatime programme *All Aboard!* Ellie had quickly become the anchor and had been with the show for twelve years at the time of the crash. She was coltish and full of bounce, her wide grin as much a trademark as Ant's Dec.

She'd carved out a secondary career writing children's adventure stories, featuring a trio of cousins who lived in a small town on the south coast that was preternaturally prone to the presence of spy rings, armed robbers, drug smugglers and kidnappers. The books had been notable for their brio, their off-the-wall sense of humour and the vividness of their illustrations. Karen remembered buying the series for her niece. They were, as she recalled, a cheerier, English version of *Lemony Snicket*. The obits said she'd brought a new zest to the traditional children's story; again, Karen wondered if there would have been a different verdict had she lived.

There wasn't much about Ellie MacKinnon's private life. She'd lived alone in North London. A detail that cropped up in only one story was that she and Caroline Abbott lived in the same building – a large detached house in Belsize Park that had been divided into two flats. The same article reported that Ellie was godmother to Caroline's younger son, Gabriel. Given Caroline's work in the theatre, it might have been handy to have a potential babysitter so close at hand. Which must have made things even worse for Gabriel. In one terrible afternoon, the boy had lost both his mother and the person he might have expected to be her surrogate. A double whammy.

Caroline Abbott came third in the coverage stakes. She'd grown up in Edinburgh, studied Drama and English at Bristol and landed a job working front of house at a West End theatre. She'd raced up the theatre management ladder, helped by a couple of lucky breaks. By the time she was thirty, she was managing one of the smaller suburban theatres in the capital. Two years later, she'd set up her own production company and was moving shows into the West End within eighteen months. 'Caroline had her finger on the public pulse,' one of her rivals had said. 'We envied her grasp of what would put bums on seats.'

She'd married Tom Abbott, a marine engineer, in 1975. Their first son, William, was born in 1976. Gabriel followed ten years later. Tom's job took him all over the world on long trips. According to another friend, 'Tom eventually just stopped coming home. Caroline said he'd died out in

Thailand not long after Gabriel was born. She didn't make a fuss about it, though. She was a very private person.'

So Gabriel Abbott had already been fatherless when his mother and his godmother had been killed. Karen wondered how a small boy dealt with something so overwhelming. She'd been devastated by Phil's death, but she had other anchors in her life. Her parents, a handful of close friends, an absorbing job. What had Gabriel been left with? A brother ten years older but still too young to take care of him. All his moorings gone. Imagining his bewilderment, his pain, his grief made her heart contract. And he wasn't the only child to have been orphaned by the crash. The Spencer children had lost both parents simultaneously.

The fourth victim, Mary Spencer, barely registered on the media radar. Karen couldn't help thinking of 'Three Craws Sat Upon a Wa'', a song they'd sung as kids. The last verse had always made her laugh – 'The fourth craw / wisnae there at a' . . .' That was Mary Spencer. Notable only for being the wife and secretary of Richard and the mother of Chloe and Guy. Pretty in that kind of way you forget half an hour later. But doubtless a huge presence in the lives of her two bereft offspring.

Karen yawned. Absorbing the details of someone else's misfortune had finally tired her brain enough to stop it fizzing and fretting. At last, she'd be able to fall into bed and sleep. And tomorrow, she'd find a way to move closer to Tina McDonald's killer.

14

A sprawling modern bungalow on the Ayrshire coast wouldn't have been Karen's first choice for her retirement, but she could see its attractions. Her parents would like it, she imagined. Her mum would love the sea views across to Arran and the small-town life on offer. Her dad would turn those manicured lawns and neat rose beds into a vegetable plot that would feed a family of ten. But even though retirement loomed for him in a year or two, he wouldn't be walking out the door of the bus depot with the cash to fund a place like this. You'd need a Chief Superintendent's pension pot to come close.

Jason had made the appointment. As they headed west along the perpetually busy M8, he told Karen about Andrew Diuguid's response. 'He said this was a call he'd been hoping for ever since we started looking at cold cases.' He sounded both surprised and relieved. Often people were less than thrilled to hear from the HCU. They didn't want to revisit dark events they'd had a tangential connection to. Their lives had moved on and they didn't necessarily want new lovers, families or workmates to know their connection to a murder or a serious sexual offence, however tangential. Police officers often saw the re-opening of cold cases as a slight on their professionalism, a black mark on their record. And sometimes the people they wanted to interview had the most to fear from the encounter – the loss of their liberty and reputation as the finger finally pointed incontrovertibly at their guilt.

Now, standing on the doorstep, Karen hoped Jason had for once got the right end of the stick. The doorbell played an electronic version of the 'Ride of the Valkyries'. Why, she wondered, would anyone choose a doorbell theme that most people associated with *Apocalypse Now* and the smell of napalm in the morning?

A figure loomed behind the frosted glass of the inner door, which opened to reveal a burly man who must barely have made the height requirement for the force. His jeans and Scotland rugby shirt fitted closely, revealing muscle rather than fat. He still had a generous amount of salt-and-pepper hair but it was shaved to a number two all over. His battered features creased into a crooked smile as he reached for the outer porch door. He looked more like a nightclub bouncer than a senior police officer, albeit retired.

'You'll be DCI Pirie,' he said, opening the outside door. 'And DC Murray. Come away in. Sorry about the doorbell, the wife's a big opera fan.' He thrust a hand out and shook with each of them as they crowded into the porch. 'I'm Andrew Diuguid. Call me Andrew.' Even in those few words, it was clear he was a Glaswegian who had not let time or rank knock any of the edges off his accent.

He ushered them into a wide hallway whose walls gleamed a white that was almost luminous. Laminate wood floor, bright rugs from, Karen guessed, IKEA. 'In to your right there,' he said.

Karen and Jason obeyed, walking into a living room with a picture window that ran the length of one wall. A spectacular

vista of sea and sky and the distant island of Arran domi-
nated the room. It was a few seconds before Karen took in
anything else – furniture chosen for comfort rather than
elegance; a couple of bookcases, one packed with biographies
and military history, the other with historical fiction; a big
flat-screen TV dwarfed to insignificance by the view; the faint
vanilla smell of air freshener.

'Sit down, make yourselves at home. My wife's just putting
the kettle on. Tea or coffee?'

He took the drinks orders and retreated briefly. When he
returned, Karen and Jason were arranged so that he couldn't
keep them both in his eyeline at once. It was a way of keeping the interviewee off balance she'd learned over the years.
And off balance meant less guarded. She had no idea whether
Andrew Diuguid had anything to hide, but it was safer to
work on the assumption that everybody did.

He settled himself in a generous armchair and placed his
hands palm down on his thighs. He looked comfortable and
in control. Karen wondered how hard it would be to put him
off balance. 'So, Tina McDonald. They're always the ones that
stay with you,' he said. 'The ones that got away. The ones
where we never got the answer.'

'I know what you mean,' Karen said. 'They drift through
your dreams when you least expect it.'

'Aye, but you're lucky. You get to be the one that closes the
cases we couldn't manage. You get to tell folk what really
happened to the ones they love.' His mouth gave a rueful
twist. 'So, how can I help you, Chief Inspector?'

Karen was about to respond when the door swung open,
propelled by a generous denim-clad hip. Mrs Diuguid's hands
were occupied by a large tray containing three oversized
pottery mugs and a plate piled with scones, butter and jam
oozing out at the sides. Karen eyed the scones with desire,
but she wasn't about to give any hostages to fortune. Jason

jumped up to help Mrs Duiguid but she tutted him aside and put the plate on a side table. She handed round the drinks with a cheery smile, as if the presence of two strange detectives in her living room was a treat. 'Help yourselves to scones,' she said, heading for the door. 'I'll get out of your way.'

'Delia made those mugs herself,' Diuguid said proudly, raising the clumsy terracotta object in a toast. And her lumpy jumper too, Karen would have bet.

'It's good to have a hobby,' Jason said, reaching for a scone.

Already wearying of small talk, Karen weighed in with, 'So, I've taken a pass through the investigation reports and, on the face of it, your team dotted all the i's and crossed all the t's.'

'Thank you. I like to think I ran a tight ship. But before we get into the nitty-gritty, are you in a position to tell me what your new evidence is? DC Murray here said you were conducting a cold case review on Tina. But I know how these things go. It takes a pretty solid piece of new evidence to get you to dust off a twenty-year-old murder.'

Clearly Diuguid hadn't lost his edge in retirement. 'We've got a familial DNA hit,' she said. 'But it's not entirely straightforward. I can't tell you more than that, I'm sorry.'

'I thought it must be something like that. Either that or a death-bed confession. Well, you've been through the paperwork, so now you know as much as I do.' He spread his hands in a gesture of openness and smiled. He seemed entirely without guile, but Karen wasn't convinced.

'In my experience, sir, there are two kinds of unsolved murders. There's the ones where the whole team have no doubt who the killer is – but they can't prove it. Lack of evidence, maybe, or somebody screws up something crucial so it never gets as far as a charge. Then there's the ones where you follow all the leads, you chase down everything that looks like a clue, you interview everybody with the remotest connection to the case, and still you can't come up with a viable suspect.'

'I've no expertise in cold cases, Chief Inspector, but as far as live cases are concerned, I can't argue with that.'

Karen inclined her head in acknowledgement and carried on. 'The thing is, you can't always tell from the paperwork which category any given case falls into. Because we've all learned to be very careful about what we commit to the files. With the level of disclosure the defence demands, nobody puts anything on paper or into the system about a suspect that might end up undermining the case when it comes to court. So which kind was Tina McDonald?'

Diuguid gave her a shrewd look from under his brows. 'We never had a single suspect worth a damn,' he said. 'We tracked down guys she'd danced with that night, guys she'd stood next to at the bar. We spoke to ex-boyfriends. Everybody checked out. The ones that didn't have an alibi fell down on the DNA.'

'And that was it? No nod and a wink? Nobody with a grudge? Nobody she'd made a fool of? No history with some guy with a temper?'

Diuguid shook his head, glum. 'Believe me, I'd be the first to tell you if there was anybody we looked at that was still in the picture when we scaled down the inquiry. It was a genuine mystery. And as far as I know, he never did it again.'

'Or if he did, he was more careful with his DNA.'

Diuguid nodded. 'Right enough. But folk watch crime shows on the telly and they think guys that commit sex murders like this can't stop at one. They're convinced they'll strike again and again till they're caught or they get terminal cancer or they top themselves. But we know that's not always the way it goes. We know there's guys that lose control and do one terrible thing completely out of character. And they're horrified at themselves. They're appalled by what they've done. But they manage to get past it and they never do anything like it again. How many cold cases have you worked where the perpetrator has kept his nose clean for ten, twenty years or more?'

Karen sighed. He was right. 'A few,' she said. 'Sometimes they're almost relieved when we turn up with a warrant.'

'Other times they're really pissed off,' Jason mumbled through a mouthful of scone.

Diuguid raised his eyebrows. 'I can imagine. But the point is, if this is the first time his DNA has produced any kind of hit, you're obviously looking for someone who has kept his nose clean for the past twenty years. Either that or a dead man.'

'Or both,' Karen pointed out. 'And you're certain there was nobody your team looked at and had their doubts about?'

Diuguid shook his head. 'I'd have known. There were no secrets on my squad.'

Karen doubted that very much. In her experience, every cop shop was like a safety deposit vault for secrets. And every now and again, robbers broke in and scattered the secrets round the locker room floor. Andrew Diuguid was, she thought, a man who needed to believe his own propaganda. She didn't think he knew anything, but that didn't mean there was nothing to know. 'Would you mind if we approached some of your junior officers to see whether there was anything they came across that they didn't think was worth pursuing at the time?'

For a moment she thought he was going to take offence. His shoulders tensed and his hands gripped his knees. Then he relaxed. 'Be my guest. I doubt any of them are still in the job, mind you. I've been to more retirement do's in the past five years than I can count. That and funerals. I've said cheerio to half a dozen men this past few years that were younger than me. Kevin Sinclair, he was exhibits officer on Tina McDonald, he had bowel cancer. Jim Brown, he ran the actions desk on nearly all my murders, he died out hill walking in the Cairngorms. Heart attack. Tam Smart, the statement collator, his liver packed up. Kenny MacGregor, the dog handler. All of them, gone to the great bar in the sky.' His eyes hardened, he heaved a sigh and rubbed his hands over the side of his head. Karen imagined it must feel like teddy bear plush.

'The job takes its toll, right enough. We lost a colleague not so long ago,' Jason said. Karen gave him a look of disbelief. 'It's hard. It's like you lose wee bits of yourself. The conversations you had that nobody else shared. The gags you laughed at together. Now it's like they're wee splinters of your history lost in space.'

'Exactly,' Diuguid said, favouring him with a smile, the wintry edge to his stare gone again. 'But anybody else that's still kicking about – ask HR, they'll have contact details, if it's only where to pay the pension.'

There was nothing more to be had here, she could tell. Karen made polite noises of thanks and disengaged from the interview. She got to her feet, taking Jason by surprise. He'd only just started on his third scone. He scrambled to the door behind her, scattering crumbs and mumbled farewells as he trailed in her wake. Karen stomped ahead of him, head down, saying nothing till they were in the car. Then she rounded on him.

'What was that about?' she snapped.

Jason's expression was a mixture of wariness and uncertainty. 'What?' he grunted through the home baking.

'All that about Phil? What did you think you were doing, talking about him like that?'

Jason swallowed. 'What he said, all those dead guys. It made me think about Phil. I knew he'd get it.'

In the grip of strong emotion, Karen struggled to express what she needed to say. 'We don't talk about Phil to outsiders. It's nothing to do with them.' She wanted to howl at him that Phil was hers and nobody else's, but she knew that would make her sound deranged so she held back. 'We don't talk about him to strangers,' she said instead, forcing her voice level.

Jason's face was wounded. 'We don't talk about him to each other,' he said, his voice cracking. 'You won't talk about him to me and I don't have anybody else to talk to about him. It was just the three of us on the old team and you won't share. It's really hard, boss.' His lower lip trembled.

She didn't want to hear this. He was right, she wouldn't share. She shouldn't have to. Phil had been hers, the only one who had ever been hers. Talking to Jimmy Hutton was one thing. He had a degree of emotional intelligence the Mint didn't even know he should aspire to.

She wanted to punch Jason for his presumption, his daring to think he was entitled to a part of her grief. She wanted to punch him hard and keep on punching him till he promised never to speak of Phil again.

Instead, she said nothing. She got out of the car, slammed the door and marched off towards the town centre, angry tears stinging her eyes.

Sod Jason, sod Diuguid and sod the lot of them.

15

Karen made it about half a mile along the road before she had her emotions back on the leash. She cast a quick look over her shoulder and spotted Jason in the car about a hundred yards back, creeping along like a punter in search of a working girl. The pair of them must look absurd, she thought. Like something out of a Coen brothers film.

She stopped and turned to face him, beckoning with a small jerk of her head. The car rolled forward and stopped beside her. Karen climbed in, fastened her seat belt and said, 'You've got a perfect right to talk about Phil with me. We were a team once. I'll try to be better about it.' It was the nearest she could manage to an apology. It wasn't Jason's fault that he was so limited. She made up her mind to think of it as talking to a favourite pet, the way she knew some people did all the time. Share her feelings without any expectation of a helpful response. But some other time. Not right now.

'I'm sorry,' he mumbled. He had a smear of jam across his cheek.

'Aye. Wipe your face, you look like a five-year-old.'

Jason's eyes widened and he scrubbed at his mouth like

the small child she'd likened him to. 'Where to now then, boss?'

'Glasgow. First we're going to pay a courtesy call to Tina McDonald's parents. Then we're going to see Liz Dunleavy. She's still running Hair Apparent in the West End. I googled her. She's got three other salons now, but she's still based in the Byres Road one. Let's see if we can catch her on the back foot.'

'Should we not phone her first?'

'No.' It was accepted practice in cold case reviews to give witnesses advance notice of interview requests so they could prepare themselves. But Karen had never felt constrained by received wisdom. Liz Dunleavy was one of a group of women who formed the core witnesses in the original inquiry and she didn't want the hairdresser conferring with her pals to come up with an agreed version of events. With the passage of time, people's memories always edited the past. A lot of details slipped from their grasp, while others that had seemed trivial at the time took on greater weight. Karen believed it was the brain's subconscious way of sorting the wheat from the chaff. Time also changed what people were willing to say about the dead. She wanted to cut straight to the chase of what surfaced spontaneously from Tina McDonald's best friend and boss rather than what collective memory decreed was the case.

'How not?' Jason asked, turning on to the main Glasgow road.

'No conferring, like your starter for ten on *University Challenge*. I don't want them putting their heads together to decide what we should and shouldn't be told.'

Jason chuckled. 'I have to watch that *University Challenge* these days. My flatmates take bets on who can get the most answers right. Me, I never know any of them.'

Karen wasn't surprised. Somehow Jason had found himself

a flat-share with a trio of Edinburgh University students. She hoped they didn't patronise him too much. The Mint might be stupid, but he had a good heart. 'Aye, but I bet they'd be rubbish at securing a crime scene.'

'No kidding. See, if you saw inside their bedrooms, you'd think we'd had a visit from extreme burglars. Totally shan. My mum would give me a skelp if I left my room like that.'

Karen had met Mrs Murray. She believed him. She tipped her head back, leaning on the headrest, eyes closed. He knew better than to interrupt her when she was thinking. Bricks without straw, that's what she was doing right now. But that didn't mean she couldn't figure out an angle of approach.

The McDonalds had moved since Tina's murder. At the time, they'd been living in a tenement in Govan within spitting distance of the shipyards where her father had worked in the drawing office. Now they were in Mount Florida, a stone's throw from the national football stadium. Karen imagined that on match days the roar from Hampden Park would drown out conversation and TV programmes equally.

Eric and Patsy McDonald occupied a first-floor flat in a red sandstone tenement. The close was spotless and smelled of synthetic pine. Karen felt they were out of order just for dragging the dirt from the street into the pristine stairway. She'd phoned ahead to arrange this meeting. There was no benefit to be had from the element of surprise when it came to the families of victims, especially those who had been dead for as long as Tina McDonald.

The door was opened by a silver-haired man in shirt sleeves and the sort of neutral-coloured trousers her father would have called slacks. His face was scored with deep lines and his eyes had the heavy look of someone who hasn't slept well for a very long time. He had a neatly trimmed moustache that reminded her of the captain in *Dad's Army*. She hadn't seen one quite like it since her parents had dragged her along to the bowling club opening day. She knew from the files he was sixty-three, but he looked a dozen years older. Behind him she could see a small blonde woman hopping from foot to foot, trying to get a better view of the visitors.

'You'll be the polis, then?' Eric McDonald's voice was resigned, expecting nothing.

Karen introduced herself and Jason. 'Could we come in?'

'Let them in, Eric, they'll be thinking we've no manners. Come away in, hen. You too, son.' Patsy McDonald had the artificial brightness and dead eyes that go hand in hand with prescription antidepressants.

They all trooped into a living room that was stuffed with furniture and ornaments. Apparently Patsy McDonald collected Toby jugs and every surface that wasn't occupied by framed photographs of Tina held a selection of some of the ugliest pottery Karen had ever seen. She sat down next to Jason on the sofa and the McDonalds angled their armchairs towards her.

'I suppose this is another one of your routine visits. Where you tell us the case is never closed,' Eric said drily, reaching for the cigarette packet on the side table next to him.

'Actually, no,' Karen said. 'We're here because we've had a breakthrough.' Eric paused with the lighter flame inches from his cigarette, eyes wide.

Patsy literally jumped in her seat, ending up perched on the edge. 'Really?' she exclaimed. 'Have you got him? Have you got the bastard who took our Tina?' Then she flushed. 'Excuse my French.'

'No need to apologise. We've not got him yet, but we're very close.'

'You know who he is, though?' Excited, Patsy was bouncing up and down.

'Not exactly. If I could explain?' The McDonalds looked

at each other, nodding in unison. 'There was a car accident at the weekend in Dundee and the driver is in a coma. But a blood sample was taken at the hospital and when it was run against the national database—'

'You got a match?' Patsy was on her feet, her hands clawing at her neck. 'Oh my God, Eric, they got a match.'

'Please, Mrs McDonald. If you'd let me finish?'

'Sit down, Patsy. Let the woman speak,' Eric said, puffing as he lit up.

Patsy subsided and looked at Karen with damp eyes. 'I don't understand.'

'It wasn't an exact match. But it was enough of a fit for the lab team to tell us that whoever attacked Tina was a close male relative of the young man in the coma. He wasn't even born when Tina died, by the way.'

'She didn't "die",' Eric said angrily. 'She was murdered.'

Sometimes you couldn't win, Karen thought. When you called a spade a spade, some relatives flinched and wept to be reminded of the horror. When you attempted delicacy, others, like Eric McDonald, took offence at what they saw as a failure to acknowledge the enormity of what had been done to their loved ones. 'And we never forget that, Mr McDonald. And we are closer to the man who killed her than we have ever been.'

'So have you arrested him? This "close male relative"?' Eric demanded.

'Not yet. There's a complication. The young man in question was adopted, so we need to trace his birth parents.'

'Does he not know who they are? Has he no curiosity?' Eric's voice was heavy with contempt.

'He doesn't actually know he was adopted,' Jason said. 'If he comes round, it's going to come as a bit of a shock to him.'

'I don't care about him. All I care about is finding who killed our lassie,' Patsy said. 'You're going to get him, right? Like Mr Diuguid said when it happened.'

'Diuguid.' Eric snorted. 'Do nothing, more like. So what's stopping you?'

'The law, Mr McDonald. We have to go to court to ask the sheriff to allow us access to this young man's birth records.'

'What's holding you back?'

'We're moving as quickly as we can, I promise you. We'll be taking this to court as soon as we can get it on the list. Then our lawyer will try to persuade the sheriff to let us see the original birth certificate.'

'But he will let you, right?' Patsy again. 'I mean, he'll understand we need to know what happened to Tina.'

'Of course he will,' Eric said. 'It stands to reason. There can't be anything more important than putting a murderer away.'

'It may not be entirely straightforward,' Karen said mildly. 'There are human rights issues at stake.'

Eric's face darkened. He looked like a man on the edge of a stroke. 'Human rights? Human bloody rights? What about our human rights? We've got a right to know what happened to our daughter. Twenty years we've lived with what that man did to her. Twenty bloody years. He wasn't thinking about Tina's human rights when he—' He abruptly ran out of steam.

'What my man's saying is you need to go away and do whatever it is you need to do to put this bastard away.' No apology this time. Patsy's dander was well and truly up.

'And that's exactly what we are doing.' Karen got to her feet. 'Before we go – is there anything new that's come up about what happened to Tina? Any wee details you might have overlooked? Anything somebody's said?'

'We'd have been straight on the phone if there was,' Patsy said. 'You think you want answers? You should walk a mile in our shoes.'

16

Liz Dunleavy always felt a sense of homecoming when she walked through the door of the original Hair Apparent. It hadn't always been like that. At first, she'd felt like a bit of a chancer. The inhabitants of the red sandstone tenement streets of the West End of Glasgow who weren't still students were mostly academics or media professionals. Liz often said to her clients that you could open a bookshop stocked only with the publications of the people who lived in the G12 postcode. By contrast, Liz had grown up in the East End of the city, in a tenement that had dodged slum clearance by the skin of its rotten teeth. Neither parent had any expectations of their six children except that they would likely be more trouble than they were worth. What Liz had lacked in advantages, she'd more than made up for in ambition, and her own transformation had been her greatest work of the stylist's art.

When she'd opened up her first salon, the location had been at the unfashionable end of Byres Road, but the world had changed to her advantage. Now Hair Apparent was surrounded by the kind of cafés where you could get any beverage except a straightforward cup of coffee; an artisan bakery; a handful of reasonable places to eat; estate agents staffed by tense and rapacious young people; and pubs that had been stripped to the bone and reconstructed in the image that attracted students and young professionals trying to stay in contact with their misspent youth.

Liz had spent the morning in the most recent of her acquisitions, a mile away on the main drag in the part of Maryhill that estate agents optimistically and mendaciously referred to as North Kelvinside. The salon hadn't quite found its feet yet. Even though it had been gutted and reinvented as a flagship for leading-edge style, baffled pensioners kept on making appointments, complaining about the music, demanding endless cups of coffee then whingeing about the prices. She needed to reach out to the young professionals who were colonising the area. She was going to have to spend some money. Leaflets with a voucher, that was the way to go. It was over the budget, but something had to be done.

When she got back, she'd had to drive round the block three times before she found a parking space. Tomorrow, she promised herself as she walked into the salon. Tomorrow she'd bite the bullet and sort out some flyers. A fiver off a cut, another fiver off a colour.

The familiar smell of the salon was enough to relax her shoulders. Coconut and lime, the signature fragrance of the products they used, and the faint underlying tang of chemicals; those were the odours that spelled comfort to Liz. That and the music, a perpetual Spotify loop of her personal favourites from the past thirty years. The three stylists working their chairs looked up as she walked in. They nodded, smiled, muttered greetings then went back to their clients. Liz swept through, stopping for a moment to touch base with Callum's customer, a middle-aged woman who was something senior in the university admin and had been coming to the salon for more than a dozen years. 'You're looking great,

Margaret, have you lost weight?' Liz asked, meeting her eyes in the mirror. One thing was certain. She was wearing better than Margaret Somerville.

At the desk she double-checked the appointments screen. Twenty minutes till her next appointment. 'I'm going through the back for a cup of coffee, Jeannie,' she said to the junior running the diary. As she spoke, the door opened and what she characterised as a very odd couple walked in. A woman in her thirties in quite a good suit – from Whistles, Liz thought – that didn't fit properly, a good head of thick brown hair in need of an emergency cut, and a ginger in his twenties who looked mortified in his cheap suit, scuffed shoes and cookie-cutter style cut to template rather than the shape of his head. Not her usual clientele. They made straight for the desk.

Jeannie turned on her sweet smile. 'Hello. Can I help you? Have you got an appointment?'

'I'm looking for Liz Dunleavy,' the woman said.

Cautious, Liz said, 'You've found her. Do you have an appointment?'

The woman shook her head, a twitch of amusement lifting one corner of her mouth. 'No, I don't. All I need is a wee bit of your time.'

Liz raised one eyebrow, casting a practised eye over the woman's hair. 'It'll take more than a wee bit of my time to give your hair the treatment it deserves,' she said drily.

'I'm not here for a cut and blow.' She produced a card from her pocket. 'I'm Detective Chief Inspector Karen Pirie from the Historic Cases Unit. And this is Detective Constable Jason Murray.'

Liz felt her face stiffen. Her mouth dried. 'Tina,' she croaked. Not dead and buried, then. She'd wondered if it would come to this one day. Every time the words 'cold case' caught her ear on the news, she'd freeze, half-expecting Tina's name.

'That's right,' Karen said. 'Is there somewhere we can go?'

Liz raised one finger. This wasn't an encounter she wanted to rush. 'One minute.' She turned to the screen, ran her finger down the next time slot. 'Callum?'

He stopped snipping and gave her an enquiring look. 'Wassup?'

'Do you mind doing my two o'clock?' She extended a perfectly manicured hand towards Karen. 'This is going to take more than quarter of an hour.'

Callum rolled his eyes. 'I was going over to Kember and Jones for some of that lovely fig and fennel bread.'

'Jeannie'll go for you when she's got a minute.' What had happened to Scottish men, Liz wondered in passing.

Callum sighed. 'Oh, all right. But you owe me.'

Liz's smile was an object lesson in insincerity. 'Jeannie, take the money for Callum's bread out of the petty cash. I'll be in the back and I don't want any interruptions.' Finally, she gave Karen her full attention. 'Come with me, Inspector. We'll get some peace and quiet and a cup of coffee.' Though a large vodka and coke would have been more welcome.

She led the way into the back shop, a small, awkwardly shaped room with a scatter of unmatching upright chairs, every other surface scattered with the detritus of the trade. Boxes of product were stacked in the corners and a shiny coffee machine hogged a narrow counter next to the door. For the first time, Liz saw it through a stranger's eyes and felt mildly embarrassed about the chaos. 'Have a seat. Sorry about the mess. All the energy goes into the front shop.'

Karen smiled again. 'You could say the same about a lot of the people we arrest.'

'Coffee? Tea?' Liz moved towards the machine. She wanted to keep control of the conversation – no, it wasn't a conversation, it was an interview, no matter how friendly this woman was trying to appear.

102

'We're fine,' Karen said. 'But don't let us stop you. Shall we sit down?'

She'd lost already, Liz realised, perching on the edge of a wooden chair with a seat covered in padded vinyl. She crossed her legs and cupped her left elbow in her right hand. Then she folded her hands in her lap, remembering all she'd read about body language. 'Have you got new evidence to open up the case, then?'

'Unsolved cases are never closed, Liz. You don't mind me calling you Liz?'

'No, it's my name.' She managed a weak smile.

'So the case was never closed. Periodically we review all unsolved murders.'

'It's just routine, then?' Liz was crestfallen. Nothing would bring Tina back, but she would have truly enjoyed seeing someone lose their freedom for what they'd done to her.

'None of our cases are routine to us. We're as keen to get a result as the original team of detectives. It gives me heartburn to think of murderers walking around scot-free.'

Liz was taken aback by the depth of feeling in Karen's voice. 'Sorry. I didn't mean to suggest . . .'

'It's all right. We're at the early stages of our inquiry, though. I'd like you to go through what you remember from that night.'

'I gave statements at the time. Do you not have copies of them?'

'We do. And chances are, Jason here will be going through those statements line by line with you. But first, I want to hear what comes to your mind when you think back to that night.'

Liz forgot all about body language and hugged herself. 'I've gone over this in my head a million times. We should have stuck together. We should have been keeping tabs on each other. But by the time we got to the club, Bluebeard's, we'd had a few bevvies and we were up for a good laugh. We started out all dancing together, but you know how it is?' She looked away.

'So, you all started dancing with other people? With guys?'

'Aye. Marie peeled off first. She was always quick off the mark, you know what I mean? Then Jan ran into a guy she knew from where she used to work, and she went off to the bar for a drink with him. Then it was just me and Tina, and these two guys started dancing with us. Only a couple of numbers, then I went to the loo. When I came back, I couldn't see Tina.' She shivered, took a deep breath and collected herself.

'It wasn't like she'd disappeared or anything. I spotted her a few times over the next couple of hours, but, I'll be honest, I was quite interested in this guy that was chatting me up, so I wasn't looking out for her.' Liz hung her head, a familiar guilt churning her stomach. 'I should have been.'

Karen shifted one shoulder in a half-shrug. 'You weren't her keeper. We've all gone out with our pals and stopped paying attention because someone we fancy has taken an interest in us. That's the way of the world, not something to beat yourself up about.' She smiled, reassuring. 'When you did catch sight of her, was she with one person in particular?'

'I didn't really notice. I'm sorry.'

'Then when it came time to go home, she was nowhere to be seen?' Karen's gaze was unrelenting. It reminded Liz of the way her maths teacher used to look at her, challenging her to do better. And she had done better. Better than any of the other lassies in her class.

'We looked for her, but we couldn't find her.' Her hand went to her mouth and she chewed the skin round her thumbnail. 'We told ourselves she'd clicked and gone home with some guy. It was the easiest thing to think, plus we were all pretty pissed by then. It was only later, the next morning when I was coming round with a cup of coffee, I thought to myself it wasn't really Tina's style, picking a guy up in a club. But I never thought ... '

'Why would you?' Karen reached across the small space and patted her knee. 'This was not your fault, Liz. None of it. Nothing you did or didn't do made this happen.'

Liz wished she still smoked, longing for the luxury of something to cling to and hide behind. 'I know that with my head, but inside, I blame myself. I blame the other two as well.' Her face screwed up in pain. 'We never see each other these days. Marie and Jan, they were both out the door within weeks. New jobs, clean slates. We never said anything, but I think seeing each other every day reminded us of what happened to Tina.' She squeezed out a distorted smile. 'She was lovely, Tina. Always had a smile for everybody. Always put herself out for folk. The customers loved her.' She blinked hard.

'When you met up in the Starburst Bar, did you notice anybody paying particular attention to you?'

Liz shook her head. 'It was my birthday. Somebody stalking us was the last thing on our minds.'

'Tina arrived last, right? She walked up from the underground? And you didn't see anybody coming in behind her?'

Liz was taken aback. 'The underground?'

'That's right. That's how she got there that night.'

Liz looked puzzled. 'I don't know where that's come from. Tina never took the underground. She was claustrophobic. She broke out in a sweat in a lift.' She saw the eyes opposite her narrow. 'I don't remember anybody asking about that at the time,' Liz said, shaking her head. 'They seemed to question me forever, but it was all about the pub and later on the club. We were all in a state, right enough, but I honestly don't remember being asked about how Tina got to the Starburst. Is that in my statement? About the underground?'

The ginger lad looked confused. 'I'm not sure. I don't think so.'

'It's probably not important,' Karen said. 'So how would she have got there? A cab, maybe?'

Liz looked doubtful. 'She wouldn't have wasted her money on a cab, not when there were buses. She'd likely have got the number 16 to Queen Street station, that would drop her round the corner from the Starburst. Does that make a difference?'

The detective frowned. 'I don't know why it would. But it's the first thing we've come across that contradicts the files. And that's always a place to start.'

17

Another clear, cold night, delicate skeins of cloud drifting across the thin sickle of the new moon. A surprising number of stars were visible above the Firth of Forth in spite of the light pollution from the city. Karen pulled on her thermal-lined gloves and gave a little shiver as she emerged from the warmth of her apartment block and the cold air hit her.

She hesitated for a moment, debating which direction to choose for her late-night expedition. She'd been promising herself a mooch through the Old Town to Holyrood, but the scene she'd witnessed on the railway path a couple of nights before had intrigued her. She wondered whether it had been a one-off or if it was a regular gathering place.

There was one obvious way to find out.

With a destination in mind, Karen moved more quickly than usual through the side streets of Leith. It wasn't the Wild West town of *Trainspotting* these days; too many people had splashed their cash on flash modern apartments like hers, too many upwardly mobile young professionals had colonised tenement closes. But after midnight, the few people she saw on the street seemed to come from the older Leith of chancers and drinkers, hookers and druggies, and the poor-but-respectable who'd failed to reach escape velocity. An old woman in a pink Puffa jacket, jogging pants and filthy trainers crossed Constitution Street to avoid Karen as she made for the heavy-handed neoclassical edifice of Pillars House and the cut-through to Leith Links. Sometimes she felt like she had a neon sign above her head that flashed 'Polis' in big blue letters.

As she walked through the dark grassy expanse of the Links and on to Restalrig Road, she thought about their interview with Liz Dunleavy. They'd arranged for Jason to go back to Glasgow on Liz's next day off, to go through her statements in detail. But on the face of it, the only problematic element in her evidence was the curious business of how Tina had travelled from her flat to the Starburst Bar. The police files said she'd been on the underground. But Liz had been unshakeable on that point. Tina would rather have walked than climbed aboard the Clockwork Orange, the local nickname for the lurid orange carriages that whizzed under the city like toy trains. It was a tiny discrepancy, but until she could make sense of it, she knew it would nag at her like a hangnail that keeps on snagging.

So after they'd driven back to Edinburgh, Karen had gone to the office to see whether she could uncover the reason why the previous investigation had got that wrong. It had taken her over an hour, but eventually she'd found the crucial detail on a list of crime scene evidence that hadn't been submitted to the lab for testing. Not everything went to the lab; testing was expensive and unless there was a good reason to believe a particular exhibit might give up some relevant physical evidence, they didn't bother. There, among the assorted litter on the list, was an underground ticket dated the day of Tina's murder.

She checked the notes that accompanied the evidence list. The underground ticket had been on the ground, among the contents of Tina's handbag, which had burst open during her final struggle. The assumption had been that the ticket had belonged to Tina. And nobody had ever checked that assumption because it had never seemed important to know how Tina had travelled into town. She'd said nothing to any of her friends to indicate there had been anything unusual about her journey, so no attention had ever been paid to it. The focus had all been on later in the evening, when she'd come into direct contact with her killer.

Karen had no idea whether there was any significance in the mistaken assumption. She suspected that a *Crime Watch* appeal asking for witnesses to a bus journey on a Friday night twenty years before would be pointless, even if she could persuade them to run one. Sometimes pulling on the loose thread in a cold case started an unravelling that led to the truth; sometimes it made an existing knot even more intractable. She had a feeling this was one that wasn't going to lead to a straightforward solution. Everything about this case had the smell of trouble.

Nothing she could do about it now, though. Maybe it wouldn't matter anyway, not if she got the right result in court tomorrow. Karen had lined up an advocate who was an expert in adoption law and they'd managed to persuade the sheriff's clerk to squeeze them in. Maybe they'd have the whole thing tied up by the end of the week. Maybe they'd finally have an answer for the McDonalds. Though she suspected that, for them, the damage done was irreparable.

Karen turned on to a flight of stone steps that led from street level to the path below and turned right towards the bend leading to the bridge where the men had been gathered.

As she rounded the curve, she could see the glow of flames licking unevenly against the graffiti on the opposite wall. She drew closer and there they were again: half a dozen of them wrapped up against the night, hats and beards giving their shadows strange elongated shapes. Again their conversation stilled as she approached. Again she found a gap in the circle and held her hands out to the flames. 'It's a cold night,' she said.

For a long moment, nobody spoke. Looks were exchanged then one of the men said, 'Every night in Scotland is cold.' His English was clear, the accent rendering the language more musical than usual.

'Sometimes in summer it's not bad.'

He shrugged. 'If we are still here in summer, maybe we will find out.' In the flickering light, he looked quite young. Mid to late twenties, maybe. Middle Eastern, certainly. Dark eyes, full lips, neat beard.

'Where are you guys from, then?'

One of the others said something sharply to the man who had spoken, but he shook his head. He gave Karen a quick tentative smile. His chin came up. 'We are from Syria.' It was almost a challenge.

She'd wondered. Syrian refugees had been arriving in Scotland for a while, finding a welcome in unlikely places. Like Rothesay, an unfashionable seaside resort populated by retirees and transplanted Glaswegian junkies, some recovering and some defiantly not. And this lot, cast adrift in a city that couldn't be less like the Middle East. 'I'm sorry for what's happened to your home,' she said.

'Thank you. We are grateful to be here.'

A short while passed in silence. The older men, who had unconsciously moved closer together when she'd spoken, relaxed again. 'So why are you down here in the middle of the night?' Karen tried to make her question sound as conversational as possible.

'We have nowhere else to meet,' the young man said simply.

One of the others leaned into the conversation. He was older, his beard streaked with wiry grey hair, his eyes nested in lines and pouches. His English was more halting, but still clear. 'Where we are living, we are not having space to meet. To talk. We are many to each apartment. Families fill everywhere.' He shrugged with one shoulder. 'We are full of thanks for being here. But it is not easy.'

The younger man spoke again. 'We have no money, we are not allowed to work, we have nowhere else to be.'

'I'm sorry,' Karen said.

'We need to be with each other,' the older man said. 'We need to share our sorrow. We have all lost friends and family in the war. Bombs and bullets and torture.'

'I understand that. My man was murdered. I know what it's like to carry that pain inside.' The words were out before Karen could stop herself. What had possessed her? She couldn't talk to Jason, but apparently she could open up to a bunch of Syrian strangers round an illicit night fire. But then, these people had endured so much; they were linked by their suffering in a way that wasn't accessible to outsiders, no matter how much they wanted to empathise.

'I am sorry for your loss,' the young man said. 'I am Miran. What is your name?'

'I'm Karen.'

The older man nodded and repeated her name. 'I am Tarek.' Then he went round the others, introducing them. Two inclined their heads towards her, but another pair glowered at the fire, refusing to make eye contact. She didn't take it personally. She understood there were cultural reasons why some of them might not be entirely comfortable with a strange woman wandering around in the middle of the night on her own.

'Is there no community centre or anywhere like that for you to meet?' she asked.

'In the daytime, when the centres are open, we are doing all the things that we have to do. We stand in line to fill in papers, then we have to wait for an interpreter.' Miran sighed. 'We have to tell our story again and again. We have to help our wives and our mothers. We need to spend time with the children. And then it's late and everywhere we can go is not open. And we have no money to go to the places that are open.'

Karen knew she didn't know enough to make a helpful suggestion. But she wondered all the same. There were churches with halls and coffee shops. Surely Christian charity might extend that far? 'Do you get left alone down here? Nobody bothers you?'

Again, that exchange of looks. Tarek said, 'Sometimes drunk men shout at us. But they are not so many as us. So they shout and then go away.'

'One time, two police came.' A third man frowned. 'They check our papers. They tell us to stop fire. They are not happy.'

Karen seized on this. 'I can stop that happening again,' she said. 'I am a police officer. A detective. I can tell them to leave you alone.'

Their looks of alarm confused her momentarily. Then she understood that even though she had neither done nor said anything threatening, the very idea of police was deeply worrying for them. 'You are police?' Miran's voice had a rougher edge now.

'Yes, but that's nothing to do with why I'm here. I told you, my man was killed. I don't sleep well since he died. I expect you know all about not sleeping, and bad dreams. That's why I come out walking. I understand why you are afraid of the police. But I can maybe help you by making sure the night patrols leave you in peace.'

Tarek looked sceptical. 'Why do you help us? We have nothing to pay you.'

'You don't have to pay me. I want to help.'

Miran said something in their language, fast and lengthy. Then he bowed his head towards her. 'Thank you. We are not used to police we can trust.'

'You can trust me.' Karen moved closer to the fire, keeping the night at bay. 'So, where did you live in Syria, Miran?'

'We are all from Homs, except for Tarek. He is from a small village near Aleppo.'

'No more village,' Tarek said, his face scrunched in pain.

'What did you do there? What was your job?' Karen asked Miran.

'I worked in my father's café. But he died in the bombing. We tried to keep going, but then the café was destroyed by tanks. There was nowhere to work, nowhere to live. We escaped to Lebanon, to a camp. We had money but it didn't last long. And then we were chosen to come here because my mother is sick and she needs me and my wife to care for her. My wife is expecting our first child and I think my child may never see our Syria.' His voice cracked and he looked away. Tarek patted his shoulder and another man thrust a cigarette at him.

'If we have café, Miran knows how to run it,' another cut in. 'But we are not allowed to work, not allowed to do things for our people.'

'All around in Leith, we see shops with boards on the windows and doors. Why can we not make café?' Tarek grumbled.

He had a point, Karen thought. She made an indeterminate noise of sympathy. 'I need to be on my way,' she said. 'Maybe I'll see you again.'

The men nodded glumly. It was clearly a matter of indifference to them. But their plight had awakened Karen's compassion, and as she walked away, she was already testing ideas for how she might help these men who had somehow breached her defences and made it possible for her to articulate her suffering. Strangers they might be, but she was determined to show them that her country was a place they might be able to call home.

18

Karen always felt vaguely intimidated by Edinburgh Sheriff Court. Even the approach seemed calculated to make people feel insignificant. The entrance was set back from Chambers Street itself, but it was of a piece with the other buildings that stood around it. They were all massive, over-sized Victorian monsters. Even the new additions, like the modern extension to the National Museum of Scotland, were larger than life, designed to dwarf passers-by. Then there was the court itself. Those elegant but imposing wrought-iron gates; the nameplate mounted on that strange dumpy phal-lic pillar that always made her think of a mortar primed to shower bombs on the city; the imposing façade that was in itself a trick – only four storeys tall, disguising the fact that there were another four levels below the street. All seemingly intended to remind the visitor that the law was a daunting institution. If she felt like that, a woman who was part of the process, how must it feel for the accused, never mind the witnesses?

She'd left Jason ploughing through the paperwork on the Tina McDonald case. He'd sift the witness statements, prioritising those it might be worth revisiting. It was a tedious job, but one that was well within his capabilities. One thing Jason did possess was an eye for detail. Neither of them expected much from this part of the investigation, but it had to be dealt with. The DNA match was significant, but on its own it might not be a clincher. Any other evidence that might potentially back it up could be crucial if they found themselves taking a twenty-year-old case to court.

Karen went through the security check then headed for the Solicitors' Room café. Colin Semple was already there, cappuccino and a scone to one side of the paperwork he was absorbed in. As she waited for her own Americano, she watched him automatically eat and drink without taking his eyes from the documents. She'd had little to do with family lawyers over the years, but she'd encountered Semple a few years previously in a complicated abduction case. She'd been impressed with his intelligence and quick grasp of complex situations, but more than that, she'd valued his calm and friendly presence. She'd met too many advocates over the years who clearly considered themselves only slightly junior to God. It had been a refreshing change to work with Semple.

She carried her coffee over and sat down opposite him. He glanced up then, seeing it was her, pushed his chair back and stood up, smiling. His brown eyes were reduced to slits by the deep crinkles at their corners. He was a big man, tall and softly fat. His disorganised thatch of sandy hair always reminded Karen of a Border terrier in need of stripping. Semple was dressed in his regular uniform – immaculately tailored black three-piece suit, brilliant white shirt and a violet bow-tie that matched the hankie peeping out of his top pocket and the silk lining of his jacket. 'Good morning, Detective Chief Inspector. I must thank you for bringing me something out of the ordinary.' His vowels were round and plummy, the product of an expensive Edinburgh education.

'Nice to see you, Mr Semple.' They sat down and Karen gestured at his papers. 'What do you make of it?'

He inhaled deeply through his nose then exhaled through his plump lips. 'It's a balancing act. The interests of the individual versus the interests of justice, to render it most simply. We're up in front of Sheriff Abercrombie, who I suspect may lean towards our side of the argument.'

'That's good news.'

'There is also less good news, I'm afraid. I know you hoped when I managed to get such an early hearing that our opponents would not have time to organise themselves. Unfortunately for us, the adoptive parents have engaged counsel to argue on their behalf. In spite of the tightness of the timetable, they've managed to instruct Alexandra Cosgrove, for whom I have the greatest respect.' He ran the tip of his index finger round the outside edge of his ear. 'And she does have a case with some validity. So I am less fulsomely confident than I was when we spoke yesterday.'

Karen's heart sank. Without the DNA, there was nothing. A discrepancy between bus and underground wasn't going to make any kind of a case for her. Her disappointment must have shown in her face, for Semple chuckled, a low rumble that shook his belly.

'O ye of little faith,' he said. 'Do not despair, DCI Pirie. I still think we can prevail.' He cast a quick look at his watch and shuffled his papers together. 'Showtime, Detective.'

The big difference between the family and the criminal courts, Karen remembered as she walked to the witness stand, was the amount of peripheral activity going on. In the criminal courts, lawyers, clerks and ushers moved discreetly in and out. Reporters slipped out to file copy – electronically, these days – then returned to catch up with proceedings. Members of the public arrived and departed according to their own particular timetables. But the family courts were different. The protection of privacy was always paramount, so the only people in the room were the ones the case mattered to. And they wanted to hear everything.

The other big difference was that the lawyers weren't disguised as refugees from the seventeenth century. No wigs and gowns, just ordinary street clothes. Well, not always ordinary, Karen corrected herself. Semple was never going to be mistaken for anything other than what he was.

Once she'd gone through the formalities, he began to lead her through their case. She explained what had happened in the wake of Ross Garvie's accident, she outlined the significance of familial DNA, the sheriff agreed that it wasn't necessary to call a forensics expert to testify to the established science, and Karen admitted that yes, without being able to identify Ross Garvie's biological father there would be no prospect of bringing Tina McDonald's killer to book.

As she responded to Semple's questions, she was aware of Alexandra Cosgrove's scrutiny. The advocate, now on the far side of her half-century, had arctic white hair sculpted close to her head. With her pale skin and fine features, she looked like a version of Audrey Hepburn with all the colour stripped out. But there was nothing cute about her pale blue stare.

After Semple had finished questioning Karen, Sheriff Abercrombie raised one finger signalling a pause while she made some extra notes. Then she nodded to Cosgrove to continue.

The advocate took her time, never taking her eyes off Karen. 'Twenty years have passed since this unfortunate young woman met her end, isn't that right?'

'Yes.'

'And the police have not so much as identified a viable suspect?'

'Until now, yes.'

'My clients have protected their son from the knowledge that he was adopted. Are you aware of that?'

'I am, yes.' Karen wondered where this was going.

'How confident are you that acquiring access to Ross Garvie's original birth certificate will allow you to develop a viable suspect?'

'I'm very confident.' Karen hoped her expression matched her words. She caught Linda Garvie shaking her head, her lips pursed in a pessimistic line.

'I suggest that confidence is misplaced. I suggest the chances are that there will be no father's name on that birth certificate. Does that dent your confidence at all, DCI Pirie?'

She was starting to see where this was headed. 'My unit is highly skilled in tracking people down. And mothers generally know who fathered their child even if they don't include that information on the birth certificate.'

'Your unit.' Cosgrove smirked and looked at her notes. 'That would be you and one detective constable?'

'That's our core unit, yes. But we can draw on other resources from within Police Scotland.'

'In all likelihood, the mother's life would have been chaotic. She may have had multiple partners. She may have been a victim of rape. Even if the two of you manage to trace Ross Garvie's birth mother and she's still alive, it's entirely possible that's not going to lead you to his father, isn't it?'

'I remain confident, Ms Cosgrove.'

Cosgrove's perfectly shaped eyebrows rose as she assumed an expression of incredulity. 'Do you really think this slender possibility outweighs the rights of my clients and their son to their human rights?'

'That's for the court to decide,' Karen said, refusing to be drawn. 'My job is to seek justice for Tina McDonald and answers for her family.'

The sheriff gave her a quick look over the top of her reading glasses, her mouth quirking in approval. Cosgrove released her after that, realising she wasn't going to get any further.

Karen found a seat at the rear of the courtroom and settled down to listen to Semple make the case. He spoke eloquently about the need for the courts to support the police's commitment to cold cases. He argued that releasing this information to the police would not necessarily have any impact on Ross Garvie. 'This case is being heard in camera,' he said. 'If the opening of this record results in a criminal trial, there is no reason why Ross Garvie's name needs to be spoken in open court. My understanding of the rules of evidence is that it would be sufficient for the Procurator Fiscal to state that, incidental to another criminal case, a familial DNA hit was obtained on the database. So there is no breach of anyone's human rights here because the knowledge remains confined to those of us in this courtroom today. I request that you grant this order, my lady.'

Sheriff Abercrombie made more notes, gesturing to Semple that he should sit down. 'Ms Cosgrove?' she said eventually. 'I'll hear from you now.'

Cosgrove stood up, thrusting one hand into the pocket of her loose-fitting jacket. 'My argument is simple, my lady. Article 8 of the Human Rights Act provides an inalienable right to a private and family life. Ross Garvie is a minor and his parents are quite correctly exercising that right on his behalf.' She waved her free hand at the Garvies. 'My learned friend Mr Semple is disingenuous in his claims that Ross Garvie's identity can be protected from both Ross himself and the wider world. If a criminal trial ensues, the media will, as usual, have no regard for his rights, especially since he will by then almost certainly be an adult in the eyes of the law. The media, particularly the online media, will leave no stone unturned to reveal his identity. As we have seen more than once in the recent past, Police Scotland is not good at maintaining confidentiality. Unlike Detective Chief Inspector Pirie, I have no confidence that my clients' rights will be protected. My lady, I ask that you not grant this request, and further that you injunct Police Scotland from revealing any information that might lead to their identification.'

There it was again. Police Scotland, the leaky sieve. Karen stifled a sigh. The Macaroon was supposed to be in charge of finding out where the information was seeping out. The trouble was he couldn't detect his way out of a paper bag without a GPS. It made the job that much harder on the front line. People didn't want to pass on confidential information if it was going to rebound on them.

Sheriff Abercrombie cleared her throat. 'Thank you both. I see no need to rush to judgement in this matter. Justice has waited for twenty years. It can wait a little longer so that I can give this conundrum the consideration it deserves. I will issue my judgement in due course.'

And that was that. The Garvies glowered at her as Alexandra Cosgrove shepherded them out of the courtroom. 'You've got no right to do this to us,' Linda Garvie hissed as she passed. Her husband shushed her, putting an arm round her shoulders and hustling her away. Karen fell into step beside Semple as he left the room.

'What do you think?' she said.

'I think we'll be all right. To put not too fine a point on it, I suspect she may want to give it a day or two to see whether or not young Mr Garvie is going to stay with us.'

Karen drew in a sharp breath. 'Harsh.'

Semple gave a sardonic smile. 'But, I fear, true.'

19

Karen had just stepped out of the sheriff court on to the bustle of Chambers Street when someone called her name. She swivelled round, trying to see who it was. An arm waved from behind a pair of lumbering American backpackers. 'Hey, Karen,' the cry came again. Then a mop of black curls emerged, followed by a familiar grinning face.

Karen grinned right back. 'Sunny O'Brien.'

Sunny sidestepped the wobbling rucksacks and pulled Karen into a hug. 'How the hell are you?' The Irish accent was thick and strong as a glass of Guinness, at odds with her brown skin, her hair and her dark eyes, the product of an Aboriginal mother and an Irish father. Sunny, whose temperament lived up to her given name, appeared delighted to see Karen.

'Not bad,' Karen said. And for a moment, on the receiving end of Sunny's smile, it was the truth. 'What are you doing here in Edinburgh?'

Sunny linked her arm in Karen's. 'I'm putting together a research proposal with a couple of chemists from the university here. We've been having a meeting and now I'm heading for a decent cup of coffee down at the Black Medicine café. Come on, bunk off and join me.'

Karen didn't need to be asked twice. Sunny was an expert in fire and explosives, a professor at Dundee University. They'd met a few years before at a mutual friend's birthday party, which could have doubled as a forensic science staff outing. For Karen, it had been the chance to make a fistful of useful contacts as well as having a bloody good night out. It was always satisfying to kill two birds with one stone.

They gossiped their way down the street and across South Bridge to the café. Armed with caffeine and brownies they settled on high-backed wooden benches near the back window. Sunny sipped her double espresso and sighed with contentment. 'It's not rocket science, so why is it so hard to get a five-star cup of coffee in these islands of ours?' Then, suddenly serious, she said, 'I'm not going to go on about this because I'm bloody sure you get it all the time, but just so's you know, I've been thinking about you. I didn't want to intrude, but I want to say, if you're ready, *when* you're ready for company, I'd be entirely delighted to go out for a pizza some night.'

It was, Karen thought, quite the most gracious offering of sympathy she'd had so far. 'That'd be good,' she said. 'I'm not quite there yet, but I'm getting close.'

'Excellent. So, what fresh hell are you dealing with right now?'

'Interesting but awkward. A familial DNA link on a twenty-year-old murder.'

'Awkward how?'

'Can't say, sorry.'

'Ach, you're such a tease, Karen.'

Karen laughed. 'I shouldn't have said anything. What about you?'

'Ach, you know, the usual. Analysing evidence from fires.

Doing some research about current practice in terrorist bomb-making.' She pulled an expressive face. 'The usual bollocks.'

Her words caught Karen's attention. It felt like another teasing hook drawing her towards Gabriel Abbott and his tragic history. 'That reminds me,' she said, slowly. 'I'm taking an interest in a case from 1994. A small plane that blew up in mid-air near Galashiels. Four people died. One of them was a former Northern Ireland minister, so the responsibility was laid at the door of the Republican movement even though nobody claimed it.'

'I vaguely remember that.' Sunny frowned. 'I was in Durham doing my PhD at the time. One of our senior lecturers did some work on it, I think, if it's the same one.'

'What struck me as odd was that neither the IRA or one of the splinter groups put their hands up. They were pretty active on the bombing front in the mid 90s – Warrington, Manchester, Docklands – and they weren't exactly shy about coming forward and taking the credit when they did it.'

Sunny nodded. 'I know what you mean. Sometimes you'd have a veritable forest of hands waving, going, "me, me", like a bunch of greedy five-year-olds. To have such a deafening silence would have been odd. But nobody really questioned it at the time, did they?'

'I don't know. I was just curious.'

'So have they reopened it, then?'

Karen stared at her hand stirring her coffee. 'No, it's only me seeing shadows in the back of the cave. One of the women who died in the crash, her son was murdered a few days ago. Or maybe he wasn't. Maybe it was suicide. And it made me wonder, because murder doesn't generally run in families.'

Sunny snorted sourly. 'Unless you live in Syria,' she said. 'Or the Democratic Republic of Congo. Or any one of a dozen places where life is cheap as chips and my anthropologist colleagues get sent to excavate mass graves.' She held up a hand to stave Karen off. 'But, yes, I know what you mean. So, your workload isn't enough for you? You have to go round inventing cases now?'

Karen pushed her hair back from her face in a gesture of impatience. 'I don't sleep much these days, Sunny. I need something to keep my head busy. I'm not arrogant enough to think I'm going to find a different answer to a case like this, but anomalies are my bread and butter, and this is an anomaly that might have got lost in the background noise in 1994.'

Sunny patted Karen's hand, sighing. 'Sure. I'm not judging you, honey. You're the one with the skills and the track record in this area. So, were you thinking I could ask a few questions and find you some food for thought?'

'To be honest, I hadn't got that far. It was just ticking away in the back of my mind. I probably wouldn't have done anything about it if I hadn't run into you today. Serendipity, the gift every cold case detective longs for.'

Sunny chewed on a mouthful of brownie and gave Karen a considering look. 'OK,' she said. 'But there's a price.'

'Of course there is. Can I afford it?'

'I want you to come up to Dundee and talk to my final-year undergraduates about police work. In spite of our best efforts, they still think you guys operate like TV cops. One grumpy inspector and a sergeant like a sheep solving all the crimes two-handed.'

'You mean, a bit like me and the Mint and the HCU?' Karen couldn't keep the wry out of her tone.

Sunny hooted with laughter. 'Right enough, youse are the dynamic duo. But I was thinking more about you talking them through major incident procedure and how their work interlocks with the investigation. What do you say?'

'It's a deal. I'll not bring the Mint, though. We don't want them running for the hills too early.'

'No, he's not the greatest recruiting sergeant for law enforcement. So, you email me the details of your plane explosion and I'll see what I can dig up. Like I said, if it's the one I'm thinking of, there's a horse's mouth I can go straight to.' Sunny knocked back the last of her coffee and smacked her lips. 'Just what the doctor ordered. But I'm going to have to love you and leave you, I've got a train to catch.'

They hugged farewell and Karen watched her bustle out of the shop and hurry down the crowded pavement of South Bridge towards the station. She wasn't sure what to do with herself. She could go back to the office and work on the schedule of interviews in the Tina McDonald case, but Jason was perfectly capable of doing that himself. She didn't want him thinking she lacked confidence in his ability to do something so straightforward. While she considered her options, she decided to drop a text to Giorsal. Karen was well aware of her tendency to let things drift on a personal level. If she didn't arrange something soon, it would slide off her agenda, and then it would get pushed aside by work, and before she knew it, months would have passed.

To her surprise, Giorsal seemed to be at as much of a loose end as she was, for she replied immediately. Within ten minutes, they had a firm arrangement to meet for dinner in a Thai restaurant near Waverley, convenient for Giorsal coming into the city by train. Cheered at the prospect, Karen decided to head back to the office after all. There had to be something she could do to push the case forward.

20

S unny took advantage of the uneven Wi-Fi on the train to access some of the background on the bee in Karen's bonnet, as she'd dubbed it in her head. So, by the time she got back to her office in Dundee, she had a list of things to ask Dr David Longford, who was now Reader in Forensic Chemistry in Cambridge.

After work, she sat down and composed a lengthy email outlining what she hoped he could tell her. The case was an old one; if he could help, he'd have to dig out some pretty ancient files. That far back, the chances were that they were either on paper or on some obsolete form of digital storage. Sunny hoped he was intrigued enough by her interest to brave the IT guys and ask them to restore his old floppies.

When she logged on the following morning, she discovered she wasn't the only one who answered work emails at midnight.

Hi Sunny. Good to hear from you. How are things in the frozen north? Are you going to the Lisbon conference? If so, can I persuade you to give a short presentation in a session I'm doing about recent refinements in IEDs?

I must admit, I was fairly gobsmacked by your questions. I haven't thought about the Cessna Skylane explosion for years. There was nothing problematic about it, as I recall, except that the incendiary device was pretty primitive. It didn't have a recognisable signature and you're right, nobody claimed it. But I should be able to access my files. We digitised all the historic archive material a couple of years ago – we got a lovely grant from an American demolition tycoon! – so, assuming it was all done correctly, it shouldn't be difficult. I'll see what I can find and maybe we can Skype? If you can make time on Thursday, my diary is clear apart from a supervision at 2pm. Look forward to talking to you.

Skype calls had become second nature to Sunny O'Brien. Her colleagues were scattered around the world, but these days, academics didn't have to wait for the next big conference to share ideas. Nowadays, it was easy to form working relationships with colleagues who had similar research interests, regardless of where they were based. So David Longford's suggestion was welcome. It was always better to see the whites of their eyes. Karen would be pleased. And given what her friend had been through lately, anything that would cheer her up had to be a bonus.

The days trickled past with nothing to show. Karen and Jason spoke to witnesses whose twenty-year-old memories added nothing new to their store of knowledge. They discussed the forensic evidence with the lab but there were no startling revelations as a result of advances in technology. They went through the motions of an inquiry that only one thing could affect.

Waiting for Colin Semple's call was killing Karen. How long did Sheriff Abercrombie need to figure out the right thing to do? If the advocate was right and Abercrombie was waiting to see whether Ross Garvie would die and save her the bother of making a difficult decision, how long would she leave it? Karen had phoned the hospital every day to check on Garvie's condition. 'Stable but critical,' was the unchanging verdict. What did that even mean?

What it meant in real terms was that Sheriff Abercrombie was sitting on the fence. So Karen kept marking time. The weather was terrible too; incessant cold drizzle, the kind that insinuated its way into every gap in weatherproof clothing, leaving you cold and clammy in a matter of minutes. Night walking was purgatory when what the locals called 'wee sma' rain' drifted down for hours on end. So Karen stayed home, wondering about the refugees. Did they brave the weather for the sake of conversation and company? Or were they, like her, stuck indoors, chafing at the inclement weather, wishing they were back where the rain was warm?

And then, late on Thursday evening, Sunny called. 'I didn't disturb you, did I?'

'No, I was box-set bingeing on *Homicide: Life on the Streets*. I always rewatch it when I'm fed up with work. It reminds me how much worse it could be.'

Sunny laughed. 'Funny, I never feel the same about *CSI*. So, I've just come off the Skype with David Longford. He did some work around the crash, analysing the bomb materials and such. And your instinct was right. It's a bit outside the usual run of Irish Republican ordnance.'

'What does that mean?'

'Boiling it down – it's very simple. It's not in the least bit sophisticated. And at that point in the IRA bombing campaign, their bomb-making was relatively high end. Between common-or-garden criminality, drug dealing and donations from across the Pond, they were raking in enough cash to afford proper explosives. Semtex and so forth. Electronic timers. There was nothing like that going on here. This was about as kitchen sink as you can get, with a couple of very vicious twists. The accident investigators got some fragments of steel and distorted metal spheres from the wreckage. Which suggests something like a paint tin with ball-bearings added to your basic mixture to up the destructive element of the explosion.'

'Nasty.'

'But effective. As to the chemicals – there wasn't much in the way of residue, but the little they got was enough to adduce that they were looking at good old sodium chlorate and sugar with sulphuric acid as the precipitating factor. With an extra dose of iron oxide and aluminium oxide.'

'Humour me. How does that work?'

'Sodium chlorate used to be quite easy to get – it's banned now, but it was a common weedkiller back when you're talking about. It was also used as a bleaching agent in recycled paper pulp. So, you mix that fifty-fifty with granulated sugar. Tip in the two metal oxides – aluminium's dead easy to get hold of, it's in everything from plastic filler to sunscreen, and iron oxide is your basic rust. Then you pour concentrated sulphuric acid into a condom – more than one, if you want to delay things – tie a double knot in it, set it on top of the chemical mix, put the lid on your tin and wait.'

'I don't get it. What's the condom for?'

'It's a very primitive fuse. The acid slowly eats its way through the rubber then it ignites the chemical mixture. And boom, you've got thermite. It burns hot and fierce, the gases build up and the tin explodes into shrapnel. With added ball-bearings.'

It was that easy? 'And you can buy sulphuric acid, no questions asked? Over the counter?'

'You can buy battery acid, which is weak sulphuric acid. You heat it in a ceramic pot till thick white smoke starts coming off it, and Bob's your uncle. You need to be careful with it, mind. You know the old verse?'

'What? You mean poetry?'

'Doggerel, more like: "Alas, poor James is dead. / We see his face no more. / For what he thought was H_2O / Was H_2SO_4." What passes for wit among chemists.'

'And that would be enough to bring down a plane?'

'Single-engine small plane? Sure. Two hundred and fifty grammes of each of the chemicals and a condom of acid and you'd be well away. It'd do terrible damage to your moving parts and the aviation fuel feeding the engine would catch fire. It's simple, but it's pretty fucking catastrophic. Look, I'll email all the tech stuff I got from David, but your bottom line is, this doesn't look like a mainstream Irish terrorist bomb of that vintage.'

'OK,' Karen said, puzzled. 'So what does that say to you?'

Sunny sighed. 'Ach, it's hard to be definitive. There were so many Republican splinter groups around at that time, all trying to make their mark. It might be as simple as a wee cell without much in the way of resources but desperate to be noticed and taken seriously by the big boys.'

'Or it might not.' One of the reasons Karen was so good at cold case work was her ability to think in tangents. Thinking aloud, she spoke slowly: 'Maybe it was nothing to do with the Irish connection.'

For a moment, Sunny was silent. Then she said, 'I suppose it's possible. But if it looks like a duck and it sounds like duck and it tastes like a duck, it's generally a duck.'

Except when it's not, Karen thought. What she said, with a laugh, was, 'Aye, you're right. I can't help myself. Flights of fancy, that's what keeps me going.'

Sunny's warm laugh again. 'You should be writing crime, not fighting it. OK, so this was a bit out of the usual run of Republican bombs, but the man on the business end of it was a former Northern Ireland minister. It stands to reason the motivation came from across the Irish Sea.'

Karen muttered agreement. But what she was thinking was that there were three other people on that plane. The obvious answer wasn't always the right one. Especially when the son of one of the victims ended up murdered twenty-two years later. If indeed Gabriel Abbott had been murdered, the voice of reason at the back of her mind insisted.

'Anyway.' Sunny carried on regardless. 'I'll ping the details over to you, to satisfy that restless curiosity of yours.'

'Cheers, Sunny, I owe you.'

'You do. And I'm hoping to collect before too long. Now off you go and get some sleep.'

As if, thought Karen as she ended the call. She looked out at the night, wondering whether the rain had eased off. She opened her sliding glass door and stepped out on to her balcony. She raised her face to the sky and miraculously, it remained dry. The air was still soft and damp, but the precipitation had stopped just in time to prevent her becoming stir crazy.

Ten minutes later, she was heading out on the route to the Restalrig Railway Path. Walking briskly, she picked up the path at an earlier point than she had the last time she'd been. She exchanged nods with a middle-aged woman tugging a recalcitrant pug along the path. When she caught sight of the now-familiar glow on the stone wall of the bridge abutment, she was surprised by how pleased she was to see it.

The weather had taken its toll on the refugees. There were only three men standing round a more subdued fire than usual – Tarek, and the two who had seemed most hostile to her before. Tarek looked up and gave a dignified nod as she joined them. 'Miserable night,' she said, warming her hands at the fire. She wasn't cold but it was a useful ice-breaker.

'We do not like Scottish rain,' Tarek said.

'Neither do we,' Karen said with a wry smile.

'So why do you come out in the night and the rain if you don't like it?'

She wondered if they were naturally direct, these Syrian men, or if it was simply that they didn't have the command of the language that would allow them to go all round the houses and tread diplomatically with a stranger. 'I don't sleep well. Walking tires me out. Then when I go home, I manage to drop off.'

'Drop off?'

'Sleep. It's an expression that means sleep.'

Tarek nodded, considering, as if filing it away for future use. 'So why do you not sleep? Do you have bad things on your mind? Bad police things? Are you guilty?'

Karen felt her shoulders rise defensively. 'I'm not a bad person. I'm not a bad police officer either. But a bad thing happened to the man I loved. Another man killed him.' She fell silent and stared at the flames.

'I am sorry,' Tarek said.

'So am I. All the time, I'm sorry. And I'm sad too. So I work long hours and I walk half the night to take my mind off what happened.'

'I understand. You have work instead of your man now.' Tarek heaved a deep sigh. 'We have sorrow too. We are sad because people we love are killed in the war. And because our homes are broken and we can't live there any more. And we have no work to stop us being sad.'

'That's hard,' Karen said. 'I don't know what I'd do without my work to take my mind off what I've lost.'

'Work is dignity.' Tarek shoved his hands deep into his coat pockets and scowled at the flames. 'We have no dignity here.'

'You're not allowed to work, are you?'

He shook his head. 'Not until we are accepted to stay. It is hard because we are men who work. We are not beggars with our hands out.' He clapped the flat of one hand on his chest. 'I am accountant.' He pointed at the closest of the other two men. 'He is chef. And he—' pointing at the third – 'he is dentist. But here, we are nothing.'

They put her to shame, Karen thought. She'd felt her own life had been emptied out with Phil's death. But these people had lost so much more. And while she could attempt to move forward with her life, they were in limbo. Desperate to begin again, but stuck fast where they'd landed.

'I'm sorry,' she said again.

Tarek shook his head. 'It's not your blame. You people here in Scotland, you are trying to help. Mostly, you are kind. Some, not so much. But mostly, yes. It's good to be where there are no bombs or bullets. We are glad for that.'

The man he'd identified as a chef looked Karen in the face for the first time. 'Why will you not let us work? Always I fed my family. Always I made a roof over the head of my wife and my children. But now we are like babies. I hate it.' He spat on the ground at his feet. 'Sometimes I think better to be dead at home than living like this.' He turned up his coat collar and walked off into the night.

'He does not mean this,' Tarek said hastily. 'He is angry, that's all.'

Karen sighed. 'He's right to be angry, right to be upset. I wish there was something I could do to help, really. Is there anything practical that you need? Food? Clothes? Blankets?'

Tarek's eyes were heavy with sorrow. 'We are not hungry. We have clothes. What we need, you cannot give us.'

There was nothing more to be said. Karen stood with the men for a few minutes longer, then said goodnight. She wasn't sure what she'd gone looking for on the railway path. But she knew she hadn't found it.

21

It was just before seven when Karen's phone woke her. A moment of disorientation – there were seldom urgent out-of-hours calls in cold cases – followed by the chill fear that something terrible had happened to one of her parents. Then she registered the name on the screen and swore.

'Good morning, sir,' she growled into her phone.

'Good? What do you mean, good, Pirie? What's good about it? Have you not seen the papers? It's all over the bloody internet.' Judging by the volume, the Macaroon's face would resemble the mottled palette of a Victoria plum.

Karen rolled upright, sitting on the edge of the bed, awake and alert. 'I have no idea what you're talking about,' she stalled. 'I've just this minute woken up.'

'Then I suggest you find out double quick. My office, eight o'clock. And I'm telling you now, Pirie, this is one step too far after what I said to you the other day.'

Silence. Karen let out a puff of breath and tossed her phone on the bedside table. Bastard, she thought, heading for the bathroom. Whatever was biting the Macaroon in the arse could wait till she'd had her shower and a brew. Everything looked worse without the mediation of hot water and caffeine, in her experience.

Fifteen minutes later she was in front of her laptop. Showered, dressed and armed with a cup of coffee, how bad could it be?

Very, very bad, was the answer. She didn't even have to go looking. The Google Alert she had set up a couple of years ago was sitting there in her mailbox, directing her to three Scottish media sites – two newspapers and an internet-based news service. The headlines screamed in her face.

COMA BOY KEY TO MURDER

JOY RIDER DNA UNLOCKS 20-YEAR MYSTERY

And finally, at greater length: LOVELY TINA'S MURDERER – THE DNA FINGER POINTS AFTER 20 YEARS. The clever concision of newspaper headlines didn't apply to the web. Nobody was constrained by the size of the page or the need for big snappy capitals to grab the passing potential reader rushing from bus stop to office.

Karen clicked on the first link, the popular tabloid her parents had read for years before finally giving up in disgust at its relentless parade of reality TV Z-list celebrities and badly behaved footballers with more money than sense. Best to get the worst over with first. Under the screaming headline, she read:

The blood of a teenage joyrider may hold the key to a twenty-year-old unsolved murder, Police Scotland believe.

When the youth's DNA was analysed after a fatal crash in Dundee last weekend, boffins realised that the killer of blonde hairdresser Tina McDonald was one of his close male relatives.

But hopes that the crime would quickly be solved were dashed when detectives discovered that the youth was adopted at birth.

Now Police Scotland's Historic Case Unit, led by Detective

Chief Inspector Karen Pirie, faces an uphill struggle to trace the birth parents of the driver, who cannot be named for legal reasons.

At a court hearing earlier this week, lawyers argued that the police should have access to the driver's original birth certificate. But his adoptive parents, who have kept the truth about his birth a secret from him, complained that this was a breach of his right to privacy and a family life.

Now both sides must await the decision of the sheriff.

Tina McDonald was 24 when she was brutally raped and murdered after a girls' night out to celebrate the birthday of her friend and boss Liz Dunleavy, owner of a salon in Glasgow's trendy Byres Road.

Her body was left in an alley behind the former Bluebeard's night club off George Square in the city centre, her brand-new sequined red dress torn and bloodstained.

Hundreds of witness statements were taken from clubbers and friends of the vivacious young stylist. But no arrest was ever made. Now, police are tantalisingly close to finally closing the case.

At the family home in Mount Florida, Tina's grieving father Eric said, 'I can't believe the police don't automatically have the right to this information. Surely justice for my wee lassie matters more than the rights of some joyrider who's already killed three of his pals?

'Tina's murder sentenced us to a life of hell. The least the courts can do is give us an answer to who did this.'

DCI Pirie was unavailable for comment last night, but a spokesman for Police Scotland said, 'We do not comment on ongoing inquiries.'

Karen gave a little snort. 'Except when it suits us,' she muttered. She skimmed the other accounts, learning nothing she didn't know, then googled the story to make sure there was nothing she'd missed. As she shrugged into her jacket, she took a quick look at Twitter and groaned as she saw #TinaMcDonald was trending locally. The Twitterati were building up a head of righteous indignation. The majority were for justice and Tina, and against the joyrider who'd wiped out three of his pals. But there was a vocal minority who championed his right to a private life even though he'd deprived others of any life at all. It was, Karen thought, enough to make you want to tear up the Human Rights Act.

If only for a moment.

She checked herself in the mirror. It was only the second time she'd worn this suit, a recent concession to the fact that she'd lost weight and everything else was hanging on her. A dark blue herringbone linen mix, it actually made her look presentable. And the shirt she'd treated herself to in the White Stuff sale was a pretty blue-and-white pattern that made her eyes more intense. Not that she was dressing up for the Macaroon. She was meeting Giorsal after work and she had a feeling there might not be time to slip home and change. She wanted to look her best; she didn't want anyone feeling sorry for her. Giorsal probably wouldn't be like that, but Karen wanted to slip back into their old friendship, not have it undermined with pity before it even got out of the starting blocks. She rubbed a smirr of moulding paste through her ungovernable hair, made sure her bag held life's necessities and set off to face the dissonance.

Assistant Chief Constable Simon Lees had been stoking his fury ever since he'd glanced at his iPad on waking. Now, an hour and a half later, he resembled a pressure cooker in the instant before the steam pushes the valve open and fills the kitchen with hissing steam. All it needed for him to blow was the arrival of that bloody woman.

This time, she'd crossed the line. She'd presided over an

almighty cock-up. One he'd specifically warned her against. Underneath his simmering rage, there was a twinge of delight that he was in the delicious position of being fully entitled to give her a full metal jacket bollocking.

He sipped his green tea and looked at his watch. One minute to go. She'd be late. She was always late. She made a point of claiming to have so much on her plate she'd lost track of time. He had time to rein in his anger and maintain the pretence of calm. He flicked open his iPad and clicked on the RPG combat game he'd become mildly addicted to. Enough time had surely passed for him to improve the strength of the main gate to his compound.

But before he could click on the icon, there was a knock on the door. As usual, Pirie didn't wait to be invited. She was in the door, across the room and in the chair while he was still desperately trying to shut down his game. He thought he'd managed it, but when he looked back at her, there was the faintest of smiles on her face.

'What the bloody hell is going on here?' No preamble, straight for the jugular. Lees took the tabloid from his top drawer and slammed it on the table in front of Karen, face up. 'I warned you about leaks. I told you specifically to get your house in order. And what do I wake up to? All hell breaking loose.'

A moment's silence while Karen cast an eye over the paper. 'I don't know where that came from, but it didn't come from my office.'

'Well, where the hell else could it have come from?'

Karen shrugged. 'Colin Semple's office. Sheriff Abercrombie's clerk. Alexandra Cosgrove's office. A court usher. The parents of Tina McDonald. You've got no grounds for assuming that it came from me or from DC Murray. We're the ones with most to lose, for one thing.'

'Really? You're not interested in the glory, DCI Pirie?

Leaking at this stage means you get the credit for not giving up on Tina McDonald, but if it all goes wrong, it's the system and not you to blame.'

She looked at him as if she wanted to punch him. He had her on the run now, he could sense it. Why had it taken him so long to figure out that her professional vanity was her Achilles' heel? He felt a smirk coming on but he forced his mouth to stay still. When she spoke, her voice was low and venomous. 'The only thing I care about is putting criminals behind bars. Tina McDonald's killer has been walking around for twenty years thinking he's got away with it. Now he knows we've got a line on him. And he also knows that we can't do a bloody thing about it till the sheriff gives us the green light. Do you really think he's still going to be around when we come knocking? Believe me, nobody is more pissed off about this than I am.'

She had a point, he had to admit. But still he thought she was the one who came out of this with most kudos. And that was what drove her, he was sure of it now. 'So you say,' he snapped, enunciating each word with precision. 'But I can't just take your word for it. We need to find out who is leaking this stuff to the press. It's not in the interests of that justice you're so very self-righteous about. So, I'm instituting a leak inquiry.'

She sighed. He was winning. She was on the run now. Time for the killer blow. 'I'll be briefing Detective Superintendent Gordon Robson shortly.' She couldn't hide the look of dismay. Her former boss. A man who was almost as fond of her as he was. Gordon Robson would make Pirie's life a misery, Lees would bet a year's salary on it. 'He'll get to the bottom of this.'

'If you say so.'

She never sirred him. No respect. Well, he'd enjoy watching Gordon Robson bringing her down. In spite of her protestations, he was convinced the leak began and ended in Karen Pirie's office. 'He'll need access to all your phone records and emails. Both you and DC Murray.'

Karen snorted. 'Well, that should induce a coma. I can't speak for Jason, but my life is an open book. I'd have thought there were better ways for DS Robson to spend his time, but be my guest.' She stood up. 'If that's all, I need to get back to work. I've got a murder to solve.'

And to his immense frustration, she walked out as if the bollocking had never happened.

22

K aren found Jason in their office, whey-faced and shaky, poring over the morning papers. 'You look like you had a good night last night,' Karen said, throwing her jacket over the back of her chair and slumping in front of the computer. 'I'm glad one of us did.'

'On the batter with my flatmates. It was Matt's birthday.' He managed a weak smile. 'I wasn't feeling brilliant to start with but this lot's made me feel shan as hell.'

'Tell me about it. I've just had what passes for the evils from the Macaroon. Kinda like being savaged by a seven-year-old that thinks it's big to say "bum". The downside is that he's bringing in Jilted John to run a leak inquiry.'

Jason looked baffled. 'Who's Jilted John when he's at home?'

'You know. Jilted John, had a hit with that novelty record during the punk thing.' Karen cleared her throat and sang tunelessly, 'Gordon is a moron, Gordon is a moron.'

Jason seemed none the wiser. 'I don't even know if my mum was born when punk was happening, never mind me. So who's Jilted John?'

'Detective Superintendent Gordon Robson,' she sighed. 'He hates me.'

'Why?'

'Because back in the mists of time I arrested my boss and he ended up going down for life. And he was Jilted John's best mate.'

'Ah,' Jason said, enlightened at last. 'You made a lot of enemies back then. I remember Phil telling me . . . ' His voice trailed off.

'Aye, and I've got better at it with practice,' Karen said, going for cheerful and almost hitting it. 'So it might be good if we can figure out where the leak sprung from before Jilted John tries to pin the tail on one of us donkeys.'

Jason's eyes widened. 'Would he do that?'

'In a heartbeat. He's going to be looking at our phone records and our email trails. Hope you've not been trying to buy yourself a Russian mail-order bride.'

He gave a weak smile. 'Not recently, boss.'

'Have a look through your contacts and see if you can come up with anybody who works for one of these rags that owes you one. And in the meantime, I think we should—'

The phone rang, cutting across Karen's words. She tutted and picked it up. 'DCI Pirie, Historic Cases Unit.'

'Colin Semple here, DCI Pirie. Bad news, I'm afraid.'

It felt like a punch to the gut. 'The sheriff said no?'

'Not yet. This is more personal bad news. Sheriff Abercrombie is demanding you appear before her without delay. She takes very seriously the "in camera" aspect of her court and she is more than a little unhappy at today's media coverage. She's considering a contempt of court finding against you.'

'But I never—'

'I said, "considering".'

Outrage and grievance swelled in Karen's heart. 'Whoever

spilled to the media, it wasn't me. So there can't be any evidence to charge me with contempt.'

'This is more about demonstrating the power of the court rather than sending you to jail to cool your heels for a day or two. Or so I believe. Sheriff Abercrombie just wants to flex her judicial muscle and show who's boss. Don't worry, DCI Pirie. You're going to get your knuckles rapped, that's all. The worst-case scenario is that she'll demand you apologise to the court.'

'That makes me feel so much better. So, what? I have to drop everything and come scurrying up to Chambers Street?'

'As soon as you like,' he said. 'The longer it takes you to get there, the more affronted she'll let herself feel. Chances are, she'll keep you waiting, but you need to be here or she'll make that an excuse to accuse you of contempt in itself.'

'Are you in court today?' Karen asked.

'I'm calling from the Advocates' Room. I've got an ex parte hearing on the list, but that shouldn't take too long. I can always ask for a short adjournment if the sheriff calls you before the bench while I'm still doing that. I've got my devil with me, I'll text you her number. Let her know when you get up here and she'll fetch me. Now get on your bike, Chief Inspector.'

Karen glared at the phone as she replaced it. 'Like I've got nothing better to do,' she grumbled, hoicking her jacket off the chair.

'What's up, boss?'

'Bollocking number two. Only I suspect the sheriff'll be a more scary prospect than the Macaroon. See if I get sent to the jail? You're in charge of the cake with the file.'

Semple had been right about one thing. The sheriff seemed intent on having Karen kick her heels for much of the day. She got herself signed into the Solicitors' Room café by

Semple's trainee, a demure twenty-something with the soft accent of the Western Isles who couldn't have looked less like a devil if she'd tried. But a cup of coffee and a slab of shortbread did nothing to improve Karen's temper. This was the kind of day that pushed her right back into the bite of her sweet tooth. She'd almost broken that habit in the wake of Phil's death. Not deliberately, but because everything tasted of ash and cardboard in her mouth. She hated to admit it, because defiance was her default position, but she felt healthier for it and now she was beginning to find food palatable again, she didn't want to fall back into bad ways. She'd have swapped being more healthy for having Phil back in a heartbeat, but since that was nothing more than a stupid fantasy, she might as well make the most of it. Karen stared longingly at a pyramid of Tunnock's Teacakes, exhaled heavily and took out her laptop. She dealt with an hour's worth of email and still there was no sign of the sheriff's summons. Nothing else for it but the case that was causing them so much grief.

Jason had painstakingly scanned in the key statements in the Tina McDonald case. She could have reread them, but she felt as if she knew them by heart now. They'd farmed out some of the reinterviews to local officers who seemed to have done a decent job. But still the only oddity remained the underground ticket among the possessions of a woman who suffered from claustrophobia.

And so Karen found herself drawn again to the puzzling deaths of Gabriel Abbott and his mother. It was none of her business, but she couldn't seem to shake it clear from her head. All the cases she worked involved people lacerated by grief. And sometimes they couldn't take the pain and killed themselves. But not twenty-two years later. There was something about Gabriel Abbott's life and death that had its hooks in her. As if focusing on him could put her own grief on the back burner, even for a short time. 'If it was my case, where would I start?' she muttered. Take nothing for granted. That was the first rule of cold case work. Examine everything in the case for its factual basis. Is this conclusion evidence-based, or merely an assumption?

Gabriel first.

But here she was stymied. She didn't have access to the case files or the interviews. All she knew was that the needle had swung from suicide to homicide then back again. Cops were only human – when a straightforward explanation presented itself and nothing contradicted it, that was generally the path they'd follow – and they were mostly right. She'd once worked with a fast-track graduate who loved to make the rest of the team feel like numpties. He was always on about Occam's razor, which as far as she was concerned was a fancy way of saying what all cops knew to be true. Maybe William of Occam had been a polis, but Karen somehow doubted it.

The thing was that sometimes the simple explanation wasn't the right one. It was a fix. A scam, a set-up, an illusion created by smoke and mirrors. She didn't know enough about Gabriel Abbott's death to decide where the truth lay. So she'd have to put that to one side for now. Maybe Giorsal would be able to join up some of the dots and colour in some of the background when they met for dinner later.

So, Caroline Abbott. And, of course, Ellie MacKinnon, Mary Spencer and her husband Richard. But it was Caroline who interested Karen, because murder didn't run in families. Except when it did. And in those cases, there were often unexpected connecting threads.

There. She'd said it. Only in her head, but she'd said it. And already she was googling Caroline Abbott, getting to know her more closely than she'd bothered with before. She'd already absorbed the bare facts – the drama degree, learning the business of commercial theatre, then her own production company surfing the wave of public taste with an impressive degree of success. But what about Caroline Abbott the woman?

Karen had read somewhere that 92 per cent of searchers never took the search past the first page. After that, she'd made a point of working her way down past the obvious to the more tangential results. And there, on the third page was buried an interview with Caroline Abbott, archived and made available by one of the classier women's magazines.

23

STAGE BY STAGE

Meet the woman who's beating the West End boys at their own game

By Fenella Drake

The chances are you won't know Caroline Abbott's name, even if you're a keen theatregoer. But you've probably thrilled to one of her shows. She's the producer behind half a dozen West End hits that have gone on from rave reviews to tour around the British Isles.

Among the shows she's brought to delighted audiences are *Call Me!*, *Thick and Thin*, *Amazing Strangers* and last year's smash hit *Starstricken*. And if that wasn't enough, she's the single mum of two boisterous boys, Will and Gabriel.

We met in her office in a narrow Georgian building in Soho. It's a welcoming room with squashy sofas as well as an imposing walnut desk and a fine view of Soho Square. Caroline, dressed in a silk Nicole Farhi ecru sweater and black jodhpurs, revealed that she loved the theatre from an early age. But she never wanted to be an actress. 'My parents loved going out to the theatre and they always took me to pantos and musicals. Right from the beginning, I was completely smitten. But I didn't want to be up there, singing and dancing. I've never craved the limelight. What fascinated me as much as the performances was how they made it happen. As soon as I was old enough, I joined the local amateur dramatic society. By the time I was twelve, I was the Assistant Stage Manager in charge of props and by fourteen I was the Stage Manager proper. I knew I'd found my vocation.'

But Caroline's parents understood how precarious a career in the theatre can be so they insisted she go to university. 'The idea was that I'd have something to fall back on. I told them I was going to study English but at the last minute I changed to English and Drama.' She laughed. 'As you can imagine, that caused a few rows. But I knew exactly what I wanted and I was determined to make it happen.'

How did she get her first break in her chosen career? 'Luck, serendipity, right place at the right time, call it what you will. I was waitressing in a greasy spoon a couple of streets away from here, right in the heart of theatreland. One of my regular customers was the front of house manager in one of the big Shaftesbury Avenue theatres and one day he came in looking really glum. I asked him what was the problem and he said his assistant had walked out on him without giving notice. I thought, "It's now or never," so I took a deep breath and said I was the person he needed. And bless him, he took a chance on me.'

But it's still a long way from a lowly assistant to a top impresario's chair. Caroline was determined to master her business and when her boss left for a job in Australia three years later, she persuaded the management to give her his job. 'I was ready, and they could see that.' Two years later and she'd persuaded another organisation to take a chance on her.

The Goddard Theatre in Epping was a struggling enterprise when Caroline took it over. But her vision for generating shows that people would love soon earned her a big local following, and glowing reviews brought audiences from much further afield.

'It was an exciting time,' she admitted. 'Not least because that's when I met my husband Tom. It was a bit of a whirlwind romance. He was a marine engineer, so he was often away for long trips, but when he came back it was like falling in love all over again.'

But the downside of those absences was that when their first son Will was born, Caroline had the life of a single parent more often than not. 'I learned rapidly that I needed a reliable support system in place, so I've always had a nanny. I used an agency that offers emergency backup for those unpredictable contingencies. And my best friend lives in the flat upstairs from me, so I've got a backup for the backup! It also meant that when Tom came home, we had time for each other as well as for being parents.'

Once she had established the reputation of the Goddard, Caroline decided to strike out on her own and set up a production company, Caroline Abbott Stupendous Theatre, or CAST as it's known. CAST's first show,

Call Me!, took the West End by storm and won a clutch of awards.

'It took me by surprise,' she admitted with a wry laugh. 'I knew it was a great piece of entertainment, but I wasn't confident the rest of the world would agree.' *Call Me!* turned out to be a great calling card for CAST, and Caroline has never looked back.

Soon after that early success, Caroline's second son Gabriel was born. 'It was a pretty hectic time,' she said. 'There never seemed to be enough hours in the day.' She had barely got her life back on an even keel when tragedy struck. Husband Tom went down with a virulent infection while on shore leave in Thailand. By the time the news reached Caroline, he was already dead.

'It seemed unreal. Because he was away so much, nothing changed on the surface. Except that this time he was never coming home. It was a slow dawning, and it was hard to explain to the boys. Because there wasn't any sudden severance, because things went along day-to-day as usual, it was hard for us all to grasp that Tom was gone for good.'

Of course, Karen thought. The days before Skype or email or FaceTime. Caroline would have had to rely on letters and postcards, the occasional phone call when Tom had been in port. Not like the contact she'd been able to maintain with Phil on the rare occasions when they were apart for a while. Tom's death would have felt like a strange, distant thing. How long must it have been before it sank in with Caroline that she was really on her own?

'And then one day, about six months after his death, I woke up with this absolutely sickening sense of loss.' Caroline looked like a lost little girl as she spoke, her professional mask slipping for a moment. 'It was as if my heart had caught up with my head. But I knew I had to keep my chin up because of the boys. And we've made a life for ourselves without Tom. He's the absence at the heart of every family event, but we've learned to celebrate what he gave us rather than mourn his loss.'

It's that positive attitude that colours everything Caroline Abbott has achieved. So which mountain will she climb next? Film or TV production? Creating a band like New Kids on the Block to storm the charts?

Caroline laughed. 'I like what I do. I want to carry on doing it, but setting myself new challenges along the way. The only other thing I want from life is to see my boys grow up happy and healthy.'

Karen closed the window. Caroline Abbott hadn't managed either of those ambitions. A stark reminder, if anyone needed it, to seize the day. As she clicked on another link, Semple's devil arrived at her side in a small flurry of excitement. 'Sheriff Abercrombie's ready for you now.'

Karen followed her back to the courtroom where they'd appeared at the beginning of the week. The sheriff was already seated, reading a sheaf of papers on the desk in front of her, pencil in hand, making the occasional note. She flicked a glance at Karen over the top of her reading glasses but carried on with what she was doing. Karen crossed to where Colin Semple was mirroring the sheriff – studying legal papers and scribbling in the margins – and sat down beside him. Five long minutes passed then, with a deep sigh, Sheriff Abercrombie laid her pencil down and frowned at Karen.

'The confidentiality of this court has been breached,' she said, her voice dark and solemn. 'I appreciate police officers have little understanding of the way we do things in the family courts, but I had thought I had made myself abundantly clear on the necessity of protecting the right to privacy of the individuals at the heart of this case.' She gave Karen an interrogative look. 'Was I in some way unclear?'

Karen shook her head. 'No, my lady. There was no room for misunderstanding in what you said.'

'So why was I confronted by these stories in the media this morning? Stories that not only breach the confidentiality surrounding these proceedings themselves but also put in serious jeopardy the anonymity of Ross Garvie himself.'

'I don't know. I can assure you—'

'I don't think you can assure me of anything,' the sheriff said sharply, her expression a mixture of disappointment and disdain.

'This didn't come from me or my team,' Karen said, standing her ground.

'I find that hard to believe. The family have no interest in communicating with the media. The officials of this court and the lawyers associated with this case know better than to violate the rules of the court. Only the police have anything to gain from leaking this information to the press. It makes a mockery of the court system and puts you and your colleagues in a good light. You are the only group of people who have access to this information with anything to gain from leaking it.'

There were many things that got under Karen's skin, but unfairness was high up the list. 'My lady, we have nothing to gain. What I want is for the court to give us access to Ross Garvie's original birth certificate. The last thing I'm going to countenance is—' She wanted to say, 'pissing off the court' but she caught herself. '—angering the court. I did not do this, and I'd stake my reputation on it not being one of my team.'

Sheriff Abercrombie glared at her with pursed lips. 'This court has the power to take action when it has been contemned. It is within our remit to fine you or send you to jail for contempt.'

Karen refused to allow herself to be intimidated. She didn't really believe the sheriff had a leg to stand on and it was a risk she was willing to take. 'There is no evidence that I have committed contempt. And no harm has been done. Ross Garvie has not been named.'

The sheriff gave a 'harrumph' of scorn. 'The names of the youths who died at his hands were published at the weekend before anyone knew he would be a key player in your historic case investigation. Anyone who wanted to find out Ross Garvie's identity would have to do nothing more demanding than walk into the local pub and listen.'

She had a point, Karen thought. Time to get on the front foot. 'You're probably right,' she said. 'But it is what it is. The court's anger is entirely reasonable. But I did not betray the confidentiality of this court. I'll commit to that under oath, if that's what you want. But I won't accept responsibility for this and I won't apologise to the court for something I didn't do.'

'You are walking very close to the edge, DCI Pirie. I see little evidence of respect for the court in your attitude. I will be watching you very carefully and if I see any indication that you have acted inappropriately, you will feel the full weight of this court's authority.' She picked up her pencil and began writing again.

Fuck this, Karen thought. 'My lady?'

The sheriff looked up, ice in her stare. 'Are you still here, DCI Pirie? Do you have no criminals to uncover?'

'I wondered if you might be able to give me any sense of when you might have a decision for us in the Ross Garvie case?' Karen thought she heard Semple groan softly next to her.

'Mr Semple will be informed in due course,' the sheriff said through clenched teeth. 'Now vacate my courtroom, all of you. We have important business to conduct here.'

Outside the courtroom, Semple wiped his shining brow. 'Do you always go around dicing with death, Chief Inspector?'

'Pompous besom,' Karen muttered. 'She was totally dancing in the dark.'

'If you say so. Let's hope nothing else happens to piss her off before she makes her decision. Otherwise your case will be dead in the water.'

24

Semple's words were still ringing in Karen's ears a couple of hours later. She trotted down the steps of the narrow close that led from Cockburn Street towards Waverley then turned into the Thai restaurant, smarting yet at her treatment at the hands of the sheriff. How could there be justice when the system treated people so unfairly?

Even though Karen was early, Giorsal was already seated, waving to her across the room. She stood up as Karen approached and the two women hugged, awkwardly air kissing. The world they'd grown up in had never gone in for that kind of intimacy but that world had changed and slowly they were adjusting.

Karen shrugged off her jacket and draped it over her chair, wondering how easy it would be to slip back into the easy camaraderie that had characterised their teenage relationship. A waiter materialised beside them. Giorsal raised her eyebrows in a question. 'After the day I've had, definitely,' Karen said. 'Bring on the Singha and keep them coming.'

Giorsal gave her a thumbs up. 'Same for me. We've come a long way from sneaking Carlsberg Specials at the rugby hop.' Karen grinned. The old complicity was still there.

Giorsal shot Karen a considering look. 'I'm guessing the case you asked my advice about is the one all over the papers this morning?'

Karen pulled a face. 'You'd be right.'

'Which would explain why you've not had the best of days, would be my next guess.'

'Also right. Some bastard leaked big time and I've been getting somebody else's kicking all day. First my boss then the sheriff. I can tell them till I'm blue in the face that the leak isn't down to the HCU, but I might as well save my breath. They've got no other obvious candidate to bollock, so I'm today's bollockee of choice.'

Giorsal's expression showed wry sympathy. 'Nice word, bollockee. But did you get a result? Is the sheriff going to give you access?'

For a fleeting moment, Karen wondered if she should trust Giorsal. After all, they were a long way from teenage confidences. But she immediately scolded herself. For one thing, Giorsal hadn't known nearly enough detail to be the leak. For another, she wouldn't have the job she had if there had ever been any question mark over her discretion. Sometimes, Karen hated that she'd become so suspicious of the world and its motives. 'She's still not decided. It's incredibly frustrating. I mean, Gus, how long does it take to make your mind up about something so clear?'

'I suppose she's got to look at precedents. A lot of human rights law is that, "on the one hand, this, on the other hand, that" kind of stuff. It's a balancing act between two contesting rights.'

'All the same ... We were wondering if she's hanging fire to see whether this lad dies. Because if he does, the ball's on the slates as far as his human rights are concerned, and we get the access we need.'

Giorsal winced. 'You don't want to find yourself wishing somebody would die just so you can solve a twenty-year-old case.'

'No. And besides, if that's what's actually going on, I don't think she's going to get off the hook any time soon. I've been speaking to the hospital every day and there's basically no significant change in his condition. There's no reason to suppose he's going to die.'

'You asked, didn't you?'

Karen remembered that cheeky smile. Back in their schooldays, it had usually accompanied Giorsal saying something everybody was thinking but nobody dared say out loud. Not much had changed, it seemed. 'I did. The consultant sounded black affronted. As if nobody was allowed to check out on his watch.'

At that point the waiter arrived with their beers and hovered by their table offering suggestions from the menu. Karen opted for her usual Tom Yum soup followed by Pad Kraprao Haggis Kai Hor. The first time Phil had ordered a dish that incorporated haggis with vegetables, spices and holy basil, all wrapped in an omelette, Karen had accused him of confusion rather than fusion. And then she'd tasted it. Now, whenever she had an excuse to come here, she never deviated from it. And not for sentimental reasons. When it came to food, Karen had no place for sentiment.

The waiter departed and Karen drained half her beer in one long swallow. 'Ah, that's better. Enough of my problems. How are things with you? How are you settling in, back in Fife?'

Giorsal was a good raconteur and her tales of resettling in her old stamping grounds were entertainment enough to get them through their starters and second beers then on to their main courses. She got to the end of an anecdote about an encounter with an old classmate, then turned serious. 'How are you coping? I imagine work is a double-edged sword? It keeps your mind occupied, but at the same time it's a constant reminder of Phil and what you've lost.'

Nail on the proverbial. 'It saves me from myself. And I talk to him in my head. I have whole conversations about what I should do next on a case. His mind worked differently from mine, and I try to figure out what he'd have suggested when I'm struggling with the best way forward. It's not that I'm trying to kid myself he's still around somewhere.' She put down her fork and shook her head. 'It's really not that.'

'You're too pragmatic for that.'

'I am. But what I don't want to let go of, what I absolutely don't want to forget is what I learned from Phil, what I gained from having him in my life. I was better when I was with him. I was a better person, I was a better polis. So I need to hold on to how he was and what being with him was like.' Her face twisted in pain. 'But sometimes, Gus, getting through the days is the hardest thing I've ever done.' She screwed her eyes shut for a moment. 'Mostly, I feel like I'll never be happy again.'

'I'm sorry.' Giorsal leaned across the table and covered Karen's hand with hers. 'I'm not going to say anything stupid like, "you'll find love again," because, even if you did, even if you met somebody tomorrow, it still wouldn't change the way you feel about losing Phil like that. I have to say, though, I know that feeling of permanent misery. Towards the end of my marriage, I thought I'd never be happy again unless I got rid of Victor for good.'

Glad to change the subject, Karen grinned. 'But you did, and since it's brought you back home, I'm going to be totally selfish and say I think that's a good thing. How is it, being single again?'

Giorsal chuckled. 'A hell of a lot different from how it was before. I didn't have two kids like an anchor round my ankle back then. It changes your perspective. Every guy you meet, you're sizing him up through your daughters' eyes. Believe me, there's nobody more judgemental than your kids. And where do you meet available guys anyway?'

'Don't ask me. I only ever meet cops and lawyers and villains, and you'd be hard pressed to decide the worst bargain out of that lot. What about online dating?'

Giorsal winced and pretended to shed a tear. 'Tried that. I swear to God, they should be turning their talent for fiction to writing novels. I've decided I'm going to sit back and wait for something completely improbable to happen like out of a Tom Hanks film.'

'That's what I felt about me and Phil getting together.'

'Improbable or Tom Hanks?'

'Both.'

'So, I'm happy to have my bed to myself. I haven't slept so well for years.'

Karen worked her way through a mouthful of haggis and vegetables. 'I wish I could say the same. I'm really struggling with sleep. Which reminds me. You might know the answer to this.'

Giorsal looked over the rim of her glass at Karen. 'What am I? Google Buddy? I thought you loved me for myself, not my boundless store of knowledge.'

Karen laughed. 'Get over yourself, Gus. I'm bloody delighted you're back within reach. But that doesn't mean I'm not going to exploit the hell out of you. That's what friends are for, isn't it? Listen, this is really interesting.' She gave a succinct resumé of her encounters with the Syrian men. 'These are serious professional guys and it's clearly doing their heads in to be stuck doing nothing all day.'

'The rules are clear.' Giorsal's voice was filled with regret. 'They're not allowed to work while their claims are being adjudicated and processed.'

'I realise that. But does it also cover volunteering?'

'It's a grey area. They can be volunteers, but they can't do voluntary work.'

Karen froze, a forkful of food halfway to her open mouth. She lowered her fork, baffled. 'You're going to have to explain that bit of doublethink to me, Gus. I'm just a simple polis.'

'OK. A volunteer is somebody who gives their time to a charity. What they do wouldn't qualify as a job eligible for minimum wage. Voluntary workers do something that would be entitled to minimum wage if they hadn't waived their right to it as a donation to the charity. As distinctions go, it's about as easy to unpick as one of those mad Escher drawings. But that's how it's defined. Why, what were you thinking?'

'As far as I can make out, the main hardship these guys and their families are facing is that they've got nowhere to go where they can sit around and have a cup of tea and a blether. When you've got no work to go to, that turns into a big deal. So what I was thinking is, there's all these empty boarded-up premises down that end of town – shops, cafés, pubs – that nobody's interested in doing anything with. Could one of them not be turned into a meeting place for these guys? A café, maybe. Like that great wee social enterprise place at the bottom of Leith Walk, Punjabi Junction. I'm always sending Jason down there for one of their curry lunches. It doesn't have to be anything special, just somewhere that's theirs. They could run it themselves as a social enterprise. One of the guys I've been talking to actually managed a café back in Homs. What do you think?'

Giorsal looked startled. She hadn't been expecting that, Karen thought drily. 'That sounds like an amazing idea, Karen.'

'So how would you go about it?'

She considered, her eyes on a corner of the ceiling as she worked it out. 'First thing, you'd need to get a charity on board to sponsor the whole thing. That shouldn't be hard, there are a lot of small local charities that might be willing to take it on. The premises might be a bit harder ... If I was trying to get this off the ground on my patch, I'd find a sympathetic councillor or, even better, an MSP to make that end of it happen. But you're not seriously thinking about taking this on?'

'No, but I wanted to check out the idea. I'll get the guys on it themselves. It'll give them something to aim for. I'll grease the wheels if need be, but they strike me as having enough gumption to make it happen. I think they need someone to point them in the right direction, wind them up and let them go.'

'Wow,' Giorsal said. 'I'm impressed.'

'Aye, well, we're not only the enforcers of the evil capitalist system,' Karen said tartly.

'You, maybe. I'm not so sure about all of your colleagues.' There was a heaviness to Giorsal's words that made Karen think it wasn't just a glib generalisation.

She swallowed another mouthful of food and washed it down with a swig of her third beer. 'Somebody been pissing on your chips?'

Giorsal shrugged. 'That DI you met in my office the other day.'

'Alan Noble? Milk Tray Man?'

She snorted in amused contempt. 'I always thought there was something creepy about a guy who would break into a woman's bedroom to leave a box of chocolates.'

'You think?' Karen was teasing now. 'I wouldn't say no. Mind, I'd rather have something a bit more classy than Milk Tray. What about Noble? What's he done to upset you, Gus?'

'It's that whole business of Gabriel Abbott's death. I think Noble's being lazy. It's like he's desperate to write it off as a suicide without digging any further. You remember I told him to speak to Ian Lesley, Gabriel's social worker? Well, Ian was in the office today so I thought I'd follow up myself. See what he'd said to Noble. And it turns out Noble hasn't bothered to speak to him at all.'

It sounded to Karen as if Giorsal wasn't wrong to feel annoyed by Noble's failure to follow through. 'It does sound like he's not covering all the bases. But if there's no reason to suspect foul play, he's maybe been told to move on by his boss.'

'Whoever made the decision, it's a rush to judgement. If Noble's not interviewed Ian, what else has he not followed up? I've got no confidence that he's looked into the rest of the circumstances surrounding Gabriel's death. What if there were other witnesses he hasn't bothered to check out?'

Given that she'd already been intrigued by the case, Karen couldn't help agreeing with her friend. 'Maybe you should talk to Noble again, give him a wee push to talk to this Ian Lesley at least?'

'You saw what he's like, Karen. He's not going to take me seriously. He'll smarm his way out of it and move on. Can you not act like you're taking an interest? Lean on him a bit?'

Karen shook her head. 'It's not my case. It's not even my division. I've got no official standing here. Sticking my nose in somebody else's investigation without anything more solid than a hunch would cause a major stooshie. I'd get seven kinds of shit kicked out of me and it would only make Noble dig his heels in further.'

'So there's nothing I can do? I just have to swallow it?'

Karen dispatched the last couple of mouthfuls of her dinner, her mind running through the possibilities. 'He's got a brother, right?'

'Will. He's a few years older than him. He lives in London. I don't think they're close, though. He spoke to Ian on Monday about coming up to make the funeral arrangements. Ian told him to hold fire until there was a clearer picture of what had happened and when the body would be released.'

'That's the way I'd tackle it. Give the brother a ring and ask if he's happy with the way the police are handling things. When he asks why you're asking, mention that you're not entirely sure they've explored all the possibilities. Then, hopefully, you can sit back and watch him set the cat among the pigeons.'

'What if he goes to the media?'

Karen wiped her mouth with her napkin. 'Then you get a proper investigation plus Noble gets a thorough bollocking. Result all round.'

Giorsal's face cleared. 'Thanks, Karen. I'll give it some thought. I don't want to create bad feeling with your colleagues. We rely on good relations with them in so much of the work we do. If Noble thinks he can make a convincing case for suicide, there's probably nothing more to be found. But I'd be unhappy if Gabriel Abbott is just written off as another nutter who couldn't cope with life. I want the right answer, not the easy one.'

'Don't we all,' Karen said absently, her mind already somewhere else. Somewhere another right answer might be hiding.

25

The two women walked down the back steps into Waverley station, laughing at one of Karen's stories of criminal absurdity. Giorsal's train was due to leave shortly, and they hugged farewell at the barrier. Karen watched her newly rediscovered friend hustle down the platform to the front. Still the same tight little steps, her body angled forward. At the door, she turned and waved, then she was gone. Karen half-turned to go but stopped, her eye caught by the departure board. The Caledonian Sleeper was due to leave for London in less than half an hour.

If she truly wanted fresh answers to the questions raised by the 1994 crash, she wasn't going to find them in Edinburgh. The people she needed to talk to weren't here. The one lead she had, apart from Will Abbott – and she didn't want to approach him because that would surely lead to endless aggravation from the Macaroon and Alan Noble, and besides, there were few things crueller than holding out false hope to victims' families – was the names of friends of Caroline and Ellie who had been interviewed in the newspaper articles she'd managed to track down. Karen had recognised one in particular. And she was pretty sure where to find him on a Saturday morning.

On an impulse, Karen made for the ticket office. Yes, there were still a few berths available. Did she want first or second class?

Ten minutes later and she was aboard, the sole occupant of a narrow cabin with a berth, a sink, a mirror and a bottle of mineral water. Hers for the next eight hours or so. She hung up her jacket and set off to find the lounge car. There was a small crowd of people there already, looking like they might be planning to make a night of it. Karen wasn't in the mood, but she was happy to see Caorunn gin on the menu. With a mental nod to Jimmy Hutton, she bought two miniatures and two cans of tonic, then squeezed her way back to her compartment.

She mixed herself a drink and perched cross-legged on the surprisingly comfortable bed. For the first time since the madcap idea had occurred to her, she asked herself what the hell she was playing at. What had possessed her to jump on a night train and run away from the hassle that had been dogging her all week? She didn't do things like this. She was steady and reasonable, not a creature of ridiculous spur-of-the-moment impulses. Especially when the impulse had nothing to do with her proper concerns. If DI Alan Noble wasn't doing his job properly, that was for his immediate boss – or, if worst came to worst, Professional Standards – to deal with.

But then, what she was interested in wasn't so much Gabriel Abbott's death as his mother's. Because somewhere in the past twenty-four hours, the tumblers inside her brain had rearranged themselves into a different configuration. She took herself through it again, step by step. There were two ways of making sense of what Sunny had told her. One was that the simple incendiary bomb in the plane had indeed been made by someone from the Irish Republican movement. Somebody outside the mainstream desperate to make a point, to get themselves taken seriously. Perhaps a young bomb-maker with ambitions, leaving a calling card.

It was a possible interpretation, but it didn't feel likely to Karen. So big a splash would have attracted a lot of attention among the paramilitaries if it had truly been a beginner, an outsider determined to make his mark. It was bound to have leaked to the British intelligence community. And from there, into some corner of the media. *Private Eye* if not the mainstream. And certainly from there on to one of the conspiracy sites online. But there had been nothing, Not a trace.

There was another explanation, and while she still had nothing concrete to support it, Karen's gut instinct was drawn to it. If it wasn't the IRA targeting Richard Spencer, then it was somebody else aiming at somebody on that plane for some other reason.

On balance, if not terrorists then the intended victim probably wasn't Richard Spencer. After the crash, his life would have been dissected, both by the security services and by the hunting dogs of the media. If there had been anything approaching a skeleton in his cupboard, it would have been dragged into the daylight in a cacophony of cascading bones.

His wife might have been their goal but it was hard to imagine Mary Spencer provoking that sort of fascination or fury. Everything written about her at the time attested to a life of bland conformity. She might have had a secret life, but the same argument applied to her as to her husband. The spotlight had been turned on them after the crash. If she'd been up to her neck in underhand financial dealings or having a clandestine love affair or covering up dark deeds in her past, it was hard to imagine them escaping such penetrating scrutiny.

Which left Ellie MacKinnon and Caroline Abbott. Best friends who lived in neighbouring flats in the same house. There was no way of telling which of them might have been the target of the person who blew up the Cessna Skylane. Except that now, twenty-two years on, Caroline Abbott's son had also died in mysterious circumstances after shadowy references to some sort of conspiracy. It was easy to dismiss Gabriel Abbott's veiled allegations as the product of his mental illness. But what if they weren't?

The train jerked into motion, making the gin and tonic slosh in the plastic tumbler and bringing Karen back into the moment. Here she was in that most romantic of places, a sleeping compartment on a night train. She and Phil had talked about making this journey together, but they never had. Now instead of romance, she was stuck with solitude, chasing shadows cast by someone else's investigation. On the run from her own life. Was this how it was going to be from now on?

She knocked back the rest of her drink and mixed another. She hated it when she let self-pity slip under her guard. 'You'd be disgusted with me,' she said softly. 'You believed in me. You'd remind me that everybody knows Alan Noble is a lazy fucker. That what I have is not women's intuition but a finely honed copper's instinct for when things aren't right.' She could hear his voice in her head, pushing her forward. He'd always reminded her that the way to find out the truth was to run towards the gunfire.

And that's what she was doing. She wasn't running away from Ross Garvie and Tina McDonald. She was running towards four unsolved murders that demanded attention. And if nobody else was giving them that, then she bloody well ought to. She was, she reminded herself, a detective chief inspector in the Historic Cases Unit.

Karen straightened her shoulders and raised her glass in

a toast to her absent lover. 'You're right,' she said. 'I can do this. Nobody else wants to, but I can.'

Euston in the early morning reminded her of a cat waking up; stretching and licking its paws, yawning and arching its tongue. Karen had slept better than she'd expected but she felt grubby. She paid for a shower, which solved that problem and also eased the stiffness in her limbs that the narrow bunk had dealt her. She climbed the stairs to the mezzanine and bought a coffee and a cardboard carton with two poached eggs, smoked salmon and avocado from Leon. While she worked her way through her breakfast, she tapped away at her laptop.

She'd woken with the Stones' 'Jumpin' Jack Flash' earworming her. The name she'd recognised from the interviews had been radio presenter Jack Ash. Back then, he'd been a Radio One DJ known as Jumpin' Jack Ash. A few years later, he'd graduated to Radio Two, where he'd lost the nickname and reverted to simple Jack Ash. Now, according to Google, he'd moved to Six Music, where he hosted a Saturday morning show that dissected a classic album every week.

This week, it was Fairport Convention's *Liege & Lief*. Reading the programme preview, Karen could put her hand on her heart and swear she'd never listened to a single track, nor did she want to start now. The only good thing about it was that she knew exactly where Jack Ash was going to be between nine and eleven that morning.

The sun was shining and she had time to kill, so she decided to walk. Even in the fumid London air it was still good to be on the move. She headed along Euston Road then cut up into Regent's Park. As she strode round the lake, she refused to listen to the voice in her head telling her she'd taken leave of her senses and instead tried to formulate an approach that might make Jack Ash open up to her.

At twenty to eleven, Karen emerged from the revolving door into the airy atrium of New Broadcasting House. Ahead of her, beyond the security barriers, she could see several floors of desks and meeting areas, splashes of bright colours apparently scattered at random throughout. It shouted at her, like children's artwork eager to impress. Out of the corner of her eye, down the hallway, she caught sight of a Dalek. And why not, she thought. If you've got it, flaunt it.

Time for the charm offensive. She walked confidently across to the long curve of the reception desk and produced her ID. 'Hi,' she said, smiling to help inject warmth into her voice. 'I wonder if you can help me? I'm here to see Jack Ash. After his show, obviously. Can you get somebody to take me up?'

The sleepy-eyed young man behind the desk gave her a cool look. 'What programme is that?'

The woman next to him glanced across and tutted. '*Both Sides Then*,' she said, rolling her eyes. 'Six Music.' She shared a conspiratorial look with Karen. 'Too young.'

The young man, whose badge said Aron, pursed his lips and tapped his keyboard. 'Hold on,' he said, picking up a phone and keying in a number. He looked everywhere except at Karen, then said, 'I got a detective here says she's here to see Jack Ash.' Pause. 'Yeah. What I said. A detective . . . Yeah, OK.' He replaced the phone. 'Somebody will be down.' He pushed a pad of visitor pass forms at her. 'You need to fill one of these in.'

Karen did as she was told, waited for him to put her pass in a plastic case and clipped it to her jacket. He waved her towards a trio of curved benches covered in muted shades of plum and green. Seven minutes later a skinny lad with a hipster beard and a topknot headed in her direction, his walk hobbled by the crotch on his jeans that reached half-way down his thighs. 'Hi, I'm Julian.' Of course you are, she thought. 'Are you the detective?' He looked dubious.

Karen smiled again. 'That's right.' She stood up and produced her ID again. 'Detective Chief Inspector Karen Pirie.'

'Police Scotland?' More dubious.

'That's right.'

'And you want to see Jack?'

'I do.'

'Is he expecting you?'

Karen spread her hands. 'I was in London anyway and I need to speak to him. He's not in any trouble, don't worry.' She gave a merry little chuckle, as if the idea of Jack Ash being in trouble was completely absurd. 'I've just got a few questions about a cold case I'm working. I'm sure he'll be happy to help.' As she spoke, she took a couple of steps towards the security gates. Keep them wrong-footed, that was the way to do it.

Julian clearly didn't have a career as a gatekeeper ahead of him. He conceded the pass right away and scuttled round her to lead the way inside the citadel of British broadcasting. They stepped into a glass lift. Karen was too fascinated by this glimpse into the programming hive to notice what floor they arrived at, and meekly followed Julian down a corridor, past an arrangement of sofas and into a small side room with a conference table and half a dozen chairs. 'If you wouldn't mind waiting here? Jack's off air in—' He glanced at a clock on the wall. 'Three minutes. He'll have a quick wash-up with the producer then I'll bring him through. Can I get you a coffee? A water?'

Karen shook her head. 'I'm fine.' She took a seat, pleasantly surprised at how easy it had been to breach Jack Ash's world. She'd expected more resistance, more sweet-talking or heavy leaning. But here she was, even if she didn't quite know what she was doing.

She didn't have long to wait. Less than ten minutes passed before the door burst open and a man she barely recognised from her online searches took a step across the threshold. His face was scarlet, his chest heaving. 'What the fuck?' Jack Ash shouted, his eyes bulging. 'I've told you people already. I've got nothing to hide. I never touched any of those silly little teenage groupies. How many times? Just because I'm gay, it doesn't mean I'm a fucking paedophile. Not every Radio One DJ was shagging their fans, you know.'

Karen jumped to her feet, hands up in a placatory gesture. 'Whoa, wait a minute—'

'Don't fucking patronise me. I'm not a child.' Ash took a step towards her, hands balling into fists. 'You're going to hear from my lawyer. You people. You destroy decent people's reputations, you wreck people's lives. This is fucking harassment.'

'No, it's not.' Karen raised her voice now. Not shouting, but brooking no easy dismissal. 'I'm not here to talk about sex crimes. I'm a cold case detective from Scotland. I've got nothing to do with historic child abuse investigations. Frankly, I don't give a flying fuck who you sleep with.' Taking the war to their territory on their terms was sometimes the only way to go.

For a moment, shock stopped him in his tracks. Then he took a step sideways, grabbing a chair and collapsing into it. 'Really?' His voice had subsided to a whisper.

'Really,' she said, matching his tone but not sitting down again. She held out her ID in his eyeline. 'I'm Detective Chief Inspector Karen Pirie. I run the Historic Cases Unit in Scotland. Right now, I'm only interested in murder. And I'm only interested in you because I need to know about two of your friends who were murdered twenty-two years ago.'

26

Jack Ash sprawled in the leather armchair and sipped his glass of champagne. As soon as he'd realised bluster wasn't going to get rid of her, he'd hustled them out of the building, away from prying ears and into the splendid hotel across the street from Broadcasting House. 'That cunt Savile,' he said, shaking his head. 'Everybody knew what he was like, the evil bastard. Girls, boys, he didn't give a shit. They were just warm bodies to be fucked and fucked over. And now we're all paying for it.' He took a longer swallow and patted his stomach as a tiny burp escaped from his lips. 'Now everybody looks at us askance. Every time I do an outside gig – a dinner, or spinning the discs at a wedding – I can see them giving me the evil eye, wondering whether I was at it too. They shepherd the kids away from me, just in case, you know?' His mouth set in a bitter line.

Karen's sympathy was tempered slightly by the fact that they were sitting in the marble-walled lounge of a five-star hotel where the fawning waiter clearly recognised Jack Ash as a regular. She reckoned the odd dirty look was a small price to pay for a lifestyle where a casual drink would set you back the cost of dinner for two at Pizza Express.

Now his rage had subsided, his resemblance to the publicity photos she'd seen online was much stronger. True, his jaw had lost the taut chiselled look he had in the eighties, and there were pouches under his eyes that marred his former high-cheekboned perfection, but Karen reckoned he'd worn pretty well. He still had a good head of hair and whoever dyed it for him did a good job of making it look natural. The only giveaway was the harsh colour of his sideburns, which she suspected he probably touched up himself every morning. He had retained the same trademark hairstyle – the casual jagged fringe that looked as if a small rodent had taken a series of bites out of it. His blue eyes still twinkled when he smiled, even though the wrinkles didn't disappear with the smile itself these days. He'd put on a few pounds round his middle, his belly straining the buttons of his shirt. Time he dumped the fitted look for a more generous cut, Karen thought. Like she had room to talk, she reminded herself.

'Aye,' she said. 'It's good that the victims have finally been listened to, but a lot of innocent people have been caught in the backwash too.' She wasn't sure how much she believed that, but what mattered now was keeping him on side.

The waiter returned with a plate of tiny pastries and placed them delicately on the table between them. Ash attacked them immediately, popping them into his mouth in a greedy flow. 'I get so hungry, doing the show. It's all that adrenaline,' he said between swallows.

'It must take a lot of energy. I don't know how you keep the chatter flowing when you're on the air. I wouldn't know what to say.'

He wrinkled his nose in a smile she reckoned must once have been cute. 'You start out with a bit of raw talent and you hone it over the years.' He emptied his glass and looked around for the waiter. 'I don't want to boast, but I'm one of the best. I've had a long successful career and I'm still at the top of my game. So, you want to talk about Caroline and Ellie?' Without waiting for a response, he continued. 'I thought that was dead and buried. It wasn't even about them. The IRA or some other bunch of Fenian bastards out to get that champagne socialist Richard Spencer, that's what everybody said at the time.' He caught the waiter's eye and signalled for another glass of champagne.

'Have you heard about Gabriel Abbott?' Time to stop pussy-footing around.

Ash frowned. 'Gabriel? I haven't heard from him in years. I stay in touch with Will. His brother, yeah?' Karen nodded to show she knew who he was talking about. 'Not close touch, you understand. Just Christmas cards. And sometimes we bump into each other around town. Parties, gigs, private views, that kind of crap. I have to show my face, make sure nobody forgets Jumpin' Jack Ash is still out there, pumping and jumping.'

'So, no contact with Gabriel?'

He shrugged, spreading his hands. A man with nothing to hide. Apparently. 'Last time I saw him, I think, was one of Will's birthday bashes. Must have been eight, nine years ago?'

'So you didn't see his name in the news this week?'

Ash frowned, irritation showing again. 'What is this? Twenty questions? Look, I said. No contact with Gabriel for years.'

'Right. Only, I thought you might have heard. Gabriel died last week.'

Surprise, curiosity, but nothing remotely like grief flashed across his face. 'That's young. What was it? Cancer? Not a heart attack, surely?'

Most people, in the thick of a conversation with a murder

detective, would make a very different assumption, Karen thought. Unless you didn't have enough room in your self-absorbed brain to bother joining up the dots when the picture wasn't going to be you. 'It wasn't natural causes.'

That shocked him. His mouth fell open, giving her the unappealing vista of pastry remnants scattered across tongue and teeth. His head jerked forward like a bird about to peck at a rival. But he recovered himself quickly and brushed a stray crumb from his shirt front. 'Killed himself, I suppose,' he said with a sigh. 'Can't say I'm surprised.'

'Why do you say that?'

Ash pulled the sides of his mouth down in a rueful expression. 'He had a shit time of it. He was packed off to boarding school at six and after Caro died, he was more or less dumped there. Will was too busy investing his inheritance in himself, exploiting his brilliant ideas, setting up his gaming empire, to be bothered much with his baby brother. The grandparents washed their hands of the boys. They weren't about to give up their retirement villa on Corsica to raise the next generation. So poor old Gabe used to spend most of the holidays at school. He was more or less fostered by a succession of house masters and their wives. And then when he was let loose on his own at university, the wheels came off. And he never really got them back on again. He's been in and out of mental institutions for years.' He smiled weakly and spread his hands wide. 'Or so Will says. As I said, I've not seen much of him over the years.' Then something clearly dawned on him. Karen couldn't remember the last time she'd seen someone with such transparent emotional responses. It was like dealing with a small child who hadn't yet mastered the art of keeping things to himself. 'So why are you here, talking to me? There must be other people who knew a hell of a lot more about Gabriel's state of mind.'

'I never said it was suicide, Mr Ash.'

Now he reared back in his chair as if trying to escape from her. 'What do you mean? Not suicide? Are you saying somebody killed Gabriel?'

'We don't know for sure. The circumstances are unclear.'

He reached for the fresh glass that had appeared as if by magic and gulped at it. 'It must have been one of the other nutters,' he said. 'I mean, in and out of those places, Gabriel must have come across all sorts. They wouldn't all have been gentle souls like him. He must have run into one of them, said the wrong thing and bang, there you go.'

'Bang?'

He shrugged, his face twisted into an embarrassed wince. 'A figure of speech, for God's sake. The other guy, he'll have lost control, gone off on one. What did you say had happened? How did he die?'

'I didn't say. But it was a gunshot to the head. Bang, as you say.'

Ash looked at her, incredulous. 'Look, I just said "bang", the way you do. Meaning, all of a sudden. You're not suggesting I knew anything about this?'

Karen gave a small, reassuring chuckle. 'Good heavens, Mr Ash. Of course not.' *But I wanted to see you squirm, you self-satisfied prick.*

'I'm sorry, I'm a bit confused. You said back at the studio that you were something to do with historic cases. And obviously, that means Caro and Ellie. But then you start on about Gabriel dying last week.' He forced a laugh. 'I know time goes faster as you get older. But even I don't think last week was history.'

'You're quite right. I asked about Gabriel only because I thought, if you'd heard about it, you might have been thinking about your old friends.'

'Well, obviously, if I'd heard about some nutter blowing Gabriel's head off, that would have brought poor old Caro and Ellie to mind. But I didn't hear about it, so no, I wasn't expecting some detective to turn up out of the blue and go all round the houses about my poor dead friends.' Peevish now, he turned his attention back to the pastries, prodding the few that remained as if that would somehow make them more attractive. Greed overcame taste and he grabbed one at random and stuffed it into his mouth whole.

'I hoped you could tell me about Caro and Ellie,' Karen said evenly. 'It's a truism of investigation that the best place to start is to understand the victims' lives. So much time has passed now, it's hard for me to get a handle on them. Their personalities, their relationships, their day-to-day life.'

He frowned. 'But I don't understand why. Their murder was solved when it happened. They were collateral damage in somebody else's dirty fight. Why are you investigating it now?'

'The case was never solved. Nobody was ever brought to trial or even arrested. We assumed at the time that the explosive device that destroyed the plane had been put in place by a Republican splinter group, but none of them ever claimed credit for it. Technically, it's still an open case. And it's my job to examine every possible angle. Now, I know it might sound daft to you, but one of the things I have to consider is whether Caro and Ellie – either or both of them – might have been the intended targets rather than collateral damage.'

There was a silence while her words sank in. Then Ash shook his head. 'That's mad. People like them don't get blown up. Not deliberately, anyway.'

'But I need to be able to rule that out. Tell me about them, Jack.' Move into the more intimate form of address, make him feel loved. 'How did you come to know them?'

'I met Ellie first. She was the BA – broadcasting assistant – on my Radio One show for a while in the late seventies. We hit it off right away. She was a cut above most BAs. She figured out what we needed and sorted it out before I even asked her. She never made a fuss or moaned about having to go the extra mile, she just got on with things. We liked the same music, so I sometimes brought her along to gigs with me. Back then, people like me had to hide the truth about ourselves, and Ellie was the perfect beard.'

'Did she know she was a beard? Or did she think there was more going on between you?'

Ash gave her a scathing look. 'Of course she knew I wasn't interested in her that way. But she liked being seen with me. It gave her kudos. People noticed her. She had all the benefits of being my girlfriend without actually having to do anything except have fun.'

'And she didn't want a proper boyfriend?'

He raised one eyebrow in a practised gesture. 'The main thing Ellie wanted was to be a star. She always said her career came first. She didn't want to waste her time on romance when she could be networking. She'd been working for my show for less than a year when she got her first TV job.'

'That was on *All Aboard!*?'

He shook his head. '*All Aboard!* came later. She started out on *TeaThyme*. It was a cookery show for kids. Ellie wasn't one of the main presenters, she was more of a kitchen porter. But she had on-screen charisma. The camera loved her. And she buttered up everybody whose path she ever crossed in kids' TV, so when they were looking for someone to present *All Aboard!*, she was front and centre in everybody's eyes.'

'You must have been pleased for her.'

His smile was as false as any she'd ever seen. 'It's always lovely when your friends get what they want. Of course, the downside was that she didn't have as much time to come out and play.' He sighed. 'And then she met Caro and she started playing happy families. The woman who had never shown any interest in kids suddenly started babysitting

Will in the evenings when Caro was working instead of having fun.'

Karen's antennae twitched. 'What? She moved in with Caro and Will?'

Ash tittered. 'Oh no, she didn't move in. What happened was they bought a house together and split it into two flats. Caro and Will – and Tom when he was home – lived on the two lower floors and Ellie had the top floor and the attic. It suited everybody, apparently. Except Ellie's friends. We saw much less of her after the move. Apart from Sundays, when Caro used to throw long lavish lunch parties for the theatre crowd. Actors, singers, scriptwriters. But it wasn't the same. I missed that old intimacy with Ellie. For a long time I'd been able to count on her in a way I couldn't any more.'

'But you did get to know Caro too?'

'Oh yes, I loved Caro. She was much more showbizzy than Ellie. And she was a fabulous hostess. Always wonderful food and endless drink and the most entertaining company. Those were wonderful Sundays. I met some lovely men ...' His voice trailed off, the distant look of reminiscence in his gaze.

There was a key player missing in all of this. A key player who might have had a motive for removing Caroline Abbott from his world. 'What did Tom Abbott make of it all?' Karen asked.

That quick flick of the single eyebrow again. 'Tom was hardly ever around. He was a marine engineer and he spent months on end at sea. When he was home, the parties stopped and nobody saw much of Caro.' He smiled. 'But at least I used to get Ellie back for a couple of weeks before Tom took off again. But latterly, he was hardly ever around. He can't have seen Gabriel more than a couple of times before he died.'

'He died?' Karen wasn't about to reveal that this wasn't

news to her. She wanted to draw from him whatever he knew that hadn't been in the clippings.

'Yes. It was out in Thailand, or the Philippines or somewhere like that. It must have been round about 1990.'

'Are you sure about that?'

'I think so. You can check easily enough – I remember Ellie phoning me to tell me, and I was watching Nelson Mandela being released from prison on TV at the time.'

Karen already knew he was right about the year but she feigned uncertainty. 'I will check it out. What did he die of?'

'Who knows? Caro said he'd contracted some sort of fever. I did wonder, though, whether she'd made it up to cover the fact that he'd left her.'

'That seems a bit extreme. A marriage ending is nothing to be ashamed of.'

His expression was pained. 'I know, what can I say? I feel a teeny bit ashamed of myself now.'

'What about Caro and Ellie's relationship? What can you tell me about that?'

The shutters came down. Apparently not everything was writ large across Ash's face. He'd learned early on to guard the secret of his own sexuality. It seemed that singular discretion might stretch to others. 'Are you suggesting they were a couple?'

'I'm asking.' Karen kept a level gaze on his narrowed eyes.

He sighed. 'Just because I'm gay, I don't assume the whole world is. It's entirely possible for two people to have an intimate friendship without being lovers. After all, that's how I would have characterised my relationship with Ellie. We confided in each other about many things, but not everything.'

'I have one or two friends like that myself.' It wasn't quite a lie, Karen thought. 'But you never asked? You were never told?'

'I never asked,' he said firmly. 'We live in a very gossipy world, my dear. If you don't know, you can't betray.'

He had a point but she thought he was bullshitting. Whatever there was to know, he knew it. But he wasn't going to give it up. He looked at his watch and seemed to gather himself together. He was going to make a break for it. 'One thing before you go. Did Ellie or Caro have any enemies? Anybody who might have wished them ill?'

His eyes widened. 'We all have enemies in this business. But not the kind that kill you.' He sounded affronted. 'And if they had, I'm not the one they would have told.'

'Meaning what?'

'Come on, Detective, you're a woman. You know how you ladies share things you'd never dream of talking to a man about, even a gay man. There would be times when I'd walk into a bar where I was meeting the girls and they'd have their heads together with somebody from the theatre – Felicity Frye, or another one of the faces from gossip central – and as soon as I reached the table they'd sit back and pretend they were talking about shoes or handbags. I told you, we were close, but we were frivolous too. People were dying all around us. We didn't want to spend all our time lost in grim reality. When I was with Caro and Ellie, it was about preserving what gaiety we could muster. But those girls were delightful, believe me. It's unimaginable to think anyone would want to kill them. Unimaginable.'

27

Unimaginable was a word Karen didn't acknowledge. As far as human behaviour was concerned, nothing was beyond imagination. What was harder to get used to was the number of things people did to each other that had never occurred to her to imagine. Sadly, what had been done to the four people who had boarded that Cessna Skylane on that May morning was horrible, but it wasn't remarkable.

She'd hoped that Jack Ash would have given her something more tangible to chase. But he'd closed down on her as soon as she'd approached the serious business of motive. She'd given him her card as he'd stood up to leave, but he'd tossed it back on to the table in front of her. 'I've told you everything I can,' he'd said, his jaw set tight around his words. 'There's no reason for us to talk again.'

Karen had paid the bill, trying not to flinch. It was almost as much as dinner the night before, beers included. This private enterprise was an expensive business. She walked back out into the sunshine, glad to be out of Jack Ash's self-absorbed ambit. As she walked back towards Regent's Park, she considered what little she had learned. The most significant fact was that Caroline Abbott had told the world that her husband was dead in 1990. Taken at face value, that meant he couldn't have killed her. But there was always the possibility that she had lied. He might still have been alive in 1994 and enraged to discover she had killed him off four years before. Far-fetched, Karen knew, but she'd fetched things from farther away before.

There was one thing that Jack Ash had let slip. He'd been in full flood on the subject of women and their exclusive conversations and he'd mentioned a name. Felicity Frye. Karen had recognised it, and not just because Felicity Frye was a popular actress with a long and lively career in film, TV and theatre. She specialised in the kind of roles where seriousness is leavened by a sprightly wit. She'd been part of Karen's viewing landscape since childhood when she'd starred in one of those perennial sitcoms that was always being rerun on some digital channel.

But there was another reason why Felicity Frye's name resonated with Karen. A few weeks before, the actress's face and her rich contralto had been all over the media when she'd revealed she had inoperable terminal pancreatic cancer. She'd spoken of the few months at most she had left and revealed she intended to abandon public life and hoped to finish writing the memoir she'd been working on for some time. Felicity Fryc was a woman with nothing left to lose. She might be the key that unlocked the lives of Caroline Abbott and Ellie MacKinnon.

Karen walked into the park and kept going till she found an empty bench in a secluded spot. What she needed right now was for Tamsin Martineau to be the duty digital forensics officer in the Police Scotland labs at Gartcosh. When it came to navigating the undercurrents of the digital world, there was nobody better. And Karen knew that the maverick Australian liked nothing better than a challenge. You only had to look at her platinum spiked hair and her nose stud to know she wasn't going to be unduly bothered about sticking to the rules.

Karen speed-dialled the number and crossed her fingers. The gods were on her side for once; the phone was answered on the third ring and the accent provided unmistakable ID. 'Digital forensics here,' Tamsin said.

'Tamsin? It's DCI Pirie from the HCU.'

'How're you doing, Karen? We've not seen you round here in a while.'

'I've been hiding. You still claiming the weekends and night shifts?'

'You bet. I get more time off that way. So, what can I do for you? You don't usually have stuff that's urgent enough to need weekend working.'

'It's so straightforward I'm almost embarrassed to ask you. It's just that I'm down in London on inquiries and I've got a lead on a new witness. I thought I might as well chase it down while I'm here.' Shut up, she told herself. Tamsin's a techie, you don't have to explain yourself to her, that's the opposite of casual.

'Fire away. I'm ploughing through a routine batch of confiscated paedo hard drives. It'll be nice to have a break from fucking with other people's encryption.'

'Thanks. I need an address and a phone number for Felicity Frye. The actress.'

'Yeah, I know who Felicity Frye is. I may be a geek but I've not been living under a stone. No worries, Karen. I'll get on to it right away. Call you back on this number, yeah?'

'Thanks.' Karen ended the call. Chances were she wasn't going to make it back to Edinburgh tonight. Time to go and find a cheap hotel. Aye, right. A cheap hotel in central London. As if.

*

Jeremy Frye accepted the bouquet from the florist's driver with his customary friendliness. They were almost becoming friends, him and the delivery woman. Pretty much every day she turned up with another floral offering from friends and fans who couldn't think of another way to express their sorrow and sympathy. Patrizia, their daily help, was developing new skills in flower arrangement. She'd become adept at plucking out the blooms that were on their last legs and distributing the remainder among the other displays. Just as well Felicity loved flowers, for these days there were loaded vases in every room.

Jeremy was less delighted. He found them too potent a token of funerals. They were a constant reminder of the event that was hurtling towards him. One day soon, far sooner than he had ever dreamed, he would be adrift in a sea of funeral flowers. She was only sixty-four, for God's sake. These days, that was no age. They had friends still hale and hearty in their eighties. Friends who had lived rackety, dangerous lives filled with booze and cigarettes and drugs and red meat and fast cars yet were still going strong. And his beloved Felicity, the love of his life, the mother of their children, who had shepherded her health with good food and fresh air and exercise, had been struck down with this horrible disease. Not for the first time, he felt a spurt of rage burn through him.

Rather than show it, he called out lightly. 'Florist, darling. Carnations and irises. From the Buchans.'

'How lovely,' came the reply from the garden room, the warm chocolate and caramel tones undiminished by illness. 'Are they lovely?'

Jeremy chuckled. 'Six out of ten, I'd say.' He continued to the kitchen, where he was making coffee for himself and a vile herbal brew for his wife when the doorbell rang. He dumped the flowers in the sink, added water then carried the drinks through on a bamboo tray with a plate of Felicity's favourite spiced oat biscuits. 'Here we are,' he said, putting the tray on the table next to her, minimising the effort she had to make.

Felicity pushed herself more upright, and Jeremy was there, plumping cushions at her back. He'd always been solicitous. Uxorious, his sister always teased. Nothing was too much trouble now. He knew there would be years to come when he'd ache for the chance to do something, anything for Felicity. He watched her now like a hawk, alert for any sign of pain or discomfort. She had drugs, carefully calibrated to spare her, but she was reluctant sometimes to take them. And so he studied every lineament and movement of her face, not least because he wanted to commit her beauty absolutely to his memory.

She reached for her cup and pulled a face as she sipped. 'I think I'm going to give this stuff up,' she said. 'If I've only got a little time left, I want to enjoy what I put in my mouth. Next time, I'll have a coffee, darling. To hell with bloody Chinese herbs.'

Before he could answer, her phone buzzed with a text message. Felicity carefully put her cup down and reached for her phone. Her movements, once so confident, were hesitant and much of her old strength had abandoned her limbs so everything now was measured. She propped her reading glasses on her nose and summoned the message. 'How curious,' she said, reading it.

'Who is it?'

'I'll read it to you. "Good afternoon, Ms Frye. I'm sorry to intrude but I wonder if you might be able to make time to see me? I am Detective Chief Inspector Karen Pirie, head of Police Scotland's Historic Case Unit, and we are re-examining the plane crash in 1994 that killed your friends. It would be very helpful to me to be able to talk to you about Caroline Abbott and Ellie MacKinnon. I am in London today and tomorrow and I would very much appreciate the chance to talk with you. Thank you." How remarkable,' she said, the low thrill of her voice still as beautiful as ever.

'But why?'

'I imagine because we were close, darling.'

'No, sorry, I didn't mean why you, I meant, why now? Why are they re-examining a case that seemed entirely straightforward at the time? Irish terrorists blow up a plane piloted by a politician who'd served in the Northern Ireland Office. Perfectly dreadful, but perfectly clear. Wasn't it?'

Felicity pushed a stray strand of hair from her face. 'We all thought so. But perhaps we were wrong.' She started tapping the screen of her phone. 'Do we have anything planned for tomorrow? Shall I invite her to come round in the morning?' She gave a wry smile. 'While I still have energy enough to think and talk at the same time.'

Jeremy felt the instinctive kick of concern that always butted in these days when Felicity suggested something he was afraid might be too much for her. 'Are you sure, my dear? I don't want you to be upset, thinking about poor Caroline and Ellie.'

'Oh, Jeremy, you're so thoughtful. But it was a long time ago now. I grieved for them at the time, and heaven knows I missed their friendship over the years, but it's scarcely traumatic to talk about them.'

'You say that now, but I know your tender heart. And besides, you said yourself, you get easily tired.'

Felicity harrumphed softly. 'I'm not at death's door yet, Jeremy. If this police officer has taken the trouble to track me down, I think the least I can do is give her the benefit of my knowledge of Caroline and Ellie. If there's any possibility at all of there having been a mistake made all those years ago, I owe it to them – and to those two boys; men, now – to provide whatever assistance I can to the police.'

Jeremy sighed. He knew there was no point in arguing with Felicity once she'd made her mind up, especially if she had summoned duty in support of her position. All he could do was make sure she was as well rested as possible ahead of the encounter. 'If you say so, darling. Why don't you ask her to come over around ten? That gives you time to have a bath and some tea before she gets here.'

'I'll do that very thing,' Felicity said, continuing to compose her message. 'An inspector calls. What terrible secrets will come to light, I wonder? Be a dear, would you, and take this horrible concoction away and bring me a coffee?'

Jeremy did as he was asked, as he had been doing for the previous thirty-five years of marriage. As he left the room, he heard his wife say softly, 'I always knew the day would come when I'd have to tell the truth about those two.'

28

Karen stretched out on the bed and flicked through the channels on her laptop. BBC Alba was showing a Raith Rovers game with commentary in Gaelic, a language no one in the club's home town had ever spoken. She'd had to endure the experience more than once when Phil had still been alive and he hadn't been able to get to the game. She'd learned that *sgiobair* sounded very like 'skipper' and meant captain. She shuddered and kept going, finally settling for a black-and-white Ealing comedy she'd seen half a dozen times before. She could afford to relax a little. She had a meeting set up for the morning with Felicity Frye, she had a decent room in a small hotel round the corner from Euston, and she had stuffed the tiny fridge with the best that the station's M&S food hall could provide.

The familiar classic lulled her to sleep and she was happily dozing, a line of drool heading for the pillow, when her phone buzzed her awake. 'Ungh,' she grunted, pushing herself upright and reaching for it. The screen said, 'Jason' and she groaned. 'For fuck's sake, it's Saturday night,' under her breath. She swiped the screen and said, 'What's the problem, Jason?' Because there had to be one.

'Hi, boss, Can I come round and see you?'

Karen was taken aback. They never socialised other than the occasional drink after work. She didn't think Jason had even been inside her flat before. When he'd picked her up on the way to jobs, she'd always run downstairs to where he was waiting in the car. 'There's a slight problem with that, Jason,' she said. 'I'm in London.'

'What? You having a weekend away? You never said.'

'What are you? My mother?' Karen knew as she spoke that she was being ridiculously grumpy, but she'd just been woken up.

'Sorry, boss.'

He sounded on the verge of tears and she softened. 'It was a last-minute thing.' Karen crossed to the fridge and took out the bottle of Pinot Grigio she'd treated herself to. She unscrewed the cap and poured out a glass, waiting for Jason to continue. But he didn't. 'So what did you want to see me about?'

He cleared his throat. 'See, it's like this, boss. You know you set me on tracking down where the leak came from?'

'Aye. Have you had any luck?'

'Not really luck, as such. But I think I know where it came from.'

'Good work. So who's the guilty party?'

'Eh . . . ' A long silence. 'I think it might be me.'

Now it was Karen's turn to be stuck for words. She could hear his breath in her ear, heavy and ragged. 'What do you mean, Jason? It *might* be you?' She kept her voice gentle, the way she would if she was trying to coax a stray dog within reach. 'Surely you must know whether you spoke to the media or not?'

'It's not that simple.'

That was a pity. Simple was within his range. 'How not?'

'I never spoke to a reporter. But, see, Monday nights we get pizza and have a few beers in the house, me and the guys I share with.'

'The students?'

'Right. And they like to hear about what I'm doing at my work. They think it's cool, like.'

Oh, dear Christ, she could see where this was going. 'And you told them about Ross Garvie?'

'I never said his name,' Jason said desperately. 'I just told them about the familial DNA and the adoption, because it was interesting and out of the usual run of things. They're all smart and full of stuff I don't know anything about, I suppose I was showing off a bit.' His voice died away. She could feel the shame from the other end of the country.

'And you think one of them sold the story to a journalist?'

'I don't think. I know. We went down the pub today at lunchtime and Liam was buying drinks. Usually, we don't buy rounds because they're all skint all the time and it's easier that way. So I was, like, "Liam, did you win the lottery?" And he's, like, "Thanks to you, Jason, my man." I didn't get it. But Matt, he said, "Put him out of his misery," and Liam told me he sold the story to a reporter that he knows.'

Karen let the silence hang while she thought of something to say that wasn't a scream of, 'You naïve fuckwit!' Eventually she said, 'Well, Jason, it is what it is. I'm going to have to think about this, see how we get you the fuck out of hot water. But here's what I think you need to do in the meantime. You need to pack up your stuff and load it into the car and move back to your mum's house in Kirkcaldy right now. Tonight. And you don't go back. And you don't pay a penny more rent.'

'But I can't leave them in the lurch. They'll never get another tenant this time of year. I can't do that. They're my mates.'

'No, Jason. They are not your mates. You're a polis. The only people you can trust are other cops and sometimes your family. These toerags are not your mates. They abused your trust. They took the piss. They are not your friends. Pack up and leave.'

His voice quivered with tears she hoped were unshed. 'What am I going to say to my mum?'

'Tell her you miss her cooking. Tell her you found your flatmates smoking dope and you can't live there now. Make something up, Jason. But go home.'

'OK, boss.' He sounded choked now.

'I'll speak to you tomorrow.' She pinched the bridge of her nose.

'I'm sorry. I let you down.'

You did, Jason, you did. 'We'll figure something out.' Karen took a long swallow of her wine. 'Now away you go and pack your bags.'

'OK. I'm sorry.'

'And stop apologising. I know you're sorry. Goodnight, Jason.' She ended the call before he could abase himself further. Karen subsided on to the chair by the counter that passed for a desk. Really, it couldn't have been worse. It explained how so many stories from her department had found their way into the press before they were ready to go public. And now Jilted John was going to be hot on the trail of, it turned out, Jason.

The one thing they had going for them was that newspapers still protected their sources fiercely. It wasn't like he was going to walk into the offices of the *Record* or the *Scotsman* on Monday morning and be handed full access to their freelance payment files. They'd fight like dogs to keep him out of their system and they'd probably win. But meantime, Jilted John would be cultivating contacts and offering a mixture of bribes and threats to uncover what nobody wanted to tell him. After all, he was the Macaroon's man and the Macaroon wasn't about to pass up a chance to make her life difficult. How he would love it if Jason was exposed as the leak. Being able to blame her at one remove would be almost as satisfying as being able to nail her directly. At the very least, she'd lose Jason and end up with one of the Macaroon's placemen at her side. She might even lose the HCU and end up back in regular CID, chasing the feckless and the gormless.

Karen knew she had to figure out somewhere else to lay the blame. Somewhere that wouldn't damage some innocent, obviously. But somewhere convincing. And she had to figure it out quickly.

But right now, she didn't have an idea in her head.

29

It took the alarm to wake Karen. She couldn't quite believe she'd slept for more than eight hours. It might have had something to do with the three glasses of wine she'd drunk before her eyelids had grown heavy, but she didn't think so. There were many nights when she'd necked more alcohol than that and sleep had been as elusive as ever.

It wasn't as if she had nothing on her mind. After her conversation with Jason, she'd paced her hotel room, trying to come up with a false provenance for the leaks that would convince Jilted John. She'd come up empty. And yet she'd slept.

The disappointing thing was that her subconscious hadn't come up with anything useful during the night, as it often had before. No brainwaves, no tangent offering a credible alternative to the truth. In the grey light of morning, she was as stuck as she'd been before she'd crashed.

Nothing for it but to ignore the problem and get on with the day. Shower, coffee, breakfast back in Euston station, and by half past nine she was on the tube heading for Notting Hill and Felicity Frye, Jason set firmly to the back of her mind. This was the make-or-break interview. Either she'd find something to get her teeth into or she'd bury her doubts, walk away and leave Alan Noble to it. Giorsal would just have to live with her uncertainties, the way that so many of them did.

Navigating by her phone, Karen walked down the hill from the tube station, soon finding herself surrounded by high white buildings with porticos and private gardens filling the space between them. It was a bit like a bleached version of the grandest parts of Edinburgh's New Town. She turned into a quiet side street and followed the numbers till she reached the address she'd been given.

It was the last house in the terrace, separated from the rest of the street by a narrow mews. Three storeys of brilliant whitewash and tall windows with swags of curtains visible from the street. A pillared portico jutted out from the glossy front door with its brightly polished brass letter box. It spoke of money, but there was nothing vulgar about it. Karen had texted ahead because you didn't doorstep the dying. But faced with this imposing house, she was glad she'd made an appointment. If she'd turned up on spec, she might have bottled it. Outclassed and outgunned, that was how it made her feel.

But there was no going back now. She gripped her bag, climbed the steps and pulled a brass knob that gleamed softly from years of other people's hands. In the distance, a proper bell jangled. Footsteps approached, muffled by the heavy door. It swung silently open to reveal a slightly stooped man with a large patrician head crowned with thick silver hair swept back from a high forehead. He wore baggy corduroy trousers and a shabby hand-knitted dark blue Guernsey. 'Detective Chief Inspector Pirie, I presume?' he said, shaggy eyebrows raised in a question.

'That's me,' Karen said.

'Come in, do. I'm Jeremy Frye, Felicity's husband.' He stepped to one side and made a sweeping gesture with one arm.

The hallway looked like something out of an interiors magazine – an elaborate tiled floor, tasteful art on the walls, toning colours of paintwork without a single scuff, nothing out of place. Where did people like the Fryes keep their crap, Karen wondered. Where were the carelessly discarded keys and gloves, the junk mail, the bags-for-life waiting to go back to the car? Even a life as stripped-down as hers seemed to accumulate clutter on a daily basis. The rich truly were different.

She followed Jeremy down the hall, exchanging meaningless pleasantries about the journey and the weather. He paused in front of a closed door, fingers closing on the handle. 'You're aware that my wife's health is . . . delicate?'

'Yes. I'm sorry.'

'She tires easily. I'd appreciate it if you would bear that in mind.'

'I'll try to keep this as brief as possible.'

A thin smile. 'She may not want you to. Felicity loves to talk.'

'I understand.'

He nodded and opened the door into a room that felt as if it was made of light and greenery. It was like stepping into one of the glasshouses in the Botanic Gardens. At the heart of the room, on a wicker chaise longue piled with silk cushions, lay Felicity Frye. Recognisably herself, but a shrunken, paler version of the woman Karen had seen on countless screens, large and small. She turned her head and her face lit up with a shadow of her familiar smile. 'How lovely,' she said, her voice still carrying effortlessly across the room. 'Forgive me for not getting up to meet you.' She held her arms out in welcome. 'Come and sit down, my dear. Jeremy, bring us some tea, please? You do drink tea, Chief Inspector?'

'Yes. Thanks.' Dry-mouthed, Karen approached.

'Sit down, here. Beside me.' Felicity pointed to a rattan tub chair set at right angles to her chaise.

'Thank you for seeing me.' Karen said, sitting down. 'I really appreciate it. I know you've not been well.'

Felicity's smile faltered. 'I'm dying, Chief Inspector. But that doesn't mean I can't still be useful. Or at least, I can try. Now, your message was rather intriguing. You said you're re-examining that atrocity in 1994 that killed my dear friends Caroline and Ellie? What on earth has happened? Has someone finally confessed? Or rather, what is it they say? "Claimed responsibility"?'

'I'm afraid not. I assume you didn't see the news last week about Gabriel Abbott?'

She looked intrigued rather than concerned. 'No, I've given up the news. What's Gabriel been up to?'

'I'm sorry to be the bearer of bad news, but Gabriel was found dead.'

What little colour Felicity had faded from her face, leaving what had been subtle make-up stark against her skin. 'Oh, that poor boy. Was it ... an accident?' There was a plea in her voice.

Karen knew she was dealing with an actress, but that didn't mean Felicity's reactions weren't genuine. She hated herself for having to deliver more bad news to a dying woman. 'Gabriel died of a gunshot wound to the head. It's not clear at this point whether it was self-inflicted.'

'You mean he might have been murdered?' Incredulity in the face and the voice. 'Why would anyone murder Gabriel? Suicide I can comprehend. But murder? Surely not.'

'We'd like to be able to exclude that possibility.'

At that point, Jeremy returned with the tea tray. As he fussed over the pouring and handing out of cups and saucers, Felicity repeated what Karen had told her. 'It's madness,' she concluded. 'Who would want to hurt that poor damaged boy?'

'Indeed,' Jeremy said, patting her hand. 'But what has that to do with an act of terrorism in 1994?'

'It was never established that the plane crash was an act of terrorism. It was an assumption, a reasonable one in the circumstances. But no terrorist organisation ever claimed responsibility, which was unusual. The case remains open. And Gabriel had spoken recently about a conspiracy that had deprived him of his rights. It's hard to think of any other event in his life that a conspiracy might centre round.'

Jeremy and Felicity looked equally taken aback. 'What sort of conspiracy?' Felicity asked.

'He didn't go into details.'

'He wasn't a well man,' Jeremy said.

'Did you see much of him?'

They both shook their heads. 'We haven't seen much of either of them,' Felicity said, sighing. 'I always felt we ought to, but—' She waved a hand. 'Life got in the way.'

'The last time we saw them, I think, was at Frank Sinclair's daughter's wedding,' Jeremy said slowly. Karen caught a quick sharp glance from Felicity towards her husband, but he continued, oblivious. 'Yes, I'm sure of it. Three years ago last summer. Gabriel seemed quite morose, as I recall. To be honest, I'd have thought he was a more likely candidate for suicide than murder.'

'You're probably right, sir, but it's my job to look at all the possibilities. Ms Frye, I understand you were a close friend of both women?'

'Felicity, please. I knew them both, of course, but initially I spent more time with Caroline because of the theatre, and because our daughter Perdita is the same age as Will. But the three of us became close friends over the years. I was probably their best friend, apart from each other, of course.' Felicity was no longer looking at Karen. She had the thousand-yard stare of someone lost in memories.

Time to tread on eggshells. But there was no other way to go. 'What was the nature of their relationship?'

Felicity dropped her eyes to the teacup she was clutching. There was a long pause, then she seemed to gather herself physically. 'I don't have long to live,' she said decisively. 'I made promises years ago, and I've kept them. But I do not want to go to my grave carrying other people's secrets.'

A look of alarm spread across Jeremy's face. 'Darling, there's no need—'

'There's every need.' She closed her eyes momentarily. 'Secrets and lies, they're poison, Jeremy. Perhaps Gabriel wouldn't be dead if I'd spoken sooner. If I hadn't kept the secrets of the dead so long.'

It was like being in a lost episode of *Downton Abbey*, Karen thought. Melodrama galore. 'What is it that you want to tell me?' she said, feeling like the prompter in the wings of a West End play.

'They were a couple, Caroline and Ellie. When they met, they fell for each other like a runaway train. They were absolutely devoted to each other. But they were also absolutely devoted to keeping their relationship secret. It wasn't an issue for Caroline. But Ellie worked in children's television. Clause 28 was in the wind and, if she'd been outed, she'd have lost her job without a doubt. So they bought the house and split it in two and made much of the fact that Ellie loved to take care of Will when Caroline was working.'

As Karen had suspected. 'But what about Tom Abbott? What was his take on all this?'

Felicity laughed, a throaty, sexy laugh. 'Tom was always away on the high seas. He had his own life. Caroline was an aberration for him. He preferred boys. That's what killed him in the end. He died of AIDS in Thailand.'

'The Philippines,' Jeremy interrupted. 'If you must tell the story, get it right.' He clamped his mouth shut again in apparent disapproval.

Felicity rolled her eyes. 'Somewhere overseas. It doesn't matter where. What matters is when. He died in 1984.' She delivered the line with all the aplomb of the curtain line at the end of an act.

It didn't make sense. 'But Gabriel wasn't born till 1986. And Caroline told everyone that Tom died in 1990.' She was sure of this; last night, she'd checked when Nelson Mandela walked free.

'She did. But it was Caroline's little white lie, to keep things simple.'

In Karen's book, it was neither little nor white. And not simple either. She reminded herself of what was becoming the mantra of the day: the rich were different, right enough. 'I'm sorry, how did that keep things simple?'

'Caroline and Ellie desperately wanted a child of their own, to set the seal on their relationship. They adored each other. So much so that Ellie persuaded their gynaecologist friend Guy to sign her off work for three months, allegedly because she had fibroids and needed a hysterectomy. That, added to the fact that her programme was always off the air for three months in the summer meant she had six months to support Caroline through the end of the pregnancy and for the first few weeks after Gabriel was born.'

'So Ellie pretended to have major surgery to keep up the pretence that they were just pals?'

'Yes. As I said, devoted.'

'And nobody noticed? What? Did Ellie stay confined to the house all those months, pretending to be convalescing?'

'They spent most of the time at their place in France,' Jeremy said. 'Lovely little cottage on the Normandy coast a dozen miles west of the D-Day beaches.'

'Heaven knows what their phone bills were like. Caroline was on the phone to the office every day.'

'I don't think that was much of a concern by that stage. Caroline was doing terribly well by then,' Jeremy said drily.

'I was pining for them dreadfully,' Felicity said. 'But we simply couldn't get away. My schedule was a nightmare. I was in *Macbeth* at Stratford with lovely Desmond Barritt and Maureen Beattie and then I was filming some dreadful sub-Henry James tosh in Boston. By the time I got back, Gabriel was a couple of months old and they were home in Hampstead.'

'And nobody asked why Tom wasn't around for the birth of his second son?'

Jeremy shrugged. 'People were so accustomed to Tom not being around for birthdays and Christmas, I don't imagine they gave it a second thought. Besides, Gabriel was born in France so nobody really knew whether Tom had been there or not.'

'Absolutely. Maintaining the fiction that Tom was still alive meant there were no awkward questions about Gabriel's parentage. And if any lowlife journalists came sniffing around with ideas about their relationship, the girls could point to Gabriel and assume an air of injured innocence.' Felicity explained this as if it were a perfectly normal way of going about things.

'So who was Gabriel's father?'

'We don't know,' Jeremy said firmly. 'The girls never told.'

'At first, I assumed it was Jack Ash, the disc jockey. With a turkey baster, obviously.' She tittered. 'Really, if you knew Jack, you'd know that was the only available route.'

Karen would have put money against that paternity. Not even a solipsist like Jack Ash could react with such equanimity to the news of a son's death. '"At first"?'

'The more I thought about it, the more unlikely I decided it was. After all, Tom had died of AIDS. There was still a huge amount of stigma around it then. I really didn't think Caroline would take the risk of impregnating herself with the sperm of a man whose sexual habits would have made him a high risk. So I had to live with the cloud of unknowing.'

'Which has never been a happy state for you, darling.' There was still a faint air of disapproval about Jeremy.

'Indeed.' That sexy laugh again. 'And then I had a blinding revelation.' She paused, clearly waiting for another prompt from Karen.

Karen dutifully obliged. Keep the witness happy, that was the way to do it. 'What happened?'

'It was the wedding Jeremy mentioned earlier. Samantha Sinclair and Toby St John Sargent. You know, the youngest daughter of Frank Sinclair. Lord Sinclair. The newspaperman.'

Frank Sinclair was a newspaperman in the same sort of way that T. S. Eliot had dashed off the odd poem. He'd edited several national newspapers and now he was editor-in-chief of the biggest stable of daily and weekly publications in the UK. He'd been elevated to the House of Lords a few years previously and was a regular fixture on TV shows where he forcibly expressed his views on any number of subjects, regardless of his level of knowledge or expertise. 'I know who you mean,' Karen said.

'Frank was a very old friend of Ellie. And later, of course, he got to know Caroline.'

Karen tried to hide her surprise. 'I wouldn't have thought Frank Sinclair had anything in common with Ellie and Caroline. Isn't he always on about families being a husband and wife and children? And how we're all going to hell in a handcart with our sinful ways?'

'Absolutely,' Felicity said. 'But he and Ellie went back a very long way. They were the star pupils in their small-town school, then they both went off to Durham University and they stayed friends. Sometimes we need people in our lives who don't agree with everything we do, Chief Inspector.'

Jeremy laughed indulgently. 'You should try it sometime, darling.'

'Very funny, you silly old boot. Anyway, we were delighted to see Caroline's boys after so long. I'd always said how odd it was that they looked so unlike each other. You'd never have known they were brothers. Gabriel so dark and Will so fair. But then genetics are a funny thing. Our two girls look nothing like each other.'

'That's because Viola looks like you and Perdita is the image of my mother,' Jeremy said. 'It happens.'

'Of course it does. Look at the Windsor boys.' Felicity raised her eyebrows suggestively. 'So, there we are, at the wedding, drinking Frank Sinclair's perfectly delicious champagne when one of those odd little moments of coincidence brought Gabriel's profile into alignment with Frank's. And suddenly all the pieces fell into place. There was no doubting it. Frank Sinclair was obviously Gabriel's father.'

30

K aren was momentarily lost for words. Felicity Frye had demonstrated for the second time that she was still the mistress of the curtain line.

Jeremy shook his head in exasperation. 'You really shouldn't, Felicity. You have no evidence for such a thing.'

'I have the evidence of my own eyes, Jeremy. You saw it too. In profile, they're almost identical. It's not quite so obvious head-on – Gabriel's face is broader than Frank's, but you can still see a powerful resemblance. And of course, their colouring is quite different. Gabriel with his dark hair and beautiful brown eyes and Frank with his sandy hair and blue eyes.'

'But how? I mean, why? It flies in the face of all Lord Sinclair's public pronouncements,' Karen blurted out.

'I imagine Ellie threw herself on the altar of their friend-ship,' Felicity said. 'Asked a favour for her friend.'

'They probably flattered him into it,' Jeremy said more sourly. 'He has an ego the size of a small planet. I can see Caroline and Ellie telling him that they couldn't imagine anyone with a better set of genes.'

'And from their point of view, he was the perfect choice. They wanted absolute discretion and they could guarantee that from Frank. Given his views and his position – I think at the time they were doing this, he'd just taken on his first editorship – he could never have even hinted at the truth. It would have destroyed him.'

'I can see that,' Karen conceded. 'But I'm struggling to get my head round why he'd do it in the first place.'

Felicity gave an elegant shrug. 'Men love to think of their bloodline continuing after they're gone. Frank only has daughters – perhaps he was gambling on a son?'

'And apparently he got one,' Jeremy said. 'Even if it was one he could never acknowledge.'

'If we're right, surely it would be easy enough to do a DNA comparison?' Felicity asked.

'Easy to do, hard to justify,' Karen said. 'I can't exactly rock up to his front door and demand a buccal swab.'

'Oh, that sounds so marvellously technical. "A buccal swab". Can't you acquire it by stealth? They're always doing that on TV. Retrieving coffee cartons from bins, stealing glasses from bars, that sort of thing.'

Bloody writers, Karen thought. Too lazy to figure out the legal way of doing things so they make it up as they go along. 'It's hard to stand that up in court. Judges take a pretty dim view of that kind of cavalier behaviour. Especially in Scotland, where everything has to be corroborated. But did Caroline not leave any letters behind? "In the event of my death . . . ", that sort of thing?'

Felicity and Jeremy looked at each other blankly. 'Not that I ever heard,' Felicity said. 'She certainly didn't leave anything for me, and I doubt there was anyone closer to her than I was.'

'What about diaries? Personal papers?'

Again they exchanged glances. 'There's nothing left,'

Felicity said. 'After the crash, Ellie's sister Maddie turned up. She was living in Italy but she got the first flight back. Will was living at home at the time, he was about to start his chemistry course at Imperial. Gabriel was still at boarding school in Scotland and they thought it was best to leave him there rather than disrupt him. He loved that school, didn't he, Jeremy? And they were very good to him. He spent most of the holidays there, because obviously Will didn't have the right sort of set-up to take care of a small boy, and Maddie was back in Italy. Living the life of Riley and turning out the occasional cookery book.' Felicity made it sound as if Maddie's books were only one step away from pornography.

'I'm sorry, but what has that to do with Caroline's diaries?'

Felicity smoothed her hair back from her forehead. 'I'm sorry. I'm not being awfully clear. Maddie burned everything. All their personal papers. If there were diaries, them too. The lot went up in flames.'

Karen's heart sank at the disappearance of another potential piece of the jigsaw. 'But why? What possessed her?'

'Anything to avoid bringing shame and embarrassment on the family.' Felicity pursed her lips.

'But did she have the right to do that? Ellie's papers, perhaps, but Caroline's too?'

'Not as such,' Felicity said, her voice grim. 'Caroline and Ellie had wills in favour of each other, and they didn't have one of those clauses that says one has to survive the other by thirty days before the inheritance kicks in. Because Ellie was a few months older than Caroline, she was deemed to have died first. So everything she possessed passed to Caroline. And Caroline had left everything to Will.' Felicity sighed and shook her head. 'I don't know what Caroline was thinking. Perhaps she drew up the will before Gabriel was born, I don't know. Or perhaps she assumed that, while Gabriel was still so young, Will would take care of him. So technically all their papers belonged to Will. But Maddie impressed upon him the need to maintain the secrecy his mother had imposed while she was alive and said the only way to make sure they protected her reputation was to burn everything that might contain a clue to the truth.'

'And so she had a bonfire in the back garden,' Jeremy said. 'Within days of the crash. Letters, cards, diaries, everything. Even photographs. Will and Gabriel were left with almost nothing of their mother.'

'We had copies made of all the photographs we had that included Ellie and Caroline and the boys,' Felicity said. 'We gave them to Will and Gabriel a couple of years after the crash, once the immediate trauma was past. They were both pathetically grateful, weren't they, darling?' She reached for Jeremy's hand and squeezed it.

'The least we could do, in the circumstances,' he said stiffly. 'Bloody awful thing to do. Bloody awful woman, Maddie.'

Doors were closing all around Karen. Really, she should take heed and walk away from so unpromising a case. If indeed there was a case, she reminded herself. 'That's terrible. But if I could turn back to the crash itself. As I said earlier, the received wisdom has always been that it was a terrorist bomb—'

Felicity interrupted her. 'But what you are saying is that if Gabriel's death turns out not to have been suicide and he'd been talking about a conspiracy, it might have been something very different?' There were two patches of colour on her cheeks. It was hard to tell whether she was excited or indignant.

'Don't put the poor woman on the spot,' Jeremy said.

'No, it's fine,' Karen said. 'But you must understand that

this is all speculative at this point. I wonder, can you think of anyone who bore any kind of grudge against Ellie or Caroline?'

The couple looked at each other blankly. 'Not the kind of grudge that leads to murder,' Felicity said, with much the same intonation as Lady Bracknell said, 'a handbag'. 'In our business, taking umbrage is an Olympic sport. Actors are always outraged at being passed over for a role or being upstaged by some up-and-coming ingénue. We bitch and moan for England. But it never comes to blows, far less murder. Caroline never spoke of anyone having genuine enmity towards her.' She laughed, a light tinkle. 'The very idea is absurd.'

'Truly, Chief Inspector, people in Felicity's world don't behave in a murderous way. Except on screen. It simply wouldn't occur to them. I'm not saying there aren't simmering resentments in the theatre, but that's where they stay.' Jeremy leaned forward to emphasise his earnestness.

Much as she disliked taking anything a witness said at face value, Karen was pretty sure Jeremy and Felicity were right in their judgement. Outside fiction, people didn't commit murder over a West End role or a TV job. They certainly didn't blow up three innocent people alongside the object of their loathing. Even in the theatre, anybody that fucked-up would have drawn attention to themselves. It looked like she'd reached the end of the road on this line of inquiry. 'Thank you for your frankness,' she said. 'Unless there's anything else you want to tell me, I think I've covered what I needed to ask you.'

'It's been fascinating. Of late, my life has become quite remarkably dull, inevitably. You've been a breath of fresh air,' Felicity said.

Karen stood up. What did you say to a dying stranger? 'I appreciate your time. I hope things are not too difficult for you.'

This time, Felicity looked away as she gave a faint smile. 'Too kind,' she said. 'I do hope you finally get some answers. Even if it only confirms what everyone thought all along.'

Walking back up the hill, Karen tried to push away the voice in her head telling her she was chasing shadows. That she was inventing things to occupy her mind. From Syrian refugees to baseless murder conspiracies, she was filling her head and her hours with stuff that wasn't real. She wasn't going to sort out the refugee crisis or an unsolved bombing that everybody but her thought was easily explicable. She needed to get a grip instead of bothering a dying woman with her pointless questioning.

For what had she learned, after all? Caroline Abbott and Ellie MacKinnon had been lovers. They'd wanted a child to cement their relationship. Frank Sinclair, Lord Sinclair, editor-in-chief of an influential right-of-centre media group, bastion of family values that even the Conservative party had moved on from, might possibly have donated the sperm to make that baby. It was a big maybe. Would you really take that big a risk for the girlfriend of your old school friend? But even if Felicity Frye was right, any evidence had gone up in flames twenty-two years ago. Short of stalking Frank Sinclair for a discarded coffee carton, there didn't seem much else she could do.

And even if she did, and even if the DNA demonstrated that Frank Sinclair had fathered Gabriel Abbott, what did that prove? That Caroline, Ellie and Frank were big fat liars. It certainly went nowhere near a motive for murder.

Unless the two women had been threatening Frank Sinclair with exposing his hypocrisy.

Karen marched along Notting Hill Gate towards Kensington Gardens mulling that thought over in her head. It was far-fetched, but not out of the question. It wasn't solely about reputation. If Caroline had identified Frank Sinclair as the secret father of her son – and presumably a collaborator in the pretence that her dead husband was still alive – he'd have been publicly destroyed. His new editor's chair would have been snatched out from under him. His own much-vaunted happy marriage might not have survived.

In Karen's world, that was motive enough for murder.

31

The sun had emerged from the clouds as Karen walked through Kensington Gardens but she didn't notice. She was lost in abstraction, leaping from problem to problem as she tried to find a way to make progress in any of her current concerns. Her mother had an expression – 'My head's full of wee motors.' And that just about covered the way her mind was running away with itself. But the very act of walking seemed to help straighten things out and as she crossed into Hyde Park, her mind snagged on something from deep down.

'Phil's laptop,' she breathed, her face lighting up. She parked herself on the first bench she came to and ran through the notion for flaws. At the time Phil had been murdered, his laptop had been sitting on his office desk. Jimmy Hutton remembered seeing it as they'd left to go out on the job that morning. And then Phil had ended up in hospital and none of their team had gone back to the office till the next day. And in that gap, some heartless opportunist had sneaked in and nicked his laptop. Could have been a cop, could have been a civilian assistant, could have been a cleaner. There was no way of knowing.

Jimmy had been raging when he told her and she hadn't been much better. What kind of arse would lift a laptop belonging to a polis lying in intensive care from injuries he'd taken in the line of duty? It beggared belief. So much for camaraderie. There was an investigation, but everybody knew it was a formality. Finding the culprit would only have made things worse. Nobody really wanted to know which of the people they had to work with was capable of such a shit's trick.

And then Phil had died and nobody cared about a laptop any more. But now, here, today, it had assumed a new significance. Karen took out her phone and called the digital forensics department for the second time that weekend. 'Digital forensics here,' Tamsin answered.

'Tamsin? It's Karen Pirie.'

'You need me to look up the phone book again?'

'That's right, keep talking yourself out of a job.'

Tamsin chuckled. 'Fair enough. What can I do for you?'

'A wee question. If somebody stole a laptop that I had guest user privileges on, is it at all feasible that they could use my account to get into whatever I have access to?'

'Only if you were too stupid to password-protect things. And you're not stupid.'

Karen's turn to chuckle. 'No, I'm not. But say my account was running in the background and I hadn't logged out before the other user logged in?'

Tamsin thought for a moment. 'It might be possible. Do you need it to be possible?'

'I'd very much like it to be possible.'

'There might be a way,' she said, thought processes slowing her voice. 'Do you want me to figure it out for you?'

'Thanks, but knowing it's feasible is all I need.'

'And I don't need to know why, do I?'

'Consider it your good deed for the day, Tamsin.'

'I haven't done one of those since I was a Girl Guide. That it?'

'It is. Thanks.'

'No worries, you're welcome.'

And that was that, sorted. One less thing to rattle round her head. She stared across the park, looking but not seeing families walking, children playing, couples leaning into each other, a scratch game of football with jackets for goalposts. Instead, she was imagining the space peopled with the Syrians from the brazier with their families. Somewhere simply to be.

Karen ran through the conversation she'd had with Giorsal a couple of nights before. Talking to a politician about the plight of the Syrians was a good suggestion but she reckoned it would have to be someone who already knew her. Otherwise she might be dismissed as another do-gooder who didn't understand how the world worked. She didn't want to waste her time on someone who wouldn't take her seriously.

That narrowed it down uncomfortably. She'd done her best to avoid encounters with politicians on the general principle that there were enough obstacles in the way of getting the job done. But every now and again, it had been inevitable. To be honest, it hadn't always gone well. But then, nobody who had ever spent any significant time in Karen's company would ever have contemplated a career in the diplomatic service for her. And if she ever felt her commitment to thrawn slipping, she reminded herself that being accommodating would only earn her promotion to ranks whose bureaucracy made her quail.

Starting at the bottom; she didn't know any Edinburgh City councillors; she didn't know any Edinburgh MSPs; but she had encountered one of the current Edinburgh MPs when he'd still been a Scottish National Party candidate with the steadfast belief that he'd never be elected in what had been, until 2014, a safe Labour seat. Craig Grassie had been an NHS administrator, lodged securely in the ranks of middle management. His wife had been a minor witness in a fifteen-year-old rape and attempted murder that Karen had finally resolved a few years before. She'd warmed to the Grassies, found them direct and uncomplicated, which wasn't what she'd expected from a man who wanted to become an MP.

Although, to be fair, he hadn't expected to be on the receiving end of a 30 per cent swing to the SNP. 'I'll never get in,' he'd confided to Karen. 'The party just want to put candidates up in every seat, that's the game. I'm window dressing.' But the voters had liked what they saw – or more likely, they'd liked the way Nicola Sturgeon put Westminster on the back foot – and Craig had been elected Member of Parliament for Edinburgh Central. Karen hadn't seen him since, but she was pretty sure he'd take her call. Even on a Sunday afternoon.

She never erased a number from her phone. Shirley Grassie's mobile number was there on her list and Karen dialled it quickly, not giving herself time to think twice. It rang so long she expected to be shunted off to voicemail, but then the ringtone cut off and she heard a breathless voice. 'Hello? Hello? Is there anybody there?'

'Mrs Grassie? This is DCI Karen Pirie. From the—'

'Yes, yes, I remember you, Chief Inspector. Hello there. How are you?' Cheery, direct. Would that everyone was like that, Karen thought, yearning.

'I'm fine, thanks. I'm sorry to bother you, but I wanted to get in touch with your husband and this is the only number I've got for either of you.' Apologetic never hurt.

'No bother, really. He's just in the other room, let me get him for you.'

Karen could hear footsteps on tiles, then a muffled shout of, 'Craig, it's that lovely detective from the cold case team,

Karen Pirie.' A low mumble. 'I don't know, it's you she's after.' Rustling and fumbling.

Then Craig Grassie's voice. 'Detective,' he said. 'This is a nice surprise. At least, I hope it is.' Rueful twist to his voice.

'It's not official business,' she said. 'But I wondered if you could spare me half an hour when you're up in Edinburgh?'

'I'm not going to be back now till Friday, I'm afraid. We're down in London this weekend.'

Karen almost punched the air. 'Actually, I'm in London myself. I don't suppose . . . '

A moment. Then Grassie said, 'Do you like coffee?'

'I do.'

'OK. We'll be in the TAP coffee shop on Wardour Street about half past two. It's a bit of a Sunday ritual for us. Does that work for you?'

Karen glanced at her watch. Plenty time to walk it. 'I'll be there.'

'Do you want to tell me what it's about?'

She gave a dry laugh. 'I think I'd better wait. I don't want you sneaking off to Costa instead.'

Jeremy Frye was in his den at the top of the house, gazing out of the small window through the trees to the mirror-image buildings on the other side of the enclosed gardens. Between his eyebrows, a pair of parallel frown lines. Felicity was asleep, worn out by her morning performance for the detective. She'd put on a magnificent show but he'd known as he watched her that she'd be wrung out for the rest of the day.

His right hand floated over his phone again then shifted away as if repelled by an opposite magnetic pole. He found himself in a quandary. He'd been deeply unsettled by what the detective had to say. All that awkward business raked up again after over twenty years. He'd listened to Felicity making light of it, appalled at the ease with which she'd given away Caroline and Ellie's secrets. Those girls had made such a fetish of discretion and it had held fast all those years. And now Felicity had broken those confidences, all for the sake of her own misguided conscience. It grieved him to think it, but misguided she was. It wasn't right to shrive herself at the expense of others.

Not only that, she'd gone off on a wild conjecture about Gabriel Abbott's paternity. She'd dragged Frank Sinclair's name into it, like trailing a cloak in the dust. Something swanky to spread out in front of the detective, who was far too shrewd to be dazzled by it. Nothing good could come of this. Had Felicity forgotten the cold rage that lived inside Frank Sinclair?

Jeremy sighed. He ran his hands through his leonine hair then let his hand fall back to his phone. He ought not to let this drift past. It wasn't right for these matters to be probed without the knowledge of the people directly concerned; it offended his sense of fair play. Someone had to be told what was stirring in the depths. But calling Frank was out of the question. There was no way of dressing this up that would avoid his fury. 'My wife has just told the police she thought you'd fathered Caroline Abbott's bastard.' Impossible to lay that out in a positive light.

Deception might have been possible for a different man, but it wouldn't play for Jeremy. 'I hear Gabriel Abbott has died and there's a rumour that the police have earmarked you as his father.' He tried the words out but they stuck in his mouth like dry pebbles. No, Frank Sinclair was not the way to go with this.

But he couldn't let it lie. Lives were going to be, at the very least, disrupted by what Felicity had revealed that morning. He had a duty, surely, to deliver a warning?

A decision finally arrived at, Jeremy lifted the phone.

32

TAP had hung on to the old-fashioned Soho shop frontage, its only concession to hip modernity being the matt black paintwork and the spartan smokers' bench outside. Karen peered through the window before she ventured inside. She approved of the clean lines, the simple wooden tables. She was less sure about the benches. She liked a back to her chair when she was relaxing over a coffee. Not everyone wanted to be doing pilates all the time.

The coffee shop was busy and its long skinny layout made it hard to see whether the Grassies had already arrived. She was going to have to go in to be sure. And if they weren't there, she could try to snag a table, though from here that looked easier said than done.

But Karen was spared that problem for, as she neared the coffee counter, she could see Craig and Shirley. They looked exactly the same as when she'd last seen them. Anonymous casual clothing you'd forget the minute you were out of their company. Craig with his lugubrious long face like a depressed Shetland pony, big luminous eyes beaming out like head-lamps from under his untidy fringe. Shirley the former nurse, who had never quite shed the expression of professional concern from a face that always made Karen think of a currant bun. Which wasn't fair, because there was nothing mean or tight about Shirley.

They were obviously looking out for her and both waved as they caught sight of her. She wove through knots of chattering people and slipped as elegantly as she could manage on to the bench. 'Wow, this place is jumping,' she said.

'The coffee's lovely,' Shirley said. 'When we grew up we thought Gold Blend was the height of sophistication. But it's like gay rights. We've come an amazing distance in the last ten or fifteen years.'

'I don't think those two things are actually connected,' Craig said, reminding Karen that his routine delivery was so deadpan she could never be quite certain when he was serious. 'It's nice to see you again, Detective.'

'Please, call me Karen. This is completely unofficial, I don't want you to think I'm pulling rank or anything.'

Shirley smiled. 'Either way, it's nice to see you again. Now, what will you drink?'

They negotiated the complexities of the coffee menu then Karen took a deep breath and dived in. 'I suffer from insomnia and I walk around the city a lot at night,' she began. As succinctly as she could, she described her encounters with the Syrian men and explained the particular problem she'd discovered. 'All they want is somewhere they can sit around and talk. Relax, like we're doing right now, right here. We've got countless places we can go and really, they've got nowhere.'

Craig and Shirley had both been nodding supportively throughout. Now Craig stirred his half-empty cup pensively and said, 'I'm assuming you have a suggestion? That you're not just bending my ear because you want to get it off your chest?'

'I wouldn't waste your time like that.'

'We know that,' Shirley said. 'But he's an MP, sometimes he has to speak to hear the sound of his own voice.' They shared a conspiratorial smile. It was clearly not the first time she had teased him with this.

'There's a lot of boarded-up shops and cafés in that part of town,' Karen said. 'Some of them have been standing empty for years. It must be obvious to the landlords – and the council too – that the economic upswing isn't happening. At least not in Restalrig and the top end of Leith, away from your Michelin-starred restaurants and the royal yacht. Why not give the Syrians a place rent-free so they can set up a wee café? A social enterprise. Any profits get ploughed back into the business. Like the Goths we used to have in Fife.'

'Goths? In Fife?' Shirley was from Cumbernauld, in the west. Karen forgave her for knowing no better.

But Craig knew what she was talking about. 'Pubs, Shirley. Run on what was called the Gothenburg system. They were owned by the community and any profits went back to the community for welfare and improvements to the environment. Quite a few of the mining villages had them. They took matters into their own hands because they refused to be gouged by the breweries and the landlords and their employers. So, Karen, you envisage a café run by the Syrians like a Goth?'

'By them but not only for them,' she said. 'Anyone could go in. Like Punjabi Junction on Leith Walk. I often get my lunch there. But primarily it would be a place they could meet and talk. Break their isolation. Get out the house, especially the women. These people have got the skills, no question. One of the guys I've met, Miran, he used to run a café back in Homs. And I'm sure the women can cook too.'

'As an idea, it has a lot to commend it.' The politician's answer. But Craig seemed willing to go beyond that. 'So what are you wanting from me?'

'They don't know where to start to go about sorting something like this. And frankly, neither do I. I'm a polis, not a social worker. I don't know the highways and byways of bureaucracy. They just need a start, a push in the right direction.' She paused. 'I wouldn't like to see them having to resort to squatting somewhere, if you take my meaning?'

Craig grinned. 'I take your meaning, Karen. Obviously, that would be something you couldn't connive at, you being an upstanding upholder of the law. But it would be unfortunate if that was the route they had to go down.'

'And a real shame,' Shirley chipped in. 'Those boarded-up shopfronts are a shocking eyesore. They must really put off potential residents and business people. It's not pleasant to walk down some of those streets. It's got to be better to have some sort of enterprise going on there, to make the place look like there's a bit of life about it. It's in everybody's interest, Craig.'

'I can see that, Shirley. In many ways, it's a no-brainer. The quicker we embed the refugees in civic society, the better the long-term outlook for them. There are good reasons why they're not allowed to work until they're formally settled here, but that shouldn't stop them being able to use their skills for the benefit of their community.' He caught himself and had the grace to look embarrassed. 'Sorry, that was a politician's answer. Look, Karen, I think this is a bloody good idea. I know very little more than you do about the mechanics of sorting out something like this, but we've got people in the party that should know how we go about it. If you give me the contact details for your guys, I'll see what I can do to get the ball rolling.'

Karen gave a wry chuckle. 'I don't have their contact details. I don't think "under the bridge on the Restalrig Railway Path after midnight" counts. But I'll get them and pass them on. Thanks, Craig.'

He shook his head. 'Wait till I've done something. Then thank me.'

'I'll hold you to that,' Karen said.

'We both will, Karen,' Shirley said. 'Now, tell me how you're getting on.' Karen's heart sank. Was the price of help going to be talking yet again about what it felt like to lose the man you loved to a murderer? But she realised almost immediately that she'd misjudged Shirley. 'How are things settling down at Police Scotland? Are you all getting used to the new set-up?' she continued.

Karen could have kissed her. They must have known about Phil, but they had no desire to watch her pick the scab. 'Well,' she said. 'It's got its pluses and minuses.' Craig Grassie wasn't the only one who could give a politician's answer.

33

Detective Inspector Alan Noble read the pathologist's report one last time, trying to look at it with the critical eye of a reader committed to finding fault with the conclusions. It was true that there was some room for doubt about the circumstances of Gabriel Abbott's death. But suicide was physically possible. The amount of gunshot residue on his hand wasn't conclusive, but it wasn't inconsistent with him having fired the shot. And the burn marks on his temple indicated that the gun barrel had been pressed against his head. So if it had been murder, his killer had been up close and personal. Either someone had crept up on him unawares or he'd known his killer. In the dark, all things were possible.

Noble wasn't the most assiduous of investigators but he knew better than to rely on a pathologist coming down on one side of a fifty-fifty call. He'd already been back through the reports from his detectives and the uniforms he'd corralled into doing the nuts-and-bolts interviews. According to the barman and a handful of other regulars in the pub where Gabriel Abbott drank, there had been nothing out of the ordinary that evening. Abbott had had two or possibly three pints. He'd been sitting at the bar in his usual seat, blethering to another one of the locals about some political stooshie in South East Asia. Apparently that was par for the course with him. He was obsessed with it in the way that some men were obsessed with a particular football team. The conversation had moved on to Donald Trump, then Abbott had left on his own.

The pub car park had CCTV footage. Just after 10 p.m., it was possible to make out Abbott emerging from the side door. He crossed the car park, paused on the street for a couple of minutes, then turned on to Kirkgate. There was no sign of anyone following him either by car or on foot. And there were no further cameras that might have picked him up before he turned on to the Loch Leven Heritage Trail path towards home. That wasn't to say he hadn't been followed at a discreet distance by someone who was familiar with his habits. But there was no evidence of it.

The crime scene itself was also innocent of anything that pointed to a third party having attacked Abbott. It was a viewpoint bench on a public trail. Of course there were traces of other people's presence – a few cigarette butts, sweet wrappers, a discarded coffee carton. But there was nothing to connect them specifically to the dead man. There were no signs of a struggle, no handy footprints or torn fabric snagged on a loose nail on the bench. Nothing remotely Sherlockian. Absent any other evidence, the logical way to go was to assume this was what it looked like – a suicide made slightly more complicated by a man who had, by all accounts, been more or less perpetually off-kilter.

Suicide, then. No further action needed on his part, not unless something changed dramatically. He'd wait a couple of hours before he signed off on it. There was no need to be too bloody eager on a Monday morning. A quick look round the room told him there were plenty of warm bodies to hold the fort. He'd nip out and get himself a second breakfast at Kitty's Kitchen while nobody was looking. Black pudding, square sliced sausage, baked beans and two fried eggs. All the things the second Mrs Noble forbade.

He'd got one arm in his jacket when his phone rang. 'Detective Inspector Noble,' he said, giving every syllable due weight.

'This is Will Abbott.' The voice was clipped and tense.

Noble rolled his eyes and fell back into his chair. Bloody relatives. Always something. 'Good morning, Mr Abbott. I was just looking at your brother's file.' Make them feel important, whether it was the truth or not. 'How can I help you?'

'You told me you were almost done with your investigation into my brother's death.'

'We are.'

'And you told me you thought suicide was the most likely cause of death.' The accusatory note in his voice was rising.

'That's right. This morning I can go further. Our investigations show nothing that contradicts the view that your brother took his own life.' Noble dropped his voice to show sympathy. You had to make the effort.

'So why have you had a detective down here in London asking questions about my brother? And our mother? You do know our mother was murdered twenty-two years ago, right? What the fuck does that have to do with my brother killing himself?' Will Abbott was almost stuttering with anger.

'I'm sorry, sir, but I've no idea what you're talking about.' Noble cut across the words tumbling into his ear. He needed to defuse this and fast. 'None of my team is in London. And we certainly haven't sought assistance from the Metropolitan Police.'

'She's not from the Met. She's from Police Scotland. Are you seriously trying to tell me you know nothing about this? One of your cops is waltzing around London asking questions about my family and you don't know anything about it? You might get away with that kind of bullshit with your local lowlife criminals, but you're not getting it past me. What the *fuck* is going on?'

Noble was starting to feel decidedly uneasy. The combination of a female officer and an ancient case was pointing in a very particular direction. One that might spell trouble. 'What exactly has happened, sir?' Play for time, slow it down, take it off the heat.

'I told you. One of your officers is going round stirring up my family's history. My mother's murder. Do you have any idea how upsetting this is? I've lost my brother. I'm grieving. And you've sent someone down here to stir things up about my mother's death? A case that was closed all those years ago. Have you no understanding of what it means to lose your family?'

'I appreciate that you're upset, Mr Abbott. But can you give me some details?'

Noble heard the sound of a sharply indrawn breath. 'What? You don't know what your own people are doing?'

'As I said, this is not one of my officers. Let's try to get to the bottom of this, eh? Maybe you can tell me what you know?'

'Yesterday, this officer turned up at the house of a family friend. You've probably heard of her – Felicity Frye, the actress?'

Noble had heard of her. His heart sank a little further because he remembered the second Mrs Noble pointing the actress out on breakfast TV a few weeks before, revealing that she had terminal cancer. What in the name of God was Karen Pirie – because it had to be Karen Pirie – doing, harassing a dying woman over a more or less open-and-shut suicide that had nothing to do with her? 'I know the name, yes,' he said, keeping his voice as neutral as possible.

'And did you also know that she's only got months to live? She's got pancreatic cancer and she's dying. And your colleague' – he made it sound like a swear word – 'interrogated her about my brother's death and used that as an excuse to dig up all sorts of gossip about my mother. What the hell business is it of hers?' Anger had reduced Abbott to a squeak.

'Do you know this officer's name?'

The rustle of paper. 'Detective Chief Inspector Karen Pirie,' he snarled. 'I've had Felicity Frye's husband on the phone complaining about this. As if it's my responsibility. As if somehow I've brought this shocking aggravation to his door. This is an outrage.'

'I understand you're very unhappy, Mr Abbott. Like I said, DCI Pirie isn't on my team. She runs the Historic Cases Unit. She must be taking an interest in your mother's murder. Nobody was ever charged with that, were they?'

Abbott made an angry sound. 'It's not like it was a mystery. Everybody knew it was the IRA or another one of those mad Irish Republican terrorist groups. It wasn't exactly rocket science to work that out. So why the *fuck* is this woman harassing a sick woman about something that we all know the answer to? How dare she?' He ran out of breath, dragging in air as if he was suffocating.

'I'm sorry,' Noble said, not entirely meaning it. 'If you'd like, I'll bring it to the attention of DCI Pirie's senior officer? And perhaps I can have him give you a call?'

'That would be fine if it was just me that was affected by this. But poor, dear Felicity . . . She's not well. And perhaps her judgement isn't quite what it should be.' There was a pause. Noble stayed quiet, waiting. He was rewarded at a level he couldn't have imagined. A deep breath at the other end of the phone, then Abbott said, 'The thing is, Felicity dragged someone else into the picture. Somebody who's got nothing to do with anything. But he's the sort of person that, if his name got out, it would cause an absolute shitstorm.'

'I'm not really following you,' Noble said. 'You're going to have to be a wee bit less opaque.'

'Oh, Christ. Look, my mother lied about the identity of Gabe's father. My father, Tom Abbott, was already dead when she became pregnant with Gabe. She lied about it because it was easier than having to answer questions about who his father actually was. There's nothing sinister about it, I've known for years. Caroline left me a letter, the lawyer gave it to me when I was twenty-one. But it was private. Family business. Nothing to do with anyone else. And Felicity Frye told all this to this Pirie woman. But she didn't stop there. Felicity's got this weird fixation that Gabe's biological father was Frank Sinclair.'

That was a name to stop the traffic. Noble didn't know what to say.

'You know who I'm talking about? Lord Sinclair. The media baron.'

'The one who's always going on about family values and family life?'

'The one who's made a career out of casting the first bloody stone,' Abbott said. 'More upright than the bloody Archbishop of Canterbury. I can't bring out a bloody console game without him and his minions predicting the end of the world – and he's a family friend, for fuck's sake. God help his enemies. Can you imagine his reaction if a stupid rumour like this starts going the rounds? He'll go off the Richter scale.'

Noble allowed himself a moment of *Schadenfreude*. 'I can see why you're upset,' he said smoothly. 'And I honestly think the best think I can do for you is to get DCI Pirie's boss to speak to you. Assistant Chief Constable Simon Lees, that would be. What I'm going to do as soon as I've finished speaking to you, I'm going to speak directly to ACC Lees and explain what's happened. Obviously, he'll have to speak to DCI Pirie to see what she's got to say about this. But I know he'll be eager to talk to you as soon as he has a clear picture of how we got here. For now, all I can do is apologise for the upset you've experienced.'

A sharp sigh. 'That'll just have to do, won't it?' Abbott snapped. But Noble sensed capitulation. They went back and forth a little longer, then ended on calmer water than they'd begun. Noble tucked his phone into his pocket and headed for the door. He wanted to make the most of this call, and he wanted to conduct it out of reach of the flapping ears of his colleagues.

Karen Pirie, to his perpetual surprise, had friends in Police Scotland, particularly in her native Fife. He wanted her to have no warning of what was coming at her. He hadn't let Will Abbott hear it, but he was furious. How dare Karen Pirie come rushing to judgement on one of his cases; a case she knew nothing about except what her arrogance told her; a case she had no right to stick her nose into. She'd never made any effort to hide her opinion of him. She thought he was lazy and that he cut corners. Just because he'd never seen the point of knocking your pan in on cases that were going nowhere. Well, now the wheel had turned and it was her feet that were about to be held to the fire. The Macaroon wasn't the only one who would enjoy it.

34

K aren knew she should have headed home on the Sunday-night sleeper, but she'd kissed goodbye to her better judgement on Friday night and it wasn't showing any sign of coming back yet. As she'd explained in her head to Phil on her way back through Covent Garden after hanging out with the Grassies, there was something about this cold-case-that-wasn't-her-case that had its hooks in her and wouldn't let go. She was breaking all the rules – not a single bit of her cock-eyed investigation had a shred of corroboration, for starters – but she couldn't shake loose the conviction that this was important and, if she didn't pursue it, nobody else would.

Phil would have shaken his head in exasperation and told her she was her own worst enemy. He'd have pointed out that all she would achieve in the long run was to create even worse feelings between her and the Macaroon. And she'd have responded that, in her world, that was a bonus. He'd have reminded her that working outside the straitjacket of the rules was the best way to make sure the case would never stand on its own two feet, and she'd have reminded him that, as things were, there was no case to stand or fall, so how could she be making things worse?

At that point, a child she'd passed in the street had strained at her parental hand, leaning back and staring at Karen wide-eyed as she beasted past, deep in conversation with herself. Karen had whirled round, walking backwards, met the child's astonished stare and said, 'Just because you can't see him doesn't mean he isn't there.'

As she swung round and continued on her way, she wondered if she was actually cracking up. Was this PTSD? Heaven knew she'd had enough trauma and stress in the past year to last a lifetime. But she didn't feel she was spinning out of control. The insomnia, the talking to Phil, the obsessions with things that were outside her remit – these were all things she was taking in her stride. People who knew her weren't acting like she'd lost it. Not her parents, not her friends, not Jason.

She was fine. Maybe a bit more driven than usual. So instead of heading back to Euston and finding somewhere to eat before she caught the train, she checked back into the hotel – 'Yes, still no luggage' – and texted Jason:

Taking day off tomorrow. Will be back in office Tuesday. Keep checking Tina McDonald statements. Think I've sorted your flatmate problem. Don't worry about it.

And then she'd sat down with her laptop to figure out how she was going to do the very thing she'd told Felicity only happened in fiction.

Which was why Monday morning found Karen heading down Tottenham Court Road, face turned up towards the sunshine that warmed her bones. She'd picked up a new shirt and underwear in the Marks & Spencer on Long Acre the day before, she was showered and caffeinated and all set to break more rules.

She stopped at a coffee shop and bought a flat white. She asked the barista for a paper bag and didn't demur when he charged her 5p for it. She folded it and put it in her pocket along with a few napkins. Now she was all set.

Back into the sunshine and on past the stores selling stylish interior fantasies; past the cheap electronic shops, their windows stuffed with things whose functions she didn't understand; round the hoardings that hid the new station; past storefronts filled with books and guitars and the quirky crap people fill their flat surfaces with; past theatres and galleries and down into the heart of Westminster.

At last, she came to the river. On one side of the street, the iconic Houses of Parliament. On the other, Portcullis House, the custom-built modern building containing offices for MPs, meeting rooms and committee rooms. Where, this morning in the Boothroyd Room, the Lords Select Communications Committee would be sitting.

When she'd discovered this, Karen had felt it was a portent. Really, she was destined to do this absurd thing that was dancing on the edge of her peripheral vision. And since her better judgement was still in a state of suspension, she walked into Portcullis House with the confident air of a woman in possession of valid police identification who has no expectation of being hindered in the pursuit of a chimera.

The Macaroon sat in the back of his official car, warring emotions surging through him. There was fury that Karen Pirie had overstepped the mark so thoroughly that she had embarrassed and undermined him in front of the lower ranks. What did it say about him that an officer in his command thought it was acceptable to ride roughshod over protocol and trample all over someone else's case?

But there was also a grim delight, and for the same reason. She had gone too far this time. There was no possible hiding place for her. Not only was Gabriel Abbott's death not her case, it wasn't even a historic case. Abbott was barely cold, never mind the inquiry into his death. For that loose cannon Pirie to treat it as an excuse to exhume a long-buried case that was only technically unsolved was egregious. (A word he'd learned from his clever daughter and seldom had the opportunity to use.) It would be bad enough in any circumstances, but when it also involved slinging muck at a peer of the realm – and one as vociferous and litigious as Lord Sinclair – it beggared belief.

No, this was the end of the road for Karen Pirie at Historic Cases. First there had been the series of leaks and now this. And this was the perfect time to do it. Her shield had always been the level of media joy that her frequent successes provoked. She was never out of the tabloids, generally associated with families gushing thanks that they finally knew what had happened to their loved ones, or victims weeping with joy that assailants they'd thought were free and clear were finally paying for their crimes. But it had been a few months since Karen had chalked up a prominent success and, in media terms, that corresponded to a geological era. She was yesterday's chip papers. Really, the only question was how far down the ranks he could bust her.

Lees caught himself rubbing his hands together in delight and laid his palms flat on his thighs. Oh, he was going to enjoy this. He rehearsed his opening as the black BMW swung into Gayfield Square and pulled up outside the police station. He was so eager that he didn't wait for his driver to open the door but rather sprang out of the car, straightening his uniform cap and making for the door.

He loved the way that everyone snapped to life when he walked into a police station. It was as if his very presence was a tiny electric shock to their synapses. The big man is in the building. He'd always dreamed of this, and now, apart from those self-styled mavericks like Pirie, everyone gave him his due.

'The HCU?' he barked at the civilian at the reception counter.

'Through the door, turn right at the end of the hall, all the way back,' she stammered, pressing the door release that allowed him access to the guts of the station. He marched down the hall, shoulders back, stomach sucked in, his cheeks pink with the anger that was driving him like a hydrogen fuel cell. Two women detectives flattened themselves against the wall as he neared them, so determined was his approach. With every step, he could feel the pressure building, the pressure he was going to release so eloquently so very, very soon.

He didn't bother knocking on the HCU door, simply threw it open and stood framed in the doorway. The ginger idiot that Pirie remained bafflingly loyal towards was so shocked his bacon roll flew into the air, deconstructing itself into its component parts as it fell. DC Murray jerked to his feet, backing away from his desk, stumbling as the back of his knees caught his chair.

Lees scanned the room, bestowing a look of contempt on Murray as his eyes skimmed over him. 'Where is she?' he demanded.

'Day off,' Murray croaked. 'Sir,' as an afterthought.

'I didn't ask you that,' Lees said, low and hard. 'I asked you where DCI Pirie is.'

'London? She went down for the weekend.'

'And that's all you know? You don't know where she is or what she's doing in London?'

The idiot looked close to tears. 'She never said. Just, a weekend away.'

'Did she tell you what she's working on?'

His eyes flicked to his screen. 'We're working on Tina McDonald. Waiting to hear if we're gonnae get Ross Garvie's birth certificate. I'm going through the statements.' His words tumbled over each other in his eagerness to please.

'The other thing. What about that?'

'What other thing?' The idiot was in a state of panic. But Lees thought it was the panic of ignorance rather than secrecy.

'Never mind. When is she due back?'

'Tomorrow. She said tomorrow morning.' He swallowed hard, his Adam's apple bobbing and his eyes wide.

'And you're not working on anything else?'

Murray shook his head rapidly. 'Well, routine stuff. Waiting for lab analysis of old evidence to see if there's anywhere to go with it. But they're still dormant cases. We're not doing anything active with them, like.' The tip of his tongue ran along his lips.

Lees turned on his heel and strode back down the hall, not bothering to close the door behind him. Back in the car, he called Karen Pirie's mobile. When it went to voicemail, as he had confidently expected, he said, 'This is Assistant Chief Constable Lees. I have just been to your office, where you are not. I require that you speak to me as soon as you get this message. And until we speak face-to-face, I am ordering you to back off from your so-called investigation into the suicide of Gabriel Abbott. Do not delay in responding to this message, DCI Pirie. And that's an order too.' He stabbed a finger at the phone to end the call and leaned back in his leather seat. He was, in the words of their national bard, nursing his wrath to keep it warm. Whenever she deigned to get back to him, he could guarantee full volcanic heat.

He was almost glad she hadn't been in her office. Anticipation was such a sweet pleasure.

35

The Boothroyd Room, according to the cop who had walked her up there, was the flagship committee venue in Portcullis House. When the parliamentarians had voted themselves a new office block, they'd clearly chosen 'dress to impress' as their motto. The building itself was stunning – a vast atrium of polished stone, glass and steel, as light as the sky allowed, saved from sterility by trees planted up the middle. It spoke of wealth and power. Karen thought it would be one of the most spectacular modern buildings most of its visitors had ever been in. Unless they'd also been to the insanely expensive Scottish Parliament. Politicians clearly understood the benefits of a workplace that had aesthetic values. A pity they didn't extend the principle to most of the spaces where public servants spent their working lives. She wondered how long their leaders would last in the cupboard she shared with Jason and the perpetual fragrance of Greggs baked goods.

Her escort delivered her to one of the best seats in the room with a clear view of the dozen chairs set behind the horse-shoe of blond wood that faced a long table where, presumably, the witnesses sat. Behind that were rows of comfortable office-style chairs with leather upholstery in an indeterminate shade lurking between grey, turquoise and aquamarine. 'There you go, ma'am,' he said politely. 'We let the rest of the public in about ten minutes before the committee starts. It's first come, first served, but with you being one of us, well, it doesn't hurt to give you a leg up.'

'Thanks,' Karen said. 'If you're ever in Edinburgh, I'll return the favour.' She hadn't had to make up an excuse for wanting to sit in on the select committee. The security detail had been happy with her ID and her vague line about wanting to check out one of the committee members. And shortly she'd be a few metres away from Lord Sinclair, the alleged provider of the sperm Caroline Abbott had impregnated herself with. Not that she'd be asking about that.

The PC had directed her to a seat in the middle of the front row, but Karen decided she wanted to be a little more inconspicuous. She chose a seat at the end of the second row by the window where she could watch the river traffic when things grew too dull. She was fairly confident that would happen. But compared to some of the places where she'd had to stake out what Lees always referred to as 'persons of interest', this had much to recommend it. The chair and the temperature were comfortable, the tapestry on the far wall – a stylised scene of trees and either fields or a river – was stitched in restful blue tones and the bust of Baroness Boothroyd was a lot less forbidding than many of the portraits they'd passed on the way to the committee room.

Karen took out her notebook and pen in a bid to look as if she had some reason to be there. A few minutes later, the door opened again and an ill-assorted group of people filed in. A handful were obviously journalists, huddling together at one side of the room, chattering with the easy familiarity of comrades if not colleagues. Some looked like students of the political wonk persuasion. A couple of hipsters; wannabe journalists, Karen guessed. A trio of jolly young Muslim women in hijabs who kept nudging each other and grinning. A scatter of the retired, keeping their minds active and their opinions under scrutiny. As the audience settled around her, the committee's administrative support trickled in, sorting out bundles of paper and chattering to each other in the easy way of people for whom this was just another day.

Next to arrive was the Canadian media mogul and his entourage, who spread themselves along the witness table, his importance obvious by the sheer numbers necessary to bolster his presence.

And finally, the committee members themselves. A dozen working peers – seven men, five women – who didn't look particularly grand. Smart, well-groomed and attentive, but none of them would have been out of place in a boardroom or on the committee of a charity. The great and the good, Karen thought. They don't look so different from us. They could almost pass.

She recognised Frank Sinclair from the images she'd studied online. In his mid sixties, he looked fit and healthy. His hair, once sandy, was greying and coarse, his skin pale and heavily lined. But his jawline was still taut and his deep-set blue eyes were never still, always scanning the room and his fellow peers. He would look at his papers for a few moments, a frown line between his bushy eyebrows, make a note with a fat Mont Blanc pen, then check out the room again. Karen had no idea how closely he resembled Gabriel Abbott. She'd only seen a couple of photographs of the dead man and that provided no real comparison. She wished she'd been able to ask Noble for a set of post-mortem pics.

The business was quickly under way and Karen soon lost the will to live. Things seemed to move at a snail's pace and she could only bear to listen when Frank Sinclair spoke and then only because she felt she ought to. She gathered that he was greatly in favour of personal privacy except when those concerned were behaving in ways that he disapproved of. Anything immoral, illegal or unethical stripped out the guilty parties' rights and rendered them fair game for the media, in his book. Given the tightness of his own moral straitjacket, Karen reckoned that meant most of the population was fair game. She was thankful to realise that his was not the prevailing view of the room.

Two hours dragged past interminably. It was hard for Karen to imagine Sinclair fitting into the sociable and louche world of theatre and TV that Caroline and Ellie had moved in. She knew that most people grew more conservative as they aged, but he must have shifted quite a distance. Perhaps his guilt at what he'd done for Caroline had kicked in afterwards and provoked an extreme reaction. Or maybe they'd just kept him around as a kind of curiosity, a dinosaur counterpoint to their lifestyle. And for him, their way of life would have been a sort of whetstone on which he could hone his sharp-edged morality.

Eventually, things drew to a close. The lords and ladies stood up, gathering their papers together. Karen hung back as the audience dawdled out and studied her phone as the support staff mingled with their bosses, chatting and handing over pieces of paper. There was a small huddle around the middle of the horseshoe, Frank Sinclair at the heart of it. He'd been sitting near the end of the table on the opposite side of the room and Karen ambled over to his place, deserted now. She looked around. Nobody was paying attention to her. Everyone was focused on leaving or on the conversation in the middle of the room or on making sure the tycoon had left nothing incriminating in his wake.

Casually, she took out the napkins from the coffee shop and, in a swift arc of movement, swept up Frank Sinclair's glass and tucked it in her pocket. Then she walked confidently out of the room and headed for the nearest toilet. Safe in the cubicle, Karen dropped the glass into the paper bag and deposited it carefully at the bottom of her handbag. She didn't want to be stopped on her way out for nicking a Portcullis House tumbler.

And breathe, she told herself. She'd done something so ridiculous she'd never be able to admit it to any of her colleagues and she'd apparently got away with it. It was madness. But it was noble cause madness.

What she hadn't realised was that she'd been spotted. Lord Sinclair had started his career as a sharply observant journalist. He hadn't lost that gift of noticing. While most of his interest had been on the people who'd come up to him with questions and comments, there had been a sliver of his attention on whatever else was going on around him. He'd caught sight of Karen out of the corner of his eye and followed her movements while he dealt with everyone else on automatic pilot, struggling not to show his incredulity at what he was witnessing.

There was no doubt about it. Whoever the woman was, she'd pocketed his drinking glass and made off with it. There was only one possible reason why anyone would do such a thing.

A coldness bloomed in his chest. But he wasn't going to panic. He hadn't risen this far by freaking out when he was under threat. He politely excused himself and drew his assistant to one side. 'That woman who's just leaving? Follow her and find out who she is.'

The assistant, who was paid well for his unquestioning loyalty, left the room without a fuss. Sinclair watched him go, his brain ticking over a series of options. Everything from a watching brief to the nuclear option. Nobody stood in Frank Sinclair's light.

36

The train was pulling out of Kings Cross when Karen realised she'd forgotten to turn her phone back on after the Select Committee. She'd been so high after her larcenous adventure that everything else had slipped to the back burner. But as she let herself relax into her seat for the long haul back to Edinburgh, she thought to check for texts only to discover the phone was still off. She gave a small groan when it fired up and revealed she had five voicemails and half a dozen texts.

The first voicemail was from the Macaroon. Then two from the Mint. Then one from a number she didn't recognise. And finally, one from Giorsal. The texts were all from the Mint. The first one asked her to call him. So did the other five, with increasing levels of urgency. The wheels had clearly come off something, but that didn't narrow it down.

Sighing, Karen took herself down to the vestibule at the end of the carriage so she wouldn't disturb her fellow passengers by swearing at the phone. Wrinkling her nose at the weird air freshener that smelled anything but fresh, she summoned the Macaroon's message in the hope of enlightenment. His tinny voice was a snappy snarl. 'This is Assistant Chief Constable Lees. I have just been to your office, where you are not. I require that you speak to me as soon as you get this message. And until we speak face-to-face, I am ordering you to back off from your so-called investigation into the suicide of Gabriel Abbott. Do not delay in responding to this message, DCI Pirie. And that's an order too.'

Ah. Well, that was enlightenment, of a sort. What she didn't know yet was how the Macaroon knew what she was up to, and how serious the situation was. He was pompous enough to be this put out by the simple act of Karen asking Alan Noble what investigative steps he was taking. And she suspected Noble was enough of a teacher's pet to have dropped her in it with the Macaroon. Everybody knew how much he hated Karen and how much he'd enjoy having something on her.

On the other hand, it might be a lot more serious than that. Whatever it was, she wasn't going to deal with it on a train. Not with the twin perils of phone signals cutting out and the prospect of being overheard. This was one to deal with on her own terms, at a time and place of her own choosing. Ideally, when she had a better sense of how deep in the shit she was.

Jason's first message was anxious. 'Hey, boss, it's me. The chief's on the warpath,' he said. 'Thought I better let you know. I said you were having a day off, I hope I didn't say the wrong thing? Anyway, I thought I better let you know, eh?' His second voicemail said much the same, except with the additional news that the Macaroon's secretary had been on, telling him to leave a message for DCI Pirie to come to the ACC's office first thing in the morning. 'She said she was going to email you, like, but she wanted to make sure you got the message. So, I'm passing it on. She sounded really pissed off, by the way, boss.'

Ramping up the pressure, Karen thought. If the Macaroon

had any notion of how to manage his officers, he'd have worked out that Karen didn't let herself be bullied. She'd got past that at school. She never backed down when the bitchy teenage cliques occasionally turned on her. She wasn't verbally quick like Giorsal, but she'd stood her ground and given them that same stubborn hard-eyed stare that drove the Macaroon to distraction. She never let the bullies see the hurt inside. Not then, not now.

The number she hadn't recognised turned out to belong to Alan Noble and it answered more of her questions. 'This is DI Noble. What are you playing at, Karen? I've just had Gabriel Abbott's brother on the phone. He's furious because you've been down in London nosing into him and his family. After I'd told him that it was pretty much a certainty that his brother was a suicide. You had no business sticking your nose in my case in the first place, but you totally overstepped the mark here. You need to stay away from other people's cases and not go about making unsupported statements that make your fellow officers look like numpties. I'm taking this up the line. I'm not putting up with this.'

Ouch. So, somebody had grassed her up to the brother. Karen suspected it had come from Jumpin' Jack Ash. She hadn't been inclined to invest much trust in him. There had obviously been stuff he hadn't wanted to tell her – perhaps some of the things she'd learned from Felicity Frye – and he'd gone running to warn Will Abbott that she was stirring the pot. Interesting that Abbott's first reaction had not been to wonder whether there were new leads in respect of his mother's death. Instead, he'd kicked off to Noble. Who had realised marginally too late that he ought to level with Karen about going to the Macaroon. She wasn't sure whether he was weak, careerist or plain stupid.

If somebody really was trying to pass off murder as suicide, they'd dropped lucky, getting Noble for the SIO.

The final voicemail was from Giorsal. 'Hey, girl. I've had the unlovely Alan Noble on with his panties in a twist. He's told me not to tell you anything about the Gabriel Abbott case. Like he's my boss or something. So, when did you want me to set up that meeting with Ian Lesley? I'm guessing we might need to aim outside office hours? Give me a bell when you know what's what.' Karen couldn't help smiling. The system hadn't ground Giorsal down in the slightest. And now she was making good on her offer to sit Karen down with Gabriel Abbott's social worker. Who better to fill her in on what was going on in the dead man's life? What was it Phil used to say? 'When life gives you lemons, make a gin and tonic.'

Thinking of Phil reminded her that it was Monday and the way things were going, she'd better cancel her Monday evening session with Jimmy Hutton. It wasn't the first time work had got in the way, but she still regretted having to do it. She sent him a text, promising to be in touch later in the week.

She went back to her seat, confident she could weather whatever was waiting for her back in Edinburgh. The only outstanding matter was the tumbler in the bottom of her handbag. Luckily, it was Monday. She did a quick calculation in her head. The person she needed to see would be changing trains at Haymarket around quarter past eight. That gave her plenty of time to deal with the one thing she needed to do in Edinburgh that night and still make a rendezvous on a windy platform. She sent a text, making the arrangement, then settled back with the latest Lee Child. Nothing like a bit of escapist fantasy to make the miles go faster.

Two chapters in and her phone started vibrating. Impatient, she checked the screen. No way was she going to randomly answer her phone on a day like this. But as soon as she registered the caller, she knew this was one she'd have to take.

She jumped up and hurried back to the vestibule, picking up the call as she went.

'DCI Pirie?' Even a poor mobile signal couldn't strip the plums from Colin Semple's voice.

'Mr Semple. Good to hear from you. At least, I hope it's good?'

'More good than bad,' he said. 'Where are you?'

'I'm on a train, heading back to Edinburgh from London.'

'In that case, it will be tomorrow before you can move on this. Sheriff Abercrombie has clearly decided that Ross Garvie is not going to oblige us with a quick quietus and so she has delivered her judgement. She has agreed that you should have access to Garvie's original birth certificate. None of the associated papers, I'm afraid. Only the bare bones.'

Karen felt a swell of excitement. At last, they could move forward on the Tina McDonald investigation. That terrible period of marking time was over and the real detective work could begin. 'That's great,' she said. 'So what do I do?'

'You need to pick up a copy of the sheriff's order from the court. If your lad is at a loose end this afternoon, he's probably just got time to get up there and collect it before they shut up shop. Then once you've got that, you need to go to General Register House – you know, on Princes Street, opposite the Balmoral? And someone there will furnish you with a copy of Garvie's birth certificate. And then it's up to you, Chief Inspector.'

'Thanks for letting me know. And thanks for doing such a great job for us.'

'It's what you pay me for,' he said, his voice warm with satisfaction. 'Good luck, Chief Inspector.'

Karen leaned against the cool train window, eyes closed momentarily. She loved nothing more than the chase, and now it was beginning in earnest. She sent a quick text to Jason: Sheriff says yes to birth certificate. Put your coat on and pick up the order from the Sheriff Court Office before close of business. See you in the morning. The game's afoot! Perfect that he had something concrete to do that would take his mind off the Macaroon on the rampage.

She could go back to Lee Child now with a clear con- science, completely unaware of the young man halfway down the carriage who hadn't stopped watching her since they'd boarded the train.

37

I t was raining when the train arrived in Edinburgh, stinging bullets of sleet carried on whips of wind that made Karen's face hurt. To hell with the bus, she was going to splash out on a taxi. This was one occasion where she was determined to show not a trace of vulnerability. The taxi rattled over cobbled streets, across the Canongate and up the Pleasance, the wipers barely managing to slap the windscreen clear of water. 'Hellish night,' the driver offered.

Not as hellish as it was about to get for somebody else, Karen thought. 'Aye,' she said.

The traffic was heavy, but the taxi driver was savvy enough to avoid the worst of it. Karen ran from the cab to the door of the Marchmont tenement, huddling in its lee as she pressed the buzzer for the third-floor flat. A garbled male voice answered. 'Hello?'

'Delivery for you,' she said. The door buzzed. These days, with everybody doing their shopping online, nobody living in a shared flat would bother to check the recipient's name.

Karen climbed steadily to the third floor. Not so long ago, she'd have struggled with the steps, but the combination of night walking and weight loss meant that a new level of fitness had sneaked up on her. She deplored the reason but had to admit she appreciated the result. She rounded the final turn of the stone stairs, coming face-to-face with a young man leaning negligently against the jamb of the outer pair of tall wooden doors. Bare feet, skinny jeans on skinny legs, grey shirt buttoned to the neck, straggly hipster beard and a wee frown. 'Where's the parcel?' he demanded. Voice cocky, posh, English; expression haughty.

'You Liam?'

'Does it matter? You said you had a delivery. And you don't.' He pushed off, reaching behind for the knob of the inner half-glass door. 'So goodbye.'

Karen moved quickly, hard up against the outer doors, ID in her hand then in his face. 'I am Detective Chief Inspector Karen Pirie.'

'Oh,' he said, a long drawn-out drawl. 'Why didn't you say? Jason talks about you all the time. If it's Jason you're after, he's not around right now.'

'As you are well aware, son, Jason doesn't live here any more.' She moved forward again, making him take a clumsy step backwards, yelping as he caught his elbow on the edge of the inner door. She grabbed the front of his shirt, ostensibly steadying him. 'Careful, son. Now, are you Liam or are you not?'

'I'm Liam. What of it?'

Now she pushed him away from her, releasing him to stumble sideways into the hall, banging into a narrow table covered in unopened junk mail. 'Ow. What the fuck? That was an assault.'

'Oh please,' she said, sarcasm extending her vowels. Again she moved forward, forcing him into a corner. 'Listen, you little fuck. And listen hard. Right now, I could arrest you for interfering with an ongoing police investigation. Perverting the course of justice, if I had a mind to. The university won't like that one little bit. Any thoughts you had of a career? Forget it. With a conviction like that, you'd be lucky to get a job as a barista. Even with the pitiful facial hair.' She reached out to tweak his beard but he flinched out of her way.

'I have no idea what you're talking about,' he gabbled, aiming for his previous supercilious air and missing by a shaky mile.

'Don't come the cowboy with me, son,' Karen snapped, making every word tight and hard. 'I know what you did. You and your smart-arsed pals pretended Jason was your friend. You'll have sniggered at him behind his back. Made fun of him to your patronising stuck-up mates. And then you betrayed him. You exploited a kind, decent, loyal guy. You wheedled stuff out of him. You made him feel important, but all the time, you were using him.'

His narrow face grew pinched. He half-shrugged with one shoulder. 'Nobody made him do anything.'

'Fair enough. And that would have been fine if you'd left it at that. Despicable, obnoxious, and treacherous, but in the great scheme of things, fine. But you pulled a real shit's trick. You broke his confidences and sold him out to the media.' Right in his face. She could feel the heat of his coffee breath on her cheeks.

'They'd have found out anyway,' he whined.

'No. They wouldn't. The stuff you leaked was sensitive. It could make the difference between a conviction and some vicious scumbag walking away to make some other poor sod's life a misery. And the way you did it? That's a criminal offence, son.'

'You're bluffing,' he said, trying to edge away from her. 'If it's such a big deal, arrest me.'

Karen let a slow smile spread across her face. 'Liam – what's your second name? Oh, fuck it, I'll find it out soon enough. Liam Wankstain, I'm arresting you. You are going to be asked questions about offences relating to perverting the course of justice. You are not bound to answer, but if you do your answers will be noted and may be used—'

'Wait! No, you can't do this.' Panic shaking his voice.

'—in evidence,' Karen continued, unperturbed. 'Do you understand?'

'Please,' he begged. 'I'm sorry. Please. I didn't mean to cause trouble. It was only a laugh.'

'And a few quid. And getting your name known as a reliable source with news editors.' She curled her lip scornfully and waited.

He hung his head. 'Yeah, that. I want to be a journalist.'

'Aye, well, you've already got the scummy morality for the job. Give me one good reason why I should let you walk away from this.'

He flashed a quick up-and-under look at her, sudden cunning in his eyes. 'Because if I go in the witness box it'll be the end of Jason's career?'

Karen gave a slow handclap. 'So it would be a win-win. You get the criminal record you deserve and I get a detective constable with half a brain.'

Liam's eyes widened. He looked shocked. 'You'd really let that happen?'

'It would be a kindness. And watching you twist in the wind would be a bonus.'

There was a long silence. 'Please,' he said finally. 'Please, don't destroy my future. And Jason's too.' He turned his head and stared at the floor. 'I've been a cunt.'

'Don't use that word as an insult. It offends me.'

He bit his lip. 'I'm sorry.'

Karen decided she was enjoying this too much. Her righteous rage had subsided, leaving her in the bully's chair. Time to recover her own sense of decency. 'You're going to write a letter to Jason detailing all the times you ratted him out to the media. A full list. You're going to apologise for what you did. You're going to enclose a receipt from a charity for the donation you're going to make tonight equivalent to the cash you got for this latest Tina McDonald story. If Jason doesn't get that letter delivered to the Gayfield Square police station by the day after tomorrow I'm coming back here to arrest you again. And this time, there'll be no backing down.'

The wretched relief in his face was pathetic. 'I didn't mean to cause trouble.'

'Save it for Jason, he might believe you.' She gave him a final push in the chest then backed out of the flat and clattered down the stairs. It was still raining when she hit the street, but it was only a few minutes' walk to the bus stop and she had a deep and abiding sense of satisfaction to keep her warm.

38

D r River Wilde hated Mondays. Not for the usual reasons. She loved her chosen calling, so work was never a hardship. It was the choices she'd made in pursuit of work that chafed. Until recently, she'd plied her trade as an anatomist and forensic anthropologist at the University of the North of England in Carlisle. But the department was small and, apart from her, undistinguished, and populated by senior academics on the gentle downward slope towards retirement. Waiting for dead men's shoes had little appeal for her and her appetite for change had been sharpened by the work she'd been doing for Police Scotland. Karen Pirie had been her initial contact north of the border, but increasingly she'd been approached by other SIOs who found themselves confronted with human remains that weren't immediately identifiable.

It made things easier all round if River did the work in a Scottish facility. She'd found herself regularly begging a spare desk at the University of Dundee, where they had infinitely better facilities than she had in Carlisle. Eventually, the prof at Dundee had bitten the bullet and offered her a permanent job at the university. Professionally, it was a no-brainer.

But personally? That was a different story. River lived in Keswick in the heart of the Lake District with her partner, Detective Chief Inspector Ewan Rigston. Even if his job had been as portable as hers, he was a Cumbrian born and bred and seriously doubted whether the air outside the Lakes was actually breathable for more than a couple of days at a time. There was no question of Ewan relocating to Dundee. Even with a view of water.

So now on Monday evenings, River said goodbye to the Lakes and took the train to Dundee, where she remained until Thursday night. She worked three long days in the mortuary and the lab, then wrote up her research on Mondays and Fridays. She loved the leap forward she'd made in terms of her achievements at work, but she hated leaving Ewan behind.

Sometimes she stopped off in Edinburgh for a couple of hours. There was a Vietnamese restaurant near Haymarket station where she and Karen would meet for a meal. But this week, there had been no arrangement in place and Karen's text suggesting a meeting had come out of the blue.

No can do, she'd texted back. Tickets already bought, specific trains. Next week?

But Karen had been insistent. And so they were meeting on Haymarket station in the brief gap between trains. River had no idea what was so urgent, but she knew Karen was no time-waster. Whatever it was she needed, there would be significance and weight to it. Together, they'd resolved cases that might have slipped through the cracks in the hands of a less determined operator. And along the way, they'd become friends.

Neither found closeness easy. Both of them had struggled to find common ground with professional colleagues. From choice, neither had kids. They both regarded shopping as a necessary evil rather than a leisure activity. They were smart enough to recognise fools at a hundred paces and neither was good at suffering their stupidity, although Karen had learned from working with Jason that other qualities were equally valuable. They had drifted into friendship warily at first, but now their bond was solid. When Phil had died, the only person Karen had shown the depth of her grief had been River. And River thought she'd never regretted it, which wasn't always how those things worked.

The train slowed as it passed the Murrayfield stadium and approached her destination. The rain that had lashed the train all the way from Carlisle suddenly stopped as if a switch had been flicked somewhere above. River stepped from the train into air heavy with its moist aftermath and caught sight at once of Karen waving damply from further down the platform.

They hurried towards each other and hugged, exchanging the easy pleasantries that required no particular response. 'So what's the big deal that won't wait till next week?' River demanded as they commandeered a couple of seats on the open platform.

Karen pulled a face. 'I'm in the bad books,' she said.

'So, nothing new there, then.' River patted her arm. 'Tell me.'

'Ha. It's kind of complicated. The five-second version is that there was a death last week that they were swithering over but it's easier to go with suicide rather than a difficult murder. The complication is that the victim's mother was murdered twenty-two years ago. Officially unsolved, but nobody looked too hard because they thought it was the IRA.'

'So you decided that made it officially yours?'

Karen wrinkled her nose. 'Kind of. Only, once I started digging, I managed to tread on a few toes and now the Macaroon is desperate to give me a good kicking.'

'And of course, you thought, who can I share this monstrously good kicking with? I know, I'll drag in my old friend River and spread the load.'

Karen grinned. 'You know me so well.'

'So what is it you need?'

Karen fished in her bag and took out a paper bag. It looked as if it contained something cylindrical, maybe ten centimetres long. 'It's a glass,' she said. 'I need DNA.'

River sighed. 'And you need it yesterday?'

'It's not quite as urgent as that. I've still got to get my hands on the profiles I want it compared with.'

'Profiles, plural?'

Karen sighed. 'Just for the sake of dotting i's and crossing t's. I've got a funny feeling about this one. I keep running up against those wee moments that make me go, "eh?" The kind of things that, when you try to explain them, sound stupid and trivial. So I don't even want to talk about them to myself, never mind to anyone else. Not till I've got some evidence.'

'And if there is no evidence?'

Karen shrugged. 'I'll look like a numpty. And not for the first time.'

'Fair enough. You know we don't have a DNA facility? That this will have to go to Gartcosh? Which makes it official, which means you might as well put it through yourself?'

Karen looked shifty. 'I was thinking, maybe the vet school?'

'The vet school.' River's voice was flat, disbelieving.

'They've got DNA analysis facilities. I remember from when there was that case in Perth about the fake pedigree dogs a couple of years back. It's the same process, right?'

River was momentarily aghast, then reason kicked in. DNA was DNA and the analysis would be the same whether it was carried out in the veterinary department of the university or the Scottish Police Authority at Gartcosh. But that didn't mean it wasn't problematic. 'You'll struggle with that in court. I can already hear the incredulity from the defence: "You took this illicitly obtained sample to the vet school for analysis? Alongside the sheep and the goats?"'

Karen laughed in spite of herself. 'That would be a problem if I was looking for evidentiary value. But right now, all I'm after is intel. If the horse whisperers come up with a match, I can use it investigatively. And off the back of that, valid opportunities will arise to take a formal DNA sample. Right now, all I want to know is whether I'm barking up the right tree.'

River couldn't help admiring Karen's ingenuity. She was no stranger herself to coming at things from an unorthodox direction. 'Are we putting this through the books? Or am I going to be begging some postgrad to run it as an exercise?'

'I haven't got a budget as such because it's not officially mine.' She made a noncommittal noise. 'On the other hand, it is technically not closed and it is definitely historic. And I have told the Macaroon I'm looking.' She came to a decision. 'Fuck it. Charge it to the HCU. I'll give you a case number as soon as I get one.'

River opened her backpack and carefully stowed the paper bag. 'Good luck with that. I'll get it done in a quiet corner of somebody's day. We'll put it through as Joe the dog.' She caught Karen's momentary look of triumph. 'But you knew that's what would happen.' She shook her head. 'You're a cheeky bastard, Pirie.'

'Somebody's got to be, in this wicked world. And make it Frank the dog, would you? For my own personal satisfaction.'

The cyclops light of a train appeared in the tunnel at the end of the platform. 'You'll have to explain Frank the dog to me another time. This is me,' River said. 'The light at the start of the tunnel.' She stood up, pulling Karen into a hug then holding her at arm's length. 'Are you OK?'

Karen nodded. 'I'm more OK than I was last week, and probably less OK than I'll be next week. Let's meet up next week, yeah? I'll come up to Dundee if need be.'

'Yeah.' River headed for the train.

As she was boarding, Karen called after her: 'And thank Sunny for her help the other day. If you need somebody to blame, lay it on her. She gave me enough straw to start making bricks.'

River turned and waved, grinning. Bloody vet school. Her world was full of bolshie women, and she loved it.

<h1 style="text-align:center">39</h1>

Getting out of bed on Tuesday morning stretched Karen's resolve to the limit. Her trip to London had been exhausting enough to make sleep seem like a distinct possibility, but she knew guilt would niggle at her till she'd managed to get contact details for the Syrians so Craig Grassie could get to work on their problem.

And so, instead of going home, luxuriating in a fragrant bath then falling into bed, Karen had forced herself to keep going. She'd caught a train for the short hop back to Waverley then stopped for a curry at the top of Leith Walk. The restaurant had been crowded and noisy; ideal for people-watching to accompany the assortment of starters she'd settled on. By the time she'd eaten and caught a bus back to the flat, it was after eleven. She'd stripped off the suit she'd been wearing since Friday, wondering if she'd get another wear out of it before it went to the dry cleaner. Maybe if she hung it up in the bathroom the creases would drop out and it would stop smelling of London.

She slipped into the comfort of her night-walking clothes and watched the latest episode of a TV drama she'd been following over the past few weeks. And then it was time to go out into the night.

Karen found them under the bridge, exactly where she expected them to be. Miran and Tarek were both there, which she'd thought might make matters easier. Tonight, there were seven of them, huddled round the brazier, smoking sweet-smelling cigarettes that reminded her of her grandfather's pipe.

As she approached, Miran stepped back to make room for her. He nodded courteously as she joined them. 'Good evening,' he said. There was a low murmur from the other men, even the two who normally glared at her.

'Good evening to you too,' Karen said. She slipped from her pocket a package of fresh dates she'd bought at the M&S food store at Haymarket earlier. 'I brought you these.' She handed the packet to Miran, who held it close to the flames to see it more clearly, then slit it open with his thumbnail and passed the dates around.

'Thank you,' he said. 'That is kind.'

She wasn't quite sure how to bring up the subject of a putative café, so she settled for her usual approach of head-on. 'I've been in London,' she said. 'I had work to do there. But while I was there, I went to see the Member of Parliament for this part of Edinburgh. I suppose he's your MP now too. And I spoke to him about you.'

Tarek looked alarmed. 'We are harming no one here,' he said. 'We find our own wood. We do not steal it.'

Miran put a hand on his arm. 'She knows this, I think.'

'I told him about your problem. That you don't have anywhere proper to go. Any place where you can all meet, with your families or on your own. We talked about helping you to find an empty shop or café. Somewhere you can turn into a place for Syrians to go. A café. Somewhere you can serve coffee, maybe some food.'

'But we are not permitted to work,' Miran said.

Karen spread her hands. 'There is a way around it. You would work with a charity. You wouldn't be able to earn money. You'd be volunteers. But you'd be working for your own community. Your wives, your children, your parents. The MP, he thinks it would be possible. He's willing to help you make it happen.'

One of the men who had never spoken before leaned forward. 'Why do you do this?' He sounded suspicious.

'Because you're here now. In our country. And you need help.'

Animated conversation in a language she didn't understand. But she didn't need the words to pick up the sense of what was being said. Most of the men were intrigued and positive. A couple glowered and shook their heads, frowning. It was always the way. You needed the dissenters to make sure everything was properly tested before you went ahead with things.

Eventually, Tarek spoke to her. 'We think you mean to help us and we thank you. How do we make this thing happen that you say we can do?'

'I don't know the details. This is way outside what I know about. What I can do to help you is connect you with the MP. His name is Craig Grassie.' She held up a finger. 'I wrote down his details.' She took a piece of paper from her pocket and gave it to Miran. 'His mobile number and his email. Can you tell me how he can get in touch with you? You have a mobile number? Or an email?'

More lively exchanges of views. Whatever the issue, Miran was arguing one side against the majority. At last he threw his hands in the air and turned to her with a sharp sigh. 'Some of us are not comfortable about giving you information because you are police.' He waved the piece of paper. 'Now we can go directly to this man ourselves and explain you have sent us. I am sorry, this sounds not polite. But we are grateful to you.'

Karen shook her head. 'I want you to have a better life here. That's all. I hope Craig Grassie can help you to get a café. Good luck with that.' She held out a hand. Miran hesitated for a moment, then he shook it. Tarek followed suit and before she knew it, all the men were shaking her hand, even the ones who seemed to think they might catch something.

It was time to go. With luck, she'd set something running that would make life better for people who'd seen too many of the worst things humans can do to each other. It wasn't much, but it was something.

And when she got home, she slept. Her sleep was full of rich and complicated dreams that disappeared from her memory within minutes of waking. They left her heavy-eyed and heavier-limbed, making the effort of getting up almost more than she could manage. But she couldn't hang about today. She had things to do and she needed to get the Macaroon off her back so she could get on with them.

Karen tried to cast off her feeling of dread with a hot shower, a black pudding sandwich and a double shot of caffeine. None of it did the trick, and even though her new favourite suit had been revivified by the bathroom steam, she still felt unimpressive and unprepared. She stood looking out over the sea, sparkling with blue brilliants in the morning light, finishing her coffee. In her head, she could hear Phil saying, 'Fuck 'em if they can't take a joke, lassie.'

Even before eight there were plenty of cars parked outside Fettes. Everybody knew cuts were coming and there were plenty of officers who didn't want to be culled. So they made themselves visible and apparently indispensable from early doors till closing time. Karen parked near the exit, ready for a quick getaway, and walked into the ugly box that was the former HQ of Lothian and Borders Police but was now nothing more than another element of the estate of Police Scotland. She wondered how long they'd hang on to it. It wasn't a proper police station, more of an admin centre, so it lacked useful things like cells and interview rooms. It could as well have been a bank or an insurance company HQ.

Karen made it to the Macaroon's office ahead of him. She parked herself in the alcove by his door on an uncomfortable wee sofa upholstered in knobbly tweed. When he appeared in the corridor, talking over his shoulder to a couple of uniforms behind him, she got to her feet, ready for the ambush. Lees literally jumped when he caught sight of her. 'Good morning,' she said brightly.

'I wasn't expecting you this early,' he said, sidestepping her and unlocking his office door.

'You said we needed to speak face-to-face.' She was at his shoulder as he opened the door. The only way to shake her off would have been to make an issue of it, and since he had an audience in the form of two superintendents on their way to other offices, she reckoned he wouldn't go for it. So she followed him in, practically treading on his heels.

Lees speeded up and quickly put his desk between them. Before he'd even taken off his uniform cap, she'd settled on the visitor's chair, legs crossed, hands demurely folded in her lap. 'Excellent news,' she said.

Lees struggled to keep his face in order. 'What are you talking about?'

'You haven't heard? Sheriff Abercrombie has granted our request. DC Murray picked up the court order late yesterday afternoon. As soon as I'm done here, I'm off to General Register House to get my hands on Ross Garvie's original birth certificate. With a bit of luck and a following wind, we should have a result on Tina McDonald's murder very soon.' Karen kept her voice lively and upbeat, giving him no chance to shoot her down in flames. 'Another feather in your cap, hopefully. It's always nice to be associated with success.'

He spluttered something that might have been an attempt at an interruption but she was refusing to be derailed. 'And another thing. You'll be very gratified about this because it not only solves a problem but it saves you the expense of an inquiry. You can stand down DS Robson. No need for a leak inquiry now.'

'What do you mean?' Lees was pink-faced, his eyes wide, his nose pinched. 'You are completely—'

'It's simple.' Karen steamrollered on. She was on the front foot and she wasn't going to stop pushing him backwards from his self-righteous voicemail. 'I've solved the leak. You probably don't remember, because it's way below your pay grade and nobody can expect you to have a grip on everything that goes on, but while Detective Sergeant Parhatka was in the hospital, before he died, somebody walked into the Murder Prevention Squad and helped themselves to his laptop. About as nasty a trick as you can get. But I never thought anything of it at the time, because obviously it wasn't high on my list of priorities. And then it dawned on me the other day . . .'

'What?' He was weakening now. Starting to crack at the edges. Time to be relentless and remorseless and robust.

'I used to use Phil's laptop from time to time. After Phil died, all his logins were cancelled. But mine are all still live and still on that laptop. I checked with Gartcosh, and right enough, whoever stole the laptop will have been able to access my emails and my case files.' She shook her head with a rueful smile. 'I'm sorry it's taken so long for the penny to drop.' She looked down and allowed a wee catch in her voice. 'I've had a lot on my mind.' Time for a swift recovery. 'But I've sorted it now. I've changed my passwords and moved all my files to new locations, so whoever has been sneaking a peek at our inquiries will meet a brick wall next time they try to log in. So we're all in the clear on that one, and, like

I say, it's good for the budget as well as clearing up that wee problem of the leaky sieve.' Karen grinned cheerfully.

Lees was struggling. She'd knocked so much wind out of his sails he was almost capsizing. But he hadn't given up yet. 'That's typical. Careless, heedless. And that brings us to why I wanted to see you—'

'Yes, there does seem to be a bit of a misunderstanding going on.' Karen spread her hands, a bewildered smile on her lips. 'I owe DI Noble a debt of gratitude. Without his investigation into the death of Gabriel Abbott, I might never have come across the cold case relating to Abbott's mother. And there's no doubt that it falls fair and square into the remit of the HCU. An unsolved quadruple murder in the skies over Scottish soil. It's my job – no, it's my duty to take a fresh look at such a serious case.'

'It's not . . . there's nothing . . . You've been sticking your nose into DI Noble's case. Which is . . . it's been decided. A suicide. No earthly justification for you stirring up all sorts of trouble.' He seemed to be having some difficulty constructing sentences.

Karen shook her head, pityingly. 'Like I said, a misunderstanding. DI Noble's very sensitive, very territorial. He thinks anybody investigating anything connected to one of his cases is trying to make him look incompetent. And nothing could be further from the truth. But it so happened that his investigation drew my attention to the original case back in 1994. And when I looked at it, I saw there had never been a review of the case.' She shrugged. 'I was waiting for the sheriff's decision on the Tina McDonald case and I thought it wouldn't hurt to give it a quick once-over. I mean, come on. Four murders, never cleared? That's a shocker to have on our record.' Her air of injured innocence was almost becoming a parody of itself. Karen reined herself in a fraction. 'And I happened to be going down to London for a weekend break, so I thought I might as well make some inquiries while I was there, to save the budget.' Always a good place to hit the Macaroon. He was obsessed with his budget.

'You're not supposed to wander through the files at random, picking cases that take your fancy. You're supposed to concentrate on unsolved cases where there is fresh evidence to focus on.'

'Absolutely. But sometimes it's important to conduct a free-standing review, to see if there are areas that could reasonably be expected to provide fruitful prospects. We need to be proactive, not just wait for moments like Ross Garvie's familial DNA hit.' She was on solid ground. Nowhere for him to go. She'd dragged herself back inside the legitimate borders of protocol. She got to her feet. 'So if it's all right with you, I'll follow up on one or two outstanding issues that slipped through the net at the time. Now, if you'll excuse me, I need to get up to General Register House and get my hands on that birth certificate.' She was halfway to the door before his voice stopped her.

'Stay away from Will Abbott,' he barked at her back. 'He's grieving for his brother. He was a mere boy when his mother was killed. There's nothing useful he can tell you about that.'

Karen rolled her eyes, then looked back over her shoulder at him. 'I'll do my best,' she said. 'Can't make any promises though.' And this time, she made it through the door.

40

The Mint, as instructed, was already at his desk, yawning over a can of Irn Bru and a slab of greasy Lorne sausage inside a roll, brown sauce oozing out of the sides. He straightened up, wide-eyed, when Karen walked in with far more bounce than anyone who'd had a bollocking was entitled to. 'How'd you get on?' He sounded apprehensive.

'Piece of piss,' Karen said. 'Everything is all boxed off and we're good to go.' Meaningless, but reassuring, she hoped.

'What happened? What did you say?'

Karen tapped the side of her nose. 'I can't be giving away all the tricks of the trade, Jason. Got to keep my feminine mystiquery.' Seeing his crestfallen look, she relented a little. 'I got you off the hook. You remember somebody lifted Phil's laptop when everybody was at the hospital with him?'

Jason nodded. 'I totally couldn't believe that. I mean, that's like grave-robbing. Burke and Hare.'

'Not quite.' Karen was impressed by his surprise erudition till she remembered there had been a Simon Pegg film about the Edinburgh bodysnatchers. 'Anyway, I used to use it sometimes. Obviously, I always signed out afterwards. But

I spoke to Tamsin at Gartcosh and asked her if it would have been possible to hack my email and files if I'd left it signed in with my details. And she said yes, it was possible if you knew your way around the systems. So I blagged my way past the Macaroon by telling him this must be how it happened.'

Jason looked astounded. 'And he believed you?'

'Why would he not? The story makes me look a wee bit careless, but that's not a hanging offence and it makes the explanation more credible. So the heat is off, Jason. And keep an eye on the post for your insurance policy.' She glanced at her watch. 'And we need to get our skates on if we're going to make our appointment at General Register House.'

Jason crammed the last of his roll and sausage into his mouth and chewed frantically. 'Hnngks,' he mumbled through the food, reaching for his jacket.

'No problem. And there won't be any blowback from your ex-flatmates. I went and had a wee word with Liam.' She gave a dark smile. 'He'll not be bothering you again.'

A look of alarm crossed Jason's face. 'Did you threaten him?'

'I've not lost my touch, Jason. Threats were just a detail.' Karen turned and made for the door. 'Don't forget the paperwork,' she added over her shoulder.

Jason grabbed the sheriff's order and the adoptive birth certificate the Garvies had been instructed to hand over to the investigation and hurried after Karen. On the way up Leith Walk to the records office, she quizzed him about his move. 'Was your mum pleased to see you back?'

'I guess. She made me a nice tea. Corned beef stovies with buttered cabbage.'

'And you're OK about being there? You understand why you had to walk away from the flat?'

'Aye,' he said, glum. 'You were right. Pals don't do what Liam did. But I want to move back to the city. I don't like the commute. I'll start looking online later in the week.'

'Good idea. Have you ever been in the General Register House?'

Jason shook his head. 'Never had any reason to.'

'I went there a couple of years ago. My dad got the gene-alogy bug from watching *Who Do You Think You Are?*. He sent me up there to dig up some family records.'

'Did you find anything interesting?'

'Only that I come from a long line of Scottish peasants. My dad lost interest pretty quickly once he realised we were just a bunch of nobodies. But it was worth it to see inside the place. It's stunning. It's one of the oldest custom-built archive buildings in the world. There's an amazing rotunda in the middle, the only light comes from one window in the roof, like the Pantheon in Rome, supposedly. You should take a look if we get the chance. And here's the best thing about it from our point of view – it was designed by Robert Adam.'

'What's that got to do with us?'

'He was from Kirkcaldy, Jason. Like us.'

Jason gave a dark laugh. 'I guess he did a bit better for himself than we have.'

'Well, not entirely. They ran out of money when they were building it. It stood half-finished without a roof for years.'

'There's houses like that up the back of the town. Started building them a few years back then the cash dried up.'

Karen rolled her eyes. 'Aye, but they're not exactly architectural masterpieces. They called this one the most magnificent pigeon house in Europe.'

They rounded the corner into Princes Street, confronted by the mounted statue of the Duke of Wellington pointing in the vague direction of Waterloo. 'The pigeons are still making themselves at home,' Jason said, pointing to a cluster perched on a stone ledge.

They climbed the stone steps and the automatic doors swept open to admit them to a completely unexceptional space. One half of the foyer held the reception desk and chairs for people waiting to be seen. The other half contained the gift shop, an odd assortment of local history books and the kind of mugs that only tourists buy. Karen introduced them to the receptionist and said, 'We've got an appointment with Bruce Andrews.'

They'd barely sat down when a glass-panelled oak door on the far side of the room opened and a man in his mid forties came in. At first glance, in spite of his greying hair, he looked more like a PE teacher than a civil servant – polo shirt, jeans, trainers. But he was clearly their man. He made straight for them, hand extended to shake. 'Chief Inspector Pirie, is it? I'm Bruce, Bruce Andrews.' He turned to Jason. 'And Sergeant Murray, right? Come away through.'

They followed him back through the door and immediately turned into a small office with a single tall window that provided a stunning view straight up the Bridges to the silvery grey cupola of the Old College of the university. The arrow-straight road was flanked by slices of a pair of grand façades: the Balmoral Hotel on one side and Waverley Gate, the old central Post Office, on the other. Up here in the centre of town, Karen often felt you couldn't turn round without getting an eyeful of amazing.

Jason was less interested in the view than in a gold-coloured wall safe the size of a bathroom cabinet. 'Is that where you keep the records?'

Andrews grinned. 'That wouldn't hold a fraction of what we've got. No, this used to be the accounts room. That would have been where cash for wages and registration fees would have been held.' He gestured towards a small blond wood table with four chairs round it. 'This is where we show people their adoption records. They make an appointment, bring in their ID and we show them what we have. I believe you've got a court order?'

Jason fumbled the paperwork out of his inside pocket and handed it over. Andrews looked it over intently. 'This all looks in order.' He stood up. 'I had to confirm that before I brought down the adoption record. We take our confidentiality very seriously. There are only two of us in the adoption unit and we're the only ones with keys to the locked room where we keep the ledgers. Not even the Registrar General gets in there without our say-so. If you'll excuse me, I'll go and get the relevant ledger.'

He left them, and Karen looked around at the impersonal space with its cream walls and blue heather mix carpet, its file boxes and its nondescript desk and computer. 'You wouldn't think so to look at it, but I bet this room's seen a lot of emotional moments.'

'I can't imagine what that would be like.' Jason's face split in a grin. 'Just as well I look the spit of my dad, eh?'

'Aye. If you don't get on with your adoptive parents, you must be hoping for something better. And if you really love the ones that brought you up, you'd have to be worried about what hand grenades your genetic history might throw into your life. Would you want to know?'

Jason shook his head. 'No. It's hard enough managing one lot of relationships. Know what I mean?'

Karen nodded. 'But I don't know if I could resist it. If I found out I was adopted, I'd have to know everything.'

'Aye, but you're dead nosy, boss. In a good way,' he added hastily.

Before Karen could react, Andrews returned carrying a fat ledger with drab green boards and tan linen binding, letters and numbers stamped on its spine. 'Here we are,' he said. 'This is the adoption register.' He opened it at a bookmarked page. 'And this is the record of Ross Garvie's adoption. Here's his adoptive parents' – he pointed to the Garvies' names – 'and here, it says they have been granted permission to adopt Darren Paul MacBride. Date of birth there, and the registration district – Dundee, as you can see – and here's the crucial piece of information we need. The number of the birth certificate. And there at the bottom, his adoptive name. Ross Stewart Garvie.'

Andrews closed the register and crossed to the desk, waking the computer. 'Now I have to input that number, and bingo.' The tapping of keys, the clicking of a mouse, the whirr of a printer. With a flourish, he presented Karen with a copy of Ross Garvie's original birth certificate.

Only when she took the A4 sheet did she realise she'd been holding her breath. There it was. The information that should lead her to Tina McDonald's killer. Darren Paul MacBride. Born in the Simpson Memorial Pavilion in Edinburgh. Mother's name – Jeanette MacBride. Usual residence: 7/43 Cambus Court, EH14 3XY. 'Wester Hailes, isn't that?'

'I think so, yes. It sounds like a block of high flats,' Andrews said.

'No mention of the father?'

Andrews pulled a wry face. 'That's often the way with adoptions. The father has to agree to being named if they're not married to the mother, and mostly they don't want to be. That's always supposing they even know about the birth.'

'It says here she was a nursery worker,' Jason said. 'Maybe we could trace her through her work if she's not still at that address.'

At the bottom of the certificate, in a box on its own was handwritten the word, 'Adopted.' Karen pointed to it. 'You write that on after the adoption?'

'That's right. Birth certificates are public documents. Anyone can access this and buy a copy of it. The written annotation is to prevent identity theft. You can't use this birth certificate to obtain any other ID, such as a passport or driving licence.'

'Is there any way to backtrack to the adoption record? To find out where that baby ended up?'

Andrews shook his head. 'It's not possible. Trust me, Chief Inspector, it can't be done.'

'I didn't think so. And it's not relevant. I was just curious.' Karen folded the sheet of paper and stood up. 'Thanks, you've been really helpful.' They walked out into sunshine lighting what Karen thought had to be one of the best views in the city. Apart from the backside of Wellington's prancing horse, obviously. But not even that could dent her mood. Finally, they had the break they needed to claw their way ever closer to the man who had murdered a young woman who'd been guilty of nothing more than having fun with her friends. 'One step closer to judgement day,' she said to Jason. 'One step closer.'

41

Karen loved the fizz of excitement that came hand in hand with forward movement after a case had been stalled. She'd marched down Leith Walk to the office so fast Jason had had to break into little skip steps to jink around fellow pedestrians and keep up with her. As they went, she'd issued her instructions. 'First thing, do the obvious. Phone book. I'll do the certificates and Google, Twitter, Facebook, Instagram. You take the electoral roll. If Jeanette MacBride isn't on the current roll, backtrack year by year till she shows up. Take a look at county court judgements, see if she shows up there at all. We'll see where we go from there.'

If they were very lucky, Jeanette MacBride would still be living in Wester Hailes on the edge of the city. But the chances of that were slim. If they could find out when she left, they could list who her neighbours were at that time then check forward in the records to see whether any of them were still around. It was a long shot and, if it failed, there would be other records to check. Marriages and deaths were the obvious ones, but there were other, less obvious places to look if they still hadn't found Ross Garvie's birth mother.

Back at the office, energised enough not to need a coffee, Karen sent a quick text to Giorsal. Just because Tina's murder had swept back to centre stage didn't mean she was going to ignore the other matter that was gnawing away at the back of her mind like a rat with a chicken carcass.

Hi Gus. Never mind Noble. Whatever he says, GA's death ties to a cold case and cold cases are mine. Can you put me together with Ian Lesley this evening? I'll buy the pizza! Kx

She smiled. Cat firmly inserted among pigeons.

Jason was already at his computer screen, head bowed, fingers clumsy on the keys, a pair of frown lines between his eyebrows. Karen made a start on her own tasks. The first thing she did was log on to the unit's account on the Scotland's People website. She typed in Jeanette MacBride's name, added a twenty-year window of possibility in the date range and chose five registration districts to start the search. She began with the ones nearest the address they already had for MacBride. There were nearly nine hundred registration districts in Scotland and if need be she'd work her way through every one till she found what she was looking for.

But the gods were smiling on her. Jeanette MacBride had been born on 27 June 1979 in Edinburgh. Her mother, Maria MacBride, unemployed and only nineteen, had been living in a flat in Portobello at the time. And as with her son, Jeanette MacBride had no father's name listed on her birth certificate. Had that been why she'd given up her child for adoption, Karen wondered. Had her own experience of being raised by a single parent made her decide she didn't want those social and economic difficulties visited on her own child? She wondered whether Maria MacBride was still in Edinburgh. She'd only be fifty-six now. If all else failed, she might know where her daughter was. 'Jeanette was from Edinburgh,' Karen said. Jason looked up, startled.

'What?'

'She'll be thirty-seven now. I'm pinging the birth certificate over to you.'

Back to her task. Google first. The dead ninety-four-year-old from Schenectady definitely wasn't their woman. Nor was the Filipino-Australian actress, who spelled her first name differently anyway.

She moved on to Facebook and worked her way through a trio of hits, dismissing them all on the grounds of geography and age. Twitter and Instagram offered no more likely options. Either Jeanette MacBride had no interest in social media or she had married and changed her name. Or she'd fallen off the grid for any one of several reasons. She could be in jail. She could have mental health issues. She could be too poor to support a digital existence.

She could be dead.

Karen thrust that annoying thought away and searched the marriage records on Scotland's People. No joy there. She tried Jeanette's mother, Maria, and eventually found a marriage certificate. In 1998, she'd married a builder's labourer called James Robertson. 'Oh, great,' Karen muttered. 'Let's hope we don't need to fall back on Jeanette's mother.'

'How?'

'She married a guy called James Robertson. Could she have picked two more common names? And he was a builder's labourer. The most casual employment known to man.' She sighed. 'You having any better luck?'

Jason grunted. 'I'm back to 2007 and she's not there yet. Just waiting for 2006 to load.' Silence fell again, broken only by the whisper and thump of two very different keyboard styles. But not for long. A couple of minutes later, Jason whooped. 'Got her. She was still living at the Wester Hailes address in 2006.' He jabbed a finger at the screen.

'Brilliant. Neighbours, yes?'

'I'm already on it.' Jason was scribbling in his notebook, listing the names of residents who lived close to Jeanette in 2006. Then laboriously he began to work his way forward through the records he'd already examined to see if any of them was still at the same address. He sucked his lower lip as he concentrated, a wet and faintly disgusting sound. Meanwhile, Karen waged a fruitless search through more marriage records to see whether she could track down Jeanette as a bride.

At last Jason pushed back in his chair and stood up. 'I done it,' he said. 'I deserve an Irn Bru. I'm away to the machine to get one. Do you want anything?'

'No. What have you got?' Karen spread her palms in a gesture of frustration. When would the Mint learn to prioritise?

'Two hits,' he said on his way out the door.

Karen bustled round to his desk and looked at his notebook. A list of ten names, all scribbled out except two. Agnes McCredie and Thomas Anderson. She checked the names against the screen. Agnes was at 7/45 and Thomas at 7/40. 'Looking good,' she said under her breath. They were on the same floor, close to Jeanette MacBride's flat. By the time Jason returned with his can to his lips, she already had her coat on. 'Come on, Jason, time for a wee run out to Wester Hailes.'

By some miracle, the lift was working. But as the door closed on the grim smells of stale urine, vomit and something unidentifiable but definitely decaying, Karen almost jammed her finger on the <door open> button so she could opt for the stairs before it was too late. But just in time, she remembered what the stairs would probably be like. Used condoms, needles, cat shit in corners, dog shit on landings and screwed-up papers drifting in the wind. No matter how hard the council – and a despairing tranche of the residents – tried to make the blocks of high flats a decent place to live, they were always fighting a losing battle.

The ridged metal walls of the lift showed faint ghosts of graffiti that council workers hadn't quite managed to erase completely, and Karen thought she recognised a couple of gang tags. The schemes of Wester Hailes seemed to change not at all from short generation to generation. Cheap booze, cheap fags and, most insidiously, cheap drugs had cheapened life to the point where escape seemed too improbable to contemplate. For these people, the escalator that had once offered a chance to rise above the poverty of their existence was permanently broken.

The seventh floor wasn't as bad as some Karen had seen. The blue doors were faded and dusty, but most of the paint was intact. A gallery ran round the four sides of the block and none of the windows facing on to it was boarded up. Some of them even had net curtains that were still approximately white. Agnes McCredie's flat was one of those. Karen knocked on the door and turned to face the kitchen window where, as she expected, a corner of the net shifted and she caught the pale half-moon of a face. She smiled; winningly, she hoped.

Time passed then the door cracked open a couple of inches, held in place by a brassy chain that Karen could have snapped with one lunge of her shoulder. But at least Agnes McCredie was showing unwilling, which was often all the deterrence it took. The eye that looked into Karen's was rheumy and faded, but queasily magnified by her glasses. 'Who are you?' she demanded, her voice reedy but strong.

Karen and Jason produced their ID. 'We're from Police Scotland.' Karen said. 'We're looking for anyone who knew Jeanette MacBride. She used to live in 43.'

The woman reared back a little. 'Jeanette? Has she done something? That doesn't sound like her.'

'No, nothing like that. We're trying to track her down, that's all. Can we come in for a wee chat, Mrs McCredie?'

'It's Miss McCredie. And none of that Ms rubbish either. Jeanette hasn't lived here in ten years. Hang on.' The door closed, the chain rattled, the door opened wider. Agnes McCredie gestured to them to enter. 'On the right,' she said, pointing to the door. It looked flimsy, like everything else in the hallway. The ugly grey carpet was threadbare but clean and framed pictures of the last four popes hung on the wall. A thin smell of bacon fat hung in the air.

The living room was furnished with a three-piece suite and a coffee table that Karen reckoned dated from the seventies. A small dining table covered with a lace runner sat against the window, an upright chair on either side. A cut-glass vase with some dispiriting plastic daffodils sat defiantly in the middle. The walls featured a crucifix, a picture of Jesus weighing the Sacred Heart in his hand as if checking whether it was good enough to cook, and a print of St Francis of Assisi charming the birds and the animals. A small TV with a rabbit ear aerial completed the furnishings. Everything was spotless. Cleanliness being next to godliness, Karen thought, settling herself on the sofa. Jason joined her and Agnes McCredie sat in the armchair facing the TV screen. She was small and neat and somehow desiccated, but the smile she bestowed on them was sweet, transforming her narrow face. Somewhere south of seventy, Karen decided. Clearly the Swinging Sixties had passed her by. But then, in parts of Scotland the sixties hadn't started till 1979.

'Now, before I tell you anything about Jeanette, I want to know exactly why you're here.' She folded her hands in her lap and gave them both a direct stare.

'We work in the Historic Cases Unit,' Karen said. 'We look

at what people generally call cold cases. We believe Jeanette can give us some information that would be useful to us in a case we're working on.'

Agnes raised her eyebrows. 'Well, Officer, that tells me absolutely nothing. I'd like some proper information.'

Karen couldn't really blame the old woman's nosiness. She'd have been the same. 'Jeanette had a baby while she was living here. Did you know about that?'

'Of course I did. I persuaded her not to have an abortion.' She sat up straighter. 'That boyfriend of hers was off like a scalded cat when he found out she was expecting. She was all for getting rid of the wee mite, but I helped her see its life was as sacred as hers. So she decided to have the bairn and have it adopted. But why are you asking about that now?'

Sometimes, honesty was the only policy worth a damn. This woman wasn't going to be fobbed off. Karen was going to have to give a little on the off-chance of getting a lot. 'Jeanette's son was involved in a car accident recently and his DNA was taken. And we learned something important from that. We discovered that one of his male relatives was involved in a serious crime twenty years ago. We need to find his father. And the only way we can think of to do that is through Jeanette.' She spread her hands in a gesture of appeal. 'We didn't have much to go on, but we figured out you might be able to help.'

Agnes took a rosary out of the pocket of her apron and absently began working it with her bony fingers. 'Jeanette moved away in 2006. She'd met a lovely man through her work. She worked at Jumping Junipers up the road at Juniper Green and Kevin was the postie. Kevin proposed but he was from Ireland and he wanted to move back there. There was nothing to keep Jeanette – her mum had died the year before.' Agnes pursed her mouth and lowered her voice. 'Breast cancer. And her so young.'

'So they got married and moved to Ireland?'

Agnes shook her head. 'No, they moved to Ireland and then they got married. Jeanette sent me a photo.'

'Have you still got it?'

Agnes shook her head. 'I kept it for a few years. We exchanged Christmas cards for a wee while but that petered out. I doubt I've heard from her in five years.'

'And do you remember Kevin's surname?' Jason chipped in, notebook at the ready, obviously reckoning there was nothing controversial in the question.

'O'Toole.' She gave a little simper. 'Like Peter O'Toole. Lawrence of Arabia, you know?'

'Do you still have an address for Jeanette and Kevin?' Karen asked.

Agnes nodded. 'Give me a minute.' She left the room and returned in a moment, clutching a battered book with a gingham checked cloth cover. 'My address book,' she said, thumbing through the index. 'Here we go.' She recited an address in Dublin and Jason dutifully wrote it down.

'Did you know Jeanette's boyfriend?' Karen continued. 'The one who got her pregnant?'

'I wouldn't say "knew". But I did meet him a couple of times, waiting for the lift with Jeanette. A handsome devil. Dark hair, dark eyes and good broad shoulders. She'd told me about him. How they were in love and he was the one, but I always say, you don't know if he's the one till you're walking back down the aisle. I disapproved of her giving herself to him, but you can't tell young people anything.' She sighed. 'And this was one time when I got no pleasure out of being right.'

'No, I can see that,' Karen said. Somehow, she thought that in spite of the obvious religiosity of Agnes McCredie, the older woman hadn't judged her neighbour harshly.

'And then she fell pregnant.' Agnes shook her head, sadness rather than self-righteousness in her voice. 'She didn't tell him to begin with. She was worried he'd think she was trying to trap him. She was going to have an abortion and carry on as if nothing had happened. But I could see she was uncertain, and in the end, she decided to keep it. And then, of course, she had to tell him.'

'What happened then?'

'He was in the army, did I mention that? He was stationed at Catterick and he used to come up to see Jeanette whenever he could get leave. Most weekends, he was here. She told him on the Saturday afternoon and instead of staying the night, he got on his motorbike and went straight back to camp. That was the last she saw of him. He wouldn't speak to her on the phone and he never answered her letters. I thought her heart would break. And then she heard he'd been posted abroad. And that was that. She had the baby, she handed him over for adoption and two weeks later she was back at her work. She was never quite the same after that. She was still a lovely lassie. A good neighbour and good company. She always had time for an old woman like me, even though she wasn't a Catholic herself. But after she gave up the baby, there was always a wee air of sadness about her. Even after she took up with Kevin, it was always there.'

Now for the sixty-four-thousand-dollar question. 'I don't suppose you remember his name? The boyfriend?'

Agnes bridled, offended. 'Of course I do. I may be knocking at the door of eighty but I've still got all the marbles God blessed me with. I do my Sudoku and the crossword every day, to keep my mind active. His name was Darren Foreman. Sergeant Darren Foreman of the Royal Highland Regiment. That's the Black Watch to you and me, son,' she added with a twinkle at Jason. 'I remember it well because I wrote the details down in Jeanette's family Bible. She wasn't very devout and I knew she wouldn't get round to it herself so I did it for her.'

'And you're sure he was the father?' Karen broke the moment.

Agnes straightened up in her chair. 'Jeanette was no good-time girl, Officer. Darren was her first serious boyfriend. She told me she'd grown up in a single-parent household and she was determined not to go down the same road as her mother.' She sighed. 'And of course, that's what happened, only a wee bit different. She was a decent lassie at heart. But Sergeant Darren Foreman, he was her Achilles' heel.'

42

Agnes McCredie closed her front door behind them, the chain rattling as she replaced it. 'Result, boss, eh?' Jason exulted, stepping out towards the lift.

'Hang on, Jason, where are you going? We've got another potential witness here.'

He turned, his expression the all-too-familiar one of bafflement. 'But we've got everything we need. Miss McCredie gave us chapter and verse. Now we just have to track down Sergeant Darren Foreman. One phone call to army records and we're cooking with gas.'

'Not so fast. Agnes McCredie is obviously a fully paid up member of the Jeanette MacBride fan club. And as we know, because we are nasty-minded, devious police officers, the version of the world people give us is never the whole truth. That's why, when we have the option of two sources, we take it, Jason.'

Comprehension dawned. 'What? You think there might be more to Jeanette MacBride than Miss McCredie was letting on?'

'No idea. But we're not going to find out if we don't try. And besides, I never trust anybody that doesn't offer me a brew.' Karen carried on along the gallery to Thomas Anderson's front door. His windows were covered with, at a guess, thin cotton bed sheets that had once been white but were now a streaky grey. She knocked, three firm raps.

A long pause, then the sound of shuffling feet. The door swung back to reveal a man who could have been any age between forty and seventy. His face was creased and yellow, patches of missed stubble dotted his slack jowls and throat, and his greasy gunmetal grey hair looked like he'd cut it himself without a mirror. Skinny white arms stuck out of a faded black polo shirt and a pair of cheap joggers flapped round stick-thin legs. He had the hard pot belly of a beer drinker. He resembled an olive pierced by cocktail sticks. Except that he smelled of cigarettes and stale biscuits. 'What d'you want?' he demanded, glaring at Karen, then peering round her to visit the same glower on Jason.

'Thomas Anderson?'

The scowl deepened, scoring his face more deeply. 'Who wants to know?'

'I'm Detective Chief Inspector Pirie of Police Scotland. And he's Detective Constable Murray. We'd like a word about one of your former neighbours.'

'Oh aye? And who would that be?' His mouth set in a stubborn line and he thrust his jaw forward.

'Jeanette MacBride.'

Anderson visibly relaxed. 'She used to live at forty-three.'

'That's the one. Mind if we come in?'

'Aye, I do. I've not been round with the Hoover lately.'

'Have you got something to hide, Mr Anderson?' Karen asked sweetly. 'Should I be talking to the local bobbies about popping round with a search warrant? Look, I don't care if you've got smuggled fags or dodgy vodka in your crib. I want one thing, and one thing only. And that's a wee chat about Jeanette MacBride.'

'Why? What's she done?'

'Nothing that concerns you. Can we do this inside? I'm sure you don't want everybody in the block to see you having a cosy wee blether with the polis?'

She'd found his weak spot. Anderson's eyes flicked from side to side and he stepped back, waving them inside. Breathing in was like an olfactory catalogue of Anderson's life. Cigarette smoke, stale fat, old farts and body odour tempered with a drift of piss as they passed the bathroom.

The living room contained a sofa whose upholstery was shiny with wear and grease and a massive TV dating from the days before flat screens were dreamed of. A spindly table with a laminated top sat by the window, a pair of wooden stools flanking it. Two upside-down cardboard boxes that had once held bottles of wine served as occasional tables. A pile of crushed lager cans lay on the floor by an overflowing pub ashtray. 'Nice place you've got here,' Karen said.

'You can fuck off any time you like.' Anderson threw himself down on the sofa.

Karen had no intention of sitting on any surface in the room. She leaned a shoulder against the wall, crossing one foot over the other. Jason was less fussy. He chose one of the stools and took out his notebook. 'So,' Karen said. 'You remember Jeanette?'

'Aye. Nice lassie. She always said hello. Well, until she took up with that Fenian bastard she went off with. He didn't like her talking to the likes of me.'

'That would be Kevin O'Toole?'

Anderston tittered. 'Tool, right enough. He was a tool, take it from me.'

Karen couldn't fault O'Toole's judgement. 'Were you living here when Jeanette had her baby?'

'Aye. It wasn't O'Toole's bairn, though. That was a good few years before he appeared on the scene.' Anderson pulled a packet of cigarettes out of his pocket and lit up with a cheap plastic lighter. Karen could see the health warning on the pack wasn't in English. She'd been right on the money with the smuggled fags.

'Did you know who the father was?' She sounded offhand, as if it wasn't important.

'She'd been going out with a soldier. I saw him in his uniform a couple of times. I suppose it must have been his, for I never saw her with anybody else.'

'Did you know his name?'

Anderson snorted. 'We were never introduced.'

'Did she have a lot of boyfriends?'

He shook his head. 'Not really. I heard she gave the bairn up for adoption and it was a long time till I saw her with another guy.'

'So there's no doubt in your mind that the army sergeant was the baby's father?'

Anderson sucked hard on his cigarette and blew out a cloud of smoke. 'That's what I heard. There's no secrets round here.' He sneered. 'Except from the likes of you. But what folks were saying was he got her up the duff then legged it. So what's he done?'

'I'm not at liberty to say.' Karen pushed off from the wall. 'Why? Is there something you're not telling us about what he was up to back then?'

Anderson shook his head. 'I'm like Manuel. I know nothing.'

That, thought Karen, was the most reliable thing Anderson had said. 'In that case, Mr Anderson, we'll take up no more of your time.' She gave Jason a tiny jerk of the head to indicate they should make a move.

'Is that it?' Having been so reluctant to let them in, he now seemed aggrieved that they didn't want anything further from him.

'That's it.' She moved towards the door, Jason on her tail. 'We'll see ourselves out.'

As they waited for the lift, Jason heaved a sigh. 'What's the matter?' Karen asked.

'See guys like that? They give me the creeps. His life's burst. How do you end up like that?'

'Bad chances, worse choices.'

Jason sighed again. 'I just think sometimes, they were kids once. They ran about the park kicking a football. They had things they wanted to be. Nobody dreams about being that guy there. Nobody sets out to be like him. And we keep coming up against folk that have got themselves completely fucked up.'

It was probably the most profound statement she'd heard Jason make. 'I know,' she said. 'If you think about it too much, you'd never get out of bed in the morning. The way I look at it, we're the lucky ones. We can't fix it for everybody, but we get to try and make it a wee bit better for some people.'

'I suppose,' he said, following her into the lift.

'And now we've got a name and a degree of confirmation that Darren Foreman is our man. So let's get on his trail.'

Karen made the call to army records as soon as they got back to the office. It was always easier to call from a landline so they could call back via the switchboard to check she was a bona fide cop. While she was on hold, her mobile buzzed with a text from Giorsal.

Ship Inn, Limekilns. Table booked for 8. Fish suppers are on you.

Karen's mouth filled with saliva at the memory of the Ship Inn's haddock and chips. That was something to hang on to as the tail end of the day dribbled away.

The phone crackled into life. 'DCI Pirie? I think I've got what you need. Darren Foreman joined the Royal Highland Regiment in 1987. He was sixteen and at the time he joined, he was living in Glasgow. He was a combat infantryman—'

'What does that mean, exactly?'

'A foot soldier. Patrols, guard duties, protecting convoys. What most people think of when they think of a soldier. The boys on the front line who get shot at.' The voice on the other end sounded mildly amused. 'The equivalent of a bobby on the beat, I suppose. He appears to have been rather good at it. He hit Lance Corporal in under three years, full corporal in six and sergeant at eleven years' service. He left at that rank after fifteen years in, in 2002. Managed to miss the second Gulf War.'

Karen was a little surprised. If pressed, she'd have marked Tina McDonald's killer as having some issues with impulse control. 'No problems with him? No disciplinary issues?'

'Nothing on his record that I can see. Good soldier, by the looks of it. There's a note here that his commanding officer recommended him for SAS training with a view to recruitment, but he didn't make the grade. No disgrace there. Only about fifteen per cent of the men who go through the training make it to the regiment.'

'I don't suppose you know what he's doing now?'

The man on the line chuckled. 'You don't know?'

'Why would I know?'

'Because he's one of yours. He's a firearms officer with Police Scotland.'

43

Karen watched Ian Lesley as he went up to the bar to get the drinks in. A short, compact frame neatly dressed in a well-pressed shirt with a subdued check, well-fitted clean black jeans, black Docs. Dark blond hair cut short at the sides with a vestigial quiff at the front. He was in his early thirties but looked younger, his face unlined and placid. He and Giorsal had arrived ahead of Karen and somehow they'd snagged a table with a view out across the Forth. Giorsal had made the introductions, they'd ordered three servings of haddock and chips, then Ian had insisted on buying the first round in spite of Karen's protests.

Giorsal followed her eyes and said, 'He's one of the good guys, I think. He's very patient with the clients. Never loses his cool. But he's dogged with it. He doesn't give up on people and he stands up for them. He's definitely a keeper, which is more than I can say for some of the bodies I inherited.'

'I know what you mean. My lad Jason, he's not the sharpest blade in the knife block. But his heart's in the right place, and the things he can do, he does surprisingly well.' Karen studied the beermat. 'And he worked with me and Phil.'

'I'd guess that helps. Having that connection.'

'It does.' Abruptly changing the subject, Karen said, 'Thanks for that suggestion about the Syrians, by the way. I spoke to Craig Grassie – the Edinburgh MP – at the weekend and he's going to see whether he can help.'

'I hope that works out.' Before she could say more, Ian returned with three gin and tonics.

'There we go,' he said. 'Our one proper drink of the evening since we're all driving and we're in the company of the law.' He grinned and handed round the glasses. 'So, Karen, Giorsal tells me you're interested in Gabriel Abbott?'

'You don't beat about the bush,' Karen said.

'Life's too short,' he said, his blue eyes on hers. She wondered how much Giorsal had told him.

'Officially, it's his mother's murder I'm interested in. Because nobody was ever charged, it's still an open case and it comes into the remit of my unit. But I'll be honest. I can't help wondering whether we've rushed to judgement on Gabriel's death. The more I find out about his family, the more of a tangle it becomes.'

Ian sipped his drink. 'It's funny you should say that. Gabriel was coming up to his thirtieth birthday. He told me a while back that he wanted to do something special. But he didn't really have anyone to do anything special with.' He shrugged. 'It wasn't like he was self-pitying. He liked his own company and he didn't make friends easily. He understood that about himself. So anyway, he told me he'd been watching *Who Do You Think You Are?* on TV one night when it came to him. He was going to draw up his family tree. It would be his present to himself.'

'So how did that go?' Karen asked, giving nothing away.

'He did pretty well on his mother's side, because she was born in Edinburgh and our records up here are so much better than they are in England because of our system of parish records. He'd got back to the eighteenth century on her side. He was having less luck with his father's side. He got stuck round about his great-grandparents. But the one thing he really wanted to get his hands on was his father's death certificate. His mother told Gabriel that his father had died in Thailand a couple of years after his birth. So Gabriel got in touch with the authorities over there. He didn't have the money to hire somebody locally to help him out, but he managed to get someone at the embassy to make some inquiries for him.' His smile had a tinge of wistfulness. 'He could be very charming, Gabriel.'

'So what happened?'

'They couldn't find any trace of Tom Abbott having died in Thailand. Not in 1990. They checked a couple of years either side, but drew a blank. Gabriel was gutted. He'd built it up in his head as something that was really important. Something that would tell him something about the father he never knew. And he'd hit a dead end.'

Before he could say more, a waitress arrived with plates laden with large slabs of battered fish and a small mountain of chips. The aroma was wonderful; none of them was going to be distracted from the food. They'd motored through a sizeable amount of their dinner, accompanied by wordless murmurs of pleasure, before Ian picked up his tale again. 'So, maybe three months ago, he had a visit from his mother's former PA and her husband. She'd always stayed in touch with Gabriel. They were heading up to Gleneagles for a golfing weekend and they stopped off to see him. He told them what he'd been trying to do, and the woman said, no, he'd been totally barking up the wrong tree. It wasn't Thailand, it was the Philippines where Tom had died. She could see how everybody got confused, because he'd been based in Thailand for a couple of years. But it was definitely the Philippines where he actually died.'

'Gabriel must have been excited.' Still she kept her face straight, eager to hear Ian's version of what Felicity had already revealed.

'No kidding. And he dropped lucky. I don't know whether you know this, but Gabriel was a real South East Asia buff. History, politics, literature. If he hadn't had his problems with his mental health, he could have taught at a university. He was like a different guy altogether when he got stuck in. Anyway, he'd built a really substantial network, and he had a good contact at the University of the Philippines. So Gabriel chivvied him into tracking down his dad's death certificate.' He loaded up his fork with more fish and shoved it in his mouth. Seeing Karen's expression, he chewed faster.

'Did he find it?' she asked.

Ian nodded. He laid down his cutlery and washed down his food with a swig of his drink. 'He certainly did. There was only one problem.' He paused.

'It was dated 1984,' Karen said. 'Two years before Gabriel was born. And six years before Caroline Abbott told everybody Tom was dead.'

Giorsal's face was a picture of disappointment. 'You knew?'

'I only found out yesterday, by chance. It's good to have it confirmed. But that must have really messed with Gabriel's head.'

'It did. This was just a couple of weeks ago, by the way, which maybe supports the idea of suicide. Anyway, Gabriel phoned me when he got the email with the scanned copy of the death certificate. He was – gibbering, I'd have to say. That's the only word for it. I told him to calm down, make a cup of tea and phone his brother, see if Will could cast any light on it. He's quite a lot older than Gabriel, so I thought he might remember things better from back then.'

Karen resumed eating, cutting her chips into very small pieces, a frown of concentration on her face. For someone who struggled to stay on an even keel, the discovery must have been a devastating piece of news. It was hard to imagine how it would have felt. 'Did Gabriel tell you what Will said?'

'I'll be honest, I was curious. We're always dealing with crises in this business. Mopping up after the wheels have come off people's lives. But mostly, they're predictable disasters. Domestic violence, child abuse, dementia getting a grip on somebody's day-to-day.' He gave an embarrassed little shrug. 'So I went round to his cottage on my way home.'

'Anybody would have done the same,' Karen said.

'I would have,' Giorsal agreed.

Ian pulled a face. 'He was much calmer than he'd been on the phone. He'd got hold of Will and told him what he'd found out. Will was shocked, obviously. But he figured it out in a matter of moments, according to Gabriel. According to Will, Caroline was always practical. Knowing Tom as she did, she'd have realised that, if she wanted another child, she might not be able to rely on him being around. So she could have got him to have his sperm frozen so she could choose when she wanted to get pregnant. And Gabriel thought it made sense. Caroline liked to be in control of things. That was how she was so good at business, he said. And if she was going to get pregnant, she'd want to do it at a time when it suited her, not when it suited Tom.'

Ian shrugged. 'Gabriel said his parents had a pretty semi-detached relationship, so I suppose it kind of makes sense. Anyway, Will was adamant that Caroline would have found a way round Tom's absences. Gabriel wasn't so sure, though. He wanted them both to have DNA tests, him and Will. Just to confirm what his big brother believed.'

Karen drew her breath in sharply. 'Sometimes you're better off not knowing,' she said. 'Why do I have this feeling that Will didn't fancy that idea?'

'I don't know. But I do know that you're right. Will was totally against the idea. He said there was no need. That he knew in his bones that Gabriel was his brother. Gabriel was really touched by that. He said he thought Will was desperate not to risk weakening the bond between them.' Ian looked dubious.

'You don't look convinced.'

'I wasn't. I thought Gabriel was getting stuck in magical thinking. Trying to make himself a close family that didn't really exist. But it wasn't the time to call him on it. I could tell there was something else going on. Something he was reluctant to tell me.'

'Something to do with Will?'

Ian sighed. 'I told myself I needed to know what was going on so I could take the best care of Gabriel. I'm sorry, Giorsal. I'm not proud of myself. I told Gabriel I knew he was holding out on me and it would make him feel better if he didn't keep things hidden. And he admitted that before he'd spoken to Will, he'd already sent samples off to one of those companies that advertise DNA analysis online.'

'He didn't hang about,' Giorsal said.

'Where did he get Will's DNA from?' Karen said, focused on the crucial detail as ever.

'That's what I wondered too. It turns out that the last time Will visited he ended up staying overnight. Gabriel gave him one of those crappy toothbrushes you get in hotels, and he never got round to throwing it out.' Ian gave a sad little laugh. 'If you'd seen Gabriel's cottage, you would know there was nothing unusual about that. He'd give squirrels a run for their money when it came to hoarding.'

'So what was the outcome?' Karen asked. Her food was forgotten now. Ian's story was even more captivating than her favourite dinner.

He swallowed the mouthful of chips he'd managed to

shovel in between sentences. 'Don't know. It hadn't come back by the time he died.'

'Which is surely an argument against suicide?' Giorsal leaned forward, as fascinated as Karen by what Ian had revealed. 'I mean, he really wanted to know. Surely he wouldn't have killed himself before he got the answer?'

'Unless he did get the answer and it wasn't the one he wanted,' Karen pointed out.

Ian shook his head. 'I don't think so. He'd have been incredibly agitated if that had been the case. I think he would have called me. But even if he hadn't, I can't believe he'd have stuck to his usual routine. At the very least, he would have buttonholed the barman or one of the other regulars. He was a spiller, was Gabriel. When things bubbled up, he let them out.'

'Do you think he told Will he was getting the DNA test done?' Giorsal asked.

That, Karen thought, might be the most significant question of the night. Almost as significant as the other one in the back of her mind. Did Frank Sinclair know Gabriel was trying to find out the truth about himself? She cleared her throat. 'I don't suppose you've got a key to Gabriel's cottage?'

44

Karen caught her foot on an uneven paving stone and almost pitched to the ground, steadying herself at the last minute against the cottage wall. Between the bloody clouds and the high hedge that surrounded the small back garden, she couldn't see a bloody thing. She felt her way along the wall, taking each step gingerly. The surface under her fingertips changed from rough harling to smooth wood. The back door. She slipped on a pair of blue nitrile gloves. The last thing she wanted was to leave her fingermarks all over Gabriel Abbott's home.

She flicked on the flashlight on her phone and shone it at the ground. Somewhere nearby there was a boot scraper and brush. According to Ian, Gabriel had kept his spare back-door key there. 'I told him he should give someone a key in case of emergencies,' he'd said. 'But he insisted it was easier to hide one and tell me and his nearest neighbour where it was.'

When Karen had revealed her plan, both Giorsal and Ian had wanted to come with her. She'd refused point-blank. 'I'm a polis. If I get caught inside Gabriel's house, I can blag my way out of it. You guys? No chance. Trust me, I won't leave you out of the loop. But this is one I've got to do alone.'

Karen spotted the boot scraper at the far side of the door and crouched down beside it. It was cast iron and heavier than it looked, but when she lifted one side, she saw the key in a shallow depression that had been hollowed out of the soil. She almost dropped it when a car suddenly revved as it passed the cottage, driving far too fast for the narrow lane.

Minutes later, she was inside Gabriel's kitchen, heart thudding even though she knew she had the place to herself. Adrenaline fizzed through her veins, setting every sense on high alert. The room smelled stale and there was a faint aroma of rotting cabbage. She could hear nothing over the sound of her own pulse.

Even by the limited light from her phone, she could see the truth of Ian's description of Gabriel as a hoarder. There was barely space on any of the worktops to prepare food. The surfaces were occupied by stacks of old newspapers and magazines, a pile of tightly folded plastic bags, Tupperware boxes of screws, nails and assorted bits of ironmongery. In spite of the clutter it was surprisingly clean, however. She'd expected a hob encrusted with dead food and splashed with fat and pasta sauce, but it was pristine, as was the tiny section of vacant worktop. Gabriel might have been flaky, but he had standards.

Karen moved through the doorway into the living room. The cottage was isolated, with no near neighbours, so she decided to take a chance and pulled the curtains across before turning on the overhead light.

The room was a dense chaos of books and papers. Shelves lined one wall, crammed end to end with books on the history, politics and geography of South East Asia. Instead of a mirror or a picture above the fireplace there was a huge map of the subcontinent, with coloured pins stuck all over it. To one side was a list of names and places that she quickly realised corresponded to the map pins. His correspondents? His contacts? A real network? Or a fantasy? She had no way of knowing. It was something she could come back to if she found any reason to consider it relevant to his death. A table by the window held a clunky old laptop, more papers and a stack of CDs. On the wall beside it was a carefully drawn family tree with neat boxes. Some were completed, others waited to be filled in. On a rickety set of shelves next to the desk, a photo album sat horizontally across a line of books.

The front door opened directly on to the living room, and there was a scattered pile of mail on the doormat. Karen scooped up the post and sat down at the table to work her way through it. Junk mail, an electricity bill, an innocuous postcard from Vietnam from someone called Dusit. A thin blue airmail envelope with a return address in Manila. And a brown envelope with a crest that said, 'Deventer Laboratories, Hemel Hempstead.'

It looked like the answer had come too late for Gabriel. Karen knew she should leave it alone. 'Step away from the envelope,' she muttered. But even as manifestly she spoke, she knew she couldn't. She turned it over and studied the flap. It was the kind that came with adhesive already applied, which was much more vulnerable to tampering than the old-school ones where you had to lick the flap.

Karen raked around in the bottom of her bag and felt her fingers close on her penknife. No new-fangled Swiss army knife for her. This steel-cased twin-bladed knife had belonged to her grandfather. It had whittled ash twigs into arrows for the sapling bows she'd played with in the woods of childhood. It had cut the string on parcels that arrived from her great-uncle in Canada. It had been whetted on the leather strop that hung by the fireplace till it was sharp as the old man's open razor. She kept it sharp, using the same steel that maintained the edge on her kitchen knives. It was the perfect tool for opening the envelope without leaving a trace.

She laid the letter flat on the table and unfolded the smaller blade. With infinite patience, she slipped it under the edge of the flap and eased it along, careful not to cut the paper. Millimetre by millimetre, she worked the blade through the adhesive, holding her breath and trying to clear her mind of everything except the task in hand.

At last the blade cleared the flap and she could open it without a sign of tampering. Karen breathed again. Carefully she pulled out the contents. There were three sheets of paper. A covering letter and two pages of graphics that she recognised as DNA analyses. She spread them out on the table and before she took note of their contents, she photographed each page.

Then finally she let herself read what Deventer Laboratories had found out.

Dear Mr Abbott,

Thank you for using our analytical services to ensure swift and accurate DNA profiles. Our results are enclosed.

In your letter, you stated that it was your belief that the two samples were related – that they were either full brothers or half-brothers with the same mother and different fathers. However, our analysis shows definitively that the two men whose samples you submitted are completely unrelated. There is no familial connection between Sample A and Sample B.

Should you require further testing, we will be happy to oblige.

Karen read the letter twice, to make sure she'd got it. Then she looked at the two DNA profiles side by side. Deventer Labs were right. There was no overlap between the two. Gabriel and Will Abbott didn't just have different fathers. They had different mothers as well.

45

The more Karen discovered, the less she believed that Gabriel Abbott had killed himself. She sat at the table staring at the papers but seeing nothing, her mind racing. Her first instinct was to get out of the cottage and take the letter with her. If she left it behind, the chances were that it would fall into Will Abbott's hands and that would be the end of that. The DNA tests – whatever they meant beyond the obvious – would disappear without trace, she felt sure.

But if she stole the letter, it would have no evidentiary value. It could never be produced in a courtroom, if it ever came to that. At least this way she had a copy on her phone. If she needed to, she could get a warrant and demand a copy of the report from Deventer. She needed to leave it behind, on the mat, in the midst of a slither of junk mail.

Karen squeezed her eyes shut and thought. What did it mean? Who were Gabriel Abbott's parents and why had Caroline pretended to everyone – including her own son – that she was his mother?

When she opened her eyes, she caught sight again of the photograph album. She reached for it and began to turn the pages. The photographs were neatly stuck in, captioned in the same neat capitals as the family tree and the map reference list. They looked as if they'd been scanned in and printed on a home printer. The first one showed Caroline holding a baby in her arms, grinning at the camera. She was sitting at a picnic table with a low building in the background that looked indefinably foreign. France, presumably. The caption read, *Mum and me at two weeks old, Sercy-sur-mer.* She turned the page, and there was Ellie holding the baby close to her chest, his head on her shoulder, her hand supporting his neck, a look of infinite tenderness on her face. *Ellie and me, six days old, Sercy-sur-mer.*

Karen had the advantage of knowing Caroline was not the mother of the baby in the photographs. But really, how had nobody understood that look on Ellie MacKinnon's face? The answer to the question raised by the DNA test was right in front of her. Ellie MacKinnon, the devoted friend, the secret lover, the reliable babysitter, was manifestly so much more than that.

She turned the pages and watched Gabriel grow up. The resemblance to Frank Sinclair grew stronger – and after all, it had been Ellie who had been Frank's friend, not Caroline. How much more likely he would have been to oblige her than her girlfriend. And as Gabriel grew from babyhood to childhood, what was also obvious was that he didn't look anything like Caroline or Will. He had Ellie's colouring – her dark eyes, her raven hair, the skin that flushed pink at the first sun. And yet it didn't seem to have crossed anyone's mind that she was his real mother.

It was always the way. People saw what they wanted to see. Karen thought about her own family. There was no doubt she favoured her father's side of the family. The stocky build, the shaggy hair. She'd seen family photos taken in the Depression, when her great-grandmother had been forced to feed her family in the soup kitchens in their mining village. Yet all the Piries in the pictures were solidly built, even running to fat in some cases. 'We're good peasant stock,' her father was fond of saying. 'Fat in a time of famine.' And yet, whenever she went to family parties, her mother's side were always trying to claim her. 'You've got your granny Welsh's eyes,' they'd tell her. Or, 'You're the spit of your great-auntie Meg that died in the war.' So really, why be surprised that nobody had ever gone, 'Bloody hell, that boy looks like the bastard love child of you and Frank Sinclair.' It would almost have been more strange if they had. And of course, Ellie and Caroline were both dead and gone before Gabriel had grown into his features in his adolescence. And by then, there was nobody around to care who he looked like.

Karen carried on flicking through the album. Then abruptly the photos ran out. Instead of pictures, there were words, printed on pale blue A4 paper.

My first memory is fireworks. We are in the garden in our house in London and I'm strapped into my pushchair. Will is there too, so it must have been the year before he went off to Glencorsie House. There's a giant box of fireworks a few yards away from us and Ellie is choosing what comes next. Then Mum comes up behind her and startles her, and she drops the taper into the box and before she can do anything about it, the fireworks start to go off. They're dazzling, all the colours of the rainbow, shooting across the lawn in all directions and for a moment Mum panics and runs to me but Ellie shouts that it's OK, we're far enough away and she starts laughing and Mum starts laughing too and they're roaring with laughter and Will starts crying because it's all over in a matter of moments.

That's my first memory and it always makes me smile when I think about it. Most of my early memories are about good times. Ellie was always laughing and playing with me because that's what she was good at. It was her job, but it was her job because she loved it. Mum was fun too but in a different way. She was more serious. She read me books and took me to museums and got me interested in other countries where they do things differently to us. Ellie took me to the zoo and the movies and we had adventures and that's what I remember when I think of her. When they died, it was like the laughter died too.

I don't think I really understood what it meant when Mr Timmins sat me down in his study and told me my Mum and Ellie were dead. Dead wasn't real to me. I was only eight years old, and dead was what happened on TV and films, only the person was still alive because they'd be in another film or a TV series before long. So I think I thought it was like that.

I didn't go to the funeral so I didn't have any sense of closure, as the therapists always go on about. It was a few weeks later than Will came to the school with Aunt Maddie. They explained that, because Mum and Ellie were dead, I would have to stay at school for the holidays because Will wasn't able to look after me. He was going off to university, but what he was also doing was setting up his company, Glengaming. He had it up and running before his first term at Imperial began. He'd wanted to do it before, but Mum said he should concentrate on his degree first. But then she died and he inherited all the money and the house, which was a good thing because he was able to start the business and it took his mind off the terrible thing that happened to Mum and Ellie. It was harder for him because he was that much older and he understood what had happened. Looking back, I'm really glad he was able to throw himself into Glengaming. Mum would have been really proud of him.

I only really started to understand how much my life had changed when the end of term came and everybody went home except for me and Terrence Smith, whose parents were both scientists and working on the British Antarctic Survey. When they came back a few months later, they gave a brilliant talk with slides and everything about their time at the bottom of the world. And Terrence didn't ever stay at school for the hols again.

Mr Timmins and his wife looked after me for most of the holidays and they were very decent to me but they didn't have kids of their own and they weren't big on fun. I used to cry myself to sleep at night. I missed Mum and Ellie so much it was like a hand was squeezing my heart.

That summer was when I started to get interested in South East Asia. Mrs Timmins – she keeps asking me to call her Briony, but that feels too weird – did Chinese and Geography at university and she spent her year abroad in Hong Kong and Shanghai. She talked to me about her time there and showed me slides of her trip. I think I was especially interested because my dad, who was a marine engineer, spent most of his working life out there, in Vietnam and Thailand and the Philippines. That's been my main interest all my adult life. I tried to study the region at university, but that was when everything really went wrong for me.

I suppose I managed to keep things together at school because it was familiar. People assume Mr and Mrs Timmins were like a second family to me, but it wasn't really like that. They were very kind, but there was always a line between term time and holidays. In term time, I had to behave like I was any other pupil. I slept in the dorm and spent all my time with the other kids and the Timminses treated me exactly the same as everyone else. And then at the end of term, I'd move into one of the spare rooms in their annexe and I'd take my meals with them and we'd be all friendly. When I tell people this, they look at me as if they can't imagine anything so weird.

But when I left school I didn't have a clue how to live.

By then, Will was really successful. Glengaming had had a couple of big successes and he was riding high. He'd just got married to Lucy so he wasn't very keen on me moving in with him. I had a place at St Andrews, so I decided to stick around in Scotland. Will helped me out with some money and I got a summer job in a bar in Kinross. And I really didn't cope well. My head wasn't right. I didn't know what to do or how to be with people, and that was when my life stopped working properly. But I think it just took me a long time to catch up with the reality. My life really fell apart on 5 May 1994. That was when the love and the happiness and the laughter all died along with Mum and Ellie. And nothing has been right since.

Karen felt tears pricking her eyes as she reached the abrupt end of Gabriel's words. If DI Noble had done his job properly he'd have found this and used it to shore up his lazy push for a suicide call. She couldn't imagine how Gabriel must have felt day in, day out, trapped in a world the joy had been sucked out of when he was only eight years old.

Eight. Karen remembered eight. That was the year they'd gone to Butlins at Ayr with two sets of aunts and uncles and five of her cousins. The weather had been cloudy but it had mostly stayed dry and they'd spent hours on the beach and on the fairground rides at the holiday camp. Glamorous Granny competitions, and her dad coming second in the Knobbly Knees contest. Fresh fried doughnuts in the ballroom before bedtime and doing a duet on the talent night with her cousin Donny. Her idea of tragedy was losing a 10p piece down a siver, hearing the splash as it hit the water below. She'd grown up with people who loved her even if they hadn't always understood what made her tick, even if they'd sometimes made her feel like shit without meaning to. She couldn't begin to imagine what Gabriel Abbott's life had been like.

And his brother. What had gone on in Will Abbott's selfish head that he'd left his little brother to sink or swim, all on his own, stripped of all the people he'd ever loved? Who the *fuck* did that to a wee boy who's just lost the woman he thought was his mum and the real mum who devoted herself to giving him fun?

She thought that was the end of the album's revelations, but tucked right in at the back, tight against the spine, was a plain white envelope. Karen pulled it out, discovering it wasn't sealed. Inside was a small bundle of newspaper cuttings, yellow and brittle with age. She spread them out in front of her and was unsurprised to see they were part of the original coverage of the crash. There was nothing to indicate who had provided them. Certainly Gabriel would have been too young to have clipped them himself, even supposing he'd had access to newspapers.

There were front-page stories from the *Daily Mail*, the *Scottish Daily Record* and the *Edinburgh Evening News*. There was nothing there she didn't already know. The four who had perished were photographed at the aerodrome before they took off on their fatal flight, grinning amiably at the camera. Ellie was giving a thumbs-up to the lens.

The final cutting didn't have a masthead to identify it. It read like local paper copy, probably from whatever weekly paper covered the Elstree airfield. It had the same photo as the other papers, but with one key difference. This was clearly an uncropped version of the picture. There was a fifth person standing on the edge of the group, next to Ellie.

It was, unmistakably, Frank Sinclair.

Karen drew her breath in sharply. What on earth had Frank Sinclair been doing at the airfield that morning? And why did none of the reports mention his presence? What did it mean? She rubbed her cheek in a nervous gesture. Did it mean anything? Was it just chance? Who could she ask?

She turned to her phone again and photographed the cutting. Coming to Gabriel's cottage had been a momentous decision, she thought. How could Alan Noble have missed all this detail?

Karen closed the album and put it back on the shelf then she folded the letter, replaced it in the envelope and pressed down on the seal to close it again. It didn't stick as well as it had, but it didn't look as if someone had tampered with it. She stuck it in the middle of the pile of mail and spread it over the mat again. When she mixed it in, she noticed that the envelope from Manila had 'URGENT' scrawled in one corner.

She picked it up and considered it. She couldn't imagine how a letter from the Philippines could have anything to do with Gabriel's death. She tossed it back on top of the pile and took one last look round the room.

Her visit had given her almost too much to think about. If Gabriel had found out the truth, he'd have realised he was entitled to much more than the crumbs from Will's table. As Ellie's son, he'd have had a claim on what she'd left in her will; everything that had been merged with Caroline's estate and passed on to Will. What would that have done to their relationship? She was going to have to talk to Will Abbott sooner rather than later.

And Frank Sinclair. What was his part in all of this? And how could she unravel it?

But first she was going to have to get her hands on the DNA evidence from the original investigation into the crash. So far, all she had was supposition. She needed something much more solid. Until now, she'd had nothing but unease to contradict the idea of suicide. Now at least she had the makings of motive.

46

Karen replaced the back-door key where she had found it and picked her way along the path to the front of the cottage. A fine drizzle had set in while she'd been indoors, making it even harder to see where she was going. She closed the front gate behind her and set off towards her car, parked in a farm gateway fifty metres up the road.

She'd only covered a few metres when suddenly, behind her, an engine raced and the lane flooded with light. Taken aback, she swung round and saw only a pair of headlights on full beam racing straight at her, the engine revving loudly, filling the night with its roar.

Surely the car was going to swerve? The driver must see her. How could they not? But no. It was actually cutting across the road towards the narrow verge where she was walking. There was no time to think. It was upon her before she could figure anything out.

Karen threw herself to one side, smashing into the hedge as the big SUV tore past, smacking her shoulder with its wing mirror. She let out a yell of pain and staggered at the impact, clutching her shoulder and stumbling. As she steadied herself, she realised tyres were screaming and headlights were casting crazy patterns on the hedges.

And then the shock realisation that the vehicle was making a tight turn up ahead, preparing to come back at her. The headlights swung round, blinding her. This wasn't accidental. This was deliberate. The horror of what had happened to Phil less than a year before flooded her and a terrible panic leached all logic from her brain.

She tried to push through the hedge but the twigs grew tight together and a wire fence ran through it, making it impassable. The pain in her shoulder was sickening, slowing her thoughts and her movements. The SUV hurtled towards her, riding the verge so this time it would hit her full on. She was going to die here. In the middle of nowhere. Chasing shadows was going to be the death of her.

And then, with seconds to spare, the unlikely cavalry. Blue lights striping the hedgerow and the road. A police patrol car coming up behind her. The SUV jerked convulsively back on to the carriageway and shot past the police car, its tail lights disappearing in seconds. The police car had braked sharply to a halt opposite Karen, the passenger leaping out in his hi-vis jacket as she stumbled away from the hedge.

'DCI Karen Pirie,' she shouted as he approached. 'Historic Cases Unit.' She reached for her ID and winced as the pain from her shoulder shot across her chest. 'That bastard just tried to run me down. Put out a call.'

The constable looked bewildered. This, Karen knew, was not the usual sort of incident he'd have had to deal with on the night patrol shift. 'What's going on?' his partner said, joining him in the middle of the road, staring at the dishevelled woman who had just climbed out of the hedge.

Karen had managed to get her ID out of her pocket. 'Look, I'm a police officer. I was walking back to my car' – she pointed down the road – 'and out of nowhere that SUV came at me. First pass, he hit my shoulder with his wing mirror. He'd just turned round to finish the job when you guys showed up. Now you need to put out a call.'

The driver scratched his chin. 'That's all very well, ma'am, but what are the boys looking for? I'm guessing you don't know make, model, colour? Maybe a damaged nearside wing mirror. He could be miles away by now. The motorway's five minutes from here.'

He was right and she knew it. Karen rubbed her shoulder. 'Fair enough. But at least you can put a report in, right?'

They exchanged looks and grunted assent. Karen wouldn't be holding her breath. The driver spoke again. 'So, can I ask you, ma'am, what you're doing, walking down a wee country lane in the middle of nowhere this time of night?'

Karen gave him a level stare. 'Pursuing inquiries, Officer.'

'Only, we got a call from a neighbour. That cottage back there' – he jerked his head – 'the owner died last week. But the neighbour spotted a light in the front room when he was closing his bedroom curtains. He gave us a bell and we came by. You sometimes get toerags who keep an eye on the death notices and break into the houses of the deceased before the families get things sorted out.' He paused, waiting for her to say something. 'Would you know anything about that, ma'am?'

She considered flippancy and rejected it. 'It wasn't a burglar, Officer.'

'You were in the cottage?'

'As I said, I was pursuing inquiries relating to a historic case. The dead man's mother was murdered twenty-two years ago, and this was our last chance to see whether Gabriel Abbott had any relevant evidence that he might not have understood the value of.' *Thin, Karen, thin.* 'I had a key,' she added with a smile.

The two men looked at each other, hesitant. Karen knew the last thing they'd want at this time of night was to make an issue out of something so nebulous, something that would tie them up for the rest of their shift and, in all probability, beyond.

'Just put it down as a false alarm on your report,' she said. 'There's no need to make a big thing out of it.'

They nodded, relieved to be off the hook. The driver headed back to the car and his partner pointed to her shoulder. 'I'd swing by the hospital and get them to take a look at that shoulder,' he said. 'You're not holding yourself right. Are you OK to drive?'

'I'm fine. Just bruised. Nothing broken. But thanks for your concern.'

'I'll walk you back to your motor,' he said. 'In case they did any damage before they had a go at you.'

Karen hadn't even considered that in the heat of the moment. Panic clutched her chest. She might, after all, be dealing with someone who had form for blowing up a plane. She trudged back to her car and studied it. Tyres intact, no sign of any forced entry to doors, boot or bonnet. She went to drop to one knee to look underneath but a stab of pain from her shoulder made her stop. 'Can you look underneath?' she asked.

He looked at her as if she was mad. 'Underneath?'

'Please. That murder? Gabriel Abbott's mother? That was a bombing.'

A flash of fear in the constable's eyes. 'OK.' He took out his torch and reluctantly lowered himself to the wet ground. He shone the light under the car, swinging it back and forth to cover the full length. 'Nothing there,' he said, scrambling to his feet and looking at his damp trousers in disgust.

Only then did Karen press the remote and unlock the car. She slipped awkwardly behind the wheel and said goodnight to the constable. Before she drove off, she searched her bag and found a pack of ibuprofen. She dry-swallowed three and set off for home, wondering all the way who she'd upset enough to warrant an attempt on her life, and exactly what she'd done to provoke it.

47

Karen considered herself to be stoic, but getting out of bed next morning made her moan out loud. Her shoulder was the centre of her pain but it radiated down her arm and across her chest and into her ribs. She hobbled to the bathroom and inspected herself in the mirror. A black and purple stain covered her left shoulder, spreading to her upper arm and across her collarbone. The muscles had stiffened and most movements hurt. She'd slept fitfully, waking every time she shifted position, and the bags under her eyes gave that away.

The shower eased the ache a little, but everything was still an effort. She found a tube of tinted moisturiser lurking in the bathroom cabinet and applied it to her face, disguising the worst traces of her pain and her lack of sleep. Dressed, caffeinated and dosed with more ibuprofen, she checked herself in the mirror one last time. 'As good as it gets,' she muttered and set off for Fettes.

The Macaroon kept her waiting for twenty-five minutes. His form of punishment for her turning up without an appointment. When she was finally allowed in, he gave her a critical glare. 'Are you limping?' he demanded.

311

'I tripped,' she said, unwilling to explain the events of the evening before.

He smirked. 'You should be more careful.'

'I should. The reason I wanted to see you is that we're pretty sure we've managed to track down the biological father of Ross Garvie.'

'"Pretty sure"? What does that mean?'

'We've got two witnesses who place him as the boyfriend of the mother.'

'What about the mother? What does she have to say for herself?'

'We've not managed to trace her yet. She moved to Ireland about ten years ago and married an Irishman. A simple DNA test will establish if this is our man, which seems a better option than dragging the Garda Síochána into things. Obviously, if we're barking up the wrong tree, that'll be our fallback position.'

Lees tapped his pen from end to end on his desk as he considered. 'So, why are you bringing this to me? Normally you make your own mind up on operational matters and I only hear outcomes. Except when it all goes wrong. Like that business in Oxford that's still grumbling away in my inbox.'

Karen kept her expression sphinx-like, refusing to be goaded. 'A matter of courtesy. Ross Garvie's putative biological father was in the army at the time he impregnated the mother. He left the army some years ago and joined Strathclyde Police, as was. He is now a firearms officer with Police Scotland. He does routine armed patrol at Glasgow Airport. I need formal permission from an officer of superintendent rank or above to interview him.'

Now the Macaroon looked worried. 'You're seriously suggesting that one of our firearms officers raped – what's her name?'

'Tina McDonald.'

'Thank you. Raped and murdered Tina McDonald?'

'It's a distinct possibility. We'll know for sure one way or another with a DNA test.' She could see he was close to vetoing her request and she was determined not to let that happen. Luckily she knew the best pressure point when it came to the Macaroon. 'Of course, if you'd rather delay until I've asked the Garda to track down Jeanette MacBride, and DC Murray and I have gone over to Ireland to confirm what we've got, I understand. But clearly we can't back away from the case after the publicity it's had.'

'And whose fault was that?' he grumbled.

'Whoever stole Phil's laptop,' Karen said sweetly. 'So, what's it to be? A quick run out to Glasgow Airport with a buccal swab kit, or dragging the Garda into a potentially expensive operation?'

Lees dropped his pen noisily to the desk. 'You leave me very little choice, DCI Pirie. You know how limited our resources are. We have to use them sparingly where possible.' He sighed. 'Very well. You have my permission to interview this officer. What's his name?'

'PC Darren Foreman.'

'Fine.' Tight lips suggesting the opposite.

Karen forgot herself and stood up quickly, stifling a gasp of pain as her bruises kicked in. 'I'll get on to it right away.'

'And make sure you come back with his DNA. I don't want him forewarned and primed to take off out of our jurisdiction. Do your job, no excuses.' He turned to his computer screen, effectively dismissing her.

Back down the black ribbon of the M8 towards Glasgow, the monotony of the ride broken by the pieces of roadside art. They were all supposed to have a traceable connection to their locale. The Horn, a giant aluminium megaphone that transmitted music and messages nobody could hear above the traffic noise; the Sawtooth Ramps, a set of grassy pyramids supposed to symbolise the shale bings that once dotted that landscape; Big Heids, a trio of giant 3D heads made from steel tubes as an engineering project for local steelworks apprentices; and the wirework and steel Heavy Horse sculpture of a Clydesdale, the local workhorse breed. Other features had appeared over the years, but Karen was never quite sure whether they were art or functional. Three crane-like structures near Livingston that looked as if they were made from Meccano, for example. The metallic cladding on a shopping centre in the East End of Glasgow. She wouldn't have bet on any of them.

She knew she was engaging in displacement activity, riffing on conceptual art when she ought to be doing the mental prep for her interview with PC Foreman. But she wasn't apprehensive about it. Either he would cooperate or he wouldn't. And if he wouldn't, she was probably screwed. He'd presumably had training both in the army and in the police on how to hold out against interrogation. None of Karen's little tricks was likely to throw him off his stride. So there was little point in running through her options.

There was one thing she could take care of. With Jason driving, she was free to make phone calls. She rang the Police Scotland evidence facility, a large warehouse near the HQ at Gartcosh. Most of their cases relied on evidence stored at the site, where physical evidence and paperwork on unsolved cases ended up. The HCU were regular visitors, staggering back to their vehicles with boxes of files.

The phone was picked up on the third ring by someone who sounded frankly far too cheerful to be working in an evidence store. Karen identified herself and explained what she was after. 'Four murders, May fifth, 1994,' she said. 'A Cessna was blown up in the skies above Galashiels. The dead were Richard Spencer, MP, his wife Mary and their friends

Caroline Abbott and Ellie MacKinnon. I'm looking for the case files. In particular, I need the DNA analysis for the four victims.'

The evidence officer recited the details back to her and she confirmed them. 'When do you want this?' he asked, a little of the shine going off his voice.

'I'm on my way to Glasgow. I'll be heading back later this afternoon. Any chance you can have them for me then?'

'If you can leave it till after four, I'll have them ready for you, Chief Inspector.'

'Excellent. See you later.' She ended the call. 'Wee detour via the evidence store on the way back.'

'Did I hear you saying "plane crash"? What's that all about?'

'It's another cold case I've been taking a wee look at. It's why the Macaroon was on the warpath with me the other day. I didn't go down to London at the weekend for fun. I was following up a couple of leads.'

'It's not on the whiteboard,' he said, referring to the list of cases in which they were taking an interest.

'No,' Karen agreed. 'I wasn't sure if there was anything for us. But the more I look into it, the more I think what happened in 1994 is not what everybody thinks.'

Jason frowned, puzzled. 'What? You mean the plane wasn't blown up?'

'The plane was blown up all right. But maybe we were wrong about the identity of the killers.'

'But . . . if we're looking at it, that means it was unsolved, right? But what you're saying sounds like we knew who did it. I don't understand.'

Karen stifled a sigh and shifted in her seat, slipping the upper half of the seat belt behind her to ease the pressure on her bruised shoulder. 'They assumed it was the IRA or a Republican splinter group because one of the victims was a former Northern Ireland minister and the Republicans were pretty active at the time.'

'And you think they were wrong?'

'I do.'

'How?'

'I'm beginning to think that Richard Spencer wasn't the target.' Karen outlined what she'd found out so far and what she suspected about Gabriel Abbott's death.

Jason's apparent confusion grew as she spoke. 'I'm not seeing what you're seeing, boss,' he said. 'It all sounds like you're making something out of nothing.'

Karen swithered for a moment. Then she decided. 'If it's something out of nothing, how come somebody tried to kill me last night?'

He turned to face her, horror in his eyes. 'What?'

'Watch the road, for fuck's sake, Jason.'

He dragged his attention back to his driving. 'Are you serious?'

'What do you think?'

'I think you don't usually make jokes about things like that. But what happened?'

Karen told him. He listened in silence, then let out a long shrill whistle. 'That sucks,' he said. 'How did they know where you were?'

'That's a good question. Either somebody was following me because they don't like the questions I'm asking or else they were staking out the cottage and they didn't like the idea that I'd been inside.'

'Or maybe . . . ' Jason trailed off, giving her a quick uncertain glance.

'Maybe what?'

'Maybe it was pure chance that they turned up at the same time as you. Maybe they were looking for the same thing you found. And they just freaked out when they saw you?'

'You're right,' Karen said. The boy was learning, no doubt about it. 'Whatever, it's clear that there's something going on.'

'Right enough, maybe you're on to something. So what are we going to do about it?'

'We're going to solve it.' What else? If someone was after her, dragging the truth into the open was the best way to defuse it. 'We'll pick up the plane crash evidence on the way home. But right now, I want your mind on Darren Foreman,' she said. 'Glasgow Airport, next exit.'

Darren Foreman's boss was a taciturn Highlander with a soft voice that belied his tough appearance. He had a face as expressive as the north face of the Buachaille and almost as craggy. He took them to a tiny interview room behind the airport's security area and left them alone. 'I'll get Darren,' he said.

The only decoration was a Home Office poster showing all the objects a traveller was no longer permitted to take on board a plane. The room smelled of synthetic lemon and, beneath that, the musky darkness of body odour. Karen tried to get comfortable on the plastic chair, but it was a big ask. Her shoulder nagged at her to find a better place to sit.

They didn't have long to wait. The door opened on a man of medium height made burly by his body armour and equipment. He carried a Heckler and Koch semi-automatic at port arms as he looked them up and down. What hair showed beneath his forage cap was as dark as Ross Garvie's. It was tempting to conjure a resemblance, but Karen couldn't put hand on heart and swear they looked alike. Foreman was eyeing her with shrewd blue eyes, weighing her up as one would a dangerous opponent.

His boss appeared at his shoulder and said, 'Darren, I'll take the piece.'

Foreman said nothing, merely lifting the gun over his head to free the strap and handing it to him. The sergeant left, taking the gun with him and shutting the door after himself.

'Please, sit down, Constable Foreman,' Karen said. As he settled into the chair opposite her, legs spread apart, hands on knees, she introduced herself and Jason.

'I don't understand,' Foreman said. 'What's Historic Cases got to do with me?'

'We'd like to interview you under caution,' Karen said. She nodded to Jason, who recited the familiar words.

Darren Foreman pushed his chair back a few feet. His eyes narrowed. 'You better tell me what this is about or I'm out of here.'

'That wouldn't be a wise move,' Karen said. 'How do you think that would look to your boss? Refusing to cooperate with Police Scotland official business? I'd guess you wouldn't have your pretty wee machine gun very long in those circumstances. Look, Darren, the best thing for everybody is if you just relax and answer my questions.'

He folded his arms across his chest. 'I might answer or I might not.'

'Do you know or have you ever known a woman called Jeanette MacBride?'

Puzzled but wary, Foreman straightened in his chair. 'I used to go out with a Jeanette MacBride.'

'Can you tell us when that was?'

His eyes moved up and to the side. 'It must have been seventeen, eighteen years ago. I was in the army then. You could check with my records. It finished because my unit was mobilised and stationed in Berlin.'

'Are you sure that's why it finished?'

He shifted in his seat. 'Why else?'

'Nothing to do with her telling you she was pregnant by you?'

Foreman clenched his fists, tucking them into his armpits. 'I was shipping out to Berlin. I told her it was over between us and she should get an abortion because I wasn't about to become a daddy. I was young and stupid in those days, Chief Inspector.'

'Did she tell you she had the child?'

'I never opened her letters, I binned them. Like I said, I wasn't ready to have kids. It took me another five years to make my mind up about that.'

'So you were unaware that Jeanette had a son?'

He shook his head.

'And that she put him up for adoption?'

Again, the head-shake. 'Look, I've got two daughters of my own now. I don't feel any connection to some teenage lad I've never seen. The man and woman that brought him up, that's his parents as far as I'm concerned.'

'Fair enough. I think they'd agree with you.'

'So what am I doing here?'

'Constable Foreman, where were you on May seventeenth, 1996?'

'What?' He looked and sounded bamboozled.

'It's a straightforward question. May seventeenth, 1996.'

'You mean, specifically where was I, or more generally?' He leaned forward, gripping his knees with his hands. 'Because I have no fucking idea what specifically I was doing that night or where I was doing it. But here's what I can tell you. That night, same as every other night in April, May, June and half of July in 1996, I was in Gun Club Hill Barracks in Hong Kong.'

48

J ason broke the long silence that followed Foreman's words. 'Can you prove that?' he asked.

'It's not my job to prove it, it's yours. You can check with army records. That'll answer your question about where I was that night. Why the hell are you asking me about that night anyway?'

Karen had gathered herself together now. 'A young woman called Tina McDonald was raped and murdered in a Glasgow back alley. Her killer left his DNA at the scene. For reasons that I imagine you have no interest in, given what you just said, we recently took a DNA sample from your biological son. We got a familial hit on the DNA database. I take it you know what that means?'

Foreman's eyes widened. 'A close male relative. And you thought it must be me?' His voice was tinged with outrage.

'You can't blame us for that,' Karen said. Until she had checked with army records, she wouldn't give up Darren Foreman as a suspect. But it would be useful to let him think she had. If only to get his DNA without further complications. 'I wouldn't be doing my job if I hadn't chased you down. Are you willing to give us a DNA sample so that we can conclusively eliminate you from our inquiries? I mean, you know it wasn't you, so you have nothing to lose.' She gave him her best smile.

'Is he in trouble, this lad of Jeanette's?'

'I won't lie to you. He's in a bad place right now. But there's nothing you can do to help him, I promise you that. So, Darren. The DNA?'

He blew his breath out in an explosive puff. 'All right,' he said. He knew the drill. He must have seen it often enough, Karen thought. Jason handed him the long cotton-tipped swab and Foreman rubbed it vigorously round the inside of both cheeks before dropping it into the proffered tube. Jason sealed it and wrote the details on the label – place, time, date, name of the donor, name of the officer taking the sample.

'Do you have any other sons?' Karen asked.

Foreman's lip curled in a sneer. 'What do you take me for? Look, I got a shock with Jeanette. After that, I was careful. I always used a condom. Until I got married, obviously. I didn't want another nasty surprise.' Then a thought clearly crossed his mind. He rolled his muscular shoulders and said softly, 'What the hell.' He sighed. 'If you're looking at close male relatives of my biological son, you should know that I have a brother. Well, I should say I *had* a brother. He died about eighteen months ago. A stupid accident on the building site where he was working.'

Karen felt the hair on the back of her neck rise. 'Do you know where he was in 1996?'

He shook his head. 'We weren't close. Chalk and cheese, me and Gary. One of the reasons I went into the army was that I didn't want to end up like him. He was three years older than me, feckless and aimless.'

'Is there anyone you can think of who would know where he was and what he was doing back then?'

Foreman nodded. 'My mother. He was the apple of her eye. It didn't matter what Gary did, it was never his fault. The world was always down on him, according to her.' The bitterness in his voice was corrosive. 'She'll be able to give you chapter and verse.'

'Thank you. And where will I find your mum?'

'Linlithgow: 39 Strathmore Court.'

Jason scribbled furiously. 'Will she be in just now?'

Foreman shrugged. 'I've no idea. Look, she doesn't keep very well. If you hold off till tomorrow morning, I'll get hold of her and make sure she's ready to see you. It'll give her a chance to tap into her memories and give you the help you need.' He stared at the floor. 'If he hadn't been my brother, I'd never have given him the time of day. But I can't believe he would commit rape and murder.'

'If he didn't, we won't pin it on him for the sake of getting a conviction,' Karen said. 'I promise you that.'

'And if he did, he got away with it, which means my mum was spared twenty years of shame. I can't say I'm sorry about that.' Foreman straightened up. 'Are we done here? Only we need to be on patrol and my partner can't do anything while I'm here with you.'

Karen gestured towards the door. 'You're free to go. Thanks for your help.'

They watched him go, then Karen said, 'Away and find his boss and tell him we want to know if Foreman does anything out of character. Till we get that DNA result back, I'm not taking anything on trust.'

The journey back across the narrow waist of the Central Belt seemed to take for ever. Roadworks, the ever-expanding rush hour, the detour via the lab at Gartcosh to drop off the DNA sample and finally the run out to the evidence store to collect six cardboard archive boxes of files from the store. 'That's the digest,' the helpful warehouse clerk volunteered. 'There's a whole stack of the original unedited witness statements, but I thought you'd be able to make a start with these. If you need more, we can always dig it out for you. No bother.'

By the time they got back to base and Jason had loaded the files into their office to spare her shoulder, he was starting to look frayed round the edges. 'Away home,' Karen told him. 'We'll be off to Linlithgow in the morning, so make sure you get here in good time.'

Jason eyed the archive boxes dubiously. 'Are you going to make a start on them tonight?'

'I was considering it.'

'It's not my place, boss, but I think you should maybe take an early bath. After last night, I mean. You look kind of rough. Tired,' he hastily corrected himself, seeing the look on her face. 'Most folk wouldn't have come in today if somebody had walloped them with a wing mirror on the way to trying to kill them.'

He had a point, she realised. But she wasn't most folk, and she had no confidence in her capacity for rest these days. 'I thought I'd just look for the DNA profiles,' she said. 'I photographed the ones from Gabriel Abbott's letter and sent them to River last night. I need to give her something to compare them with.'

Jason lifted the first box on to his desk. 'I'll give you a hand, then. But only if you promise you'll knock off when we find them.' He gave her an uncertain grin, not sure if he'd overstepped the mark.

Karen had an unsettling moment of recognition. What Jason had said was the sort of thing that Phil would have said back when they all worked together. She nearly tucked it away without further examination, but then she remembered Jason's plaintive words. She really should try harder. So, 'That's the kind of deal Phil would have made,' she said.

Jason's eyes flared with panic, then he realised she was reaching out to him. He came up with a tentative smile. 'I managed to learn some things from him.' He propped the box lid with its index list against his monitor and started sifting through the files. 'The first round's on you. That's one of the other things I learned from him.'

Karen couldn't help smiling. A poignant, sad smile, but a smile nonetheless. It was a start. She sat on the floor next to one of the boxes, trying not to grimace as her shoulder complained. She began the slow task of sorting the paperwork. They had a system they'd developed over the years. It involved a series of piles. Evidence, crime scene photographs, analysis, witness statements, suspect details. Then those piles themselves were sorted into separate stacks, depending on how Karen and Jason were approaching the material. Sometimes they arranged them by date, sometimes by subject, sometimes by individuals. It was Karen's idiosyncratic method and Jason, trained up in it since he'd joined the unit, had adopted it uncritically.

So they worked through the paperwork, which seemed to have been dumped in the boxes at random, no organising principle apparent. 'This is chaos,' Jason complained.

'It was a big case,' Karen said. 'There will have been a lot of people working on different bits of it. And there will have been a review at some point, which is why the index sheets in the lids have no relationship to what order things are in, or even if they're in the right boxes.' She tutted. 'I don't know why people can't put things back where they found them,' she muttered.

Halfway through the second box, she found what she was looking for. There, in a plastic envelope, were the DNA profiles of all four victims of the Cessna crash. It was how they'd confirmed their identities. Samples had been taken from their homes – hairbrushes, toothbrushes, laundry baskets – and compared to the DNA extracted from the fragments of flesh and bone that had rained down on a Borders hillside. 'Got them,' she said. 'You can stop now.'

Jason looked up, a dazed expression in his eyes. 'Sorry?'

'I've found the DNA. You can knock it on the head for tonight.'

He gave her the straightforward smile of a child. 'Brilliant. I was kind of lost in what I was looking at. I'm glad I wasn't one of the guys on the ground after that. Bits of bodies and bits of plane, like the world's worst jigsaw.'

Karen got up, making what she called 'old people noises' as the pain kicked in again. 'You and me both. I need to scan Caroline and Ellie's DNA profiles and send them off to River. It's a Wednesday, she'll still be in the lab. Then we can go to the pub. Just for one, mind, because you're driving back to Kirkcaldy.'

He curled his lip in an expression of disgust. 'I need to sort out someplace else to live. It's great getting my breakfast cooked, but it's too much hassle to drive back and forward every day. I'll start looking at the weekend.'

'No more students, though, Jason. Maybe it's time you started thinking about buying?'

He looked aghast. 'I don't think so,' he said. 'Buying? That's for grown-ups.'

Karen laughed as she laid Caroline Abbott's profile on the glass plate of the scanner. 'You are a grown-up now, Jason. Time to take responsibility for yourself.'

He shook his head. 'I'll leave that to you, boss. You're better at it than me.'

She scanned the second sheet, shaking her head. 'I'll tell you a secret, Jason. I just talk a better game. Deep down, I'm as scared as everybody else.'

49

Dr River Wilde was indeed still in the lab. Whenever she was in Dundee, she worked as long as she could bear, partly to justify the deal she'd negotiated with the university and partly because there was nothing to love about the tiny modern studio flat she was renting near the Victoria Dock. She was eating pizza at her desk while reading a revised PhD thesis on the chemical analysis of tooth enamel when Karen's message pinged into her inbox.

She opened the attachments and sent them to the printer, thoughtfully chewing a chunk of crust as she read the email. She set the PhD to one side and summoned up the DNA analysis of Frank the dog's DNA, which had come back from the vet school that afternoon with the comment, 'Doesn't look much like a dog to me!'

Now she had five DNA profiles to compare. So that she wouldn't prejudge that comparison, Karen had not told her who they belonged to. The two she'd sent from her phone were labelled A and B; the two she'd just sent over were C and D. And of course, there was Frank the dog.

River laid the five sheets in front of her. They looked like elongated barcodes. To the untrained eye, there was little connectivity between them. But although it wasn't her area of specialism, River had been looking at DNA comparisons for years and she'd learned how to make sense of the patterns.

She moved them around so they formed different relationships to one another. And finally, she had the patterns clear in her head. In all probability, C was the mother of A, whose father's DNA was not one of the selection in front of her: B was the child of D and Frank the Dog. A and B were completely unrelated.

She double-checked her findings then put them together in an annotated email attachment to Karen. Hope this is helpful, she added in her message. Give me a call if you need to talk it through.

Almost instantly, River's FaceTime icon started chirruping at her. She connected with Karen, who looked both exhausted and excited. 'Thanks for this,' she said. 'I just need to run through it with you to be sure I've got it right.'

'OK. But you look more like you need to be in bed,' River said.

'I had a wee run-in with an SUV late last night.'

'What? You had an accident in the car?'

'I had an accident, but I wasn't in the car. Somebody tried to run me over. If it hadn't been for a patrol car coming along in the nick of time, they'd probably have managed it.'

'Jesus, Karen, that's terrible. Who the hell was it? Do you know?'

'I've no idea. The main suspect in the cold case I'm working officially is probably dead, so I don't think it's him. If I've stirred things up in the Gabriel Abbott case, I don't have a clear enough idea of where I'm going with it to know who might be trying to stop me.'

River gave a shaky laugh. 'You'd better get a move on before they succeed, girl. Did they catch them?'

'No. By the time the night patrol boys realised what had happened, they were long gone.'

'Where was this?'

'Near Kinross. Loch Leven side.'

'Could they not have checked the ANPR cameras?

Karen shrugged. 'No point. He could have gone six different roads within five minutes of where it happened.'

'Oh, come on, Karen. Stop being so bloody heroic. Kinross late at night isn't the bloody North Circular. Even that close to Perthshire, there can't be many SUVs hurtling around late at night. Get on to it. Talk to the guys at Traffic. Whoever tried this might try again.' River's voice rose in anger. 'I don't want to be going to another bloody funeral.'

Karen looked shocked. 'I'll be careful,' she protested.

'Phil was careful.' River spoke quietly and clearly.

'I know,' Karen said. 'Every time I woke up in the night, I relived the moment when that SUV was heading for me and I was thinking, this is what Phil felt before he didn't feel anything ever again. And that's why I'll be careful.'

'Careful isn't enough. You need to get Traffic on to this. Promise me you'll do it.'

Karen looked away. 'I will. OK? I will.'

'So did they actually hit you? Because you look very pale and you're holding yourself awkwardly.'

'The wing mirror caught my shoulder, that's all. Look, it's only bruised. Nothing's broken. And I have cases to work. Cases the Mint can't manage on his own. Cases like this one. I need you to run me through this, to make sure I'm understanding it. What you sent me is clear, but I need to be certain I'm on solid ground before I start acting on it.' She drank from a tumbler of clear liquid with bubbles studding the glass.

'Good painkiller, gin,' River said drily. 'Just don't use too much of it.'

'What, not unless you or Jimmy Hutton is around to share it?' Karen chuckled. 'So, take me through your results.'

'As you know, I did the comparisons blind. I don't know who any of these people are. C is the mother of A. The father isn't present in this group of profiles.'

'That's Carolyn Abbott, Will Abbott's mother. The father was presumably her husband Tom but he's been dead since the mid 1980s and there's no prospect of getting his DNA now. But B definitely isn't her son?'

'That's right. B – is that Gabriel Abbott, then?'

'Yes. And D is Ellie MacKinnon, Caroline Abbott's bidie-in. And they're definitely mother and son?'

'That's right. And Frank the dog is his father.'

'So two boys who have grown up thinking they were full brothers are completely unrelated?'

'That's what the science says. But of course, biology isn't the determinant of family relationships that it once was.'

'No, but when it comes to matters of inheritance, blood is still thicker than just about anything else.'

'You look pensive.'

'I'm going to have to go away and think about what this means and how it comes together,' Karen said slowly.

'If you need to talk it over, I'll be here. I'll maybe stop off on my way south tomorrow night, if you like? Take a look at your shoulder?'

Karen nodded. 'At this point, there's no reason why not. I can buy you dinner, say thanks for sorting this out for me.'

'Works for me. We'll talk tomorrow. And Karen?'

'Yes, I know,' she sighed. 'Talk to Traffic.'

River broke the connection and tried to refocus on the PhD. But she couldn't help fretting about her friend. Karen had always been a law unto herself. But River had hoped that if Phil's death had taught her one thing, it was that she wasn't invulnerable. Right now, it didn't look as if that lesson had taken very well.

Normally, Karen would have ventured back out into the night to walk through what she knew and what she surmised in the light of that information. But her whole body felt bruised and shaken. Even walking around the flat was uncomfortable. Instead, she ran a hot bath, topped up her glass with the appropriately named Bathtub Gin, put her Blue Nile playlist on shuffle and settled down to try to make sense of what had happened twenty-two years ago and whether it had any connection other than familial with Gabriel Abbott's death.

Twenty-two years ago, four people had been murdered. Everyone had jumped to the obvious conclusion – that it had been orchestrated by Irish terrorists. There were good reasons for that assumption. Richard Spencer had been a Northern Ireland minister, hated by Republican sympathisers on principle. The IRA had been active around that time, with some very high-profile bombings. It was a convenient place to lay blame when there were no other obvious suspects.

But there were arguments that ran counter to that reasoning. First, the failure of any group to claim responsibility. Terrorists generally liked to shout their triumphs from the rooftops. It was part of the way in which they spread terror. It was also how they bolstered their own feelings of power.

Secondly, in spite of the best efforts of Special Branch and the anti-terrorism unit, there was no evidence of the security at the aerodrome having been breached. Admittedly, it was hardly the tightest of cordons, but because it was a relatively small airfield, strangers who had no business to be there were easy to spot. It wasn't impossible that a terrorist had managed to get on to the airfield and into the hangar where Richard Spencer's plane was housed, but according to the files she'd already skimmed that afternoon, the general feeling was that it would have posed problems. But of course, someone had planted an incendiary device on the plane, so the security must have been breached somehow.

Thirdly, there was the device itself. According to Sunny O'Brien, it was what was generally called an IED – an Improvised Explosive Device – rather than one of the much more sophisticated bombs the well-funded IRA of that period had come to prefer. It wasn't a complex device, and it had none of the hallmarks of known Republican bomb makers.

'So let's assume it wasn't an Irish bomb aimed at a former minister,' Karen said aloud. 'Let's twist the kaleidoscope and see what the picture looks like if we take Richard Spencer out of the equation. What possible motive could anyone have for killing Caroline Abbott or Ellie MacKinnon? Two successful women, but not doing the kind of jobs that you can imagine providing much of a motive for murder.' It was only in a certain kind of traditional detective novel where actors murdered producers who passed them over for lead roles, or bumped off presenters whom they perceived to stand in the way of their greater glory.

When Felicity Frye had told her that Gabriel's father had been Frank Sinclair, that perpetual preachy occupant of the moral high ground, Karen had felt the stirrings of an idea. When he'd agreed to be the sperm donor for the child the two women wanted to cement their relationship, he'd been a lot lower down the greasy pole. He'd had less to lose. If he'd been exposed as fathering a child outside his famously devoted marriage, it wouldn't have been the end of the world.

But by the time of the murders, he'd gone through a meteoric rise. He was editing a national newspaper and beginning to assume a role in the public eye as a commentator and controversialist on radio and TV. Although his elevation to the Lords hadn't happened until the millennium honours list, he was already being talked about as someone who could have an influential career in public life. If Caroline or Ellie had somehow threatened that, if they'd wanted to tell Gabriel the truth about his paternity, that would be a very potent motive for wanting rid of them.

And now she'd seen a photograph that proved he'd been in the right place at the right time.

It had been hard to picture Lord Sinclair skulking about an aerodrome with a bomb, but her years in the police had rendered Karen immune to surprise. The casual cruelties and deliberate destructiveness that people visited on each other no longer shocked her. She'd been leaning towards the idea of Sinclair being responsible, not least because she found his politics vile and his attitudes oppressive. But she'd also been in the job long enough to recognise the danger of letting her own prejudices run away with her. Sinclair might be loathsome but that made him no more likely to be a killer for personal reasons than someone who shared her own world view. Except that she'd never seen any trace of a 'live and let live' philosophy in his utterances.

But everything had been thrown up in the air by the DNA revelations from River. Karen picked up her slippery glass carefully and took a swig of gin and tonic. Everything changed because it wasn't Caroline who was Gabriel's mother but Ellie. Ellie who had supposedly been off having a hysterectomy, but who was actually having a baby. Ellie who had been the devoted friend, allegedly spending the three months post-convalescence, when her show was off air during its annual break, taking care of Caroline through the end of her pregnancy. Ellie who had wanted motherhood but desperately feared losing her career working with children at a time when a hostile government was clamping down on the very idea of talking about homosexuality in schools.

And Ellie who had conspired with Caroline to break the

law. Which meant they were equally vulnerable to exposure as Frank Sinclair. They were the ones who had broken the law, not Frank Sinclair. Making a false declaration on a birth certificate was a serious matter. Karen imagined it would be at least as serious in France, where Gabriel had been born. The revelation of the truth about Gabriel's parentage would have done terminal damage to Ellie's career as well as Frank's public persona. Really, her vague suspicions about Frank and Ellie had been right on the money. It had after all been Ellie who had been Frank Sinclair's friend, not Caroline. Ellie was the one he'd have done such a colossal favour for, not her girlfriend.

And yet, Frank Sinclair had been in the right place at the right time.

When it came to Gabriel Abbott, a fresh set of questions popped up. Here was a man in search of his own history, a man on the edge of discovering who he really was, a man desperate to find a place in the world where he belonged. Such a man might pose a very real threat to what Frank Sinclair had become. There was every reason why the man with the ermine robes might want rid of his unacknowledged son.

The big question was how much Frank Sinclair knew and when he knew it. Karen drained her glass and edged gingerly upright. Finding the answers to those questions wasn't going to be easy. Especially if the Macaroon found out she was planning to ask them.

50

Karen wiped the bathroom mirror and checked out her bruise. The purple had turned blue in the middle but it hadn't spread any further. She took her time getting dry then pulled on jogging pants and her thick velour dressing gown. She curled up on the sofa with another drink and scoured Netflix for something to watch. She was ten minutes into an episode of *Modern Family* when she realised nothing had sunk in and she had no idea what was going on.

'For fuck's sake,' she muttered, clicking the TV off. This was when she missed Phil most of all. Something was nagging at the back of her mind and she needed first to figure out what it might be and then how to track it down. They had always bounced ideas off each other, using each other as a sounding board. They could be as outlandish as they wanted with each other, and know they were safe from mockery. And neither was shy about making suggestions on the other's cases. The last months of his life, when Phil had been working with the Murder Prevention Squad, had been among the most intense and creative of their time together. Now she was inching out on a limb again, she felt isolated and slightly crazy.

She knew she could talk to River. She reckoned she could probably talk to Giorsal. But neither was a polis. Neither had that visceral understanding of the job that she'd shared with Phil. She was on her own again, just as she had been before they'd got together. But now it was worse because she'd known what it was to have someone to share with.

On an impulse, she texted Jimmy Hutton. It was after eight. If he was at home with his feet up, he wouldn't be up for listening to her daft theories. But if he was still at work, as the MPT often were in the evenings, he might have time for her. Nothing ventured ...

> Hey, Jimmy. You up for a blether? Something I'd like to run past you. No big deal if you're busy.

The answer came quickly:

> Hiya K. I'm wrapping up a bit of business in Dunfermline, I could be at yours in half an hour if that suits?

Just enough time to get dressed and throw some pasta in a pan.

> Cheers, pal. Arrabiata or puttanesca?

Jimmy wiped the back of his hand across his mouth and smiled. 'That was what I needed. It's been a long day, going nowhere slow.' He took a drink of water. 'So, what's all this about, then?'

Karen had insisted they eat before she talked through what was bothering her. She'd known Jimmy would be hungry and she didn't want him to have half his attention on shovelling penne puttanesca into his mouth. They moved across to the comfy chairs that looked out across the Firth of Forth and she fixed them both a glass of Edinburgh Rhubarb and Ginger liqueur. 'It's kind of weird. It started out as none of my business, except that Alan Noble wound me up with his laziness.'

Jimmy gave a harsh bark of laughter. 'You're not the first person to say the likes of that. I have no idea how he got his inspector's pips. He gives me the pip, that's for sure. So what did he do, or not do?'

'He did that really crap thing of writing something up as a suicide without properly investigating the alternative. And he'd have probably got away with it if I hadn't been in a bloody-minded mood.' Karen sighed. 'I hate that kind of thing, Jimmy. The dead have only got us to act for them, so we should do it properly, you know?'

'I know. Believe me, I know. Tell me the story, Karen.'

So she did. With more detail and subtlety than she'd given Jason. Horses for courses, after all. He listened attentively, only interrupting a couple of times, seeking more detail. When she reached the point where she'd realised Frank Sinclair might well have a motive for the murder that Alan Noble had wanted to deny, she stopped. 'What do you think?'

Jimmy exhaled noisily. 'What is it with you?' He had a smile on his face and his words were warm rather than critical. 'Most folk would think running the HCU was enough of a plateful without going out looking for more hornets' nests to poke sticks in.'

'Don't give me that. You're the same. Digging every last particle of dirt on violent men to stop them abusing the women in their lives.'

'Fair enough. Though I don't know why you think you need me for this one, Karen. It's Murder 101.'

'What do you mean?'

'You've been so busy looking at abstract reasons for murder – reputation, jobs, maybe getting nicked for telling a few lies on a birth certificate – that you've forgotten the first question, the concrete one. The starting point of every murder investigation.'

Karen looked blank for a moment then slapped her forehead. '*Cui bono.*'

'Exactly. Who benefited back in 1994?'

'There are two obvious candidates: Frank Sinclair and Will Abbott. For Frank Sinclair, it meant the chance to get rid of the two people who could torpedo his public persona. And maybe his marriage as well.'

'But you've no evidence to suggest he had anything to do with it.'

'Not quite no evidence.' Karen fumbled with her phone and brought up the photograph of the newspaper clipping. 'See who that is on the far right? Appropriately enough.'

Jimmy frowned. 'Looks like Sinclair. What's the significance?'

'The other four were dead by teatime. That picture was taken at the aerodrome before the others set off for Perthshire. You have to wonder what the fuck Sinclair was doing there.'

Jimmy gave a low whistle. 'You do indeed. Well, well, well. That's a very interesting photo. But' – he held his hands up as if to ward off a blow – 'it's still not really a motive. You said "two obvious candidates".'

Karen sighed. 'The other one is Will Abbott. That crash made him a rich young man. Both women had wills in favour of each other, but they didn't have one of those clauses that say the survivor has to outlive them by a certain number of days. So because Ellie was a wee bit older, the law says she died first and her entire estate went to Caroline. The big surprise was that Caroline left everything to Will in the event of Ellie being dead already. Not a brass farthing to Gabriel.

But it makes sense to us tonight, knowing what we know now. Caroline left Gabriel out because, in spite of what the paperwork said, he wasn't her son. If she'd made her will in Scotland, Gabriel would have got a share because of forced heirship. But under English law he was cut loose without a penny. I've looked at the probate, by the way. Most of the money was Caroline's, but Ellie left a substantial estate too because the mortgage insurance paid off her half of the house.'

'So Will got Gabriel's share as well as his own?'

'Not to mention he gets pats on the back all round for supporting his little brother by paying his school fees for years and paying his rent on the cottage in Kinross. Win-win.'

'It's pretty extreme, though. I mean, how old was he at the time?'

'He was eighteen. He was about to start a degree at Imperial College in London. But what he wanted was to set up a computer gaming company. According to Jumpin' Jack Ash, he had a killer game idea that he was developing but Caroline wanted him to get his degree first.'

'You think that's a motive?'

Karen pulled a face. 'I don't know. It's a difficult age. Teenagers notoriously get things out of proportion. All they can see is what they want. Most of us hate our parents at some point in our teens. It's like, all they want is to thwart us. If it wasn't for them, the world would fall into line and everything would be fine. Did you never feel like that?'

He shrugged and poured himself another drink. 'A bit, I suppose. But the only thing I wanted to be was a polis and they thought that was a pretty good idea so it could have been a lot worse. I know what you mean, though. I had pals who maybe would have blown up their parents if they'd known how to. But how sure are you that the two things are connected? The plane crash and Gabriel Abbott's murder?'

'I don't like coincidence, Jimmy. Gabriel was doing fine. A bother to nobody. Taking his meds and behaving himself. Then he decides to draw up a family tree and a couple of weeks after discovering that the man he thought was his real dad was pushing up daisies two years before he was even born, Gabriel ends up dead. You don't think that's too much of a twist of fate?'

'I'm not saying you're wrong, Karen. All I'm saying is you've got nothing in the way of evidence. A coincidence and a funny feeling isn't enough, you know that. And you also know how hard it is to get evidence at this distance. If you really think Gabriel's murder is a consequence of what happened in the past, you'd have more chance of success. Maybe you should sweet-talk Alan Noble into letting you lend a hand.'

She snorted. 'Not going to happen. I've already been warned off by the Macaroon and Alan is at full gallop on his high horse. I need to do some more research, Jimmy. Find something a wee bit more solid. I've not been through all the files yet. Maybe there will be something there that will ring a bell for me.'

'Maybe,' Jimmy agreed. He knocked back the last of his drink and stood up. 'I need to get down the road. I've got an early start in the morning. Evil men to charge with silly wee crimes till they get the message that they need to change their ways.'

'Good luck with that. And thanks for coming over. It always helps to talk things through.' She walked him to the door.

'It cuts both ways, Karen. You've listened to me often enough. At our level, we need to be able to talk to people outside our own team who understand the job. Now don't you be staying up too late. I can see you're suffering with that shoulder.' He patted her undamaged shoulder on the doorstep and walked away. Then he suddenly stopped and swung round.

He had a quizzical expression on his face. 'Something just popped into my head. I don't know when exactly this was, and it might be long after the plane crash and all that, but was there not a big stooshie when Sinclair was running the *Examiner* about them paying an Irish terrorist for serialising his book? Does that ring any bells with you?'

Karen frowned. 'Not really. It doesn't sound like his kind of story. I don't see him giving the IRA the oxygen of publicity,' she said, ironically referring to Margaret Thatcher's famous dictum.

Jimmy rubbed a hand over the nine o'clock shadow on the side of his head. 'That's the thing, it wasn't a Republican terrorist. It was on the Unionist side, so Sinclair's rag could paint him as a man defending Queen and country. Only the Press Complaints Commission didn't see it that way.'

As he spoke, she realised that was what had been lurking in the dim recesses of her brain earlier, nagging at her memory. Karen smiled. 'I'll check it out.'

Jimmy grinned and tipped his head towards her. 'Don't stay up too late.'

Karen thought about taking his advice, but she knew she wasn't tired enough to guarantee falling down the rabbit hole into sleep. She might as well go back to her laptop. There might be answers in the stack of boxes in her office, but there might also be threads to follow in cyberspace.

At first, she struggled. Her search terms were too broad, resulting in a tsunami of results, impossible to mine for anything useful. But gradually she began to refine what she was looking for to the point where she was finally able to click on a link that took her to the website of a political journalist who'd specialised in writing sympathetically but not uncritically about the wilder shores of Ulster unionism.

And there, buried in the backwater of a blog post from half a dozen years before, was what she was looking for. The journo had written a short and pithy account that gave her all the keywords she needed to flesh out her account.

Peter Boyd had, by his own admission, started off as a boy soldier with one of the militant protestant militias that had waded into the Troubles with gusto and the conviction that God was on their side. His devotion was coupled with a sharp intelligence and a knack of staying out of trouble with the law. His career of escalating violence had culminated in a series of pretty primitive bombs that had been responsible for blowing up cars and taxis belonging to IRA men. Then one of his bombs had caught his target's family, killing the man's wife and four children.

Boyd had walked away from his fanatical friends, some of whom decreed that walking away was not an option. He'd had to go on the run, spending half a dozen years in Canada. Then his daughter had a baby and the pull of seeing his granddaughter was more than he could resist. To finance it, he'd written a warts-and-all account of his years waging war. Some reviewers cast doubt on whether he'd actually had a finger in all the pies he'd claimed, but it made for a decent read.

Frank Sinclair had been editor of the *Examiner* in 1992 when Peter Boyd's book had been published and he personally did the deal to buy the serial rights. The *Examiner* took Boyd at his own estimation, painting him in heroic colours, making much of the fact he could never take a drink in a London pub with his back to the door, never mind go home again.

There was, predictably, outrage. The toothless Press Complaints Commission got on its high horse. Sinclair – with the support of some of John Major's government colleagues – told them to go fuck themselves in barely coded terms, and six months later everyone had forgotten about the story.

It was no kind of evidence, Karen knew that. But it did put Frank Sinclair in the same room as a man who had made bombs that worked. A man who presumably felt some cordiality towards an editor who had stuffed a wedge of money into his bank account.

She leaned back in her chair. She'd thought Frank Sinclair wasn't much more than window dressing when Felicity Frye's revelations had forced her to include him as a suspect. But now he was starting to look disturbingly credible. She knew better than to keep worrying at the idea, though. The best thing she could do was to set it to one side and let her subconscious have its wicked way with it while she concentrated on something else.

Which might as well be Will Abbott. She started with Wikipedia. It wasn't evidence she would necessarily choose to rely on, but it would give her pointers as to where she might more profitably search.

The basic information seemed accurate enough. Date and place of birth, parents, early years. His first school had been Glencorsie House, where Gabriel had been a student from six to eighteen. But Will had left Glencorsie at sixteen to move to the Ada Lovelace School in London, a private academy that specialised in science and computing. From there, he'd gone on to Imperial.

Out of curiosity, Karen checked out the Ada Lovelace School website. It trumpeted the school's credentials in the teaching of chemistry, physics, biology and every aspect of IT, claiming to focus both on the theoretical aspects and the practical applications of its subjects. 'Nothing like a bit of practical chemistry,' Karen said, thinking back to what Sunny had told her about easy ways to blow up planes.

Poking about the sitemap took her to a page dedicated to Prizegiving Day. Scrolling through the assorted awards, she found a button that took her to archived lists of the awards.

She clicked on 1994 and discovered Will Abbott was no stranger to the podium. He'd won the Geoffrey Challoner Hanley Prize for Best Designed Chemistry Experiment and the Ludwig Horner Award for Programming. The best-designed chemistry experiment. It was probably too much to hope there was anyone still around at the Ada Lovelace School who might remember what that was. But it might be worth a try.

What was clear was that Will Abbott had studied chemistry and knew how to apply his knowledge. It was circumstantial at best, but it did take her one step closer to the point where she could justify questioning him.

She was about to call it a night when her phone buzzed with a message from River.

> Speak to the traffic camera guys about the SUV. I know you haven't done it yet, so do it now! Xxx

'Bloody woman,' Karen muttered. Life had been simpler when she'd kept the world at arm's length. She found the number for the Automatic Number Plate Recognition analysts in Hendon. There would be someone there. They operated in real time so they had to be staffed up to deal with emergencies. Eight thousand cameras round the UK, twenty-seven million reads per day. Karen couldn't do the maths but she knew it was a number well beyond the capacity of the human brain. Then she brought up the map that showed Kinross and the immediate area around it.

The phone was answered on the third ring. 'ANPR authorisation.' A woman's voice on the other end.

'This is Detective Chief Inspector Karen Pirie of Police Scotland. I need access to cameras around Kinross last night between eleven and midnight.' She rattled off a list of roads to the accompaniment of keystrokes from the other end.

'How far do you want to go on the M90? We've got eyes all the way up and down.'

'Ten miles either side of Kinross should do it.'

'OK . . . I've got product from eight cameras showing on my list. And you're coming up on my system as an authorised officer. So that's all fine. I'll email you authorisation and access codes.'

It was that simple. Except that it wasn't. There was only so much the technology could do. Without a registration plate, there was no shortcut. She'd have to go through the footage camera by camera, minute by minute. Normally, Karen would have handed over a task of such routine tedium to Jason. But she was still working in that grey area between legitimate inquiry and complete flyer. If anyone was going to end up neck-deep in shit over this, it really shouldn't be Jason.

'The sooner I get started,' she muttered, opening the newly arrived email and logging herself on to the system. It took less than two minutes for her to be up and running. She compared the camera positions to the road maps. A local who knew what he was doing could have left the scene on lanes and back roads without being picked up. She'd have to hope her attacker wasn't from round there. In that case, the SUV would definitely show up.

Karen opted to go for the minor roads first. If she'd been making a getaway, knowing what everybody seemed to know these days about roadside cameras, that's what she'd have done. Balanced against that was the possibility that her assailant didn't know the territory and had headed back the way he or she had come. But there would be less traffic on the back roads at that time of night, so she could exclude them more easily.

She ran the camera films on fast forward, only slowing when a vehicle came into shot and speeding up again as soon as she saw it wasn't a boxy dark SUV. She zipped through more quickly than she'd expected. It took less than an hour to cover the four minor road cameras. Now for the motorway. There would be more traffic there, but at that time on a weeknight, it wouldn't be hard to check it out.

The whole search was over in a little more than two hours. She had identified three dark-coloured SUVs at the approximate time of the attack. Now she had to run the number plates through the database to see who owned them. Karen took a deep breath. She almost wished she was religious so she could say a wee prayer. *Please, God, let one of these belong to Will Abbott or Frank Sinclair.*

She was out of luck. A Perthshire farm, a village in the hills behind Dundee and a company in Newcastle. No obvious connection to anyone involved with the case. Of course, if Gabriel's death was completely unconnected to his past, if she'd been building castles in the air, his killer could have come from anywhere. Dispirited, Karen closed down her computer, popped a final dose of painkillers and dragged her weary body to bed.

Sometimes Scarlett O'Hara's final line felt more like a curse than a promise.

51

Linlithgow town centre always struck Karen as a random act of violence by town planners. It was hard not to be charmed by the striking romantic ruin of the late medieval palace, or the clutch of interesting and attractive buildings from the eighteenth and nineteenth centuries lining one side of the main street. Then, slapped down right in the heart of the main street, was one of the ugliest brutalist blocks of flats she'd ever seen. It overlooked the marketplace, with its statue of St Michael, promising to be *kinde to straingers*. Somebody had been very unkind indeed to the citizens of Linlithgow.

Darren Foreman's mother lived in an enclave on the fringes of the town centre that had been provided by the council for the elderly. Short terraces of single-storey cottages alternated with small blocks of four flats. The uniform grey harling gave the whole cul-de-sac a depressed air. A tiny square of scrubby grass sat at its centre with a redundant sign prohibiting ball games. It would have been a struggle to play anything more territorially adventurous than marbles, Karen thought.

They left the car in the residents' parking area and walked up the pavement to number 39, one of a pair of ground-floor flats. The woman who opened the door was bent almost double. She had to crane her head back to let them see anything more than a thin frizz of unnaturally brown hair. She couldn't have been much more than her mid-sixties, but she seemed to have the fragility of a much older person. She peered through smudged and greasy glasses at them. 'You'll be the polis,' she said, her West Coast accent obvious even in those few words. She gave a sigh of resignation. 'Darren said you'd be coming. I suppose you'd better come inside. I don't want the whole street knowing my business.'

They followed her into a living room that barely had room for a pair of armchairs and a massive TV set. Two dining chairs sat in either corner, their cushions still covered in plastic. The room was stiflingly hot; Karen could feel sweat springing out the length of her spine as she walked in. The smell of air freshener rasped in her throat, its overwhelming purpose to kill the odour from the ashtray that sat on a table by one armchair.

'You'd better sit down,' Cathy Foreman said grudgingly. She collapsed into her own chair with obvious relief. 'Now, what's this nonsense about my Gary? Darren says you think he had something to do with some lassie's murder? You're barking right up the wrong tree, hen.' Already she was on the defensive.

'We're from the Historic Cases Unit,' Karen said. 'When we're revisiting old cases, all sorts of names come up in the course of our inquiries. Part of our job is to eliminate people from our inquiries. That's why we were talking to Darren, who was very helpful. We were able to discount him completely—'

'Of course you were,' Mrs Foreman said, the sarcasm obvious. 'Nothing was ever Darren's fault. Total Teflon boy. Nothing ever stuck to him. Whatever went wrong, it was always Gary got the blame, never Darren.' She shook her head and fished a packet of cheap cigarettes out of the pocket of her ratty cardigan.

'So why we're here today is to do our best to take Gary out of the picture so we can focus on the guilty party in this case.' Karen hoped Jason's face wasn't giving away any surprise at her blatant lies. Although, judging by the way Mrs Foreman was peering at the end of her cigarette, trying to bring the lighter flame to the right place, her eyesight probably wasn't up to spotting the nuances of facial expression across a room, even one this small.

'So you say,' the old woman grumbled. 'Gary was always getting the blame for things he never did. Darren was always on about Gary having a drink problem, but that wasn't true. He had awful bother with his stomach. Some days he could hardly get out of bed with the pain. And sometimes he was driven daft with it. It's not surprising he sometimes lost the place with folk and got into all kind of rows over nothing.'

'That must have been hard for you to see.'

'It was. But I'd happily have it all again if I could have my boy back.' She shook her head, her mouth twisted in bitterness. 'It's always the same. It's the poor working folk that get the blame. That accident on the building site, if we had the money, we could have sued them into the middle of next week. Health and safety, my backside. And they had the nerve to say it was Gary's fault. As if he'd take stupid risks.'

'Had he always worked on building sites?'

'No, hen. He had a good job on the buses.'

'Here in Linlithgow?' Karen hoped she knew the answer.

'No, that was back in Glasgow. I was still living in Castle-milk then, before I moved out here to the sticks to be near my sister and her family. Gary was driving buses for years.'

'Can you remember when he started?'

Mrs Foreman sucked on her cigarette and tilted her head back. 'It must have been 1993. His father walked out on us in 1992 and he was on the buses within the year.'

'You must have been proud of him.'

'I was. He looked that handsome in his uniform.'

'Did you get on his bus often?' Jason with a supremely helpful question for once, sounding like he was interested.

'No, son. He never had a route out my way. Mostly he was on the 16. That was a good long run, from Clydebank to Auchinairn. You had to be somebody to count on to drive a route like that, right through the city centre and out the other side in the rush hour. They didn't have the bus lanes like they have now, by the way.' She folded one arm across her chest, as if she was holding her pride in.

The 16 was the bus Liz Dunleavy had identified as Tina's likely choice to get into town. 'And that was his usual route?' Karen clarified.

'Aye. I went in once to Queen Street and rode out to the terminus and back with him. My, but he was a good driver. It was a pack of lies they told to get rid of him. I think they were jealous.'

'When did he leave the buses?' Karen asked.

'It was 2002 when he got his jotters.' She shook her head, tutting.

'Do you know why?' Jason asked, his voice surprisingly gentle. He was learning, Karen thought. Not before time, but he was learning.

Mrs Foreman looked away. 'Like I said, there were always folk that were jealous of my Gary. Somebody told a pack of lies. They said they'd seen him drinking on the job. They even planted a quarter bottle in his locker. It was a disgrace. The union never stood up for him. All those years paying his dues and when push came to shove, they told him there was nothing they could do.'

'That must have been hard,' Karen said.

'Bastards,' the old woman said primly. 'Never gave him a reference either. After that, Gary had to take what he could get, and that's what killed him. You'd have thought Darren would have stepped up to the mark and taken care of me. But no. Not Darren. It's always been self, self, self with that one. Not a patch on my Gary.'

'Did Gary ever mention a girl called Tina? Tina McDonald?'

Her head snapped up and she fixed Karen with a glare. 'Is that the lassie got herself murdered?'

Karen had no time for blaming the victim. But there was still information to be had from this bitter self-deluding woman. 'It's Tina's murder we're looking at, yes. She was a hairdresser in the West End.'

Mrs Foreman harrumphed. 'Hairdressers. No better than they should be. Flighty types. I know hairdressers. My Gary wouldn't have taken up with anybody like that. He kept himself clean, Gary did. He was very fussy who he asked out.'

'Did he have a partner? A regular girlfriend?'

'He got married in 2000 but it didn't last. She was a real bitch. She didn't deserve a man like Gary. They got divorced in 2004. Thank goodness they didn't have any bairns. She was the kind of bitch that would have kept him from his kids. Better off without the heartache. Since then, he never really bothered with women. He spent a lot of time on his computer, buying and selling stuff. And going out with his pals, the way men do.'

'So he never mentioned Tina McDonald?'

'Are you not listening to me? He wouldn't have wasted his time on the likes of that.'

'It's just that she regularly used that route. The 16.'

'That doesn't mean he knew her.' Her mouth was a line carved in stone. 'You can't prove he knew her.'

'I wondered, that was all. If he'd maybe seen anybody bothering her on the bus. And maybe mentioned it to you.'

She thawed a degree or two. 'He never said anything like that. He'd have stepped in, Gary would. If a lassie was getting bothered, he'd have put the man off the bus. Make no mistake about it.'

'I understand. You're helping me to get a clear picture of Gary. But my boss, he's a stickler for crossing the t's and dotting the i's. It's not enough for me to go back and say, "I've spoken to Mrs Foreman, Gary's mum, and what I've learned is that Gary was not our man." I need to bring back proof. Do you still have any of Gary's possessions? His razor, maybe? Or his hairbrush? Maybe a coat or a scarf he used to wear?'

She looked put out. 'What? You want to test his DNA? Oh, don't give me that look. I might be old but I'm not stupid. I watch the telly, I've seen *CSI*, I know all about forensics. Aye, well, I'd give you his DNA like a shot if I had it because I know my son and I know he's not the man you're looking for. But I haven't got anything like that.' Now she had the air of a woman who has trumped a winning hand.

'That's a pity.'

Cathy Foreman shook her head. 'I don't need your kind of proof to know that my Gary was a good man. Even after he died, he was still doing good. He carried a donor card, you know. There's bits of Gary all over the place, saving other people's lives. I don't know how you can even countenance the idea that a man like that could have anything to do with a murder.' She struggled out of her chair. 'Now, if that's all you've got to say for yourselves, I need to get on. Everything takes longer when you have to walk about like a half-shut knife.'

It was a dismissal. And in all honesty, Karen didn't think there was anywhere else to take the interview. Jason trailed after her and they walked back to the car. 'I don't know what it is about this case, but nobody wants to make us a cup of tea,' he complained. 'Never mind chocolate biscuits.'

'Still, we got a bit of a result. There's a connection between Tina and Gary Foreman. The number 16 bus is the link. He could have talked to Tina about her plans for the evening.

Or he could have overheard her telling somebody else on the bus.'

'If she'd told somebody on the bus, they'd have come forward at the time.'

'Probably. But they might have had their own reasons for keeping shtum. Sometimes they think that what they know isn't important and they don't want to get involved. Speaking of not getting involved, do you think Mrs Foreman was telling the truth when she said she didn't have anything that might have Gary's DNA on it?'

He shrugged. 'I don't know. She was quick enough to hustle us out after that came up, so maybe.'

'Either way, we're not going to get our hands on it. We need that DNA and I think we've got zero chance of getting it.'

Jason stopped in his tracks. 'Zombies,' he said.

Karen turned, regretting the movement as her shoulder kicked in. 'Jason, what are you talking about? Zombies?'

'See, when a zombie bites you, you get infected, right? Part of the zombie enters into you, yeah?' He was as animated as she'd ever seen him. 'But the zombie eats a bit of you too, and you become part of the zombie. It's like you share each other's flesh. What if it's like that with transplants?'

'You're not making sense,' Karen said. 'This is a high watermark in the surreal, Jason. Standing in the middle of a council estate in Linlithgow in the middle of a murder investigation discussing the zombie apocalypse? I mean, what the fuck?'

'You're not listening,' he protested. 'Zombies and their victims, they share themselves. What if that happens with transplanted organs? What if the people that got Gary Foreman's organs are still walking around with his DNA in them? I mean, it makes sense, right? It's still his flesh.'

Karen realised her mouth was hanging open. 'Jason,' she croaked. 'You might just be a genius.'

52

In the car, Karen googled furiously. Jason clung to the steering wheel as if he needed something to ground him. 'You're right,' she said, not quite believing what she was seeing. 'A transplanted organ retains its donor's DNA. There's a research paper here saying that donor DNA is detected in the recipient's blood for years after the transplant.' Her face was radiant with wonder. 'Who knows how many people are wandering about this country with Gary Forcman's DNA in their blood?'

'The transplant people,' Jason said, ever literal. 'They'll know how many and who they are.'

Karen was still reading. 'Doctors used to have to do regular biopsies to check whether an organ was being rejected. But now they can tell by doing a blood test. They can see how much donor DNA is in the recipient's bloodstream and that lets them know whether they need to change the doses of the anti-rejection drugs. Jason, a simple blood test will tell us all we need to know.'

Jason looked less excited than he had when he came up with his idea. 'Yeah, but how are we going to get our hands

353

on it? How do we find out who got the bits in the first place? And how do we get the info? We can't just go up to somebody and say, "See that nice new heart you got? Well, we think it might belong to a murderer, how's about you let us take some blood and check?"'

It was an idea that brought Karen up short. She shook her head. 'I don't know the answer, Jason. I suspect Colin Semple's going to be getting another pound of flesh from Police Scotland, though.' As she spoke, she was searching for his number.

She put the phone to her ear, waited, then tutted. 'Voicemail.' Cleared her throat. 'Mr Semple, this is Karen Pirie. DCI Pirie. I'd like to talk to you about an interesting issue that's come up relating to the Ross Garvie case. Can we get together at some point today? Thanks.' She ended the call and stared unseeingly ahead, her brain racing over possibilities. Then Karen shook her head like a dog emerging from water, yelped at the pain from her shoulder and said, 'Back to the office, Jason. We might as well get stuck into the Abbott case while we're waiting for Colin Semple.'

'OK.' He started the engine.

'That was a brilliant idea, by the way. Whether we go down that road or not, it was still a brilliant idea.'

His ears turned an unflattering shade of pink. 'See, it's not a waste of time watching horror movies.'

Karen laughed. 'It mostly is, Jason. Trust me, it mostly is.'

'Maybe. But you have to think about these things. I mean, in the event of a zombie apocalypse, what weapon would you choose to defend yourself?'

This time, they weren't skimming the files. They were scanning every page to see where it fitted in the big picture they were trying to put together of the events leading up to the mid-air explosion that had killed four people. Slowly, the timeline of the day was starting to emerge. Close attention had been paid to the movements of Richard and Mary Spencer, but Caroline and Ellie hadn't been ignored in the process.

Most of the paperwork was routine; dull, possessed of no evidential significance, but testament to the thoroughness of the investigators, both police and Air Accident. Keeping alert was tough. It was late in the afternoon when Karen found something that sharpened her attention and set the adrenaline coursing through her. Halfway through a report from one of the investigating officers was a single sentence: *Caroline Abbott and Ellie MacKinnon were driven to the aerodrome by Mrs Abbott's son Will.*

'Yes,' she hissed, lips drawn back in a harsh smile.

'You got something, boss?'

She passed him the page. 'It's a very wee something, but it's a start. It puts Will Abbott on the scene. There's got to be more. There must be a timeline in here somewhere. And there should be a statement from Will himself. This investigation was done with such a fine-tooth comb, they wouldn't have missed him.'

'It's a pain in the arse that nothing's in order,' Jason complained, not for the first time.

'On the other hand, it makes us look more carefully. If the files were all properly indexed, we'd go straight to what we thought we needed and we might end up missing something crucial.' Out of the corner of her eye, she saw the exasperated look he gave her. 'All right, I know I'm a pain in the arse too. But you know I'm right.'

She was almost at the bottom of the first box when Jason interrupted her. 'I've got the timeline,' he said, waving some sheets of paper above his head. 'And he didn't just drop them off. He drove into the aerodrome and he had a look around. Look, here: "Ten fifteen to ten thirty RS completes paperwork and flight path details. MS, CA, EM, FS, tour of control tower. WA to hangar."'

'Bingo. Not just Will but Frank Sinclair too. Anything that explains what he was doing there?'

'Hang on. "Ten thirty. To hangar. Already present in hangar, mechanic Christopher Barnes, Will Abbott, son of CA." He was definitely there, in the hangar, before they left.'

Karen whooped in delight. 'We're getting somewhere. There's got to be a statement from the mechanic, and one from Will Abbott too. That's our priority now.'

Jason flicked through the bundle he was looking at. 'Here we go, boss: "Mr and Mrs Spencer arrived at the aerodrome with Mr Frank Sinclair, newspaper editor. They were driven by Mr Sinclair's driver. Mr Sinclair was discussing the possibility of Mr Spencer contributing a column to his paper. He toured the site with the three women then posed outside the hangar for photographs taken for the local weekly paper by freelance photographer Don Mayhew. Mr Sinclair left before the plane took off." Is that what you were hoping for?'

Karen smiled. 'Pretty much. It's circumstantial, but enough circumstantial adds up to a case.' Buoyed up, she returned to the tedious task, only to be interrupted by her phone.

'Mr Semple, thanks for getting back to me,' she said.

'DCI Pirie. You wanted to talk to me. Are you in Edinburgh?'

'I am.'

'Good. I've been in court all day but I'll be back at my stable in twenty minutes or so. You know where we are?'

'You're off the Canongate, right? Down by the kirk?'

'That's it. If you can get here then, I've got a small window in my diary.'

'I'll be there.' She ended the call and pushed herself upright. 'I'm going to see Semple at his stable.'

Jason tittered. 'I know, I know,' he said, holding his hands up defensively. 'I've had the lecture. It's Scottish legal tradition. Part of our heritage and all that. But talking about advocates hanging about in their stables, it's ridiculous. How can they not have offices like the rest of us?'

'It's not just tradition.' She put her jacket on, struggling less than she had the day before. 'It's a way of excluding the rest of us from their world. It reminds us that they're set apart from the likes of you and me.'

'So they should call their firms "palaces", not stables. That makes me think of a bunch of clapped-out old nags.'

Karen laughed. 'I think you're supposed to imagine sleek racehorses with gleaming flanks, going flat out on the final furlong.' She groaned. 'I wish I hadn't said that. Not on my way to see Semple.'

'You sure you don't want me to come with you?' Wistful tone, big puppy eyes.

'I'll be fine. You get on with this and see if you can find those statements.'

Semple's office was exactly as it ought to be, in Karen's opinion. Dark wood panelling, diamond-paned window looking out on a grey stone tenement courtyard and a fragment of grey Edinburgh sky; scarred old desk polished deep mahogany from long years of cleaners' elbow grease; stacks of files tied with ribbon; and shelves of books whose titles alone might cure her insomnia. And at the heart of it, the advocate himself in his distressed leather chair, hands folded on his stomach, gazing equably at her.

Karen explained as best she could the status of Gary Foreman's DNA. 'So we don't know how many people benefited from his organs or where they are now,' she concluded. 'But we don't have to engage in any invasive procedures to get at the DNA. We just need to be able to examine the DNA results from their routine blood tests. What are our chances, do you think?'

Semple probed his left cheek with his tongue, brows lowered. It was a theatrical performance of thought. He looked up at the ceiling, then back down at Karen. 'There's certainly an interesting argument to be made. On the one hand, you are seeking to breach medical confidentiality in the matter of transplant donation and further in the matter of blood test results. On the other hand, I could argue that since there is no need for the identity of these patients to be disclosed to the police, the courts or indeed the patients themselves, there is no breach and the public interest is such that it should be granted.'

'And you think that argument could carry the court?'

'I do consider myself an able enough advocate to win the argument. Or at the very least to set up grounds for appeal. I could certainly run this for you.' He unfolded his hands and folded them again. 'On the other hand . . . ' His eyebrows raised in a question.

Karen obediently let herself be drawn. 'On the other hand, what?'

'What is driving you here, Chief Inspector? It seems to me that you have already demonstrated the validity of your case. It's rather like Sudoku, where you've filled in so many of the squares that the last two or three are inevitable.' He unclasped his hands to tick off the points on his fingers. 'Firstly, you have established a familial DNA connection between Ross Garvie and Tina McDonald's murderer. That points to a father, an uncle, a brother or, I believe, possibly a cousin. Ross Garvie's biological father has an absolute alibi, and you fully expect his DNA to exonerate him. Apart from Ross he has only daughters, so far as you have been able to ascertain. The only other close male relative that you are aware of is Gary Foreman, Ross Garvie's uncle. Who also had no sons. He had a potential link to the victim, in that we know he drove the bus on the route she regularly used to travel in town and which she almost certainly used on the night she was murdered. The man is dead, Chief Inspector. There is never going to be a trial, so "beyond reasonable doubt" is never going to be tested in this case. I would suggest you simply declare the case closed. Tell Tina McDonald's family that the killer's identity is now known but he is beyond human justice.' He smiled, a pitying, indulgent smile. 'I entirely understand your drive towards certainty. Not to mention the headlines such a novel approach will bring. But anything other than the course I've put forward is about you and not the case, I would suggest.'

His words shocked her. A lawyer rejecting a paying brief on moral grounds hadn't featured on her expectations of how the day would go. 'There's still room for doubt.'

'Only the kind of doubt that afflicts the blinkered and the partial. His family won't like it, but you have to weigh that against the closure it will give Tina McDonald's family.'

'You're right, Gary Foreman's family won't be happy. His mother in particular. She'll be all over the tabloids, shouting the odds.' It was a valid point, but Karen suspected she was using it to cover up her own desire for absolute answers. Because she had a sneaking suspicion Semple might be right about her motives.

'No, they won't be happy. But nothing you do at this point is going to make them happy. Besides, you can step up on to the high moral ground and say that you're confident you have reached the correct conclusion without wasting Police Scotland's budget or potentially invading the privacy of innocent transplant recipients.'

Karen breathed deeply. 'But this isn't Sudoku. It's not about playing word-games for the media. It's about truth and justice.'

He shifted in his chair and leaned forward, forearms on the desk, hands clasped in front of him as if in earnest prayer. 'Karen, you know better than that. You don't have to wrap yourself in that tattered cloak to feel proud of the job you do. I'm not pressing you for a decision now. But I think you should go away and think about what really matters here. I'll take it on if you are determined to go ahead with it, but I would advise you to consider what's really in the best interests of your department and the victim's family.'

53

C hastened, Karen took the back way from the Royal Mile to her office, down past the graffitied hoardings and the grimy stone of the railway viaduct. Sometimes her thoughts were too ugly and uncomfortable for the drama and beauty of the Edinburgh skyline. Semple had been right. She'd been so excited at the prospect of nailing a case with a flashy new trick that she hadn't looked at the whole picture. She was getting things all out of proportion, something Phil would never have let her get away with.

Which reminded her that she had half-promised River that they could meet between trains that evening. She leaned against a hoarding and sent a text suggesting they meet for a quick Vietnamese meal near the station. Karen could unburden herself and discuss the options with a friend, as opposed to a lawyer who couldn't know what really mattered to her.

She arrived back at the office to find Jason with his feet on the desk, a can of Irn Bru in one hand and in the other, a doughnut leaking what looked suspiciously like blood and pus. 'Good to see you hard at work,' she said, sounding as sour as she felt.

'I found the statements,' he said, not even pretending to sit up. 'Both of them. So I went to the shop. There's one in the box for you. I got you the chocolate cream one.'

Sometimes, Karen thought, she didn't deserve the people in her life. She flipped open the box and stared greedily at the sticky brown glaze dripping on to the greaseproof paper. 'That's a glorious sight,' she sighed, reaching for it before she even took her coat off. She sank her teeth in, unable even to remember the last time she'd had so much sweet sugary pleasure. 'Oh man,' she groaned, muffled by chocolate crème pat. This, she thought, was utter self-indulgence. And maybe enough self-indulgence for one day.

'How'd it go with the stallion?'

Karen spluttered crème pat over her desk. 'Not fair!' She wiped her mouth with a tissue from her drawer. 'I think there's something wrong with him. He thinks we don't need the DNA to point the finger at Gary Foreman. There's enough on the balance of probabilities, since we're never going to have to stand up in court and prove it beyond a reasonable doubt. So he says it's a waste of money to set him on the medics.'

Jason hoicked his feet off the desk and sat up straight. 'What? Is this the invasion of the bodysnatchers? A lawyer turning down money?'

'Apparently. I've to go away and think about it. But never mind that. I'll think on my own time. What did you find?'

He handed her a couple of sheets of paper stapled together, holding another close to his chest. 'This is the statement from Christopher Barnes.'

It began with the usual official introduction. Place, date, time, full name, address, date of birth. Christopher Barnes, an aircraft mechanic, had been fifty-three at the time. His words had the traditionally stilted air that came from a police officer translating them from colloquial English to officialese.

I attended my place of work at Elstree Aerodrome at 8 a.m. on the morning of 5 May 1994. Upon arrival I changed into my overalls and collected my toolkit from my locker. I performed routine maintenance on a Piper Cheyenne III on the airfield apron. I then proceeded to the hangar where Mr Richard Spencer kept his Cessna Skylane. I arrived there at approximately 9.15. I unlocked the hangar, which was padlocked as usual and showed no sign of forced entry. I was to prepare the plane for a flight to Scotland that morning so I performed a series of checks on the plane itself and on the engine. There was nothing untoward about the body of the plane or the engine. When I checked it over, I could see nothing out of place.

At no point did I leave the hangar unattended. At one point the airfield manager John Saroyan came in and asked me about another customer's plane. We spoke for about five minutes then he went away. Later, a young man came into the hangar and introduced himself as Will Abbott. He said his mother was to be a passenger in the plane. He was interested in the plane so I told him a bit about it. While he was there, I opened up the hangar and walked out to check there were no hazards outside or on the runway. I was gone for perhaps five minutes at most but Will Abbott was still there when I returned so the hangar was never left unattended.

It is possible that a foreign object such as a bomb could have been hidden in the plane. There are enclosed areas of fuselage which I had no reason to check. Mr Spencer had a key for the padlock and there is also a spare in the office safe. I suppose someone could have got in without it being obvious. We do have security and the local police routinely check the hangar is locked up, but if someone was determined to get in at night they could. But nobody could have interfered with the plane that morning.

Karen read the last sentence aloud and looked at Jason. 'One person could have.'

He nodded. 'But who would suspect a teenager whose mother died in the crash?'

'We would. Let's see what he has to say for himself.'

A similar preamble then a short statement:

I drove my mother Caroline Abbott and her friend Ellie MacKinnon to Elstree Aerodrome on the morning of 5 May 1994. We got there about ten o'clock. They were flying up to Scotland with their friend Richard Spencer and his wife Mary. Richard was a qualified pilot and had his own plane. Richard was filling out paperwork and the ladies were having a tour of the control tower. I was interested in the plane. I'd never seen a small plane up close before so I went to the hangar.

Mr Barnes, the mechanic, showed me the plane. Then he opened the doors and went outside to check everything was OK for take-off. He was gone for a few minutes and I was there the whole time so nobody could have got in then and planted a bomb. Then Mr Spencer and the passengers came out to the hangar. I gave my mum a hug and said goodbye to her and Ellie, then I watched as they got in the plane and taxied out to the runway and took off. That was the last time I saw my mum.

She put the statement down. 'Means, motive and opportunity. That'd be good enough for Miss Marple.' She sighed. 'Unfortunately we have the small matter of proof.'

'How do we get that?'

'I don't know. I don't know if we can. We need to pull together as much circumstantial as we can.'

Jason produced another piece of paper with a flourish. 'And speaking of circumstantial, see what I found!'

It was a statement from Frank Sinclair's driver. Jason stabbed one paragraph with his finger. 'Look at that. Either the mechanic was lying or he forgot.'

Karen read the key passage. '"Mr Sinclair told me to park the car behind the hangar so he could get away quickly after he'd said goodbye. So I did that. The mechanic came out of the back door of the hangar when he heard the car. He was interested in the Bentley's engine so I opened up the bonnet to let him have a look. I suppose it took about ten minutes, but nobody went into the hangar past us."' She sighed. 'But anyone could have gone in the front of the hangar, presumably. I wonder if they arrived before Ellie and Caroline and Will?'

Jason went back to the timeline. 'According to this, they arrived a good twenty minutes ahead of the others.'

'Where was Sinclair then? Before the tour of the control tower?'

'It doesn't say. Everybody thought it was the IRA, all they were looking at was access to the plane. They weren't checking every movement of the passengers or the people with them because they were all above suspicion. Do you still think the plane crash is tied in with the Gabriel Abbott murder?'

'I do. It's too much of a stretch not to. Gabriel takes an interest in his history and boom, next thing he's dead.'

'But why?'

'I think because finding out the truth about his past would make him reconsider what he'd always believed about the plane crash. Not to mention that he'd be pretty bloody angry with Will for doing him out of his inheritance, which he'd realise as soon as he saw Ellie's will. And who knows where that would have ended up, if he'd pursued it? All sorts of awkward questions start to rear their heads then. They'd probably already started, which was why Will – or Frank Sinclair – decided Gabriel had to be taken out of the picture.'

Jason scratched his armpit while he considered. 'It's a bit harsh,' he said. 'I mean, what kind of person kills his mother then kills his brother just because things might get a bit sticky?'

'There's a thing called narcissistic personality disorder. People who have an inflated sense of their own importance, a lack of empathy for others. They're vain, they crave the power over others they think they deserve. They can be arrogant and callous. They think they're better than everybody else and they don't care who they trample on in their desire to get what they want.'

'A bit like Donald Trump, then?'

Karen grinned. 'Nail on the head, Jason. Controlling, blaming, self-absorbed, intolerant. And always that high opinion of themselves.'

'Maybe that's how Will Abbott is so successful in business.'

'And Frank Sinclair. Which reminds me. The SUV that tried to run me over. It could theoretically have got away without being caught on a camera if the driver knew the roads round here, but I think it's more likely that it wasn't a local. The most likely one was a company car from an outfit in Newcastle called Spartacular. I need to check it out . . . ' As she spoke, she was already logging on to a company search website that Police Scotland subscribed to. 'Spartacular,' she muttered, waiting for results. 'Gotcha.' She skimmed the page. 'CGI specialists, apparently. Image rendering.' Then she stopped scrolling. 'Fuck.'

'What?' Jason got up and looked over her shoulder. '"Wholly owned by Glengaming plc since 2014." That's Will Abbott's company. We've got him bang to rights.'

'Hang on, Jason. Hang on. It's just another bit of circumstantial flim-flam. It doesn't prove anything yet.'

But even as she spoke, Jason was reaching for the phone. He keyed in the number displayed on the screen for Spartacular. Dismayed, Karen said, 'No, wait.' But it was too late.

'Hello. This is Detective Constable Jason Murray from Police Scotland. We have a report of an incident on Tuesday evening involving a vehicle registered to your company ... Yes, I'll hold.' He gave Karen the thumbs up. He covered the mouthpiece. 'Gimme the reg, quick!'

Karen scrambled through her phone where she'd noted the SUVs' registration plate details. She passed him the phone and pointed out the one she was interested in.

A moment passed, then Jason repeated what he'd said before, adding the registration number Karen had shown him. 'And so I need to know who was driving the vehicle at the time of the incident ... Yes, I appreciate that ... Aye, well, I'm trying to spare you the embarrassment of having uniformed police turning up at your offices for something so trivial ... No, no question of charges, it's only a witness statement ... ' He rolled his eyes and made the sign of hanging himself with his free hand. 'I appreciate that. But honestly, I'd like to get this sorted out asap, you know how it is? I only need a name to finish off my paperwork. You will? Excellent.' He recited his official email address and the Gayfield Square office number. 'You've been very helpful, thank you.' His grin was so wide she thought it must hurt. 'He's going to email me the details soon as he gets the chance to look at the vehicle logs.'

'I can't believe you just did that.'

Jason looked embarrassed. 'Sometimes I say to myself, "What would Phil have done?" and I do it.'

An unexpected wave of emotion brought a lump to her throat. Phil would have laughed like a drain at the thought of being a role model for the Mint. 'Me too,' she said. 'He'd complain that we never paid that much attention when he was alive.'

'You did,' Jason said. 'You do. You pay attention all the time. There's not many bosses would have pulled my nuts out the fire the way you did the other day.'

Karen chuckled. 'You might be a numpty sometimes, but better the numpty you know.' She contemplated the papers on her desk. 'I think we've done a pretty good day's work, Jason. Let's knock it on the head now before we screw up.'

He looked at her out of the corner of his eyes. 'Do you fancy a pint?'

He'd never suggested that before, always waiting for her to take the lead. But a lot of things seemed to be happening for the first time between them. Karen nodded. 'Why not?'

54

Karen wanted to be near Haymarket to make it easier for her to meet River. So Jason decided he'd have two pints and take the train home. They crossed Leith Walk and caught a 26 to the West End, heading into Ryrie's Bar. They found space at the polished wood counter, where Jason ordered a pint of Flying Scotsman. Karen stuck with gin, going for a Blackwood's with tonic. Shetland botanicals, fresh and fragrant. The first burst of flavour on her tongue lifted the grey from the day.

Neither of them noticed that the man in the North Face jacket at the other end of the bar had been in the same bus queue. Even after the attempt on her life, Karen had no thought that anyone would be on her tail. She was used to being the watcher, not the watched.

'So, what will we do if it turns out Will Abbott was driving that SUV?' Jason asked, filling his mouth with crisps.

'I'm not talking about work,' Karen said firmly. 'I need to not think about what comes next. Let it churn away in the background for a wee while. Talk to me about football or politics or where you fancy living in Edinburgh.'

Jason thought for as long as it took him to demolish the rest of the crisps. 'Did you know that between January and the play-offs, Raith Rovers scored ten more points than any other Championship side?'

Karen, who knew this from her irrepressible Twitter feed, feigned ignorance. 'That's amazing,' she said. 'Phil would have enjoyed that.'

It was all the encouragement Jason needed to talk about the vexed questions of Scottish football for the rest of his pint and most of the next one. When he finally ran out of facts and opinions, he stopped dead and gave Karen a blank look. 'I don't really do politics,' he said. 'That Ruth Davidson's a bit of a comic turn sometimes, though.'

Karen smiled. 'It's OK, Jason. You're off the hook. I'm meeting River off the train in ten minutes. We're going to the Vietnamese café up the road for a bowl of pho.'

He gave a weak smile. 'That's spicy, right?'

'Pretty much.'

'I don't really do spicy.'

'I know.'

'Unless it's a vindaloo after a few pints, you know?'

'Away home to your mum's cooking.' Karen finished her drink and patted him on the shoulder. 'I'll see you in the morning. I'll have slept on things. I'll know then what we're going to do next.'

Karen and River perched on stools at the window counter of the Vietnamese café, waiting for their bowls of pho to cool down. River didn't look like a professor in Scotland's leading forensic science establishment. With her mane of red hair, her battered waxed jacket and disreputable old work boots, she looked more like a spruced-up traveller. Karen always half-expected to see a mongrel of dubious temperament at her heels. But underestimating River would be a serious mistake.

Karen had explained her dilemma on the short walk from the station. Now they were settled with food, River was ready to engage. 'You're doing your usual thing,' she said with weary good humour.

'What do you mean, my usual thing?'

'You're overcomplicating the issue. You've got this brilliant idea and you've picked it up and run with it without stopping to think. You always do this. You're so smart you never stop at the first step. You can't help yourself running all the way up the stairs.'

Karen made a show of pretending to be offended. 'I have no idea what you're talking about.'

'Jason made a smart connection. And by the way, what's that about? Jason showing signs of life above the neck?'

'He's learning,' Karen said defensively. 'He keeps asking himself what Phil would have done.'

River raised her eyebrows. 'It's not a bad mantra, as these things go. Anyway. Jason made a connection. And you were so excited by the prospect it opened up that you went straight from nought to ninety in no time at all without pausing to consider.'

'Consider what?' Karen sampled her pho and decided the temperature was acceptable.

'Yes, Gary Foreman's DNA will be present in the bodies of the recipients of his organs. But just take one step backwards. When the medics are analysing the recipients' blood, how do they know it's the donor's DNA that they're seeing in the mix?'

Karen processed the question then buried her head in her hands. 'I am so fucking stupid,' she said.

River tested her soup and winced. 'What is it about you Scots and your asbestos mouths?'

'They'll have had to analyse the donor DNA before they even started doing the transplants. Gary Foreman's dead so he's got no right to confidentiality, he's got no human rights. There's no reason for the transplant authorities not to release that DNA to us. OK, we might have to get a sheriff to sign off on it, but this way doesn't compromise a living soul.' She made two fists and punched the air. 'You are a genius, River.'

River shrugged. 'I'm just slower off the mark than you. So, does that resolve your moral dilemma?'

'Pretty much. I'll talk to Semple in the morning, see what he thinks.'

'It's not a hard case to argue, particularly since this is probably the last chance the victim's family has for closure.'

The two women concentrated on their soup. In a spirit of celebration, Karen ordered an iced coffee with condensed milk, the speciality of the house. She was about to take her first sip when her phone alerted her to an incoming text. It was from Jason.

Bingo. Email from Spartacular transport guy. On Tuesday night, the SUV was signed out to Will Abbott.

Karen closed her eyes, saying a silent thank you to the fates.

'Something wrong?' River asked.

'Quite the opposite,' Karen said. 'Something very, very right.'

55

Karen waved River off on the last train back to Carlisle. The revelation that had emerged from their meeting had set half her mind at rest. But Jason's text had provoked fresh tumult in her thoughts. What was she to do about the Gabriel Abbott case? Did she have enough to go to the Macaroon and demand that Alan Noble open his case files to her? Was there any obvious way to get beyond the circumstantial to solid probative evidence? Or was she going to have to walk away? Her personal certainty that a five-times murderer would walk free if she did that wasn't actually a valid reason for arresting someone.

She walked back through town. It would have been quicker to follow the path beside the Water of Leith but there were a few places where there wasn't enough light pollution from the city to illuminate the way clearly. Karen wasn't afraid of being attacked, but she didn't trust her own sure-footedness in the dark and she was already carrying an injury that compromised her movements.

As she walked, she turned over possible ways to resolve what she saw as the irrevocably entwined cases of the plane crash and murder of Gabriel Abbott. Once he'd uncovered the true identity of his mother, he'd only have been a couple of careless conversations away from discovering Frank Sinclair was his biological father, a revelation that would have been embarrassing at the very least.

To a man like Frank Sinclair, possessed of a towering ego and the power to pander to it, the idea of being exposed as a liar and a hypocrite would have been unbearable. And it would undermine his public position as an arbiter of other people's morals. How far would such a man go to protect position and reputation? Did he have the sort of people around him like that English king who had wanted rid of Thomas à Becket, the kind who would do what their boss hinted he wanted? 'Who will rid me of this lying crooked little bastard?' It was all a bit melodramatic, a bit medieval. But she never ceased to be amazed at the lengths apparently respectable people would go to in order to keep the aspidistra flying. She knew not to underestimate the petty bourgeoisie.

And then there was Will Abbott. How far would a single-minded eighteen-year-old with a killer idea have gone to realise his dream? A narcissist wouldn't hesitate to put his own certainties ahead of the lives of others. If he'd known the terms of Ellie and Caroline's wills, he would have known he'd have all the capital he needed to get Glengaming off the ground. But how much did he know about Gabriel's parentage and how long had he known it? Did he know when he took possession of his inheritance that a sizeable chunk of it wasn't morally his? What would Gabriel have done once he found out? By all accounts, he was a smart man with a hefty dollop of paranoia in his make-up. Would he have been smart enough to work out that his non-brother had had a powerful motive for murder all those years ago?

But noodling around with motive wasn't taking her any closer to finding the sort of evidence that would impress the fiscal. These days, they wouldn't countenance a prosecution unless they were more than 50 per cent certain of a conviction.

She turned on to Hamilton Place, distractedly dodging a group of young men heading down towards Stockbridge. Where was the evidence coming from? They had Will Abbott signed out as the driver of a black SUV that had been seen close to where a black SUV had tried to run Karen down. But that was will-o'-the-wisp thin. And the cameras wouldn't have sufficient definition to reveal the driver. Will could have handed the keys to anyone. He could even argue that the SUV had been taken without his knowledge or consent and returned before he needed it next. What Karen was sure of and what she could prove were two very different things.

She still needed to place him in the area on the night of Gabriel's murder. Had he supposedly been in Newcastle then too? What vehicles had he had access to? If they could find that out, she could set Jason up with hours of camera feeds to work through. And what about the gun that had killed Gabriel? People talked a lot about violence in video games. Could somebody have given Will Abbott a gun as a kind of joke?

'Get a grip, for fuck's sake,' Karen said aloud, to the surprise of a middle-aged couple walking past. She was reaching absurdly for things she didn't even know, never mind that she could prove.

Was there anything about 1994 that might lead somewhere? The only loose end she could think of was the experiment that had won Will Abbott a school prize. If that had anything to do with the mechanism of the bomb that had blown up the Cessna, it was another piece of circumstantial evidence that would add to the pile. Sometimes circumstantial could be enough to convict, if you could only amass enough of it.

As she neared home, Karen stopped to buy milk and ibuprofen at the supermarket. Her shoulder had started to ache again. It was distracting her from her surroundings, making her concentrate all her attention inwards. She popped a couple of pills on the final walk back to the flat, but they seemed to have no effect. She stood under the shower for what felt like ages, but the nagging throb didn't ease up.

Wrapped in a towel, she sat with a cup of tea staring out at the night. Low cloud, no moon, the sea a dark shapeless presence in the gap between her and the lights of Fife. There was a low point in every investigation, a place where all roads seemed to lead nowhere. Tonight she was in that nowhere zone. Once she could have counted on Phil to dig her out of her depression, to remind her that it was like this every time and she always got past it in the end, even if every case didn't end with a conviction. But now she was on her own to face the bleakness.

Angry with herself, knowing sleep was a million miles away, Karen decided to go out again. Without even thinking about it, she headed straight for the Restalrig Railway Path. As usual, it was deserted at this time of night. Even the dog walkers seemed to give it a miss for that last turn of the night. Karen turned up her collar against a sudden sharp wind and kept walking, trying to ease her pain and get her thoughts off their repetitive treadmill.

And then everything changed. Some instinctive apprehension kicked in. Animal instinct told her she was under threat. She heard heavy breathing, felt the heat of another body close at hand. Karen half-turned, needing to know what the adrenaline was telling her to flee. The movement deflected something hard and heavy that had been heading straight for her head. Instead, it landed full force on her already bruised shoulder. Karen screamed in pain, a terrible rending sound that cut a ragged slice through the night. She had a confused awareness of another body crashing into hers, the momentum carrying her to the ground, a knee in her ribs. Karen tried to wriggle away, but her left arm was a useless drag holding her back.

She squirmed her right arm free and clawed at the shadowy face of her assailant. She was rewarded with a yelp as her nails made contact with flesh. He jerked his head back before she could find his eyes, grabbing her jacket and pulling her towards him before slamming her into the ground again.

Karen found her breath and yelled at the top of her voice. Noise was her friend right now. The louder the better, the more chance of rescue. She smashed her right fist into his ribs and felt his weight shift off her chest. As she prepared to punch again, he went on the attack, grunting with effort. She saw an arm and something else cutting across the light. Then darkness and silence.

56

The first thing she knew was that she felt sick. A deep, heavy weight of impending nausea that filled her senses. Her whole body was swaying. Karen opened one eye a crack. A swim of blue light against white. It hurt her head so she closed her eye again. She heard a groan and wondered who was in pain.

'Can you hear me, Karen?'

That was her name, right? But she didn't recognise the voice. Not Phil. Not one of her pals. No need to answer.

'You're going to be all right, Karen.'

She knew that was risible. Wanted to laugh but couldn't be bothered. That groan again, and this time she recognised the sound. It was her. She tried to speak, but all that came out was another unformed groan.

'Take it easy, Karen. Can you hear me?'

What would it take to make this stranger shut up? 'Aye,' she managed to force out.

She felt a hand patting her shoulder. The good one. The one that didn't feel like a red-hot burn. 'We're on our way to the hospital,' the voice said.

She turned her head and threw up. Then everything went black and quiet again.

The next time she opened her eyes, Jason was standing next to the bed, his expression stricken. The nausea had passed and the pain had been replaced by a distant feeling of vague discomfort. 'Take that look off your face, Jason. I'm not going to die,' Karen croaked.

A huge grin spread across his face. 'You're awake. Brilliant.'

'What time is it? What happened?' Karen tried to move but there was something obstructing her. She looked down to see her left arm strapped in a sling across her body.

'You broke your collarbone. Well, probably Will Abbott broke your collarbone, but either way, it's broken. It's nearly four o'clock. In the morning. You were knocked out cold.'

'I don't remember. The last thing I know is that I went for a walk down the Restalrig Path.'

'Well, we've got Will Abbott in a cell at Gayfield Square. When the uniforms arrive, he said he saved you from being mugged by three Arab-looking guys. He's not said a word since then. We've also got three Syrian refugees in custody who are claiming they weighed in to save you getting a beating from Will Abbott. I know who I believe, but the bosses are dancing on hot bricks, waiting to hear from you.'

Karen closed her eyes momentarily, trying to focus. 'All I can say is that I know the Syrians and I have a good relationship with them. And I believe Will Abbott tried to run me down earlier this week. So that's got to be enough to interview him on, if not to charge him. Oh, and I think I scratched his face, so you should probably take scrapings from under my nails. Did they find what he hit me with?'

Jason shook his head. He clearly hadn't paused long enough to comb his hair, which stuck up in five different directions. 'One of the Syrians says he saw Abbott throwing

something up the embankment, but there's no point in looking till it's daylight.'

'So we've got Abbott in custody right now? With a strong
probability he's going to be charged with assaulting me?'

'Maybe even attempted murder,' Jason said. 'He must have
hit you really hard.'

'Has anybody told the Macaroon?'

Jason nodded. 'The duty sergeant called the chief super
and he called the ACC. He hasn't shown up yet, though.'

'Where's my clothes? My phone? For fuck's sake, help me
up, Jason.'

'I'll get a nurse,' he said, leaving her lying fuming and
impotent.

It took half an hour and a lot of forcefulness before Karen
managed to get out of bed and into her fleece. Two nurses
and a junior doctor kept telling her they wouldn't be held
responsible, that she might have a concussion, that she was
taking risks with her health. 'There's no point arguing with
her,' Jason had said glumly as he took scrapings from under
her fingernails.

Karen limped out to the car with Jason, wincing as she sat
in the passenger seat. 'I'm not putting the seat belt on,' she
said. 'Get over it.' Then she slid her phone out of her pocket
and keyed in the Macaroon's number. 'Head for Fife,' she
told Jason.

Her boss answered the phone eventually, sounding extremely
unhappy about it. 'Do you know what time it is, DCI Pirie?'

'I do, as it happens. I've just got out of the hospital with a
broken collarbone and a head injury. We have my attacker in
custody. And I want permission to access DI Noble's files on
the murder of Gabriel Abbott because I believe my attacker
may be his killer.'

'What?' Lees shouted. 'You're making no sense. Obviously,
that blow to the head—'

'Will Abbott attacked me. I think because I'm the only person investigating his connection to the murders of his brother and his mother twenty-two years ago.'

'You're raving. I understood that Abbott rescued you from a mugging?'

'That's the opposite of what happened. The Syrian refugees are my friends.'

'Oh, for heaven's sake, Pirie, keep your politics out of this.'

'It's nothing to do with politics. I know these men. I've spoken to them several times. I've arranged for them to meet with Craig Grassie, the local MP. They're the last people in Edinburgh who would mug me. Will Abbott, concentrate on him. I need access to those files while we've still got him in custody.'

'On what basis?' Lees was sounding less angry now, more cautious.

'On the basis that he's tried to derail any investigation into his actions. First by complaining to DI Noble about me, and now by trying to kill me. For the second time this week, actually.'

'The second time?'

'He tried to run me down on Tuesday night.'

'Why am I only hearing this now?'

'Because I only had circumstantial evidence. But the circumstantial evidence is growing into quite a pile now. All I'm asking is a look at the case files. How can that be a problem?'

The Macaroon said nothing.

'I know Abbott is the kind of high-profile businessman that the government loves. But that doesn't mean he should get away with murder,' Karen said. 'You've got to let me do my job.'

Lees sighed. 'Fine. A look at the case files. That's all. You've got no operational authority here.'

'Thank you.' She ended the call before he could change his

mind. As they headed round the ring road towards the Forth Bridge, Karen leaned against the headrest. Whatever lovely drugs they'd pumped into her were still working very nicely. It would be easy to drift into sleep, but she knew that wasn't a good idea. Not with a head injury. 'Where's DI Noble based? With the Gabriel Abbott investigation?'

'Glenrothes, I think.'

'That's where we're going, then. It's time Gabriel Abbott got some proper police attention.'

57

It would have been fair to say that DI Alan Noble was less than thrilled to be rousted out of bed at half past five in the morning by a nervous duty sergeant who claimed he was under orders from DCI Pirie. Who claimed to be under orders from ACC Lees – a claim Noble wasn't about to contest, since that would involve waking his commanding officer. That would have to wait till later. As it was, he took his time showering, dressing and drinking two cups of coffee before he ambled into the station just over an hour later.

'You're an embarrassment to your rank, Inspector,' was the greeting he got from Karen. 'This is a murder inquiry, not a community policing assignment. When a superior officer gives you an order, you don't dawdle. You carry it out.'

'Aw, come on, it's the middle of the night. And it's not a murder. Nothing's that urgent in a case that's been sitting for a couple of weeks already.'

'It is when there's a suspect in custody with the clock ticking for a different offence.'

Noble looked shocked. 'A suspect? In my case? I already

told you, it's not a murder. It's a suicide. You can't be a suspect in a suicide.'

'Just because you've written it up as a suicide doesn't make it one. It's murder now, all right? Now let me see the case files.'

'But I—'

'Do you really want me to wake ACC Lees again? Because he was really pissed off when I called him earlier. I don't fancy your chances of getting a civil word out of him.'

Noble looked like he'd bitten into a chocolate and found a scorpion. 'This isn't your case.'

'Stop being so bloody pathetic and give us access,' Karen snapped, brandishing her phone. 'I'm going to count to ten, then I'm calling the ACC to report your insubordination.'

Noble flushed. 'They're in the incident room.' He wheeled round and marched down the hallway. He unlocked an office and waved them inside. It was small; a cluster of chairs around four tables pushed together, five computers at the ready. Archive boxes piled in one corner. Crime scene pictures pinned to a corkboard wall. 'Our so-called incident room. One step up from a broom cupboard.' Then he looked at Karen as if seeing her for the first time. 'What happened to you?'

'The killer you didn't catch took a pop at the boss,' Jason said, a mutinous set to his jaw.

'Don't you speak to me like that, Constable.'

'Don't give him cause, then,' Karen hit back. 'Now, if you'll just give us access to the case files, you can get away back to your bed.'

'No way. If you're looking at my team's product, I'm going to be in the room.'

Karen liked him a little better at that moment. 'Fair enough. Maybe you could organise some coffee and bacon sandwiches?'

'I'm not the tea boy. I'm the SIO on this case.'

'I've not seen much evidence of that so far,' Karen snorted.

Noble flushed. 'You don't get to come in here throwing your weight around. You cold case cops, you swank around the place getting results because the lab can finally make sense of the evidence samples that mugs like me on the front line have been collecting for years. You think you're better than us. Well, you try running a case in real time, with the bosses and the press and the families breathing down your neck twenty-four seven and see how well you do then.' He stopped abruptly, his neck redder than a turkey's wattle.

Karen eyed him up and down. Buried under his indignation was a valid point, though she didn't recognise herself in his characterisation. 'I've run plenty of cases in real time,' she said calmly. 'And never with anything less than one hundred per cent. But this is not about your wounded pride. It's about practicality and hospitality. If we were in our office, Jason would be rustling up the coffee and sandwiches because he knows where to find them. You can either speed the plough or you can fuck off, Alan. It's all one to me.'

Rage seethed off Noble, but he had more sense than to fight with a senior officer, especially one with Karen's record in direct combat. He bit his lip but he set them up with file access, then reluctantly left to rustle up supplies. He returned in moments, grumbling that there would be something to eat and drink soon. Karen, already deep in the pathologist's report, barely acknowledged him. Jason, who was normally more interested in food and drink than any satisfaction work could provide, didn't even look up.

They worked on through the arrival of strong bitter coffee and stale muffins, absently eating and drinking. 'Don't get crumbs on the keyboards,' Noble complained. Jason gave him a hard blank stare and carried on eating.

A couple of hours passed slowly in the tedious consumption

of other people's work; little of it possessed of any interest to them. Karen's head had begun to hurt, a dull ache behind her eyes. 'Do you know what they gave me?' she asked Jason.

He shook his head. 'No idea.'

'Or when?'

He shrugged. 'Probably about five hours ago?'

Karen popped two pills from the blister pack the reluctant doctor had given her and swallowed it with the rancid dregs of her coffee. She sighed and returned to her examination of the crime scene reports.

A couple of minutes later, Jason cleared his throat. She looked up. 'Something?'

He nodded. She got up and moved behind him to read the screen. Noble jumped up and joined her. It was a witness statement. Douglas McCloskey had been taking his dog for a bedtime walk in Kirkgate Park. He knew Gabriel Abbott by sight; they both drank in the same pub. He'd seen Abbott walking down Kirkgate towards the Loch Level Trail path.

Then a man came from the opposite direction, from the path itself. And he walked up to Gabriel. I could see him quite well because they were under a street light. They knew each other all right, because they did one of those handshakes with half a hug. They spoke for a wee minute then they walked back together to the path. I didn't see if they actually went down the path, because I'd turned round to go back by then. The man who met Gabriel was a stranger to me but I think I would know him if I saw him again. He was a couple of inches taller than Gabriel, quite lean and wiry. Maybe a few years older. He was wearing a suit jacket and jeans and a dark T-shirt. A younger man's clothes, I would say.

Karen looked at Noble. 'You haven't put this description out,' she said flatly.

He looked pained. 'It's not much of a description, is it? It could be half the blokes in a Kinross pub.'

'I don't think so,' she said. 'Have you had him in to do an E-FIT?'

'I didn't see the point. Those things never look like the real thing. And eye-witness testimony, it's notoriously unreliable.'

'Jesus,' Karen said. 'Have you got any other witness statements like this?'

Noble shook head. 'Nothing. It's an uncorroborated sighting in the dark, for fuck's sake.'

'For fuck's sake, *ma'am*, Inspector.' Karen sighed. 'You've got an unidentified stranger walking towards the locus where the body turned up and you didn't think that was indicative of something other than suicide? Christ.' She turned away in disgust. 'Print that out, Jason. And you're sure there's nothing else remotely similar? Nobody seen walking around Kinross with a gun or anything?'

'Obviously not. Look, there was no indication of anything other than a chance encounter between people who knew each other. It's not like we had a suspect to put in a line-up. We thought, it's just an old guy in his seventies walking his dog, trying to make himself look important.'

Jason collected the statement from the printer. 'We're out of here,' Karen said. 'But there's every chance we'll be back. So make sure all your paperwork's in good order and there's no more unexploded bombs in there.'

She headed for the door, willing herself to put one foot in front of the other without stumbling. Was this concussion, that sense of being light-headed and heavy at the same time? Once they were clear of the police station, Karen gave Jason his instructions. 'Let's get back to Edinburgh. I want you to put together a six-pack including Will Abbott and send someone from Fife to pick up Douglas McCloskey and bring him to Gayfield Square. It's got to be an officer from outwith the inquiry that does the ID from the six-pack, but there's plenty of bodies around the place that we can rope in. Let's get this thing moving.'

'And what about you, boss? You need to rest.'

'I'm OK, really. My head's still working, which is the main thing. But you need to tell me if I'm going off the air, OK?' Jason met this with a troubled look. 'I know, I know. How will you tell?' She smiled. Even the muscles of her face felt weary. 'Let's get this done before some smart-arse from Health and Safety decides to send me home.'

58

They were met at Gayfield Square with a degree of contained panic. Four men in custody, one lawyered up, three whose first language wasn't English, and no statement from the victim that might clear up who were the heroes and who the villains. Karen sat down with a sergeant from CID she'd drafted in before when she'd needed an extra body. He was good in the interview room; he'd done the courses and he'd actually assimilated what he'd been told.

She repeated what she'd told Jason – that, as far as she was concerned, the Syrians were her friends and Will Abbott was a potential suspect in five murders. 'I don't have much recall of the attack itself. But I think I scratched my attacker's face.' She held up her right hand. 'Jason took scrapings at the hospital. Witnessed by a nurse.'

'That's helpful. He's got a scratch on his face. He was accusing the Syrians, but if you've got his DNA under your nails, that blows him out.'

'I'm told there might be a weapon on the embankment?'

The sergeant grinned. 'We had a team out at first light. It appears that what you were battered with was a heavy-duty power strip with a surge protector. Much more likely to be the weapon of choice of a software millionaire than a trio of Syrian refugees, if you ask me. It's away to the lab now for DNA and prints.'

'So what are you waiting for?'

He grinned and went off to the interview room. Karen took herself off to the observation room where there was an audiovisual feed from the interview. Nothing else to be done while Jason was organising a photo ID parade, unless she snuck back to her office for a nap. How long did you have to wait after a head injury before you were actually allowed to go to sleep unsupervised?

Will Abbott and his lawyer were facing the camera. Abbott leaned back in the chair, all nonchalance and confidence. He had his mother's good looks, sharp symmetrical features and thick head of honey-coloured hair. He was, she thought, distinctive. With luck, Douglas McCloskey would pick him out of a line-up.

Abbott's solicitor, a well-known face called Cameron Campbell, read out a prepared statement. 'My client was spending the night in Edinburgh prior to meetings with business associates tomorrow. He decided to go for a walk to clear his head before bed and chose the Restalrig Railway Path. He had been walking for a short time when he came upon a woman being attacked by three men of Middle Eastern appearance. He tried to fight them off but he too was overcome. The police arrived before matters escalated into something more serious. He will be making no further comment on the occurrence.'

The sergeant leaned back in his chair, mirroring Abbott's body language. He chuckled. 'Really? Mr Campbell, you know as well as I do that your client's statement has got more holes than Blackburn, Lancashire. It begs so many questions it should be sitting on Princes Street with a dog on a string and a cardboard cup in front of it.' He shifted to a more upright position. 'Mr Abbott, are you booked into a hotel in Edinburgh?'

'No comment.' Abbott's voice was more reedy than she expected.

'Where is your car parked?'

'No comment.'

'Why were you stalking DCI Karen Pirie? Was it to do with her Historic Cases Unit investigation into your mother's murder?'

He blinked half a dozen times but said, 'No comment,' without flinching.

And so it continued. Abbott was good at this. But if he was as narcissistic as she thought, he would pride himself on being able to outwit them. She was about to give up and go in search of a decent cup of coffee when Jason stuck his head round the door. 'Result, boss. Douglas McCloskey picked Will Abbott without any hesitation. We've got it all on video. Do you want to come and have a wee word with him?'

Douglas McCloskey was a sprightly seventy-two-year-old with loose, lined skin that reminded Karen of a Shar Pei. His blue eyes were sharp enough, though. He'd brought his dog with him, a grumpy-looking terrier who sat on his lap. McCloskey stroked the dog's ears compulsively, which Karen thought might explain the dog's bad mood. 'That was very interesting,' he said as soon as they'd introduced themselves. 'I was worried I might not be as good a witness as I thought, but as soon as I saw those photos, I knew that was the man I'd seen with poor Gabriel.'

'You did very well, Mr McCloskey,' Karen reassured him. 'I've seen the statement you gave to my colleagues. Do you know what time it was when you saw this encounter?'

'It would have been about quarter past ten. I'd been watching a repeat of *Scott and Bailey* and when that finished at ten,

Roxy and I went out. It takes me about fifteen minutes to get to the place where I turn around, and that's where I saw them.'

'And was there anything that struck you about their meeting?'

'I thought Gabriel seemed a bit taken aback. Hard to be sure, I know, but he looked a wee bit startled. But they greeted each other very friendly.' He fondled the dog's soft ears. 'There was certainly nothing antagonistic about it, which is why I thought it was probably nothing to do with poor Gabriel's death. The bench he was found on was quite a step away from the start of the path, and the other man didn't look like he was dressed for walking. Town shoes, you know?'

'But you didn't see him come back into town?'

'Well, no, but I wouldn't have. I had my back to the path, walking home. I don't go about spying on my neighbours.' He sounded mildly offended.

'I know, Mr McCloskey. But even though I've been a police officer a long time, I still hold out for the lucky break.'

He chuckled and pointed to her sling. 'Looks like you got an unlucky break there.'

She sighed. 'You could say that. Thanks, Mr McCloskey. We'll get an officer to drive you back home.'

'The neighbours will be thinking I've been breaking the law.'

'I hope not. We'll be in touch.'

In the lull while they waited for someone from the fiscal's office to come round and make legal sense of what they had, Karen hid in her office and called Colin Semple. 'I've been thinking about what you said,' she began. 'And I think you're right. But I was discussing it with a colleague and she pointed out that I was trying to run before I could walk.'

'I'm not sure I follow you.'

'In order to identify the donor DNA in the recipients' blood, the medics have to know what they're looking for. So before they do the transplants, they take samples of the donor DNA for later comparison. That DNA will be on the record—'

'And Gary Foreman, being dead, has no human rights.' Semple had caught on faster than she had. 'And the hospital owes him no duty of confidentiality.' He groaned. 'We've both been rather stupid, Chief Inspector. Overcomplicating things. Thank goodness for your clever colleague. I shall get on to it first thing on Monday morning and, with a following wind, we should have a conclusive answer very soon. Well done.'

'Not really. Thank you for making me stop and think about what I was doing. Sometimes I get so focused on the prize, I forget the human dimension.'

'We all do, Chief Inspector. We all do.'

Karen put the phone down and allowed herself a moment of pleasure at reaching this point in the case. It would be closed, and closed soon. In a sense, justice had been thwarted because Gary Foreman had never passed a night in jail for the murder of Tina McDonald. But he'd had to live with it every day, and she suspected he'd known his own torments. The main thing was that the people who loved Tina would finally know the truth. No more moving through the city where they lived, wondering whether the man they'd passed on the street, stood next to in a bar, sat beside on the underground was the one who had killed their Tina. No more fearing they could somehow have prevented her death.

Karen built a picture of that night in her head. Tina, dressed up to the nines, on the bus. Did she know Foreman from her regular trips on the number 16? Had they grown pally over time? Had he thought there was more to her open, friendly manner than there was? Or did some trip switch in his brain flick on that night for reasons that were nothing to do with Tina?

Either she'd told him her plans for the evening or he'd overheard her telling someone else. And he'd come off his shift determined to make her his that night. He'd taken the underground back into town and picked up Tina's trail at some point. Maybe asked her to dance. Maybe suggested they go on somewhere else. And then something went badly wrong. Was he too insistent? Did she have second thoughts? Did she sense something off about him?

Whatever the reason, Gary Foreman turned savage. And what had started as a fun night out ended in fear and pain and death.

Karen heaved a sigh. It was a horrible story, but at least now it was one with an ending. One more case closed. But another lay in wait, one that was far less tractable. It was a never-ending task. She remembered a poem they'd done at school, a poet called Robert Garioch with a Scots version of the myth of Sisyphus. 'Bumpity doun in the corrie gaed whuddran the pitiless whun stane / Sisyphus dodderan eftir it, shair of his cheque at the month's end.' Sometimes that was exactly what life in the HCU felt like.

59

The Fiscal Depute was unfamiliar to Karen, who had hoped for someone she'd worked with before. Someone who knew what she'd achieved and how she worked. Someone who might cut her a wee bit of slack. The fiscal's job was to work with the police to discuss whether there was enough evidence to bring charges and to direct the investigation where more was needed. Karen thought a good fiscal required a dash of imagination and a core of trust for the best results. Those were not always qualities found among lawyers, in her experience.

What she knew about Ruth Wardlaw: she hadn't been in the Edinburgh office for long. Now in her early thirties, she'd cut her teeth in the Highlands where, frankly, there wasn't an overwhelming amount of serious major crime. Murder was thin on the ground, as was armed robbery. But Karen acknowledged that they did have their share of sex and drugs and rock 'n' roll up there; it wasn't the lovely idyll that Sunday-night TV drama projected. So Karen hoped the new FD was adept, experienced and adroit enough to take a chance on her case against Will Abbott.

Karen brought Ruth through to the HCU office, away from

the hurly-burly of the main station. She sent Jason off to make tea for Ruth – 'no coffee for me, it gives me the illusion of intelligence' – and tried to take the measure of the FD. She looked extremely businesslike – lawyer's black suit with severely cut jacket and trousers, no jewellery except for a pair of gold knots in her ears, mid brown hair in a tidy bob, watchful eyes and a surprising slash of scarlet lipstick. Karen was aware of Ruth engaging in the same assessment and reckoned she was going to come off a lot worse. She didn't want to think about how shit she looked right now, still in last night's jeans and fleece, hair like a bag lady, arm in a sling and eyes sunken and bruised with lack of sleep. 'I don't usually look as rough as this,' she apologised. 'It's been a tough week and somebody tried to kill me last night.'

'Ah yes. That's the first item on our docket, I believe?'

'Your docket, not mine. I'm staying well clear of the process on that. I'm the victim, so I'm taking no part in anything except giving a statement. Which is probably less helpful than I would have liked,' she added wearily.

'So while we have Mr Abbott in custody for this matter, you want to make progress on another case?'

'Two cases, actually. One historic, one current. I don't think we have enough on the historic case. It's very circumstantial and I don't see how I can progress it any further.' Karen went through everything she had uncovered about the plane crash and the complex relationships that coloured in the background. Ruth was recording her, but also making extensive notes in a grey leather notebook. At the end of her recital, Karen rubbed her eyes with the heel of her hand, feeling the ache coming back to plague her.

Ruth scratched her chin and frowned at her notes. 'You need to follow up on that chemistry prize. It may just offer something we can use. I suppose it's possible Maddie MacKinnon may have something to add.'

'I doubt it very much. Maddie burned those papers to avoid a scandal back then. She's not going to backtrack on that now. She won't say anything that reflects badly on Will. But we shouldn't forget Frank Sinclair in all of this. He was at the aerodrome that morning. And he had the kind of connections to arrange for a bomb. I'd certainly want to talk to him about 1994. Because I wouldn't be surprised if he'd goaded Will into getting rid of Gabriel when it all looked like it was coming on top.'

Ruth's eyes widened in surprise. 'You really think so? A peer of the realm?'

'I think these are greedy selfish people who will do whatever it takes to keep their grip on the power and wealth and status that they live by.'

The silence between them held for a long moment, then Ruth spoke. 'Karen – it's all right if I call you Karen? – I think we have to let this one go. It might be worth running alongside the contemporary case if we get anything on the chemistry prize, but otherwise it's very slender. Though, for what it's worth, I do think you're probably on the right track. So, tell me all about Gabriel Abbott's death.'

Ruth Wardlaw put her pen down and breathed deeply. 'You're right. It's thin.'

Karen smiled. 'But it's the kind of thin that could well be fleshed out quite conclusively. Establishing Abbott's whereabouts on the night of the murder would be a start. Searching his home in London and finding forensic traces on his clothes would be another. Checking the ANPR cameras between Newcastle and Kinross for that night also moves us forward. Triangulation on Abbott's phone needs to be done, and that might pin him down even more precisely. Publicity around the case might even give us the source of the gun. We've got a motive that we can boil down simply to the threat of Gabriel coming after his share of the empire Will built on a partially stolen inheritance.'

'Agreed. But those are all contingencies that might not come good. Still ... there's no doubt in my mind that he did commit a serious offence against you.'

'So, what? You think we should go ahead and charge him?'

'Generally, in this sort of situation, I would want to err on the side of caution. My job is to prosecute cases that will result in convictions. But there is one thing that marks this case out as a wee bit different.'

'What's that?' Karen was intrigued.

'Ellie MacKinnon. She was a star before TV became completely fragmented, before kids' channels were common as chips. She was hugely popular with anyone who was a child while she was presenting. She's embedded in people's souls like John Noakes and Valerie Singleton. We'd only have to suggest that Will Abbott might have blown up that plane and already we've turned a chunk of the jury against him.'

'That's very devious,' Karen said, admiring the tactic. Perhaps she'd found an unexpected new ally.

'And not to go beyond this room.' Ruth gave a wry smile.

'So, you'd support me charging him?'

'I think you need to interview him. He'll "no comment", obviously. But for the record, you need to try. And unless the wheels come off at some point, then you charge him. And we will, of course, be opposing bail. Because otherwise it will be very difficult to access some of the potential sources of forensic evidence.' She pointed at Karen's sling. 'I hate to say this, but being able to charge him with attempted murder on a police officer makes my life a lot simpler.'

Karen snorted. 'Happy to help. So, let's get this show on the road.'

*

Cameron Campbell looked astonished when Karen and Jason walked into the interview room. As Jason set the recording equipment running and completed the litany of formalities, the solicitor interrupted. 'This is completely inappropriate. DCI Pirie, you're the victim in an assault case in which my client is a witness. At the very least, this could be seen as interfering with a witness.'

'We will not be touching on the events of last night. My inquiries are related to a completely separate matter. Two cases which I have been investigating. One comes under the remit of the Historic Cases Unit, of which I am the commanding officer. The other is ancillary to that.'

Campbell, with an air of affront, leaned over and whispered to Abbott, who was now sitting more erect in his seat, still and alert. His eyes never left Karen as he listened to his solicitor. He turned his head to mutter a low reply but kept his gaze locked with hers. 'My client will be making no comment at this stage.'

Karen stared at Abbott. She was gratified to see a long scratch along the line of his jaw. She hoped it stung. The dull ache in her shoulder was competing with the one in her head and all she wanted to do was take more painkillers and go to sleep. Instead, she knew she had to go through the motions. 'Will Abbott, did you murder Gabriel Abbott?'

A tiny smirk lifted one corner of his mouth, as if to say, 'Is that your best shot?' What he said was, 'No comment.'

'Are you the owner of a Smith and Wesson 457 handgun?'

'No comment.'

'Is your company, Glengaming, the beneficial owner of Spartacular, based in Newcastle?'

'No comment.'

'How long have you been aware that Lord Sinclair is the biological father of Gabriel Abbott?'

And so it continued. Karen's questions dodged hither and

thither in a bid to unsettle Abbott. But nothing disturbed his calm, although his solicitor's professional demeanour did suffer a few ripples along the way. After thirty minutes of getting nowhere, Campbell grew restive. 'This is a fishing expedition,' he complained. 'Either charge my client or release him.'

Karen smiled. 'I'm happy to oblige,' she said conversationally, buoyed up by the thought of the Macaroon's inevitable apoplectic response. 'Because, Will, you're an amateur. People like you, smart, successful people, you think you can turn your hand to murder and get away with it because you're smart and successful. You've watched all the forensics dramas and the true-crime shows on the telly, you've listened to the podcasts and you've read the books. You've watched how the little people get caught out. And you think that won't happen to you because you're smart and you're successful.' More smiles.

'I asked you whether you were in Kinross on the night of your brother's murder. You said, "No comment." And from your point of view, it's really good that you didn't deny it, because it never looks good in court when we demonstrate that a suspect lied in their interview. So you're lucky. We didn't catch you out in a lie. Because we do have a witness who doesn't just put you in Kinross that night but has you greeting your – what shall we call him? Your "not-brother"? – with a warm embrace. He's identified you from a photo line-up.'

She could see muscles twitching under the skin of his face. Amateurs. They thought they could handle themselves. But if your only practice with lying came from the occasional little white lie to your spouse or bigging yourself up to your shareholders, you'd really struggle to survive in the interview room against someone with the killer instinct she'd honed over the years.

Karen kept her voice light and pleasant. 'That's the first thing you're going to struggle to wriggle out of. And trust me, Will, there are going to be a lot more of these awkward pieces of information to sidestep.'

'Is there going to be a question here at any point, Chief Inspector? Some evidence, perhaps? As I said, charge my client or release him.'

'I know you're expecting me not to charge you, Will. Your lawyer will have told you we've not got enough evidence. But the Fiscal Depute thinks different. And I know that when we get the lab results back, you're toast. You'll have been really careful, I know that much. But even if you wore gloves when you were loading the gun, I will guarantee that your DNA will be on those bullets. And that'll be goodnight, Vienna. So, Will Abbott, I am charging you with the murder of Gabriel Abbott ...' The familiar words rolled out, and at last she saw a response from Abbott. A flash of outrage, a tensing of his shoulders. His mouth tightened and he breathed heavily through his nose.

'Wait,' he shouted before she got to the end of the charge. 'I need to talk to my lawyer.'

Karen and Jason leaned against the wall outside the interview room, heads down, breathing deeply. 'Is he going to cough?' Jason said.

'I don't think so,' Karen said. 'He's the kind that'll make us go to the wire.'

Ruth Wardlaw emerged from the viewing room. She carried herself as if she was walking on eggshells. 'Good job in there. I thought he was going to tough it out, but then you got under his defences.'

'Hit them where it hurts. In the vanity,' Karen said. 'Make out that he's not as smart as he thinks he is. Get that worm of doubt growing. Right, Jason?'

Startled, he flinched. 'Aye, right,' he gabbled. 'Like you say, boss.'

Ruth looked at her watch. 'Shall we run a book on how long they take?'

60

Campbell opened the door after twenty-two minutes and seventeen seconds by the stopwatch on Jason's phone. He looked as comfortable as a man who has inadvertently sat in a puddle. 'If you'd like to continue?' he said, resignation in his voice.

Once they were settled, he spoke: 'My client would like to make a statement.'

Will Abbott was back in command of himself. He sat upright, his upper arms tight against his torso. 'I did not kill Gabriel,' he said. 'I admit I was there in Kinross the night he died, but I swear I did not kill him, nor did I know he was going to die. I thought I was just setting up a meeting.'

'So who did kill him?' Karen asked quietly.

'I'd like to explain this in my own way, then you can ask questions.'

Karen knew that, ironically, that was the best way to get the interview moving from her point of view, the style of interview that provoked genuine revelations. The more they talked, the more they gave away, however much they thought they were in control. But she wanted to make him work for it, so she shook her head. 'That's not how it works, Will. You're not in charge here. You've made a very serious accusation against a third party which we need to explore.'

'Why don't you go and arrest him like you've arrested me?' Anger flashed in his eyes. 'Frank Sinclair. Lord Sinclair to you. He's staying at the Balmoral. The J. K. Rowling suite. He'll be waiting for me to debrief him.' He gave a sharp little bark of scorn. 'I wasn't supposed to be set upon by a gang of immigrants.'

'I'm not here to talk about what happened earlier. I must ask you not to discuss that in this interview,' Karen said. 'Why would I want to arrest Lord Sinclair?'

Abbott gathered himself together again. 'Because he killed Gabriel. Look, let me tell this in my own way, please. I need you to understand how this happened.' He sighed, shook his head and looked down at the table. 'I've been in hell since it happened. It's been a nightmare.' He met her eyes. 'It brought it all back to me. Mum and Ellie, dying in that plane crash. I feel as bereft as I did then.'

He was good, Karen thought. 'Why did Lord Sinclair kill Gabriel?'

'It's a very long story.'

'I think I already know most of it. He was Gabriel's biological father and Ellie MacKinnon was his mother. It was a secret only three people knew, and then two of them were dead. But you told DI Noble that your mother left a letter for you to be delivered when you were twenty-one, and I'm guessing she told you the truth. Quite a secret to have in your hand, I'd have thought.'

His eyes had widened as she spoke. She loved that moment when they realised she had them on the back foot.

'Probably a mistake to let Frank know that you knew, though. Pretty high-risk strategy. I'm thinking of that old saying: two can keep a secret, providing one of them is dead.

And I'm thinking of how the other two secret-holders died. But of course, you'd have no reason to fear Frank if it had been you that blew the plane up.' Karen kept smiling, kept her voice gentle. 'Do you want to tell me about that?'

'I'm trying to tell you about what happened to Gabriel,' Will said, the tightness in his throat evident in his voice. 'Gabriel had started taking an interest in genealogy. He wanted to draw up a family tree.' He looked away again, shaking his head. 'Since you already know so much, you presumably know that was hardly straightforward. He was talking about having DNA tests and all sorts. I was afraid of what that might reveal and I went to see Frank to discuss how we should handle it.'

Karen frowned, pretending puzzlement. 'I don't understand why you went to Frank. Why not just tell Gabriel the truth?'

He ran a hand through his hair. 'Gabriel was ... unstable. I had no idea how he would react. He was quite capable of posting it online. The fact of his paternity. The claim that I'd done him out of his inheritance.' He spread his hands and tried a boyish smile. 'I have shareholders to keep happy. Frank has a position in public life. I don't want my wife and kids to think of me as some kind of crook. I wanted to make sure Gabriel understood that he needed to be discreet.'

'I see that,' Karen said. 'So what was Frank's reaction?'

'He wasn't happy,' Abbott said. 'At first he wanted to keep the lid on things. For me not to give Gabriel a DNA sample and, if I had to, to keep Frank's name out of it. But I knew that wouldn't work. People love to gossip, you know how it goes. If Gabriel started going round all Mum and Ellie's friends looking for a potential father, it wouldn't be long before Frank's name came up. I said it was better to make a clean breast of it.'

'And that's what you were planning that night in Kinross?'

Abbott nodded. 'Frank said he didn't want to give Gabriel advance warning of the meeting in case he started shooting his mouth off about it. Frank's driver brought him up to Newcastle – I've been working with a new subsidiary company there recently – and the two of us came up to Edinburgh together. We both checked into the Balmoral and then we went across to Kinross. I knew Gabriel's habits. He was like clockwork. I knew I could meet him coming out of the pub and walk him along the path towards his cottage. And Frank was going to wait for us on the bench.'

'Why all this rigmarole? You could just have turned up at Gabriel's cottage, surely?'

Abbott gave a derisive snort. 'Because Frank's a public figure. He thinks everybody recognises him wherever he goes. He was terrified someone would spot him and wonder what he was doing there. I told him there was no chance of that, but he was adamant. Of course, I realise now why he didn't want to meet at the cottage. He didn't want to leave forensic traces.'

'He was planning to kill Gabriel all along?'

Abbott pressed his fingertips against his forehead in a mime of pain. 'I didn't realise that, obviously. I believed him. He sits in the House of Lords, for God's sake. I've known him since I was little. Why would I think for a nanosecond he was going to murder my brother?'

'So what happened?'

'I met Gabriel in the street near the pub. He was surprised to see me, but I explained that I'd brought someone who wanted to talk to him about his personal history. He was excited by the idea.'

'You told him it was Frank?'

'No, I said it was to be a surprise. We walked down the path by the loch for about quarter of an hour and when we came to the bench, Frank was there. Gabriel was thrilled to see him. He'd not seen him for a couple of years or more. They sat down and started talking. I hung back a bit, to keep a lookout in case anyone came along. I had my back to them. The next thing I knew, I heard a shot and, when I turned round, Frank was standing over Gabriel.' He covered his face with his hands. Karen couldn't have said why, but she didn't believe his performance of shock and grief. 'I couldn't believe it.'

'What did Frank say?' Karen knew she had to keep pushing forward.

Abbott dragged his hands down his face. 'He was totally calm. He just said, "There's nothing to worry about now, Will." Like he'd fixed a leaking tap or something. He leaned over Gabriel and put the gun in his hand. I noticed he was wearing gloves. I was in a state of shock; you notice the strangest things.'

'You could see what he was doing? From where you were standing?'

He froze for a moment, almost imperceptibly. 'I must have moved closer, I don't remember doing that. Look, you have to believe me. I loved Gabriel. I grew up thinking of him as my brother. I took care of him, I paid his school fees, I paid his rent, I looked after him.'

'In fairness, what he should have inherited from his real mother would have paid for all that several times over.'

His mouth tightened. 'I was legally entitled to everything I got.'

'Legally, maybe. But morally? You know you stole Gabriel's money. And who knows what the courts would have to say if he'd decided to sue you?'

'I didn't know the truth at the time. Not till I was twenty-one.'

Karen gave him a more-in-sorrow-than-in-anger look. 'Not good enough. You must have seen both wills at the time.

And it's quite clear that Ellie's intention was that Gabriel should inherit her estate if Caroline wasn't around.'

'I don't make the rules,' Abbott said. 'The money was legally mine. Look, when are you going to arrest Frank and make him answer for what he did?'

'Where did the gun come from?'

'How would I know? Frank has all sorts of contacts and they're not all in the government.'

'And you never touched the gun?'

'No, I told you. I had no idea he had a gun with him. It's all been down to Frank. It was his idea to keep tabs on you when you started sniffing around. He got one of his minions to follow you and let us know where you were and what you were doing. Frank thought you'd give up, but you didn't, did you?' The bitter words were out before he could stop himself.

Campbell leaned forward and whispered urgently in his ear. Abbott looked angry but he controlled himself. 'My client has given you full and frank disclosure, Chief Inspector. In the light of that, I suggest you consult with the FD and consider waiving the more serious charges against him. To ensure his continued cooperation.'

'I don't think so, Mr Campbell. We're going to have to speak to Lord Sinclair and check out your client's story. In the meantime, Will Abbott, I am arresting you on suspicion of murder . . . ' This time, she got to the end of the necessary words.

And that was that. A furious Campbell lingered after Abbott was taken away to the cells. 'This is an outrage,' he kept repeating.

'Continually repeating that doesn't make it so,' Ruth Wardlaw said, walking up to them. 'I suggest you sit down with your client and explain the sentencing advantages of a guilty plea. Because he knows and we know that there are a lot more skeletons in his cupboard. And DCI Pirie is not about to leave them there.'

Karen left them, Campbell spluttering and Ruth calmly asserting the upper hand. Abbott's story hung together. It was credible. Right now, she didn't know what to think. Somebody had to go and bring in Frank Sinclair and, given her current bag lady image, she didn't think she'd get past the front lobby of the Balmoral. Maybe a pair of uniforms would do the trick. At the very least, it would annoy the living shit out of Lord Sinclair.

61

F rank Sinclair glared at Karen across the interview room table, his bushy brows pulled down low over his bright blue eyes. 'You were at the Lords Select Committee on Monday,' he said. 'I never forget a face.'

'I was,' Karen admitted. 'I wanted to see you in the flesh.'

'I thought you were up to no good. You stole a glass at the end of the meeting.' He cocked his head to one side, a predator sizing up his prey. 'My glass.'

'You're very observant.'

'If you used that as a source of DNA, it has no evidential value.'

Karen nodded. 'I know. Not everything our labs analyse is for evidential purposes. Sometimes it's just for investigative value.'

'Why are you investigating me? And why am I here?'

'Your name came up in two separate but possibly connected investigations. The fatal bombing of a small plane in 1994, and the recent murder of Gabriel Abbott.'

His frown deepened. 'I understood from his brother Will that Gabriel's death had been classified as suicide.'

'Initially there was some doubt, but we have revised that opinion. We consider his death to be suspicious.'

'That's sad. But I fail to see the connection to me?'

Karen left a long pause while they held each other's gaze. At last, she said, 'He was your son.'

Sinclair snorted. 'Only in the way that a sperm donor is the father of the babies born to women treated with his genetic material. I had no emotional connection to Gabriel Abbott. I scarcely knew the boy.'

'Yet his mother was one of your oldest, closest friends.' She saw the involuntary shift in his seat. 'Yes, I know the truth about that too.'

'They wanted a child. I provided sperm. I saw very little of Ellie after she took up with Caroline. I did not approve of their relationship.' He sighed. 'But Ellie persuaded me against my better judgement. I suppose you could say it was a mixture of flattery and emotional blackmail. I regretted it almost as soon as I did it. I knew the damage it would do me if it ever became known. But I was not his father. I am father to my daughters, but I was never a father to Gabriel.'

'Not everyone would understand that. You're seen as someone who occupies the high moral ground on pretty much every issue. Fathering a love child for a pair of lesbians is the kind of thing your papers put on the front page. And not in a good way.'

He said nothing. Fair enough, she thought. It hadn't been a question.

'You were at the Elstree aerodrome on the morning of the crash.'

Now he looked surprised. 'It's not a secret. I spoke to the police at the time. I gave Richard and Mary a lift. I was trying to persuade Richard to write a regular column for me, so I thought it might be helpful to do him a small favour. I did a courtesy tour of the control tower with the ladies and I was gone before the plane was even on the tarmac.' His face twisted in an expression of distaste. 'I was deeply upset by the accident. Even though I saw very little of Ellie by then, she was, as you said, one of my oldest friends.'

'And you didn't plant the bomb?'

Sinclair looked completely astonished. 'Are you mad? Of course I didn't plant the bomb. These were my friends. How ...? How could ...? How could you consider such a thing?'

'I have to ask. Nobody ever stood trial for the murder of your friends.'

He shook his head with a baffled air. 'Madness. Is that why you dragged me down here? To make a preposterous allegation going back twenty-two years?'

'A very serious allegation has been made against you,' Karen said. 'Not to do with the plane crash.'

He frowned. 'Well. If it's as ridiculous as your last question, I have nothing to fear.'

'Will Abbott alleges you murdered Gabriel.'

Sinclair's mouth fell open. His face screwed up in an expression of utter incredulity. If it was an act, the man could have auditioned successfully for any major theatre company. He twisted his neck like a man hard of hearing thrusting his good ear towards the speaker. 'What?'

'Will Abbott alleges you murdered Gabriel.'

He shuddered. Karen had never seen anyone actually do that in an interview. 'I've woken up in a Kafka novel,' he said faintly. 'This is madness.'

'Gabriel was trying to draw up his family tree. Discovering the truth about his parentage would have been deeply embarrassing for you.'

'That's true. It would have been personally difficult.' He gave a wry smile. 'But the world has changed a great deal in recent years. And ironically, a revelation of that sort might serve, bizarrely, to raise my standing in some quarters. My daughters would find it hilarious. Chief Inspector, I am far from perfect, but I do try to adhere to my Christian principles. I have found that "Thou shalt not kill" is one of the easier precepts to stick to.'

'So you say. You also have a reputation for ruthlessness. Coveting your neighbour's columnists, if not their asses.' There was nothing humorous in Karen's tone.

'When am I supposed to have done this?'

'A week past Sunday. Some time between quarter past ten and midnight.'

He threw his head back and laughed. As he struggled to regain his composure, he gasped an apology. 'You have no idea . . . ' And he laughed again.

'So tell me.'

He gathered himself together. 'I did come up to Edinburgh from Newcastle with Will. We had a business meeting in Newcastle to discuss some cross-promotion between our online platform and his new company, Spartacular. And I was continuing to Edinburgh where I had a series of meetings on Monday morning. Will wanted to continue the conversation, to iron out some creases. He offered to drive me, so I agreed. We both checked in at the Balmoral. He said he was going to go over to Kinross to see Gabriel. I told him I was going to have an early night. We said our farewells in the lobby.'

He shrugged. 'I was lying. I did, in fact, have a meeting that evening. A meeting of absolute confidentiality.'

'You're going to have to do better than that.'

'I appreciate that. You are probably aware that my newspaper titles and our online presence were deeply hostile to the independence movement during the referendum here in Scotland.'

No shit, Sherlock. 'I had noticed a certain level of vitriol.'

'It has become regrettably clear that Ms Sturgeon and her nationalist cohort are here to stay, both in Scotland and in Westminster. Our position is hurting our sales. So I set up a meeting with a senior Holyrood minister and a couple of high-ranking party officials to discuss the terms of a rapprochement.'

As alibis went, it was a stonker. If it was true. 'I'm going to need names.'

'I am not going to say them aloud. Not for the tape.' He took a small notebook and pen from the inside pocket of his beautiful grey suit. He scribbled a few lines on the page, then tore it out and handed it over.

Karen, who was far from an assiduous student of politics, recognised the names. She'd been right. A stonker, right enough. She couldn't imagine any set of circumstances that would unite those three people behind Frank Sinclair. 'And they'll confirm this?'

'Reluctantly, I imagine. But I will ask their indulgence.' He leaned forward, his forearms on the table. 'I have no idea who killed Gabriel, if indeed anyone did. But it really wasn't me.'

'Did you see Will Abbott again on that trip?'

'We ran into each other in the breakfast room. I asked him how Gabriel was doing. He told me he was worried that he was heading for another of his episodes. That he seemed depressed. That he was getting wound up about some friend of his in Myanmar being persecuted. To be honest, it sounded like almost every conversation I'd had with Will about Gabriel. I wasn't really paying attention.' He paused, working his jaw from one side to the other. 'Are you . . . ? Do you . . . ? Is Will a suspect?'

'A wee bit more than that,' Karen said. 'He tried very hard to push it on to you. He didn't know about your meeting. If you'd had your feet up in your hotel room, it might have been kind of difficult for you to talk your way out of it. Just one thing – Abbott said you'd had me followed. Why?'

He shrugged, dismissing the question as insignificant. 'I didn't know who you were or what your game was. I wanted to be sure you weren't up to something nefarious. I am targeted by all sorts of people. As we've both discovered this morning,' he added, acid in his voice.

Karen slid carefully between the sheets, her assorted aches dulled by the drugs. She couldn't remember ever feeling this tired. River, summoned by Jason, was in the living room with her laptop and instructions to wake Karen every two hours. 'Good luck with that,' Karen had said, emerging from a shower that had done the opposite of waking her up.

There were, she thought, different ways of serving justice. Sometimes it was enough to have the answer. Nobody could fault the cops on the original inquiry into Tina McDonald's death. Even if they'd realised the underground ticket wasn't hers, it would have taken them nowhere. The evidence that had nailed her killer simply hadn't been available to them. Three more people had to die a horrible, stupid death before the crucial piece of evidence fell into her lap. Sure, it would have been more satisfying to put Gary Foreman behind bars. But at least Tina's family had their answer now, and without having to relive those terrible days through the medium of a trial.

But when it came to Will Abbott, there was only one way to serve justice. And that was to put him behind bars for the rest of his life. Karen knew in her bones that he had blown up that plane. But she had to let that go. She was never going to nail that. But he would pay for taking Gabriel's life.

So far, her best efforts had taken away his liberty. Charged with assault, attempting to pervert the course of justice, and murder. No sheriff would grant him bail. Not with the evidence against him on the police assault. The problem was, that was only temporary. There was still a long road to travel before she could be sure a jury would convict him of at least one murder. In her heart, Karen believed the necessary proof was there, somewhere. And if anybody could find it, it was her. Justice would be served. Somehow.

Epilogue

Three months later

They walked down Leith Walk in step, Karen and River keeping pace with each other in the mild early evening. Only in the past week or so had Karen felt herself walking as freely as she had before Will Abbott broke her collarbone with the business end of a power strip. She still hadn't recovered full strength or mobility in her left shoulder, but every week, the physio got easier and the range of movement improved. What baffled her about her recuperation was that hand in hand with her physical healing had come a restoration of the possibility of sleep. She had rediscovered the ability to go to bed at a reasonable time and sleep until her alarm woke her.

She'd been so spooked by this she'd gone back to see the doctor who had given her the all-clear after her blow to the head. He'd run some tests, given her a CT scan and pronounced her well within the range of normal. 'First time for everything,' River had commented drily.

So she was sleeping through the night again. Oddly, she almost missed her night walks, that quartering of the streets that had made sense of the city for her. But she had come to relish the alertness that came with long hours of good sleep. She was better-tempered too. Better able to deal with the Macaroon with equanimity.

She'd even managed a moment of compassion for Ross Garvie. Just a moment, mind. He'd eventually surfaced from his coma to the news that he'd never walk again, he'd be in nappies for the rest of his life, blind in one eye and deaf in one ear. The speech centres in his brain were permanently damaged. The next debate would be whether he was fit to stand trial for the culpable homicide of his three friends.

As they reached the bottom of Leith Walk and turned into Duke Street, Karen could wait no longer. She'd been hugging to her heart a piece of extraordinary news that had landed in her inbox moments before she'd walked out of the office to meet River. 'Something to tell you,' she said.

River half-turned, alerted by some note in Karen's voice. 'The Macaroon's taking early retirement?'

'Even better than that.'

'Hard to imagine.' River thrust her arm through Karen's. 'Come on, tell me.'

'I got a message from the lab this afternoon. I don't know why it's taken this long, but apparently sometimes it just does. They've found Will Abbott's DNA on two of the bullets in the gun that killed Gabriel.'

River stopped in her tracks, pulling Karen round to face her, forcing an elderly woman to execute a clumsy sidestep, tutting at them. 'You're kidding!' she yelped.

'No kidding.' Karen couldn't hold her face in check any longer. She stood grinning like a kid in a sweetie shop. 'We've got him. We've nailed the devious slippery arrogant bastard. Ruth Wardlaw will crucify him. He's never going to sit in his lovely Notting Hill games room playing Glengaming's latest blockbuster again.'

River lit up. 'That's great news. It's hard to see how he can explain that away.'

Karen swung her round and carried on walking. 'It's the final brick in the wall. Add that to the ANPR data that confirms Frank Sinclair's statement that they drove up to Edinburgh then Abbott travelled on alone to Kinross and back. And the jacket he was wearing? They found that when they searched his house. He'd taken it to the dry cleaner's, so we lost any gunshot residue. But there were minute traces of Gabriel's DNA deep in the fabric – the blowback from the wound.'

River shook her head. 'I can't believe he kept the jacket. You'd think these days that everybody would be forensically aware.'

'It was bespoke Oswald Boateng.'

'If he can afford Boateng, he can afford to bin it and buy a replacement.'

Karen chuckled. 'I met his wife. She was outraged that we were taking the Boateng. So maybe he was more worried about his wife noticing it was missing. Anyway, most people, if they think about it at all, would imagine that dry cleaning would destroy DNA.'

'You've nailed him.'

'It's never over till the jury has had their day in court. But yes, I think we've nailed him for Gabriel. It's a shame we couldn't make the cold case stick. But once he's been sent down, I will be talking extensively to the media about the different angle we've been taking in that investigation.'

River smiled. 'Which, technically, is ongoing.'

'Which, technically, is ongoing,' Karen agreed. 'Oh, and there's one more odd thing. Do you remember me telling you that Gabriel had supposedly been going on about some mate of his in Myanmar who was being persecuted by the government and had supposedly disappeared? There was a letter from him in the cottage, full of paranoid ramblings that made no sense, according to somebody we tapped up in the Foreign Office. For a wee moment, we wondered if Will was going to try that as his second attempt at shifting the blame. Well, this week, a postcard turned up from his mate. Not in a government jail. Eloped with his girlfriend to another island.'

River giggled. 'I'm glad somebody got a happy ending for once.'

They came to a halt outside a freshly painted shopfront. The signboard said, ALEPPO – SYRIAN CAFÉ, and beneath that, a line of Arabic script that Karen presumed repeated the same thing. The interior was crowded with people, Middle Eastern and locals, glasses in hand. Teenagers moved among them with bowls of olives and plates of meze. She took a deep breath, mentally girding her loins. 'Come on, then. Let's be sociable.'

They had barely crossed the threshold when Miran appeared in front of them. 'Inspector,' he shouted. 'I have been waiting for you.' He turned and ushered a woman forward. Fine features, big brown eyes and a wide smile, a small gap between her front teeth, the bump of her pregnancy preceding her. She inclined her head towards Karen. 'This is my wife,' Miran said. 'This is Amena. Amena, this is the inspector. She is the reason we are here.'

Karen shook her head. 'No, Miran. You're the reason we're both here.'

Before anyone could say more, the hubbub of conversation was broken into by the tinkle of metal on glass. The noise died away. Time for speeches. Someone gave a short speech in Arabic, then Tarek took over. 'Welcome, everyone. Welcome to the new Aleppo. Now we have a place to meet, we can start to belong here. We thank everyone who helped us. We thank Inspector Pirie because she started this. And MP Grassie who help us make it happen. We thank too the city council and all our friends who work on the café to make it good. Enjoy tonight and enjoy coming back to Aleppo many times.' Applause, then conversation broke out again.

River squeezed her arm. 'You did a good thing, Karen.'

'River, they probably saved my life. What I did for them doesn't even come close.'

'Yeah, but you didn't know that when you helped them make the right connections.'

Karen thought about the past year. Things lost, things found. And in the thick of it, an unimagined way forward. 'Right enough,' she said. 'But this isn't my place. Come on, let's walk.'

Acknowledgements

Because Karen Pirie always has one foot in the past, I need to find people with arcane bits of knowledge to help me get the details right. Thanks to everyone who chipped in, and in particular, thanks to:

Andy Preece for period bus details;

Professor Niamh Nic Daeid for explosive information and for letting me blow things up in her lab;

Professor Dame Sue Black for the Vet School suggestion;

Rachael Kelsey for Scots family law and legal standing of a dead man's DNA;

Tom Phillips for that crucial wee detail about Fife office buildings;

Ellie MacKinnon for generosity in donating to Breast Cancer Now and the Sick Kids Friends Foundation in exchange for lending me her name;

The McCredie brothers for their totally shan help;

Pete Wishart MP for parliamentary detail;

Steve Bruce from the General Register Office for making sure I got the adoption details right.

I have a team of hard-working and committed people whose support makes my life so much easier. My perceptive and demanding editors David Shelley and Lucy Malagoni at Little, Brown and Amy Hundley at Grove Atlantic; copy editor Anne O'Brien who knows how many days there are in the week; publicist Jo Wickham who knows where I should be on every one of those days; the rest of the design, sales and marketing teams who help to get my books out there and into the hands of readers; and the booksellers and librarians who have generously supported every one of my 30 novels with enthusiasm and persistence.

Finally, my staunch friends and family, particularly my bidie-in Jo and my son Cameron, who treat my addiction to words with compassion, pity and humour.

Read on for the opening pages of *Insidious Intent*,
the new Tony Hill and Carol Jordan novel
from Val McDermid.

"Powerful . . . McDermid's prose is pure pleasure
to read . . . A master operating at the height of her
considerable powers. Prepare to be swept away."
—*Mystery Scene* on *Splinter the Silence*
Available now.

1

If Kathryn McCormick had known she had less than three weeks to live, she might have made more of an effort to enjoy Suzanne's wedding. But instead she had adopted her usual attitude of resigned disappointment, trying not to look too disconsolate as she stared at the other guests dancing as if nobody was watching.

It was just like every day at work. Kathryn was always the outsider there too. Even though the title of office manager wielded very little in the way of actual authority, it was enough to set her apart from everyone else. Kathryn always felt that when she walked into the kitchenette to make herself a coffee, whatever conversation had been going on either stopped altogether or swerved away from the confidential to the inconsequential.

Really, it had been stupid to think today would have been any different. She'd once seen a quote that had stuck with her – the definition of insanity was, doing the same thing over and over again and expecting different results. By that standard, she was definitely insane. Sitting on the fringes of a wedding reception on a Saturday night but expecting to be at the centre of conversation and laughter fell smack bang at the core of repetitive behaviour that never produced anything but entirely predictable failure.

Kathryn sneaked a look at her watch. The dancing had only been going for half an hour. But felt like a lot longer. Nikki from accounts, hips gyrating like a pole dancer, opposite Ginger Gerry, slack-jawed with delight. Anya, Lynne, Mags and Triona in a neat shamrock formation, elbows tucked in, bodies twitching and heads bobbing to the beat. Emily and Oli, feet shuffling in sync, eyes locked, grinning at each other like idiots. Idiots who would probably be going home together at the end of the night.

She could barely remember the last time she'd had sex. She'd split up with Niall over three years ago. But it still stung like a razor cut. He'd walked into the house one evening, the sharp sour smell of lager on his breath, a faint sheen of sweat on his skin. 'I've been headhunted for a job in Cardiff. Running my own design team,' he'd said, his excitement impossible to miss.

'That's great, babe.' Kathryn had slid off the stool at the breakfast bar, throwing her arms around him, trying to stifle the voice in her head shouting, 'Cardiff? What the *fuck* am I going to do in Cardiff?'

'Big salary increase too,' Niall said, his body curiously still, not responding to the hug.

'Wow! When are we moving, then?'

He disentangled himself. Kathryn's stomach clenched. 'That's the thing, Kath.' He looked at his feet. 'I want to go by myself.'

The words didn't make any sense. 'What do you mean, by yourself? You're just going to come home at weekends? That's mad, I can get a job down there, I've got transferrable skills.'

He took a step back. 'No. Look, there's no good way of saying this ... I'm not happy and I haven't been for a while and I think this is the best way for both of us. For me to move away, start again. We can both start again.'

And that had been that. Well, not quite. There had been tears and shouting and she'd cut the crotches out of all his Calvin Kleins, but he'd gone anyway. She'd lost her man and she'd lost her dignity and she'd lost her home because half the lovely terraced house in her favourite Bradfield suburb had been Niall's and he'd insisted they sell it. So now she lived in a boxy little flat in a 1960s block too close to where they'd lived together. It had been a mistake to move somewhere so near the place she'd been happy, the house she had to walk past to get to the tram stop every morning. She'd tried making a ten-minute detour to avoid it, but that had been worse. An even sharper slap in the face, somehow. Every now and then, the couple who had bought the house emerged as she walked past and they'd give her a little wave and an embarrassed half-smile.

Since then, Kathryn had made a few tentative attempts at getting back to dating. She'd signed up for an online dating site and swiped her way through dozens of possibles. When she pictured herself standing next to them, none of them seemed remotely credible. One of Niall's old workmates had texted her and invited her out for dinner. It hadn't gone well. He'd clearly thought she'd be up for a pity fuck, and had been less than happy when she'd told him to sod off. At her cousin's fortieth, she'd hooked up with a sweet lad from Northern Ireland. They'd ended up in bed together, but it hadn't exactly been a raging success and he'd escaped back to Belfast with a broken promise to call her.

That had probably been the last time she'd had sex. Fifteen months ago. And this was supposed to be her sexual prime. Kathryn stifled a sigh and took another swig from her glass of Sauvignon Blanc. She had to stop feeling so sorry for herself. All the magazines she'd ever read were agreed on that point – nothing was a bigger turn-off for a man than self-pity.

'Is someone sitting here?' A man's voice. Deep and warm.

Kathryn started and jerked round. Standing with his hand on the back of the chair next to her was a stranger. A not bad-looking stranger, she noted automatically even as she stammered, 'No. I mean, they were but they're not now.' Kathryn was used to sizing up potential clients. Not quite six feet tall, she thought. Thirty-something. Mid-brown hair with a few silver strands at the temples. Full, well-shaped eyebrows over pale blue eyes that crinkled when he smiled. Like now. His nose looked a bit thick around the bridge, as if it had been broken at some point and poorly set. His smile revealed slightly crooked teeth, but it was an engaging smile nevertheless.

He sat down beside her. Suit trousers, brilliant white shirt with the top button undone, blue silk tie loosened. His fingernails were square and manicured, his shave close and his haircut crisp. She liked a man who took care of his grooming. Niall had always been meticulous that way. 'I'm David,' he said. 'Are you with the bride or the groom?'

'I work with Suzanne,' she said. 'I'm Kathryn. With a y.' She had no idea why she'd said that.

'Nice to meet you, Kathryn with a y.' There was amusement there, but not in a piss-taking way, she thought.

'Are you a friend of Ed, then?'

'I know him from the five-a-side footie.'

Kathryn giggled. 'The best man milked that in his speech.'

'Didn't he, though.' He cleared his throat. 'I noticed you sitting here by yourself. I thought you might like some company?'

'I don't mind my own company,' she said, regretting the words as soon as they were spoken. 'But don't get me wrong, it's really lovely to meet you.'

'I don't mind my own company either, but sometimes it's nice to talk to an attractive woman.' That smile again. 'I'm guessing you don't much like dancing? So I'm not going to suggest we strut our stuff on the dance floor.'

'No, I'm not much of a dancer.'

'I'm a bit fed up with the music. I prefer conversation, myself. Do you fancy going through to the bar? It's quieter there, we can talk without having to shout at each other.'

Kathryn couldn't quite believe it. OK, he wasn't exactly George Clooney, but he was clean and polite and attractive and, extraordinary though it seemed, he was acting like he was interested in her. 'Good idea,' she said, pushing back her chair and getting to her feet.

As they weaved through the tables to the ballroom door, the man who called himself David cupped her elbow in his hand in a solicitous gesture. Kathryn McCormick's killer was nothing if not solicitous.

2

Detective Chief Inspector Carol Jordan shrugged into her heavy waxed jacket and pulled a thermal hat over sleep-tousled hair. A black-and-white collie danced around her feet, impatient to be out into the morning chill. She tied the laces on her sturdy walking boots and stepped out into a flurry of rain. She shut the door of the converted barn behind her, letting the tongue of the lock click softly into place.

Then they were off, woman and dog cutting up the moorside in sweeping zigzags. For a few blessed moments, concentrating on what she was doing drove the turmoil from Carol's head, but it was too insistent to be kept at bay for long. The phone call that had come from out of the blue the night before had stripped her of any chance of a restful night and now, it seemed, of any peace this morning. There had been no running away from the blame her caller's bitter voice had directed at her.

Years of policing at the sharpest of sharp ends had provided Carol with ample cause for regret. Every cop knew the acrid taste of failure, the tightness in the chest that came with delivering the worst news in the world. Those cases where they'd failed to bring any kind of consolation to people who had a sudden gap in their lives where a loved one should be – those cases still rankled, filling her with a sense of raw inadequacy when she drove down certain streets, crossed particular landscapes, visited towns where she knew unspeakable things had happened.

All those things were generic, though. All cops everywhere who had an ounce of sensitivity to what they were doing carried these loads. But this was different. This latest quantum of blame was a personal burden.

She'd thought she could escape these outcomes that twisted inside her like a tightening rope when she walked away from the job, from the badge and the rank. Her relentless pursuit of a multiple murderer had cost the life of her brother and his wife. What possible reason could there be for staying? She'd wanted nothing more to do with a job that demanded such a high price.

But other people had known only too well the buttons to push to draw her back to policing like a moth to a flame.

#1: Boredom. She'd spent six months stripping her brother's barn conversion to the bare bones then rebuilding it, learning the skills she needed from YouTube videos and old men in the local pub. She'd been driven to erase all traces of what had happened there, as if by remaking it she could convince herself Michael and Lucy's death had been a hallucination. She'd been close to the final stages of the project when her rage had finally cooled enough for her to understand she was growing bored with her choice. She was a detective, not a builder, as the man asleep in her spare room had forcibly told her.

#2: Loneliness. Carol's friendships had always been inextricably linked to her job. Her team were her family, and some of them had made it past her barriers to become her friends. Since she'd walked away, she'd pushed them all to arm's length and beyond. One of her neighbours, George Nicholas, had tried to breach her defences. A generous man, he was the reason she had the dog. Flash was the offspring of his own sheepdog, an anomalous pup who was afraid of sheep. Carol had taken the misfit because she thought they belonged together, somehow. George had seen that as a signal for a closer connection, but he hadn't been who she wanted. George could never be home for her. A return to policing, though? That would take her back into the orbit of people who made her believe she belonged somewhere.

#3: Pride. That had been the killer vulnerability that had left her open to an offer she should have refused but couldn't. Pride in her skill, pride in her smarts, pride in her ability to find answers where nobody else could. She knew she was good. Believed she was the best, especially when she had the right hand-picked team around her. Others might have thought her arrogant; Carol Jordan knew she had something to be arrogant about. Nobody could do this job better. She had doubts about all sorts of things but not about her ability as a guv'nor.

And finally, the killer button to press. #4: Temptation. They'd held out so much more than the simple chance to return to a job that had defined and rewarded her for so long. They'd invented something new, something bright and shiny, something that might change the future of the way they did policing. And she was their first choice to lead it. A regional Major Incident Team – ReMIT – that would scoop up all the sudden violent deaths, the most vicious sexual assaults and the sickening child abductions from six separate police forces. The first tentative step towards a national agency like the FBI, perhaps. Who else could do it if not Carol Jordan?

But she'd screwed up before they could even ask her.

A screw-up so breathtakingly stupid that the only way to rescue her was an audacious act of noble corruption that she should never have considered accepting for a nanosecond, never mind buying into heart and soul. She'd been blinded by the vote of confidence in her abilities, flattered that a man of honour should risk his integrity to place her where she belonged, and, at the last ditch, doomed by the demands of her own ego.

And now there was more blood on her hands and nobody to blame but herself.

Carol drove her body harder against the gradient, making her muscles complain and her lungs burn. Flash quartered the hill in front of her, a sudden flurry of rabbits scattering before her, dirty white scuts bouncing across the moorland grass like a random release of old white tennis balls. Carol didn't even break stride, registering nothing around her, locked into the fury she was directing entirely towards herself.

What was she to do now? The one principle she'd always clung to was her drive for justice. It had taken her to dark places and forced her down reluctant paths but it had never failed her. To deliver criminals to judgement had always fulfilled her. That sense of restoring some kind of balance in the world also gave balance to her life. But there could be no justice here.

If Carol admitted the conspiracy she'd been part of, she'd only be a tiny part of the damage and destruction. It would kill ReMIT before it was even up and running properly. And that would improve the chances of serious criminals escaping the consequences of their actions. She'd have screwed up the careers of other officers who had counted on her. She'd likely go to jail. Worse still, so would other people.

The guilt was hers. The blood was on her hands. There was only one road to redemption. She had to make a success of ReMIT. If she could turn it into an elite team that really did deliver arrests and convictions in the most exacting of circumstances, if they could put killers behind bars before more lives were needlessly taken, if she really did make a difference ... She'd still owe a debt for those other deaths. But at least there would be something to put on the other side of the balance sheet.